MW00831462

ENERGY
IN CHINA'S MODERNIZATION
Advances and Limitations

East Gate Books

Harold R. Isaacs
RE-ENCOUNTERS IN CHINA

James D. Seymour
CHINA RIGHTS ANNALS 1

Thomas E. Stolper
CHINA, TAIWAN, AND THE OFFSHORE ISLANDS

William L. Parish, ed.
CHINESE RURAL DEVELOPMENT
The Great Transformation

Anita Chan, Stanley Rosen, and Jonathan Unger, eds.
ON SOCIALIST DEMOCRACY AND THE CHINESE LEGAL SYSTEM
The Li Yizhe Debates

Michael S. Duke, ed.
CONTEMPORARY CHINESE LITERATURE
An Anthology of Post-Mao Fiction and Poetry

Michiko N. Wilson
THE MARGINAL WORLD OF ŌE KENZABURO
A Study in Themes and Techniques

Thomas B. Gold
STATE AND SOCIETY IN THE TAIWAN MIRACLE

Carol Lee Hamrin and Timothy Cheek, eds.
CHINA'S ESTABLISHMENT INTELLECTUALS

John P. Burns and Stanley Rosen, eds.
POLICY CONFLICTS IN POST-MAO CHINA
A Documentary Survey, with Analysis

Victor D. Lippit
THE ECONOMIC DEVELOPMENT OF CHINA

James D. Seymour
CHINA'S SATELLITE PARTIES

June M. Grasso
TRUMAN'S TWO-CHINA POLICY

Bruce L. Reynolds, ed.
REFORM IN CHINA
Challenges & Choices

Pat Howard
BREAKING THE IRON RICE BOWL
Prospects for Socialism in China's Countryside

Vaclav Smil
ENERGY IN CHINA'S MODERNIZATION
Advances and Limitations

ENERGY
IN CHINA'S MODERNIZATION
Advances and Limitations

VACLAV SMIL

An East Gate Book
M. E. Sharpe, Inc.
Armonk, New York/London

East Gate Books are edited by Douglas Merwin

Available in the United Kingdom and Europe from M. E. Sharpe,
Publishers, 3 Henrietta Street, London WC2E 8LU.

Library of Congress Cataloging-in-Publication Data

Smil, Vaclav.
    Energy in China's modernization.

    Bibliography: p.
    Includes index.
    1. Energy policy—China. 2. Power resources—China.
3. Energy industries—China.   I. Title.
HD9502.C62S644   1988   333.79′0951   87–12922
ISBN 0-87332-423-4

Printed in the United States of America

This book
and royalties from its sales
are dedicated
to
Amnesty International

This is a book about China's prospects for modernization, a task necessarily requiring huge sums of energy. The book looks ahead— yet the ancients would readily recognize the aspirations: energy is just a key unlocking access to affluent life. Definitions of affluence change but the basics remain.

> If you do not interfere with the busy seasons in the fields, then there will be more grain than the people can eat; if you do not allow nets with too fine a mesh to be used in large ponds, then there will be more fish and turtles than they can eat; if hatchets and axes are permitted in the forests on the hills only in the proper seasons, then there will be more timber than they can use. When the people have more grain, more fish and turtles than they can eat, and more timber than they can use, then, in the support of their parents when alive and in the mourning of them when dead, they will be able to have no regrets over anything left undone. . . . When the aged wear silk and eat meat and the masses are neither cold nor hungry, it is impossible for their prince not to be a true king.

> Meng Ke, Book 1

Would Deng Xiaoping disagree?

CONTENTS

Preface xi

**1 CHINESE ENERGY:
COMMONALITIES AND PECULIARITIES** 3

2 RESOURCES: RICHES AND POVERTY 7

2.1 Renewable flows 9

　　2.1.1 Solar radiation and wind 10
　　2.1.2 Geothermal potential 15
　　2.1.3 Biomass 19
　　2.1.4 Hydroenergy 24

2.2 Fossil fuels 30

　　2.2.1 Coals 31
　　2.2.2 Hydrocarbons 35

**3 EXTRACTION AND UTILIZATION:
TWO ECONOMIES** 41

3.1 Rural energetics 44

3.1.1 Traditional biomass fuels 49
3.1.2 Biogas generation 54
3.1.3 Water power 63
3.1.4 Energy flows in rural China 69

3.2 Industries and cities 84

3.2.1 Coal as the foundation 85
3.2.2 Oil and gas industry 95
3.2.3 Electricity generation 104
3.2.4 Uses and conversion efficiencies 121

4 MODERNIZATION:
ENERGY FOR THE QUADRUPLED ECONOMY 133

4.1 Modernization goals 134

4.2 Energy needs and strategies 136

4.2.1 Conserving fuel and electricity 141
4.2.2 Doubling coal output 148
4.2.3 Searching for hydrocarbons 162
4.2.4 Expanding electricity generation 171
4.2.5 Providing energy for the countryside 189

5 THE OUTLOOK: APPRAISING THE LIMITATIONS 201

5.1 Reforms and innovations 203
5.2 Environmental complications 214
5.3 Sustainable strategies 224

References 229

Appendices 237

Index 249

PREFACE

When I was finishing my first book on China's energy, in the spring of 1976, I was fairly pleased with the work. This feeling was not a result of uncritical self-appraisal but rather of relieved satisfaction that I was able to put together a comprehensive and reasonably detailed review and analysis of China's energetics on the basis of decidedly inadequate information.

In those years any deeper understanding of Chinese affairs required a thorough immersion in what Alexander Eckstein called so aptly "economic archeology": extensive, diligent, time-consuming searches for shards of information which, one hoped, could be reassembled to resemble the reality camouflaged from the foreigners by effusive official pronouncements about glorious achievements and by the arrogance of Maoist slogans. This quasi-detective work was challenging, intriguing, even rewarding—but it was also frustrating, wasteful, and, not infrequently, well off the mark: often too many shards were missing and even a critical observer could fill the void with more substance than was justified—or, conversely, could be unduly pessimistic or conservative.

Ten years later one faces the very opposite problem: a decade after Mao's death and seven years after Deng's rise to an innovative helmsmanship there is an information overload coming from China. Leading periodicals carry fairly involved discussions of economic, technical, or environmental problems, hundreds of scientific journals publish each year thousands of contributions ranging from general reviews and international comparisons to detailed site-specific analyses, official statistical yearbooks and almanacs offer thousands of pages of tables and comprehensive summaries, and yet more information is carried out of the country by the incessant stream of Japanese and Western experts who are now delving into almost every facet of the Chinese economy.

This information flood swept away most of the pre-1980 work on China's performance during the two "lost decades" (1958–1978). Critical observers may point out with satisfaction that their general conclusions, formulated after pondering the badly incomplete evidence, were only confirmed by the new data flow—but countless particulars of their work are clearly superseded by better understanding. Consequently, in the text of this book there will not be a single reference to its 1976 predecessor.

The old book's basic conclusions about the weaknesses and limitations of China's energetics were abundantly confirmed by the post-1978 candor, and its forecasts held quite well. The things I predicted for the 1980s—opening of large surface mines, construction of giant mine-mouth power plants, high-voltage long-distance links, first steps toward nuclear generation—are all happening now, and even my aggregate energy production forecasts were very close to the mark. For 1985 I had the primary energy use at between 734 and 828 million tons of coal equivalent (tce); the actual total was about 800 million tce, nicely nestled within my range. But many of those painstakingly assembled specific production and performance figures were in considerable error; hence the book will be relegated to a place among the sources of historical interest.

But this new work is not going to recapitulate the "two lost decades" on the basis of new data: it looks forward. To do so in a sensible manner one must, of course, appreciate the foundations, and so I will look in sufficient, but definitely not overly particularistic, detail at the resource endowment and current status of China's energetics before focusing on strategies and approaches aimed at securing enough energy for the country's ambitious modernization endeavor.

This is a book with a clear mission: a critical appraisal of the foundations and prospects of China's energetics. This goal required comprehensive coverage, but, as with all of my books the stresses and omissions reflect strongly my perceptions and convictions.

An engineer might find too few descriptions of particular Chinese energy technologies—but I reviewed them in detail a few years ago, and plenty of such information is now readily available in Western

technical journals. With only a very few exceptions, Chinese achievements have little to offer. Hence only an essential coverage of the topic
is to be found in this book. An economist might point out a brief
discussion of energy pricing as the book's weak spot—but why spend
pages on what can be summed up so easily? Namely, energy pricing in
China is arbitrary, centrally dictated, inimical to proper management
and market functioning, and, as the Chinese now readily admit, must be
totally reformed.

On the other hand, I devote a good deal of attention to hydroenergy
because China has the world's largest untapped capacity to produce
electricity from water, and because its plans for the next two decades
add up to the greatest hydro construction program in history. And the
book includes an extended look at the environmental implications of
energy production because they will be of key importance in pinpoint-
ing and limiting the options for future development, a fact recently
broadly acknowledged by one of China's most forward-looking techno-
crats, Vice-Premier Li Peng.

A book such as this one would have benefitted from an open, infor-
mal exchange of views with Chinese researchers, but I had no opportunity for such intellectual intercourse. I had access to detailed sectoral
reviews prepared by China's leading energy experts for the International Development Research Center's (IDRC) Energy Research
Group project in 1984–85, but in Beijing, when I got a hearing, I could
not learn anything beyond the facts already available in published
Chinese sources.

As with *The Bad Earth*, this book is based solely on a critical evaluation of Chinese sources, and I hope that it will be a
useful contribution to a better understanding of aspirations and limitations of modernizing China. I would not have written it without Ashok Desai, who, during his tenure as director of the IDRC's
Energy Research Group, asked me in 1984 to write a comprehensive
review of China's energetics, and who later suggested its upgrading,
reworking, and expansion into a book. Needless to say, the views and
interpretations contained in the book are mine and not those of the
IDRC.

And the book could not have been published so speedily without
Doug Merwin of M. E. Sharpe, who gave me another welcome chance
to write a book on China without resorting to the sanitized blandness
preferred by many lesser editors.

Editorial notes

Before the Chinese resumed the publication of comprehensive official statistics, detailed reviews, and in-depth analyses, it was important to reference every major fact or claim, as their provenance was a key indicator of their reliability and utility. With a new profusion of Chinese statistical and review sources, I have decided not to burden the text with references in the sections giving general background and describing basic production records or sectoral arrangements. Instead, the one hundred or so publications reviewed topically in appendix A provide details on all of these basics. References in the text are used only when introducing facts or appraisals that are highly specific, very remarkable, or little appreciated, or, naturally, when quoting directly. All the sources are arranged alphabetically in the list of references.

Chinese place names in this book are romanized in pinyin according to *Zhongguo renmin gongheguo fen sheng dituji (Hanyu pinyinban)* (Atlas of the PRC [Pinyin edition]). Beijing: Ditu Chubanshe (Cartographic Publishing House), 1977. Measures in this book are in metric units.

ENERGY
IN CHINA'S MODERNIZATION
Advances and Limitations

CHINESE ENERGY:
Commonalities and Peculiarities

When China was rediscovered by the Western media, after the Nixon-Kissinger pilgrimage in 1972, numerous apologists for the Maoist regime tried hard to create the image of a country truly apart: an admirable, efficient society dedicated to economic advancement and well-being, a nation of vigorous growth rates, plenty of food, and a smile on everyone's face. And, a feat in such startling contrast to post-1973 Western woes, a nation with self-sufficient and vigorously expanding energy supplies.

When two years after Mao's death the Chinese started to tell the world the truth about the country's affairs all the admissions reinforced a simple fact: China is a poor country, and most of its huge population lives barely above the basic subsistence level. Being such a big economy, its aggregate performance figures are large, some of them—including total energy output—ranking among the world's top five, but its per capita achievements are decidedly modest.

China's per capita GNP of around U.S. $ (1986) 400 puts the country just into the top third of the world's poorest group of nations (the World Bank's thirty-five or so low-income economies), some 30 percent ahead of India and roughly at par with Pakistan. Recently released income statistics show that historical disparities between rich coastal and poor interior provinces have actually intensified. By the late 1970s most Chinese ate no better than they had two decades before, a depressing stagnation reversed only through the recent de facto privatization of farming. Countless accounts in resuscitated professional journals have detailed widespread economic mismanagement and shocking production inefficiencies.

In the late 1970s, after three decades of impressive, although un-even, growth, China became the world's third largest producer and consumer of commercial energy. China's large population, however, shrinks this absolute accomplishment to a very modest relative figure of about 700 kg of coal equivalent energy (or 20 GJ) consumed annually per capita in 1985, still slightly below the consumption average for all developing nations and an order of magnitude below the rich world's use.

In annual per capita energy consumption China is ahead of such populous nations as India, Pakistan, and Bangladesh—yet far behind those countries that, from conditions not unlike China's a generation ago, have risen to, or beyond, the economic take-off stage. In Asia, South Korea and Malaysia are, of course, the best examples (even more successful Hong Kong and Singapore are peculiar city-states that should not be compared with true countries).

However, most Chinese (nearly four-fifths), like most Indians or Nigerians, are villagers, and their annual per capita energy consump-tion is just between 200 and 400 kg of coal equivalent. Most of this inadequate supply comes from traditional biomass sources; fossil fuels and electricity are used with low efficiencies in industrial production and, to a much lesser extent, by urban households.

Commonalities of Chinese energetics with those of other populous poor nations are thus obvious: a low-income society with a predomi-nantly rural population, still heavily dependent on biomass and using inadequate amounts of fossil fuels and electricity in an inefficient man-ner to industrialize its economy.

Shanghai, China's foremost industrial center, consumes commercial energy at a level approaching per capita rates of poorer European Mediterranean countries (nearly 2 tons of coal equivalent) while peas-ants on the loess highlands of Shaanxi dig out tree roots and collect dung cakes to cook their thin gruels and heat their cave houses. China's domestic energy gaps are thus no less wide and no less common than those between the urban elites of Bombay, Lagos, or Rio and the subsistence peasants of Bihar, Kano, or Ceara, respectively.

But there are peculiarities. Since the Communist Party assumed control in 1949, China is the only large, populous poor nation that has guided its modernization by the quite rigid central planning of, until most recently, a decidedly Stalinist variety, and this strategy has had a profound effect on levels, modes, and efficiencies of energy extraction, transfers, and consumption.

The Stalinist obsession with heavy industries, an unusually high share of coal in primary energy consumption, an excessive promotion of inefficient small-scale enterprises, and the ubiquitous mismanagement characteristic of systems lacking personal responsibility have combined to set China apart as perhaps the world's most wasteful convertor of commercial fuels and electricity. On the other hand, this deficiency presents a huge potential for efficiency improvements and conservation so that a significant part of energy needed to drive China's modernization can come from the existing production.

The size of China's population—1.06 billion at the end of 1986, about 22 percent of the global total—and the inevitable gain of at least another quarter billion people during the next generation will make solution of the country's energy problems extraordinarily challenging, especially as the choices should not worsen the already much degraded environment and should harmonize with maintenance of the intensive agriculture needed to assure food self-sufficiency (after all, one-fifth of humankind can never rely on imports to secure its food).

Fortunately, China, unlike other large, poor nations—oil-rich Mexico excepting—is very well endowed with virtually every kind of energy resource and can thus confidently plan for long-term energy self-sufficiency. Yet a closer look at this impressive endowment reveals many limitations: a few absolute shortages, some qualitative and many distributional limits, and the omnipresent relative ceiling as the country's riches prorate to only a modest patrimony when divided among more than one billion people.

In addition to its recent tumultuous history and its unequaled population size, the third of the greatest Chinese peculiarities is the unprecedented experiment of the post-1978 years. Although it is just the latest of repeated efforts to reconcile the irreconcilable—a one-party bureaucracy running an enterprise system—and as such it could easily be dismissed as a doomed temporary aberration or extolled as an admirable quest, it is undeniable that the new policies have already improved the lives of hundreds of millions of Chinese to an extent that they would have considered impossible just a decade ago.

These changes have ranged from fundamental physical betterment (most significantly, average per capita food availability shot up to within less than 10 percent of the Japanese mean) to a much looser spiritual milieu (from prospering Buddhist temples to frequently daring writing), and they are all part of a grandiosely conceived dash to national prosperity. Modernization in one generation is undoubtedly more of a mobilizational slogan than a realistic possibility, but the rush is on—and its energy requirements, even with the best conceivable conservation, can be characterized only as stupendous.

Consequently, this book, after first describing the country's energy resources, appraises the existing production and consumption patterns (subdivided into the two disparate realms of rural and industrial-urban energetics) and presents a detailed review and assessment of the ways Chinese are proposing to provide the energy supply for an economy whose output is to quadruple in two decades.

Adherence to Communist ideology continues, but the traditional pursuit of *fu qiang*—wealth and power—has been asserting itself conspicuously since 1978. This book will enable a persevering reader to judge the possibilities and limits of energizing the grand visions of Chinese prosperity in the coming generation and beyond.

② RESOURCES: Riches and Poverty

China's large territory—more than 6 percent of the world's continental surface—may not in itself be a guarantee of substantial energy endowment, especially as far as fossil fuel deposits are concerned: Brazil's poor mineral fuel fortunes come obviously to mind, and India's relatively small and poor-quality coal deposits and rather meager oil reserves are yet another example of unfulfilled expectations. But a large territory increases greatly the probability of substantial altitudinal differences and voluminous water flows: both India and Brazil have huge hydroelectric potentials, and China, with the world's highest plateau in the Southwest and large eastward-flowing streams dropping toward the coastal lowlands, is unsurpassed worldwide, leaving behind even the USSR's immense hydroenergy resources.

But the great eras of sedimentary minerals did not bypass China either, and the recoverable resources in the country's extensive coal basins are rivaled only by those of the United States and the Soviet Union; moreover, the quality of China's northern coals is mostly outstanding. Hydrocarbon reserves have been so far much less impressive, although they have been sufficient to support annual crude-oil output large enough to place China among the top half-dozen producers worldwide. However, a major offshore search, underway since the late 1970s and so far without any sensational discoveries to its credit, will in time certainly amass significant new reserves, and the latest policies of allowing the experienced foreign oil companies to take part in onshore exploration will surely result in the development of new oil and gas fields. China's sedimentary basins are simply too numerous

Table 2.1

Comparison of 1985 fossil fuel reserves in China, USA and USSR (all values are in J)

Country	Coal	Crude Oil	Natural Gas	Total	Per capita
China	2.5×10^{21}	1.1×10^{20}	3.2×10^{19}	2.65×10^{21}	2.5×10^{12}
United States	5.5×10^{21}	1.5×10^{20}	2.0×10^{20}	5.85×10^{21}	2.5×10^{13}
Soviet Union	4.0×10^{21}	3.5×10^{20}	1.5×10^{21}	5.85×10^{21}	2.1×10^{13}

Sources: Coal reserves from World Energy Conference (1983); crude oil and natural gas reserves from *The Oil and Gas Journal*.

and too extensive for this not to happen. At the same time, only an ignorant analyst could now join those irresponsible promoters who a decade ago were presenting China as the future Oriental Saudi Arabia.

Even when leaving unequaled (but difficult to compare) hydro potential aside, superior coal deposits and substantial crude-oil reserves put China's mineral fuel reserves into the same order of magnitude as the United States and the Soviet Union, the world's two resource-richest nations (table 2.1). Yet, as the last column of table 2.1 shows, China's enviable energy patrimony shrinks to an order of magnitude below the U.S. or Soviet levels once divided by more than one billion people. This fundamental limitation brought on by the country's large population must be kept in mind when assessing China's modernization outlook. In per capita terms, China's fossil fuel reserves and hydroenergy potential are surpassed by dozens of countries, and although the known endowment is certainly large enough to energize the nationwide economic modernization and to allow for maintenance of a decent standard of life, it clearly sets major limits on the country's developmental strategy.

Even with the Japanese levels of energy conversion efficiency, the Chinese cannot contemplate achieving the levels of Western affluence of two generations ago. Increasing ownership of electronic gadgets, impressively improved life expectancy (especially in Asian comparisons), and better everyday diets are most welcome tangible signs of China's developmental success, but the great attributes of affluent Western civilization—cheap and varied food, comfortable housing, personal mobility, and easy access to higher education—are subsidized by energy flows averaging annually at least 60–80 GJ per capita, a level the Chinese simply cannot reach during the next two generations (as already noted, their current annual consumption averages about 20 GJ per capita).

The other notable complicating factors concerning China's modern energy resources are extremely uneven spatial distribution of coal reserves and a no less unbalanced location of the huge hydroelectric potential. And although among the alternative energy resources geothermal potential should eventually be of major local importance, opportunities for direct solar energy conversion are relatively limited, as is any modern, efficient conversion of biomass energies traditionally used in an inefficient manner throughout China's countryside.

Altogether, then, this is a story of dichotomies: absolute riches dissolved in relative poverty; development of large resources made difficult by staggering regional disparities; promising theoretical potentials negated by technical considerations. The following sections will document the main points made in this brief opening, first for the renewable flows, then for fossil fuels.

2.1 Renewable flows

One of the beneficial legacies of the heightened worldwide interest in energy affairs has been the emergence of a more systematic look at resource endowment. Before 1973, surveys of energy resources rarely went beyond fossil fuels, whereas after that great divide, inclusion of renewable capabilities appears to be obligatory even when the practically exploitable potential adds up to merely marginal contributions. Fortunately for the Chinese, theirs is not such a case: the country is endowed with impressive geothermal energy flows whose harnessing can translate into far from negligible local heat and electricity supplies; it has an abundance of slope land suitable for fuelwood plantations, which can make, with proper species selection and careful management, a fundamental and sustainable difference in easing severe shortages of heating and cooking fuels throughout rural China; and its hydroenergy potential, by far the largest in the world, can be tapped both in the form of tens of thousands of small hydro stations suitable for local electrification and in scores of multigigawatt projects, including several of the world's largest hydro sites whose development is planned to make a critical contribution to China's modernization effort.

The only major weakness in the renewable realm concerns direct solar radiation, whose flux is lowest in the most densely settled regions. Consequently, I shall start a review of the renewable flows with a rather brief look at this relatively marginal source and end it with a detailed appraisal of the rich hydroenergy capabilities.

2.1.1 Solar radiation and wind

China's first nationwide map of insolation became available in 1978 (fig. 2.1). It confirmed the expectations based on the country's location at the eastern fringe of the Eurasian landmass: solar radiation has a generally declining NW-SE gradient, with the peaks on the high Xizang-Qinghai Plateau and with the minimum in the southern interior basin and valley locations. This distribution, reflecting the pronounced influence of the Siberian anticyclone in the Northwest and the strong cyclonic (monsoonal) flows in the Southeast, makes for a nearly perfect mismatch between the total radiation received at the ground and population density. The peak values are on the virtually uninhabited Xizang (Tibetan) grasslands, and the minima embrace all of Sichuan, by far China's most populous province with over 100 million people. A newer map, published in the inaugural issue of a new solar energy journal (Wang, Anang, and Li 1980), differs in numerous details but displays the same unmistakable gradient (fig. 2.2).

Sichuan's scarcity of direct sunlight is well illustrated by the fact that during the first decade of LANDSAT operation it was possible to acquire only two completely clear images because morning clouds or fogs over the basin are rarely absent and the LANDSAT satellite scans all regions at about 9:30 A.M. local time. Chengdu, the province's capital, receives no more than 1,150 hours of sunshine a year, and its foggy reality is mirrored in a local saying about dogs barking at the sun. In contrast, virtually the whole Northwest and much of the North get over 2,000 hours of sunshine annually—but the more than 3,000 hours of insolation, the high altitude, and the extraordinarily clean atmosphere above the Xizang-Qinghai Plateau mean that the total energy received there at the ground is much higher than in the often naturally dusty or industrially polluted air over the northern provinces.

In international comparison, the densely settled farmlands and cities of the coastal and interior South receive annually no more solar energy than the Pacific Northwest, Maine, or parts of northwestern Europe, all places of little appeal for direct solar conversions. On the other hand, practically the whole Xizang-Qinghai Plateau gets yearly more solar energy than Arizona or New Mexico or the northernmost Sahelian part of Nigeria. This sharp resource population mismatch is,

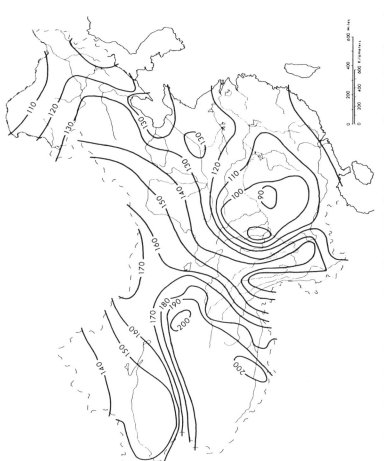

Figure 2.1: Distribution of average solar radiation (in kcal/m²·year) according to Beijing Planetarium (1977).

Figure 2.2: Distribution of average solar radiation (in kcal/m^2·year) according to Wang, Anang, and Li (1980).

naturally, an irremovable obstacle to any widespread convenient use of solar energy in households, as well as to promising large-scale commercial conversions.

Not surprisingly, the overall contribution of direct solar conversions has been negligible (Gong, Lu and Tian 1984). Applications have been confined overwhelmingly to the sunnier regions of China, most notably to the cities and suburbs in the North (Beijing, Tianjin, Xi'an) and to rural areas in the northwestern interior (Gansu, Xinjiang, Xizang). A 1983 survey listed about 200,000 m² of hot water collectors used largely in the public service sector (bathhouses, barbershops, restaurants, hotels, hospitals). Their prices ranged from Rmb (renminbi, "people's currency") 100 to 150/m², until recently clearly beyond the reach of most private users. By 1983 only 5,000 small household units (with a capacity of 60 liters) costing about Rmb 70–90 were in use, an insignificant number considering China's more than 200 million families—or the hundreds of thousands of domestic hot water heaters now installed in the United States, Australia, Japan, and Israel.

Even were the total collector area 100 times larger than in 1983 (i.e., 20 million m²) and all these solar water heaters could operate at a North Chinese average of five to eight months, nationwide fuel savings would not amount to more than about three million tons of standard coal (as a typical heater saves 100–200 kg/m²•year), a fraction of one percent of the current coal consumption. Prospects for solar cooking are similarly limited in nationwide impact. By 1984 there were some 35,000 parabolic dish cookers in use in Gansu and Qinghai provinces, where severe deforestation, extreme fuel shortages, and abundant sunshine made their introduction appealing in spite of their relatively high cost of Rmb 60–80 per unit. Poor quality of the whole assembly and deterioration of reflective surfaces have been the other two key persistent problems. Heat balance analyses and operational testing established the desirable sizes at 2–2.5 m² with 1–1.5 kW of thermal power, resulting in annual fuel savings equivalent to about half a ton of standard coal per cooker.

Solar energy conversions for uses other than water heating and cooking have been mere curiosities: a prototype 54 m² dryer for Chinese dates in Shanxi; a 64 m² timber-drying kiln (Feixi county, Anhui); a 385 m² solar still on Hainan Island (Guangdong); and two smaller installations, 50 and 128 m², on the Xisha Islands in the South China Sea. Photovoltaic research and applications are much behind Western levels, with total annual production of less than 80 kW in 1983 compared to the annual combined Western output of about 10 MW, and costs of Rmb 60 per peak watt (no sensible comparisons are possible here because of the Renminbi's artificial exchange rate). Current Western averages, however, are around \$5/W for the best first-generation single-crystal silicon wafers and \$2.5–3.0/W for the spreading second-generation semicrystalline and amorphous silicon devices. Aside from railway stations, ports have been the most frequent recipients of photovoltaic cells, and there are also more than 100 electrified fences in the pastures of Nei Monggol.

Interior areas receiving plenty of solar radiation are also among the windiest places in China, again the consequence of the influence exerted by strong seasonal pressure cells. Coastal areas south of Jiangsu province are also quite windy, whereas several densely populated interior areas—above all the Sichuan Basin, central Hunan, and the valleys of the Wei He and the Fen He—have calms for at least 30, and in some places even 50–70, percent of the year (Yang and Ding 1980).

China's total wind-generation capacity was estimated at 1.6×10^{12}W, and about 1×10^{11}W is in the near-surface flows that could be tapped, the same order of magnitude as China's total hydroenergy potential, but only a very small part of this huge flux will be eventually recovered. By far the greatest potential is in the area of 200,000 km² between 90°–100°E and 40°–45°N at the narrow end of a huge funnel formed by the Altay, Kunlun, and Tianshan ranges, but, once again, this region is only sparsely populated. In most of Nei Monggol, where some grasslands have relatively dense pastoral populations, winds faster than 3 meters per second are present more than 200 days a year, and this area has become the main focus of Chinese efforts to develop small wind generators.

There have been numerous reports about construction and utilization of such devices ranging from 100 W to 20 kW. By the end of 1985, 3,000 small wind-powered generators, mostly with capacities of a few hundred watts, were working not only on the grasslands of Nei Monggol, but also in Gansu, Xinjiang, and Heilongjiang, and several larger units were installed on Sijiao Island of the Zhoushan archipelago off the coast of Zhejiang. About 8,000 wind-powered pumps are produced annually, most of them going to coastal salt ponds. As with the direct solar conversions, the overall contribution of wind power to China's energy supply will remain negligible for decades: as yet there are no plans for any large-scale projects akin, for example, to recent utility-managed wind farms in California.

2.1.2 Geothermal potential

China's geothermal resources should be among the world's richest, given its otherwise hardly cherishable tectonic position. The country is affected by the movements of both the large Pacific plate and the fast-advancing Indian plate. The latter collided with Eurasia in what is now southern Xizang (the suture line is more or less along the Yarlung Zangpo Jiang, or Brahmaputra, valley), and it is in southern Xizang and western Yunnan where the potential for larger-scale commercial utilization of geothermal energy is by far the highest; otherwise, only smaller areas along the southeastern coast and most of Taiwan belong to this highly promising category (fig. 2.3).

Distribution of hot springs is, of course, the simplest indicator of geothermal capacities. A nationwide inventory now lists 2,412 separate sources, of which 279 have temperature exceeding 60°C. Predictably, Xizang, Yunnan, and Guangdong dominate. The annual heat discharge of China's hot springs sums up to 111 PJ (a thermal equivalent of 3.8 million tons of standard coal) of which Xizang has 43, Yunnan 26, and Guangdong 4 percent (Ren, Yang, and Tang 1984).

Resource assessment for purposes of electricity generation must distinguish between convection- and conduction-dominated geothermal fields. For convection fields estimates based on heat volume calculations and geochemical thermometry add up to 220 MW of electricity-generating capacity for identified resources and to 3,513 MW for possible installations. Further, 494 MW of identified and 3,491 MW of potential resources can be used directly in other thermal applications. Yangbajing field, located 90 km northwest of Lhasa, has by far the largest identified geothermal reosurces: at least 26 MWe in 160°–172°C flow from depths between 150 and 200 m as well as 54 MWe from nearly 5,400 m³/hr of lateral flow. Preliminary evaluation of forty other Tibetan convection-dominated fields puts their possible capacity at 3,200 MW, or 91 percent of the national total.

In the conduction-dominated basins the temperature gradient in cap rock must be over 3°C/100 m, and a permeable thermal reservoir must be no deeper than 3 km to consider any possible geothermal generation. Total area of these fields, estimated from geotectonic maps, is 114,000 km² (about 1.2 percent of China's territory), and the total identified and possible capacities are, respectively, 26.613 and 588 thermal GW. Bulk of the identified resources are in the Songliao (1,415 GW or 54 percent)

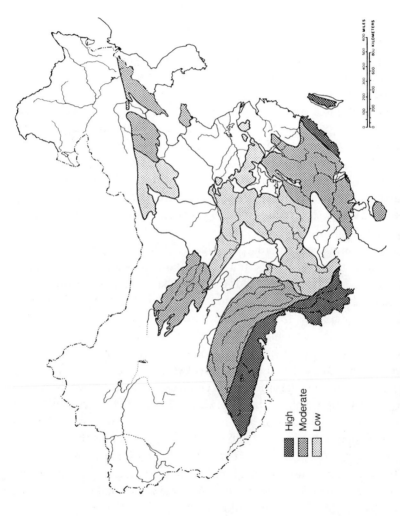

Figure 2.3: China's principal geothermal regions (State Geological Bureau 1979).

and Huabei (680 GW or 26 percent) basins (in both instances reservoir temperatures are mostly 80°C and their thickness is 500 m). Locations of the ten conduction-dominated geothermal basins as well as those of sixty-five identified convection-dominated fields are shown in figure 2.4.

Nationwide aggregates of geothermal resources suitable for electricity generation—200 MW in identified and a further 3,500 MW in the possible category—are much less than expected given China's tectonic history: their full harnessing would expand the 1985 installed generating capacity by less than 5 percent, but the location of the most viable sites guarantees that only a tiny fraction of even the identified resources will be exploited during the next few decades. In view of the currently very small installed geothermal capacity I will briefly review the existing projects in this resource section rather than include them in a later survey of thermal electricity generation.

Of China's seven geothermal stations six have capacities below 1 kW and four are inefficient binary installations where the hot water between 67° and 91°C is used first to vaporize a working medium (chlorethane or butane) with a lower boiling point. Yangbajing station is still the only medium-sized wet-steam project. Its first 1-MW unit, put into operation in 1977, has never reached the full designed capacity (at best it peaks at 620 kW), but the two 3-MW units put on line in 1982 work more satisfactorily, so that by 1983 nearly two-fifths of Lhasa's electricity came from Yangbajing. In 1986 another 3-MW unit went into operation. Xizang's second large (7-MW) geothermal station is under construction at Lunjug field in Ngari prefecture. The 1984 total of 8.356 MW of China's geothermal capacity was still less than one-tenth of El Salvador's installations (95 MW) and two orders of magnitude below the U.S. capability, and it represents less than half a percent of the worldwide geothermal power on line.

The identified total heat flow harnessible for direct thermal uses, 2,613 GW, is impressively large as its continuous recovery would provide annually some 82 EJ, or roughly four times the total of China's primary energy production in the mid-1980s. Prorated over the total area of conduction-dominated fields this works out to an average flux of 23 W/m^2 or nearly 400 times higher than the mean global geothermal flow of 0.063 W/m^2—but given the necessities of deep drilling and insulated-conduit distribution (often also of water treatment) and logistic problems of harnessing the diffuse flow over large areas, it is obvious that practical prospects are for no more

Figure 2.4: Distribution of conduction and convection-dominated geothermal fields in China (Ren, Yang, and Tang 1984).

Convection-dominated fields, high temperature

Convection-dominated fields, middle and low temperature

Conduction-dominated fields

than restricted local uses.

Current direct heat applications include heating of greenhouses (80,500 m² in 1983, mostly in Liaoning, Hebei, and Xizang) and fishing pools (205,000 m² in the same year, above all in Tianjin, Fujian, and Jiangxi); hot water for washing and dyeing in the textile industry (predominantly in the capital and in Tianjin); and space heating and public bathing. Of 400,000 m² of geothermally heated housing in 1983, 230,000 m² were in Beijing and 160,000 m² in Tianjin, and both cities have plans for further considerable expansion of both heating and public bathing. The total equivalent of these agricultural, industrial, service, and domestic uses is estimated at 247 MW at 40°C, an insignificant fraction of the huge conductive flux, illustrating well the limits of practical exploitation of this large but diffuse source of energy.

2.1.3 Biomass

No other Chinese energy resource is so contrastingly dichotomous as the country's biomass: so critical for everyday rural needs yet so ubiquitously scarce, its potential production so large yet the current sustainable harvest so low. At the most fundamental level is the relative poverty of China's biomass, its disproportionately low share in global primary production and storage. Although all such figures, be it on a national or a global level, can be only rough approximations, recent advances in the study of various ecosystems make it possible to put China's standing phytomass (all above- and underground parts of trees, shrubs, grasses, crops, and aquatic plants) at about 30 billion dry tons and its annual net productivity at no more than 4.3 billion tons (table 2.2).

These aggregates represent about 3 percent of the respective global totals, whereas China's territory covers nearly 6.5 percent of all dry lands. Another way to express the country's low photosynthetic output is to compare the overall conversion efficiency of the process. The global net energy fixation of terrestrial plants is nearly 0.3 percent of annual solar radiation, but the Chinese efficiency is no more than 0.15, and possibly as little as 0.1, percent. Extensive areas of highly stressed ecosystems in China's large, dry, high-altitude interior (deserts, semideserts, poor grasslands), degradation of previously fine grasslands owing to overgrazing, conversion to cropland, and desertification, and low and low-quality forest coverage combine to produce these poor outcomes.

Table 2.2

Areas, standing phytomass, and net primary productivity of China's major ecosystems in the early 1980s

Ecosystems	Area (10⁶ha)	Average standing phytomass (t/ha)	Average net primary productivity (t/ha)	Total storage (10⁸t)	Total production (10⁸t)
Boreal and temperate forests	70	200	8	140	6
Subtropical and tropical forests	45	220	10	100	5
Shrublands	45	50	7	2	3
Tall grasslands	40	20	7	8	3
Medium grasslands	100	15	6	15	6
Desertified and de-generated grasslands	120	10	1	12	1
Grassy hills	80	10	4	8	3
Arable land	100	10	10	10	10
Tree crops	5	100	10	5	1
Swamps	10	80	10	8	1
Deserts	110	5	1	6	1
Settlements, trans-portation, mining	15	5	5	1	1
Barren land	220	2	1	5	2
Total	960			320	43

Source: Author's calculations based on a variety of Chinese sources and on Smil (1983).

In terms of substantial, long-term contribution to national energy supply, forests are the source of most of the phytomass. Crop residues, above all cereal straw, which are now so critical for China's rural energy needs (see section 3.1.1), should not be even calculated in terms of their energy potential: in a properly run agroecosystem they should be reserved for animal feeding and bedding, small-scale manufacture, and, above all, for extensive recycling (directly or indirectly via traditional composting).

Yet China's forests are among the world's poorest. Results of a comprehensive 1976 survey showed the total coverage of just 121.6 million hectares (ha), no more than 12.7 percent of China's territory. However, 65 million ha (53 percent) were middle-aged and young forests, including 28.2 million ha of new post-1949 planting, survivals of the repeated mass afforestation campaigns during which more than 100 million ha were planted but more than two-thirds did not survive.

Adding shelter-belts (which Chinese count as a part of their forest total) to the 65 million ha means that in 1976 about 73 million ha, or three-fifths of China's forested area, were in poorly stocked secondary growth.

Clearly, Chinese count as forests many plantings that would not easily fit into the "closed" category (forests whose canopies cover at least 25 percent of the ground from a perpendicular view). Even if all of China's forested land were under mature trees, this area, prorated to about 0.11 ha per capita, would not put China higher than about 120th place among the world's 150 nations (many of which also use dubious forest definitions).

In terms of commercial wood resources China's position is no better: with about 9 m^3 per capita it is about sixtieth among the seventy-five nations for which this ratio is available. This reflects not only China's large population and the relatively small forested area but also the poor state and low productivity of Chinese forests. Whereas a typical North American forest will store about 110 m^3 of timber per ha, the Chinese mean is only around 75 m^3. Even the most productive Chinese forests yield annually no more than 0.7 m^3 of timber per ha; Scandinavian means are nearly three times higher.

Low storages and productivities are made economically and environmentally even more distressing owing to their extremely uneven distribution (fig. 2.5). In the Northwest the mountains of Nei Monggol, Heilongjiang, and Jilin (above all the Daxing'an and Xiaoxing'an ranges) were covered in 1976 with 33.8 million ha of forests, storing 3.08 billion m^3 of timber. In the Southwest, in Yunnan and in western Sichuan, 17 million ha of forest had 2.34 billion m^3. These two regions at the opposite ends of China had about 42 percent of all forests and contained 56.8 percent of all timber resources. This higher share is easily explained by the fact that the Northeast's boreal and the Southwest's subtropical forests have most of China's remaining rich, climax, primary growth. And, most unfortunately, widespread deforestation which has cut climax forests by some astonishing shares during the past three decades—55 percent in Yunnan, 30 percent in Sichuan—still has not been eliminated. The demand for new cropland, industrial timber, and household fuel continues to diminish the area of remaining natural forests (for many details on this environmental degradation and its consequences see Smil 1984). Sustainable fuelwood harvests from China's forests are thus very limited, and the recently released data enable one to fix this sensible utilization rate with some accuracy.

Figure 2.5: Distribution of China's forested areas. Lighter tone in the Central-South and Southeast indicates broken distribution of thin, secondary growth.

According to the 1976 inventory, four-fifths of the 121.6 million ha (that is, 98 million ha) were in "industrial" forests with timber suitable for commercial harvesting, 7 percent (8.25 million ha) were "economic" forests (mostly trees yielding edible and industrial oils, lacquer, shellac, and other raw materials), 6.4 percent (7.85 million ha), shelter forests (mainly in the dry North and Northwest as barriers against desertification), bamboo groves covered 2.6 percent (3.15 million ha) and forests maintained specifically for fuelwood extended over only 3.67 million ha or 3 percent of all forested land. These firewood forests are spread in an uneven, patchy pattern across the country, and their wood reserves were estimated at 44.71 million m^3, or a mere 12 m^3/ha. Annual wood fuel production is not known with any certainty.

Depending on the species and the region, fuelwood yields can range from just 1–2 tons per ha a year in the arid Northwest to as much as 25–30 tons per ha a year in the southern, rainy subtropical provinces. Typical averages throughout most of the North are 3.75–4.5 tons/ha, and in the lower Chang Jiang basin, between 7.5 and 11.5 tons/ha a year. Should the mean be about 6 tons/ha the nationwide annual yield would be 22 million tons of firewood. Naturally, woody phytomass for combustion can be gathered from all other forests: taking their total area (about 118 million ha) and an average firewood yield of 600 kg/ha (equivalent to 20 percent of the mean timber yield of 3 tons/ha year) would provide an annual supply of just short of 71 million tons of woody matter. The total sustainable (or, as the Chinese have repeatedly called it, rational) harvest of firewood would be about 93 million tons a year. Yet, as will be seen in section 3.1.1, actual annual firewood consumption has been recently about double this sustainable rate.

Consequently, China cannot contemplate using natural forest biomass as an important ingredient of overall energy supply, that is, a resource for direct combustion or for subsequent conversions to electricity or fuel alcohols. In fact, even the traditional use of forest woody matter as household fuel should be curtailed as much as practicable, and new fuelwood groves and plantations should be set up on usually plentiful barren slopes and oddland: that the Chinese have finally started to move in this direction is certainly encouraging (see section 4.2.5).

Although biomass energies are still critical for everyday rural life, and although their supply must be expanded on an environmentally acceptable basis to satisfy the needs of the large rural population, neither wood nor straw and organic wastes can figure prominently in industrial modernization efforts of the coming decades: only further expansion of coal and hydrocarbon extraction and substantial expansion of electricity generation can fill this need, and Chinese are fortunate enough to possess not only very large coal reserves and promising hydrocarbon deposits but also impressive resources of hydroenergy.

2.1.4 Hydroenergy

As with the geothermal potential, China's location at the eastern rim of Euroasia explains the country's extraordinarily large resources of hydroenergy: large rivers originating on the world's highest plateau in the western regions of China have steep gradients during their eastward descent, and their deep valleys present many outstanding opportunities for construction of large hydrostations. Moreover, hilly terrain throughout the southern provinces, inland or coastal, combines with abundant monsoonal precipitation in offering literally countless possibilities for local small-scale hydroelectricity generation.

About 50,000 Chinese rivers have drainage basins of over 100 km², and some 1,200 of these streams have catchments larger than 1,000 km² (major streams and their basins are shown in figure 2.6). Altogether, these rivers carry annually about 2,640 km³ of water, the fifth highest volume worldwide after Brazil, the USSR, Canada, and the United States. The first systematic survey of their generating potential was undertaken in 1954–55, and it put the total theoretical power at 540 GW under average water flows, with 300 GW suitable for eventual development (Cao 1981). A reappraisal carried out between 1977 and 1980 raised the total to 680 GW, with 379 GW, or about 55 percent, actually exploitable. This puts China in the first place worldwide, well ahead of the USSR with 269 GW, Brazil with 213 GW, and the United States with 197 GW; steep gradients of Chinese rivers more than make up for their lower runoffs.

In its special insert in August 1982 *Shuili fadian* (Water Power) carried detailed results of the latest survey, with breakdowns of China's hydroenergy resources both by major river basins and by provinces. Figure 2.7 shows the distribution of exploitable hydroenergy by river system according to possible annual output rather than by installable capacity. Of the nationwide total of 1.9 PWh, slightly over 50 percent come from the Chang Jiang (Yangzi) basin, roughly one-seventh from the Yarlung Zangbo, and one-tenth from the deep parallel valleys of the three southwestern rivers near the Burmese,

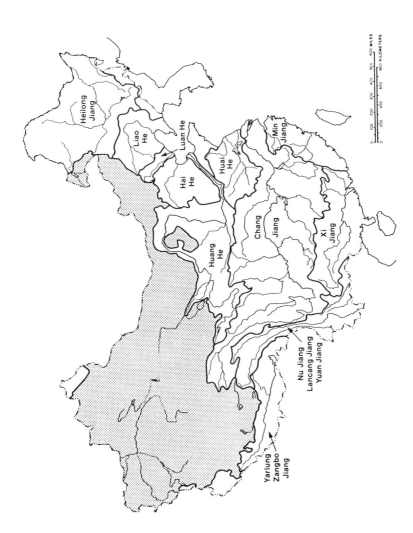

Figure 2.6: China's principal river basins (dotted area is without an outlet to the ocean).

Figure 2.7: Potential hydrogenerating capacity of China's principal river basins in GW (*Shuili fadian* 1982). See also table 2.3.

Table 2.3

China's exploitable hydro resources by river system

River system	Installable capacity (GW)	Annual output (TWh)	Percent of total
Chang Jiang	197.25	1,027	53.4
Huang He	26.00	117	6.1
Zhu Jiang	24.85	112	5.8
Hai and Luan He	2.13	5	0.3
Huai He	0.66	2	0.1
Northeastern rivers	13.71	44	2.3
Southeastern rivers	13.90	55	2.9
Southwestern rivers	37.68	210	10.9
Yarlung Zangbo Jiang	50.38	297	15.4
Northwestern rivers	9.97	54	2.8
National total	378.53	1,923	100.00

Source: *Shuili fadian* (Water Power Generation), 1982(8), special insert. See also figure 2.7.

Thai, and Laotian boundary (table 2.3).

The Chang Jiang is both the longest and most voluminous Chinese stream. With Tuotuo He now given as its main headstream, the river measures 6,300 km (compared to the Nile's 6,650 and the Amazon's 6,437 km), gathers its waters from a basin of 1.8 million km² (nearly a fifth of all China), and its annual runoff of over 1,100 km³ (42 percent of China's total) results in an average discharge of 35,000 m³/sec, third worldwide after the Amazon and the Zaire. Of its total descent of 5,060 m (or 0.8 m/km), 95 percent occurs between the source and Yibin county in Sichuan; a cascade of stations with a total capacity of 49 GW (generating 260 TWh a year) is planned between Yibin and the town of Shigu upstream in Yunnan.

Only 4 percent of the descent falls between Yibin and Yichang in Hubei, but this section includes the spectacularly narrow (300 m) and steep confines (cliffs up to 500 m) of the Three Gorges (San Xia, made up of Qutang, Wu, and Xiling Xia), a unique site offering an opportunity for a giant hydrostation whose installed capacity could be surpassed only by the planned Inga project on the Zaire (see section 4.2.4). The point where the river leaves the gorge and enters the alluvial plain of western Hubei is now the site of the largest Chinese hydrostation so far, Gezhouba, planned for 2,715 MW; from there to East China the river descends a mere 40 m over 1,800 km, offering no good dam sites.

Narrow valleys and large drops of major tributaries of the Chang Jiang, above all the Dadu and the Yalong, also provide sites for multigigawatt projects, as do the main southwestern (Lancang) and southern (Hongshui) streams.

Dominance of the southern and southwestern rivers originating on the Xizang Plateau and in the Himalayas is thus obvious: regional breakdown shows the Southwest with 61.4 percent of producible hydroelectricity, the Central-South a distant 12.8 percent, the Northwest 11.1 percent, the densely populated East only 4.7 percent, the Northeast 3.2, and the North a mere 1.8 percent. These great regional disparities are not, of course, anything specifically Chinese, but the great distances separating the best potential sites of giant hydroprojects in the interior Southwest from major load centers in the East, North, and Northeast (2,000–3,000 km) and uncommonly rugged terrain (including transects of steep mountain ridges and deepcut valleys with repeated height differences of up to 5 km) make any plans for large-scale development extraordinarily difficult.

As a result, remaining hydroenergy resources are still very large: only 0.04 percent of the exploitable potential was tapped in 1949; two decades later this share rose to just 1 percent; and long-delayed completion of several major projects during the 1970s brought the fraction to 5.3 percent by 1980 and to about 7 percent by 1985. Plans for the next two decades envisage pushing the share to over 15 percent, still far behind the three- to fourfold higher North American or European shares (for example, the U.S. share is now about 40 percent, the West German over 60 percent).

Approximately one-fifth of the exploitable hydrogeneration capacity is in sites suitable for small-scale (up to 12 MW but more typically just several hundred kW) projects. A detailed regional breakdown published in 1983 shows that of 71.313 GW available in small sites, nearly one-half (33.382 GW or 46.8 percent) is in the Southwest, and a bit over one-fifth is in the South-Central region, which has more than two-fifths of installed capacity as well as the largest share of developed resources (table 2.4).

Although the spatial distribution of small-scale hydro capacities is predictably uneven, about 1,104 of China's 2,133 counties can tap more than 10 MW in small sites; in 600 counties the exploitable capacities range between 30 and 100 MW; in 134, over 100 MW, and in a large part of the country, especially in the Chang Jiang basin where 249 of 932 counties have sites with total capacity of over 10 MW, water-

Table 2.4

Regional distribution of hydrogeneration capacity exploitable by small stations and their capabilities as of 1982

Region	Exploitable capacity (GW)	(%)	Exploited capacity (GW)	(%)	Exploited capacity as percent of the exploitable one
Northeast	1.96	2.8	0.19	2.3	9.7
North	1.64	2.3	0.22	2.7	13.4
Northwest	9.36	13.1	0.48	5.9	5.1
East	9.42	13.2	1.95	24.2	20.7
South-Central	15.54	21.8	3.42	42.3	22.0
Southwest	33.38	46.8	1.82	22.6	5.5
Total	71.30	100.00	8.08	100.00	11.3

Source: Xiao Dianhua (1983).

driven electricity generation for local use has become an important ingredient of rural modernization.

The rich opportunities for construction of hydrostations of virtually any capacity would alone guarantee hydrogeneration's prominent place in any sensible strategy of China's energy development—but this importance is further strengthened by multipurpose utilization of most Chinese reservoirs: river flow control in a nation whose settled areas are so prone to recurrent floods and droughts naturally has a high priority, and aquaculture has always occupied a critical place in supplying high-quality protein for predominantly grain- and vegetable-consuming peasants. Finally, traditional Chinese skills in hydraulic engineering are also helpful in executing many small projects.

Before closing the review of renewable resources it should be mentioned that the country has also a fairly large tidal energy potential. Its detailed appraisal (Xu 1984) put the total at 20 GW, capable of generating annually about 58 TWh. This is a substantial potential, especially when compared to the currently operating thermal power plant capacities in the East (about 13 GW), the region with about 90 percent of tidal sites. However, only a small fraction is utilizable, a relationship even more obvious as far as the estimates of the near-shore wave energy potential are concerned (150 GW in total). By 1985 seven small tidal stations were in operation with an aggregate generating capacity of about 4 MW. Jiangxia station in Leqing Bay (Zhejiang), tapping the tides up to 8.39 m, is by far the largest; its designed capacity is 3 MW with six 500kW turbines (Li 1984). Baixiakou in Rushan county (Shandong) is second with 960 kW.

2.2 Fossil fuels

China has an ancient tradition in extracting coal and natural gas. Local preindustrial burning of coal was not uncommon in many other countries with outcropping coal seams, but drilling for salt water in land-locked Sichuan led to numerous discoveries of natural gas in the province. Bamboo drills, human and animal power, and bamboo pipes were used to complete relatively deep natural gas wells centuries before the introduction of modern technologies. But all of these efforts went ahead without any systematic appraisal of mineral fuel deposits, and it was only during the last decades of the last dynasty when some reliable assessments of rich coal resources became available for most Chinese provinces.

Detailed systematic resource evaluations got underway only after 1949, first with a heavy reliance on Soviet personnel and expertise, during the 1960s and early 1970s with inadequate domestic capabilities, and since the late 1970s with increasingly important Western and Japanese participation. The work is still far from finished: although there will be no major surprises as far as coal deposits are concerned, the figures available for other solid fossil fuel, peat, and oil shale resources are, in the absence of any serious commercial interest, mere order of magnitude estimates.

But as neither peats nor oil shales will figure prominently in China's long-term development strategies (the country has too much excellent coal to turn to those inferior fuels as anything but marginal local sources), the most important uncertainty concerns China's hydrocarbon resources. With extensive exploratory drilling finally underway in the South China Sea—a region seen by many petroleum geologists as one of the few remaining untapped oil provinces with potentially large, conveniently located deposits—the wide-spread expectations of sizable discoveries that would greatly expand China's current oil reserves are now undergoing their critical test. The verdict is far from complete, but the first few years of partial returns indicate far fewer riches than those envisaged by many enthusiasts of the 1970s.

2.2.1 Coals

In spite of nearly a century of appraisals of China's coal deposits, the numbers still keep changing substantially. As coal-bearing sediments cover about 550,000 km² (or over 5 percent) of Chinese territory, total resources must be enormous. During the years of exaggerated Great Leap Forward claims they were put at as much as 9.6 trillion tons, more than the best current estimates for the global total. The much more realistic latest Chinese value is 3.2 trillion tons up to the depth of 1,500 m in the North and 1,000 in the South, a total that would put the country second in the world, not far behind the USSR (with 3.99 trillion tons) and well ahead of the United States (with 2.28 trillion tons).

Yet in the Chinese case this resource total is much more of an estimate than the more carefully established Soviet and American aggregates. Even what the Chinese call "explored reserves" within a depth of 1,000 m, a category claimed to total 781.5 billion tons in March 1985, is not of immediate economic interest: it has to be shrunk by an order of magnitude, to between 70 and 100 billion tons of coal the deposits of which were carefully prospected and hence correspond to the commonly used Western category of verified reserves. Using this figure for the most meaningful comparisons puts China again third worldwide, after the United States' roughly 220 billion tons and the Soviets' 188 billion tons, and leaves it with about 14 percent of the known global economically recoverable coal deposits.

Exploitable reserves are not only abundant, they are also mostly of good or exceptional quality. Twenty-six percent of the deposits originated in the Carboniferous and Permian periods (mainly in the North, centered on Shanxi province); early to medium Jurassic formations comprise about 60 percent (again, mainly in the North and the Northwest); and the post-Jurassic and post-Permian periods contribute, respectively, just 7 (in the Northeast) and 5 percent (throughout the South). No less than 35 percent are coking coals, and bituminous varieties provide 69.9, anthracite 16.2, and lignites a mere 13.9 percent, a qualitative breakdown superior to the distribution of U.S. coal reserves (53 percent bituminous, 2 percent anthracite, 45 percent subbituminous and lignites). Most of the currently exploited deposits contain abundant reserves of generally low ash and medium sulfure coals with relatively high energy content (table 2.5). The only unfavorable

Table 2.5

Characteristics of major Chinese coal reserves

Coals	Moisture (percent)	Ash (percent)	Volatile fraction (percent)	Sulfur (percent)	Heat content (MJ/kg)
Lignites					
Zhalainuo'er	30–36	5–17	41–46	0.3–0.8	10.5–15.1
Yima	5–15	10–25	40–43	0.8–3.1	14.6–21.8
Non-caking coals					
Jinyuan	4–8	6–16	25–35	0.4–1.0	23.9–26.8
Weakly-caking coals					
Datong	5–10	5–10	28–34	0.5–1.5	26.0–28.5
Baotou	2–5	14–22	24–26	0.3–1.0	22.2–24.7
Bituminous coking coals					
Kailuan	—	15–17	28–39	0.4–2.5	22.2–29.3
Fushun	—	5–29	41–47	0.4–1.0	24.3–31.0
Huainan	—	11–26	33–40	0.4–2.0	23.4–29.7
Pingdingshan	—	10–29	28–34	0.8–1.8	23.9–29.3
Xuzhou	—	5–29	35–47	0.4–7.7	26.8–32.3
Anthracites					
Yangquan	3–8	7–18	7–10	0.4–1.9	35.2–36.0
Jiaozuo	3–8	12–18	3–8	0.3–0.5	34.7–35.6

Source: Yang and Chen (1982).

complication in terms of quality is the rather high ash content of some coking coals.

Mining conditions are also predominantly favorable. Average extraction depth in the currently worked mines is only about 300 m, and the calculated mean depth of all of their reserves is just 500 m. Only 13 percent of the total output originates from seams thinner than 1.3 m, 44 percent comes from 1.3–3.5 m-thick deposits, and 43 percent from thick seams above 3.5 m. Moreover, 84 percent of all seams are either flat or only gently dipping, and only 5 percent have difficult steep inclines. On the negative side, 45 percent of the operating mines have high potential for methane accumulation and explosions, and half of the seams must be watched for possibilities of spontaneous combustion.

Yet another advantageous consideration are China's extensive, and so far virtually untapped, possibilities for large-scale and highly economical surface mining. A new geological survey now underway—more than 100 exploration teams and some 100,000 people are available to carry on comprehensive multidisciplinary surveys—is designed to fix in a much more detailed manner the extent and the characteristics of China's exploitable coal reserves by 1990 in order to provide a better foundation for long-range development of new collieries, which will provide the bulk of the country's primary energy in the next century.

But nothing can change the most burdensome reality of China's coal industry—the great regional disparities in economically recoverable reserves. This inequality is about as pronounced as that in distribution of hydroenergy resources, except that in this case the northern half of the country dominates. Although some coal reserves can be found in all of China's provinces, deposits anywhere south of the Chang Jiang are greatly inferior in terms of magnitude, quality, and exploitability to rich reserves in the northern provinces, above all in Shanxi, Nei Monggol, Hebei, and Shandong (fig. 2.8).

Shanxi province has by far the largest explored reserves, 203.5 billion tons or nearly 30 percent of the national total; its eight large coalfields cover altogether 57,000 km² and are currently exploited by sixty-three large and medium and two thousand small mines. Datong coalfield (1,827 km²) in the northernmost part of the province, with reserves of 37.58 billion tons, has China's best steam coal (table 2.5), which is burned by locomotives all around the country and increasingly shipped out of the province for domestic industrial use as well as for export (see section 3.2.1). Nei Monggol is a close second with 190 billion of explored deposits, but much of this fuel is not in excellent bituminous coals but rather in medium-quality lignites which will be increasingly extracted in large surface mines (see section 4.2.2). Most of the North's remaining coal reserves are in Hebei, above all in the Kailuan mining region whose center, the city of Tangshan, was destroyed in August 1976 by a powerful earthquake and has been rebuilt since.

The region with the second largest coal reserves is the Northwest, but its small and widely dispersed population and its remoteness from major industrial centers do not make the exploitation of these rich deposits of bituminous and lignitic coals appealing. The South-Central provinces have the smallest and, moreover, only low-quality reserves of bituminous coal. However, the fuel the Chinese call "stone-coal" is abundant throughout the South—more than 100 billion tons of proven

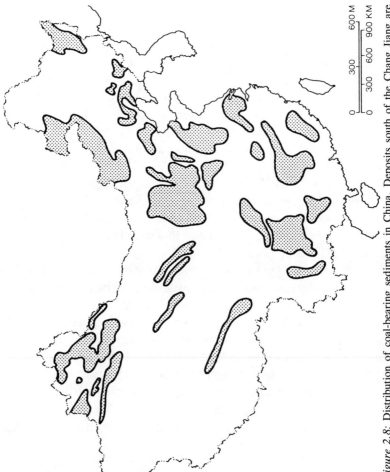

Figure 2.8: Distribution of coal-bearing sediments in China. Deposits south of the Chang Jiang are extensive but of poor quality and costly to extract.

reserves (Hunan, with 27.3 billion tons leads), with 19.49 billion tons less than 100 m underground in layers mostly 10 m thick. Extensive utilization of this resource solely for energy is unlikely: with 60–80 percent ash and a mere 4.6 MJ/kg (compared to standard coal's 29 MJ/kg), neither the environmental costs (capture and disposal of copious fly ash) nor engineering considerations (too low energy density) promise widespread conversion. Its multipurpose use is more encouraging as the deposits contain relatively high concentrations of valuable metallic elements (most common being vanadium, molybdenum, copper, and gallium), potassium, and phosphorus and are also a good raw material for cement, lime, and brick production. According to *Zhongguo meitanbao*, the 1983 extraction of 5.37 million tons was accompanied by production of 750,000 tons of cement, 2.35 million tons of lime, and more than 200 tons of vanadium.

Actually, "stone-coal" has lower energy content than coal mining and cleaning wastes of which about one billion tons are lying around northern provinces, with 50–60 million tons added each year. With 6.2–7.5 MJ/kg, this gangue is still a poorer energy carrier than straw, but its local use may make it a marginal subsidiary fossil fuel "reserve."

Unfortunately for China, neither water power nor coal, two of its richest energy resources, is distributed in ways that minimize the expenditures for large-scale development (table 2.6). Hydroelectricity from large southern and southwestern plants will have to be transmitted eastward and northward over long distances of rugged terrain, and the northern coal has to be transported, by rail and by coastal shipping, southward to supply the fuel-deficient Jiangan (provinces south of the Chang Jiang). These shipments, however, could be greatly reduced if the large-scale hydrocarbon exploration now underway in the South China Sea results in discovery of major oil and gas reserves.

2.2.2 Hydrocarbons

Chinese oil and gas potential has been a frequent topic of unbounded speculation since the early 1970s when the Chinese, in order to attract Japanese purchases and investment, started rumors about a new Saudi Arabia in the making. Top Japanese officials returned from China in the mid-1970s offering predictions of Chinese crude oil output surpassing 400 million tons within a decade, a level of production in the class with Saudis, Soviets, and Americans and requiring, with reserve production

Table 2.6

Regional shares of population and energy resources in 1980 (all figures are in percent)

Region	Population	Coal reserves	Hydroenergy potential	Oil and gas reserves
Northeast	9	3	2	48
North	11	64	2	14
East	30	6	4	18
Central-South	27	4	9	3
Southwest	16	11	70	3
Northwest	7	12	13	14

Sources: Cao (1981), Li and Chen 1983.

ratio at least at 20–25, reserves of no less than 8–10 billion tons of crude oil.

Indeed, 8–10 billion tons were the highest speculative reserve estimates published by many eager Western promoters of China as the looming new Middle East—and I do not think that even the prevailing tenor of those days (the OPEC-generated scare and search for a new source of supplies) can excuse those grotesquely exaggerated figures. Such totals could have been permissible speculations on the unknown resource base, but they should have never been used in connection with verified reserves: just a simple matter of basic geological ignorance. Cessation of formerly rapid oil production growth rates, years of stagnating crude oil output from onshore fields, and initiation of extensive offshore searches are, of course, most eloquent proofs that China's current onshore oil reserves are only a small fraction of the just cited huge totals.

Significantly, the Chinese never disclosed the actual number while giving detailed accounts of coal and hydroenergy riches. In 1979 they placed their oil reserves thirteenth in the world, a ranking implying some 1.4 billion tons. Since then one could read repeatedly—be it in the *Yearbook of China's Economy*, in Fang's (1984) survey of all energy resources, or in numerous publications of the Ministry of Petroleum—about China's 4.2 or 4.5 million km² of sedimentary basins with rich oil and gas potential, but such a figure is basically worthless even as an approximate guide to China's hydrocarbon stores.

Perils of extrapolation from known basins of similar stratigraphy—most often by volumetric-yield techniques—are now sufficiently appreciated (White 1986) to view the earlier attempts at reserves evaluation by analogy as mere order-of-magnitude fixes. A very good example of this procedure is Terman's (1976) gross appraisal based on analogy with the U.S. basins, crediting China with 40–60 billion barrels, or 5.8–8.25 billion tons, of recoverable oil.

Similarly, the recent Chinese speculations on the magnitude of offshore reserves are of little meaningful help. In April 1982, just as the first round of bidding for offshore drilling contracts was getting underway, China announced that it had "reserves" of 225–450 billion barrels, that is, roughly 30–60 billion tons of crude oil, of which one third (10–20 billion tons) was in offshore fields. This was, of course, yet more misinformation aimed at influencing foreign interest as the given range can refer only to the total of unexplored, speculative oil resources; after all, the crude oil reserves of Saudi Arabia are less than 170 billion barrels, and the total non-Communist world reserves are about 600 billion barrels!

Chinese estimates have also credited the South China Sea with "reserves" at least as rich as those of the North Sea (that is, no less than 25 billion barrels), and the three basins off Guangdong (Beibuwan, Yinggehai, and Zhujiang kou) have been said to have more than 2.5 billion tons of crude oil reserves (Jiang 1984). All such estimates based on geophysical exploration alone (at that time exploratory drilling had barely started) are, naturally, quite uncertain, and it will take at least two decades of extensive drilling to ascertain China's offshore and onshore crude oil reserves with satisfactory certainty.

The only evidence supportable by facts—by the current level of onshore production, by plans for output expansion of recently developed onshore fields, by the published figures on annual addition of new oilfield capacities, and by the confirmed discoveries of offshore commercial wells—is that China's 1985 reserves were no larger than 4 billion tons, with the most likely range between 2 and 3 billion tons. Indeed, the 1986 global survey of crude oil by the *Oil and Gas Journal*, perhaps the most widely accepted summary of its kind, puts China's reserves at about 2.6 billion tons.

We do not know what is the current total of Chinese oil reserves, but we know enough about the country's sedimentary geology to outline in much detail the setting for the existing reservoirs and the probable location of substantial new discoveries. Figure 2.9 delineates China's principal onshore and offshore basins, and numerous details on their setting, stratigraphy, exploration, and production history can be found

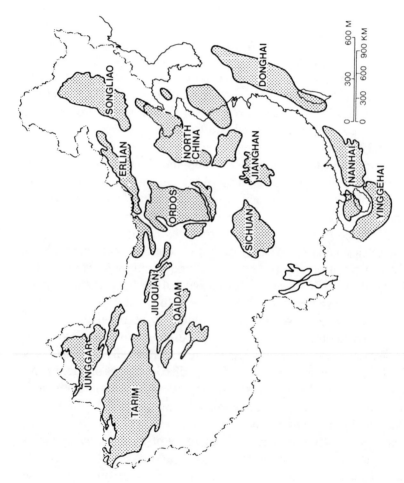

Figure 2.9: China's principal hydrocarbon basins.

in Meyerhoff and Willums (1976), CIA (1977), Li (1982), and Bai (1985).

Although the large majority of the world's crude oil resources are associated with structural traps in relatively undeformed marine sediments of the Mesozoic and Cenozoic eras, almost all of the Chinese basins with significant hydrocarbon production or potential are made up of continental deposits. Moreover, most of them consist of variously deformed structures containing the fuels in stratigraphic traps. Such complicated conditions are a result of grand geotectonic forces—subduction of the Pacific plate from the east and compression of the Indian plate from the southwest.

These stresses brought much faulting, which, together with multiple deposition cycles, led to the formation of numerous secondary oil pools and smaller multilayered reservoirs rather than a few big "bubbles." More than anything else, this clear deviation from the "normal" geological expectations based on extensive experience in the Middle East and North America was the principal reason for earlier Western assumptions about China as an oil-poor territory.

The Soviet experience from prospecting in continental basins, transferred to China during the 1950s, changed the Chinese prospects, first slowly with several minor developments in the Northwest and then abruptly with the 1959 discovery of the giant Daqing oilfield in the northeastern quadrant of the Songliao Basin in Heilongjiang. Daqing has been the largest source of China's crude oil since the early 1960s, currently producing about half of Chinese oil from three principal Cretaceous horizons (see also section 3.2.2). In spite of intensive domestic effort during the 1960s and 1970s and extensive foreign participation in offshore search since the late 1970s, no other discoveries have equaled the riches of the Songliao (for details on the offshore exploration currently underway see section 4.2.3), although Shengli oilfield, which now produces one-fifth of China's crude oil, is to double its capacity in the near future.

Both Daqing and Shengli crudes are rather heavy and waxy but have low sulfur content and low gasoline yield during primary distillation (table 2.7). The high pour point of these two principal crudes means problems with winter shipments, but low gasoline cut is quite acceptable in China where until recently there were no private cars at all and where the demand for refined fuels is led by diesel and distillate oils.

As for the natural gas, recently stagnating, even declining, output is clearly indicative of only modest reserves. But, as in the case of crude

Table 2.7

Characteristics of Daqing and Shengli crude oils

Properties	Daqing		Shengli	
	Saertu	Lamadian	Bangnan	Gudao
Specific gravity	0.8615	0.8666	0.9024	0.9640
˚API gravity	32		20–24.61	
Pour point, (˚C)	32.2–35		12–28.3	
Sulfur (percent)	0.06–0.14		0.88–1.35	
Nitrogen (ppm)	1,600		5,100	
Wax (percent)	22.4		15.3	
Distillation yields (percent)				
Gasoline (180˚C)	8.0	8.7	7.3	1.9
Light diesel oil (180˚C – 350˚C)	20.8	18.7	23.3	14.0
Heavy distillates (350˚C – 500˚C)	27.1	28.7	24.0	28.9
Residuum (>500˚C)	44.1	43.9	45.4	55.2

Sources: CIA (1977), *Acta Petrolei Sinica* (1980).

oil, the situation may change considerably with new major discoveries offshore: Atlantic Richfield's 1983 find of natural gas in the Yinggehai Basin off Hainan may be only the first installment, but it also may be the largest find for years to come. Again, by the end of the 1980s, when most of the basic exploratory drilling in promising offshore areas is completed, we shall know much better.

Finally, before leaving the discussion of China's energy resources, it should be mentioned that China has about 10 percent of the world's reserves of peat (some 27 billion tons, mostly in Heilongjiang), and that verified reserves of fissionable uranium (in addition to military use, as the Chinese put it) are sufficient to support installed capacity of 15 GW for three decades of full-load generation.

In spite of considerable uncertainty regarding the magnitude of hydrocarbon reserves, and in spite of the complications introduced by uneven distribution of huge coal and water power resources, it is obvious that the country's overall energy endowment is considerable, and with careful management certainly adequate to support the ambitious modernization drive. But for most of the people in China development of fossil fuel extraction and building of large generating stations is of only indirect importance as they continue to live within traditional solar-dominated agroecosystems.

3 EXTRACTION AND UTILIZATION: Two Economies

The great cleavage characterizing energy consumption throughout the poor world—and reflected in numerous other socioeconomic variables—is very much in evidence in China. As low as the nationwide average of the country's primary energy consumption is, it hides a much lower rural mean: four-fifths of China's population continue to live in a still predominantly solar economy while disproportionately large shares of fossil fuels and electricity are destined for large cities where a multitude of inefficient industrial enterprises consume the bulk of China's commercial energy.

Increasing amounts of coal, refined liquid fuels, and electricity have been reaching the Chinese countryside, both directly (to energize irrigation pumps and tractors and to fuel small rural industries) and indirectly (mostly invested in the synthesis of nitrogenous fertilizers whose heavy use is essential for the needed high yields), but hundreds of millions of poor peasants continue to depend on inadequate supplies of crop residues, forest fuels, and dried dung for all their everyday household needs.

Even when all nonhousehold fossil fuel and electricity rural uses are included, per capita energy consumption in the countryside is still heavily dependent on biomass fuels, whereas the urban average, elevated largely owing to industrial uses, is dominated by coal (fig. 3.1). Comparisons only for household use would show the rural-urban dichotomy in even stronger relative terms.

As already noted in chapter 1, both the make-up of China's commercial energy consumption and the shares of final use are highly idiosyn-

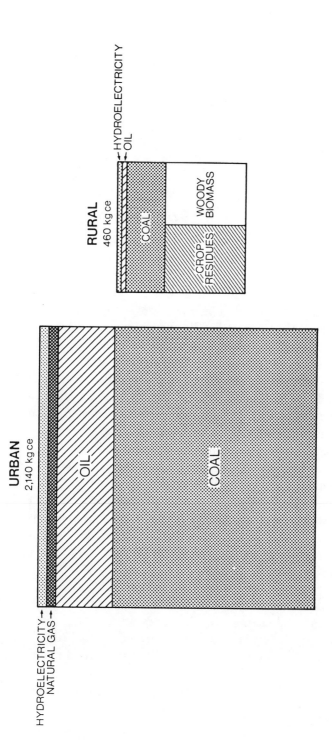

Figure 3.1: Comparison of 1983 urban and rural averages of primary energy consumption (squares are proportional to total per capita values in kg of coal equivalent).

Table 3.1

China's primary energy consumption and its structure, 1953–1984

	Total (10⁶tce)	Coal	Crude oil	Natural gas	Hydro electricity
1953	54.11	94.33	3.87	0.02	1.84
1957	96.44	92.32	4.59	0.08	3.01
1962	165.40	89.23	6.61	0.93	3.23
1965	189.01	86.45	10.27	0.63	2.65
1970	292.91	80.89	14.67	0.92	3.52
1975	454.25	71.85	21.07	2.51	4.57
1978	571.44	70.67	22.73	3.20	3.40
1979	585.88	71.31	21.79	3.30	3.60
1980	602.75	71.81	21.05	3.14	4.00
1981	594.47	72.42	19.92	2.85	4.49
1982	619.37	73.92	18.67	2.56	4.85
1983	656.48	73.71	18.56	2.47	5.26
1984	704.70.	74.00	18.80	2.35.	4.85

Source: SSB (1985).

cratic. When the first set of official statistics was released in 1979, after a twenty-year absence, it was revealed that coal supplied 70.2 percent of all primary energy, crude oil 23.5 percent, natural gas 3 percent, and hydroelectricity 3.3 percent. These shares have since undergone only slight changes (table 3.1). Among the world's five largest energy consumers this represents a unique pattern, with China's dependence on coal being more than twice as high as that of West Germany, the most coal-oriented Western nation (table 3.2). Available breakdowns of final uses show considerable discrepancies, but at least 60–65 percent has gone recently into industrial production. China's sectoral consumption pattern is unusual in its combination of very high industrial share and very low transportation use (table 3.3).

Detailed looks at rural energetics with its shortages of biomass fuels and at the industrial-urban sector with its dependence on modern commercial energies (which, too, are in short supply) will elaborate the dual nature of Chinese energy provision and use and outline all important features of both modernizing systems.

Table 3.2

Sources of primary energy for the world's top five consumers in 1981.

Country	Total energy consumption (10^6tce)	Primary consumption shares (percent)				
		Coal	Crude oil	Natural gas	Hydro electricity	Nuclear electricity
USA	2,345	23	42	31	2	2
USSR	1,536	33	34	31	2	0
China	594	73	20	3	4	0
Japan	421	21	66	8	2	3
FRG	346	34	44	19	1	2

Source: UNO (1983).

Table 3.3

Final uses of primary energy in the world's five largest consumers in 1980 (all figures are in percent)

	Industry	Transportation	Farming	Households and commercial	Nonenergy uses
China	66	4	8	18	4
United States	29	34	1	32	4
USSR	54	13	7	19	7
Japan	53	21	1	21	4
West Germany	37	21	1	39	2

Sources: For China Lan, Hu, and Mao (1984), for the OECD countries OECD (1984), for the USSR Melent'ev and Makarov (1983).

3.1 Rural energetics

Although the focus of energy studies in China and abroad remains disproportionately on the problems and options of commercial fossil fuel and electricity supplies, the latter half of the 1970s saw a laudable shift toward critical appraisals of the world's real energy crisis—the shortage of fuels for billions of poor peasants in Asia, Africa, and Latin America. Chinese researchers have contributed to this growing understanding by numerous publications reviewing both the nationwide situation and the cases of the most acute regional and local fuel shortages. But before detailing many alarming facts on how rural Chinese households get by, some basic statistics are necessary to appreciate the setting.

According to the July 1, 1982, census of China's 1.008 billion people, almost exactly four-fifths (79.4 percent) lived outside cities and towns. As befits a country of continental size and great variety of environments, these 800 million villagers are earning their living in many different ways and with far from egalitarian rewards. With the rapid diffusion of the post-1978 rural economic reforms, increasing numbers of villagers are not engaged anymore in farming but work instead in local small and medium-size industrial manufactures and in newly expanding trades and services. And within the farming sector there have been recent impressive gains in specialized cropping, animal husbandry, and fisheries resulting from the abandonment of the narrow and unproductive "grain-first" policy.

These shifts are well illustrated by the shares of official rural output statistics: in 1970, 75 percent of the total value of farm production came from crop farming, 15 percent from animal husbandry and fisheries, just over 2 percent from forestry, and the rest, less than 9 percent, from small-scale industrial works and services; by the early 1980s, the shares had shifted substantially—away from fields and into the workshops (table 3.4). As for incomes, suburban villagers growing vegetables and specialty crops, delivering meat and fish to the cities, and using their surplus labor for contract manufacture of light industrial products are now by far the best-off segment of the Chinese rural population. Their per capita income is often higher than the very good wages in the city, and among these villagers there is the largest number of families with annual incomes surpassing Rmb 10,000, that new yardstick of rural opulence.

Another income cleavage is easily discernible along regional lines (fig. 3.2). Although the national peasant income averaged Rmb 310 in 1983, in seven coastal provinces and two municipalities (from Liaoning to Guangdong) it was Rmb 390, and in the nine inland provinces west of 110°E it averaged less than Rmb 250 (obviously, there were also considerable intraprovincial disparities). The contrast is unmistakable: millions of villagers in Jiangsu or Guangdong are now enjoying incipient prosperity (when measured by the frequency of meat eating or ownership of televisions) while their counterparts in Gansu or Guizhou are still barely above the subsistence level.

Regardless of large income and lifestyle differences one essential limitation is common to localities as disparate as relatively rich and

Table 3.4

Composition of China's gross agricultural output, 1949–1983 (all values are in percent)

Year	Crop cultivation	Animal husbandry and fishing	Forestry	Sideline production
1949	82.5	12.6	0.6	4.3
1953	81.8	12.9	0.7	4.6
1957	80.6	13.4	1.7	4.3
1960	80.2	8.7	3.4	7.7
1965	75.8	15.7	2.0	6.5
1970	74.7	14.4	2.2	8.7
1975	72.5	15.5	2.9	9.1
1978	67.8	14.6	3.0	14.6
1979	66.9	15.2	2.8	15.1
1980	63.7	17.0	4.2	15.1
1981	63.2	16.9	4.2	15.7
1982	62.8	17.1	4.1	16.0
1983	62.1	16.4	4.1	17.4

Source: SSB (1985).

warm coastal plains and impoverished mountainous regions in the cold interior: widespread and seasonally very acute shortages of energy for basic household sustenance which have brought to hundreds of millions of Chinese peasants hardship easily comparable to that experienced by rural inhabitants of the world's other most densely populated or most deforested regions in Asia and Africa. Unless otherwise indicated, the following discussion of this genuine energy crisis is based on information published in Smil (1981b), Wu and Chen (1982), Smil (1984), Deng and Wu (1984), Wu (1984), and Deng (1985).

Besides the essential requirements for cooking three meals a day and boiling of drinking water, the only other fuel uses figuring prominently in rural household consumption throughout China (with the exception of pastoral areas) is preparing the feed for pigs. Lighting needs have been relatively negligible, and heating, imperative in the northern half of the country and in Xizang for up to six months, is generally dispensed with in Jiangnan (although only the southernmost provinces have less than five freezing days a year). Rural energy surveys done in various regions of all provinces in 1979 established the average daily effective energy requirement of only 16.2 MJ (Wu and Chen 1982) to

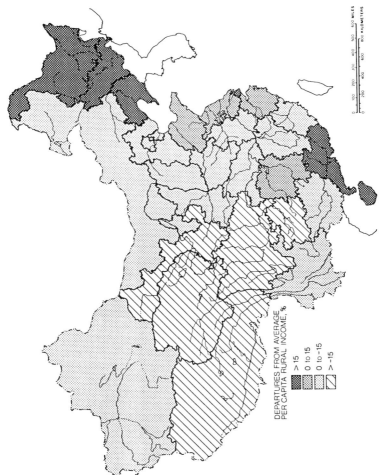

Figure 3.2: Departures (in percent) from average per capita rural income by provinces: relatively rich Northeast and coastal areas contrast with the poor interior (based on the data from the State Statistical Bureau 1984).

18.7 MJ (Deng and Zhou 1981) per family, or a mere 3.25–3.74 MJ per day per capita. This means that the nationwide annual need of 800 million villagers would add up to as much as 1.1 EJ of effective energy. As it would be unrealistic to assume that the average fuel combustion efficiencies in Chinese rural households are in excess of 10 percent, the actual annual energy requirements are about 11 EJ. In terms of standard coal (29 MJ/kg), the common energy measurement in China, this translates to roughly 380 million tons of coal equivalent.

Practically, this means that a typical Chinese rural household of five people should burn each day at least 12 kg of straw (14 MJ/kg), or about 11 kg of woody matter (16.5 MJ/kg), or any mixture of these two fuels dominating the energy consumption in the Chinese countryside, to obtain, with average 10 percent efficiency, effective energy of nearly 19 MJ. The 1979 consumption survey, however, indicated that the actual daily availability of effective energy is only 14.5 MJ per family (or 5 kg of standard fuel), a difference resulting in an average shortfall of some 22 percent. Obviously, the supply differs regionally and also fluctuates with the seasons, and different quantitative and temporal appraisals of this deficit are available.

Yang Jike, speaking at the Second National Symposium on Energy Resources in December 1980, stated that 500 million peasants (63 percent of the total) suffered from a "serious" fuel shortage for at least three to five months, and that in the best-off provinces only 25 percent of all families were so affected but in the worst-off areas 70 percent of villagers were short of fuel for up to six months every year. In May 1981 a Xinhua news release estimated that "more than half" of the country's 160 million peasant households were short of firewood, with the share over 60 percent in Xinjiang, Hebei, Hunan, and Sichuan, and with the worst situation in twenty-two counties in the valleys of the Yarlung Zangbo, Lhasa, and Niamcha rivers in southern Xizang.

A year later the same source claimed that "about half" of China's peasant households are short of firewood for "over three months of the year," and in November 1982 an unsigned *Renmin ribao* article put the share of households lacking firewood for at least three months at a curiously precise 47.7 percent, whereas another of the paper's stories on rural fuel shortages in January 1983 reverted to the earliest cited estimate of a mean nationwide 22 percent shortage merely in the energy required to satisfy the basic subsistence needs.

According to the 1982 edition of *China Agricultural Yearbook*, of the country's 2,133 counties only 397 (19 percent) in or near the forested mountains have fuelwood supply adequate to meet all household energy demand for more than six months, that is, for the whole heating season, and 915 counties (43 percent) could cover their basic household energy needs with fuelwood for less than one month. Precise figures must be suspect and are, of course, irrelevant. Without them it is easy enough to appreciate the staggering dimension of China's rural energy shortage: about half a billion people lacking enough fuel just to cook three meals a day for three to six months a year!

Some published descriptions portrayed a life of incredible misery. A few years ago in Yongjing county of Gansu province average annual food grain allocations were merely 220 kg per capita, and no more than 50 kg of crop residues were available per person for burning in this deforested area (Zhang Qinghai 1981). This translates to less than 10 MJ a day per family, while China's mean rural biomass fuel availability was about fifteen times higher—and Gansu is a province with very cold winters. Not surprisingly, one could read that when the country's housewives "face the stoves, tears come to their eyes."

Throughout most of southern Xizang firewood is more expensive than grain, and in 1980 a sack of dried cow dung cost as much as Rmb 10 (Zhou 1980), easily an equivalent of a two-month income for a poor peasant. What makes this dismal situation still more critical is the fact that even these meager supplies are secured at a heavy, and mounting, environmental cost through burning of crop residues and animal dung and through widespread deforestation because the Chinese countryside remains critically dependent on combustion of traditional biomass fuels.

3.1.1 Traditional biomass fuels

Combustion of cereal straws, corn stover and stalks and vines of tubers, leguminous and oil crops, and cotton is the single largest source of household fuel in rural China and also the one that can be accounted for with by far the greatest accuracy. Crop residues have always been critically important in providing organic fertilizer, feed, fuel, and raw material for a wide variety of manufactures, and in today's China they continue to be treated with nearly as much care as the crops themselves: as the harvesting remains overwhelmingly manual, straws, stalks, and vines are cut very near the ground, carefully gathered, and stored in any suitable place around the farm houses.

Total mass of annually harvested residues can be estimated with fair

Table 3.5

Production of crop residues in China in 1983

	Annual (1983) crop harvests (10^6 t)	Crop residue ratios	Total crop residue output (10^6 t)
Rice	168.9	1.0	169
Wheat	81.4	1.3	106
Corn	68.2	1.2	82
Other grains	39.5	1.3	51
Tubers	146.5	0.2	29
Oil crops	10.6	0.6	6
Sugar cane	31.1	0.2	6
Cotton	4.6	2.0	9
Total			458

Source: Author's estimates based on SSB head counts.

accuracy on the basis of newly available detailed crop output statistics and typical residue/crop ratios. My calculations for the 1983 harvest total 458 million tons (table 3.5), a sum identical to a differently derived estimate by Wu (1982) and very close to Shangguan's (1980) 450 and Chen's (1982) 443 million tons. To determine reliably the fraction used for fuel is considerably more difficult. According to the large-scale rural energy use survey conducted nationwide in 1979, 51 percent of harvest crop residues were left for combustion (Shangguan 1980), but Wu and Chen (1982) put the share at 60 percent, and Shi Wen (1982) claims that 75 percent of all residues are burned.

An independent check of these claims is possible by estimating the roughage requirements of China's large animals (cattle, horses, water buffaloes) and pigs. Using the official head counts, average roughage requirements of 2.6 tons a year for cattle, 2.5 tons for horses, 0.55 tons for sheep and goats, and 0.35 for pigs, and assuming that one-half of these roughages are provided by grazing on China's extensive grasslands and hills, one arrives at animal residue requirements of about 215 million tons a year. The rural energy use survey put feeding and raw material needs at 220 million tons: this is a very close agreement, and consequently I will assume that half of all crop residues are currently used for fuel.

These roughly 230 million tons of dry residues are (at 14 MJ/kg) equivalent to about 111 million tons of standard coal, or to about one-half of all biomass fuels burned in China's countryside in recent years. Without them over 100 million peasant households on the long-deforested and densely populated plains and lowlands of the eastern third of China as well as in the barren northwest interior could not survive—but if this large amount of biomass were recycled as organic fertilizer rather than burned, assuming average nitrogen, phosphorus, and potassium contents of 0.7, 0.1, and 1.2 percent, then about 1.6 million tons of nitrogen, 230,000 tons of phosphorus, and 2.76 million tons of potassium could be theoretically returned to China's soil. Naturally, phosphorus and postassium are conserved in the ash, which could be composted, but nitrogen is irretrievably lost, and about 15 percent of the current Chinese output of nitrogenous fertilizers is needed to make up this loss. Moreover, there is no substitute for heavy crop residue recycling to improve the soil structure and to provide the best protection against the water and wind soil erosion that is now degrading at least 15 percent of China's farmland (Ma and Chang 1980).

Similar but smaller nutrient and soil improvement losses arise from the burning of dried animal excreta. This practice, in the West usually associated with the Indian subcontinent, has been the only means of cooking fuel provision in China's extensive interior grasslands—mainly in Nei Monggol, Xinjiang, and Xizang—and with continued deforestation and growing shortages of straw it has been spreading recently, above all in the northwestern region. Wu and Chen (1982) calculated the total animal waste production at about 103 million dry tons in 1980; my 1983 estimate is close to 150 million dry tons (table 3.6).

Almost all pig wastes are collected but only about 25–30 percent of cattle, horse, sheep, and goat excreta are gathered, and hence the total of available animal wastes is at most some 80 million tons annually. Of this amount just one-tenth, mainly cattle dung, is used as fuel. Even when crediting these dry wastes with a high heat value of 15.5 MJ/kg, the total contribution of dung to Chinese rural energy use is just over 4 million tons of coal equivalent, or only about 2 percent of all biomass energy consumption. Crop residues and animal wastes thus contribute slightly more than one-half of all traditional fuels; the other half of rural consumption must come from trees and forests and any other accessible harvestible phytomass.

Using the common term fuelwood would be misleading in the Chinese context. Naturally, villagers in forested regions cut a great deal of roundwood, both from fuelwood lots and from illegally felled trees in protected forests—but the fuel comes from literally any burnable tree

Table 3.6

Output and availability of animal wastes in China in 1983

	Total (1983) head counts (million)	Annual output of solids (kg/head)	Total solids output (million t)	Collection rate (percent)	Total solids availability (million t)
Cattle	78.1	800	62	30	19
Horses	12.2	900	11	30	3
Pigs	298.5	200	60	90	54
Sheep and goats	167.0	80	14	25	3
Total			147		79

Source: Author's estimates based on SSB head counts.

and forest biomass: not only branches and twigs, roots and stumps, but also bark off the living trees, needles, leaves and grasses, and carved-out and dried pieces of sod. People carefully raking any organic debris accumulated on the floor of even small groves, peasants drastically pruning the summer growth of shrubs and trees, and children gathering tufts of grass into their back baskets are common sights in China's fuel-short countryside.

Environmental consequences of this often desperate search for fuel are predictably severe: rapid nutrient loss and erosion of slope sites stripped of trees or of the protective floor-debris cover not infrequently result in the total loss of the site for eventual revegetation. The extent of this dangerous environmental degradation can be best appreciated by comparing the recent forest phytomass removals with estimates of sustainable harvest.

As estimated in section 2.1.4, total annual net primary production of China's forests is about 1.1 billion tons. Net ecosystem productivity (that is, phytomass remaining after subtracting heterotrophic respiration equivalent to about two-thirds of the net photosynthesis) of about 400 million tons is thus theoretically available for sustainable harvesting. With stemwood accounting for an average of two-fifths of the new productivity, cuttings of about 160 million tons of timber can be sustained indefinitely. For comparison, the best available Chinese estimate puts the annual stemwood increment at 220 million m^3 or (with an average of 650 kg/m^3) about 145 million tons, an excellent confirmation of my differently derived approximation (errors of less than ± 10 percent in calculations of this kind are most unlikely).

Yet the recent timber harvests have been between 50 and 55 million m³ (or up to 36 million tons), and the 1979 rural energy survey put the total firewood consumption at 181.6 million tons a year for a total of almost 220 million tons of wood. This total would indicate a massive overcutting of between 60 and 75 million tons a year. Although there is no doubt about continuing deforestation throughout China—the nationwide forest cover declined from 12.7 to 12 percent between 1976 and 1984—the actual overcutting in terms of stemwood (what the foresters call merchantable bole) is considerably smaller. As already stressed, the 180 million tons of forest phytomass used for household fuel include anything combustible, not just split stemwood, and an important part of these fuels comes also from the country's extensive shrublands whose production (equal to about half of that of boreal and temperate forests) is not included in the calculations of sustainable wood harvest.

I do not think it will soon be possible to determine the most likely margin of wood overcutting. That it is no less than 10–15 million tons (about 15–25 million m³) a year is almost certain, and that cutting for fuelwood, together with excessive lumbering and conversion of forest slopes to grainfields (during the decades of the misguided ''grain-first'' policy), has been one of the three largest reasons for China's rapid deforestation is indisputable. There are no disaggregated data apportioning the blame and, once again, I doubt they could become soon available. But if only a third, or even just a fifth, of all recent Chinese deforestation would come about as the result of the increasingly more taxing (in both human and environmental terms) search for fuelwood, the chronic rural energy shortages would have to be credited with disappearance of many millions of ha of forests since 1949.

In the early 1980s many provincial and county figures became available, the most staggering ones being clearly Hainan's 72 percent, Yunnan's 55 percent, and Sichuan's 30 percent forest cover loss in three decades. On the basis of these data, I have estimated the total nationwide 1949–1980 forest loss at about 20 million ha (Smil 1984), of which certainly no less than 7 and possibly as much as 7 million ha may be ascribed to the quest for basic (and mostly still inadequate) provision of cooking and heating fuel.

China is just one of many poor countries whose biomass is far from sufficient to supply the rising amount of fuel needed for basic rural subsistence. Crisis regions abound around the world: Sahelian Africa, Namibia, Nepali hills, Gujarat, Haiti, western Bolivia. Some of these acute energy crises, most notably the Sahelian shortages, have received much Western media attention. Digging of sod, breaking off the branches of just planted trees, guarding piles of drying dung cakes, or, in utter desperation, burning sweet potatoes—these are not images associated with the post-Mao China of Deng's bold reforms. Yet they are, unfortunately, true and all too widespread. Farming reforms have pushed the average peasant from a bare food subsistence to fairly comfortable sufficiency in just a few years, but easing of the rural fuel shortage will be a much more intractable process.

Flows of commercial energies are on the rise throughout the Chinese countryside, but the critical dependence on traditional biomass fuels cannot be shed for decades to come. The best estimates calculated or cited in this section—230 million tons of straw (110 million tce) 8 million tons of dried dung (4 million tce), and 180 million tons of forest fuels (104 million tce)—add up to some 220 million tce in 1983. This is roughly 275 kgce for every Chinese villager, a total accounting for three-fifths of all rural energy inputs. Such a dependence cannot be shed easily.

Not surprisingly, Chinese have been looking for ways to eliminate the worst rural energy shortages while protecting their environment through an innovative conversion of traditional biomass fuels—and the spectacular expansion of biogas generation during the 1970s persuaded many outside observers that methanogenic fermentation is the best answer to the problem in deforested farming areas. A closer look, however, will reveal a much less impressive reality.

3.1.2 Biogas generation

Diffusion of the technique was unusually rapid. In Sichuan, where the mass construction campaigns started in the early 1970s, digester numbers rose from 30,000 in the spring of 1974 to 4.3 million by the end of 1977, and the nationwide total surpassed 7 million units by 1979 (table 3.7). Relatively simple design of the digesters, use of locally available materials in their construction, and some indisputable lifestyle advantages—ranging from less time spent on fuel collection and reduced expenditures for commercial fuels to improved hygienic conditions and easing of many household chores—have combined to make the strong case for officially sponsored diffusion compaigns and for an often eager acceptance of peasants.

Unlike in India, where the focus has been on larger village digesters, most of China's units are single-family devices with a capacity up to 10

Table 3.7

Diffusion of biogas digesters in Sichuan and in China

	Year and month of the reported total		Number of biogas digesters
Sichuan	1974	January	30,000
	1975	June	410,000
	1976	August	2,800,000
	1977	December	4,300,000
	1978	December	4,800,000
	1979	June	5,000,000
	1982	November	2,700,000
China	1975	May	400,000
	1977	May	4,300,000
	1978	May	5,760,000
	1979	June	7,100,000
	1980	July	6,570,000
	1982	November	4,500,000
	1984	July	3,760,000

Sources: Smil (1981) and Xinhua releases.

m³. Many digester designs have been tried in China, and exhaustive construction and operational details of these digesters have been available since the late 1970s in numerous reviews and manuals, most notably in the Sichuanese how-to booklet (in English translation Van Buren 1979). The most popular designs are different kinds of fixed-dome water-pressurized tanks developed in central Sichuan. They are fairly simple structures consisting of loading, fermentation, and sludge compartments (fig. 3.3). Fermentable materials pass from the loading chamber into the main compartment in which the biogas is pressurized below the rigid cover; digested material should be removed from the sludge compartment at least twice a year. Pressure inside the tank is maintained with the aid of a small hole in the wall between the fermentation and sludge chambers.

To maintain the pressure necessary for transporting the biogas through plastic, bamboo, or natural rubber pipes to a household, the digester must be tightly sealed. A simple glass pressure gauge is usually connected to the gas outlet to monitor for tank leaks, estimate the quantity of the stored biogas, and prevent the cracking of the containment. Inexpensive, locally available materials, rather than scarce and costly steel, are used to build the structure: mortared rocks, bricks,

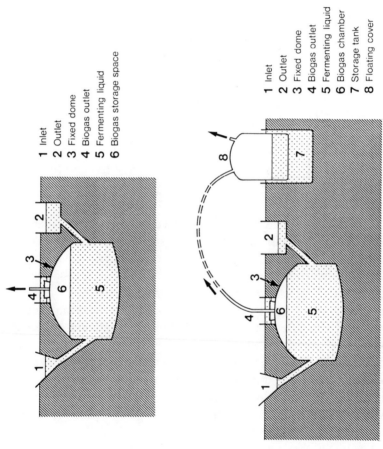

1 Inlet
2 Outlet
3 Fixed dome
4 Biogas outlet
5 Fermenting liquid
6 Biogas storage space

1 Inlet
2 Outlet
3 Fixed dome
4 Biogas outlet
5 Fermenting liquid
6 Biogas chamber
7 Storage tank
8 Floating cover

Figure 3.3: Typical designs of fixed-dome biogas digesters, without storage and with a floating storage tank.

cement. A typical well-built 8-m³ unit requires about two tons of quarried stone or 500 kg of cement or bricks; one meter-long PVC or steel pipe of about one centimeter in diameter is inserted at the gas outlet into the covering plate. Not surprisingly, then, the cost of such a structure is much cheaper than that of an Indian installation. The earliest available figures clearly exaggerated the cheapness, claiming only Rmb 30–40 between 1973 and 1978 for a typical family unit, with the smallest digesters costing a mere Rmb 10; the latest estimates are around Rmb 100, a more considerable sum in a country where the average rural per capita income, although rising rapidly, was still only Rmb 310 in 1983.

Fixed-dome digesters without auxiliary storage were dominant during the 1970s, but more recently the fixed-dome design with floating tank storage or with plastic bag storage has been diffusing successfully (fig. 3.4). The latest addition is the plastic-covered digester, with or without storage, which is simple to build and easy to clean. These considerations are critical for proper operation and maintenance of digesters. In principle, the operation is rather simple but several environmental factors must be maintained within desirable limits to achieve high fermentation efficiencies and steady biogas output. Proper carbon/nitrogen ratio of digestible materials, optimal concentration of substrate solids, and stable or only narrowly fluctuating pH and temperature inside the tank are the most important variables.

Variety of feedstocks available for small-scale biogas generation falls generally into either carbon-rich or nitrogen-rich categories. The first ones, composed mostly of cellulose, hemicellulose, and lignin, include crop residues, grasses, aquatic plants, and tree leaves, and to speed up their biodegration they should be first chopped to smaller pieces (3–5 cm) or undergo a short aerobic fermentation before methanogenic digestion. The second group consists, of course, of animal and human wastes; some food-processing wastes are also fairly rich in nitrogen.

Both kinds of feedstock can be fermented to release roughly comparable volumes of biogas per kg of dry substate (table 3.8)—but only if the C/N ratio is within the optimum range of 25–30. Obviously, this requires mixing of various feedstocks in correct proportion. There is no simple precept as the C/N ratios range from less than 3 for human wastes to 13 for pig manure and 18–25 for cow dung, while for the plant feedstocks the spread is from as little as 20 for some grasses to 50–90 for cereal straws.

58

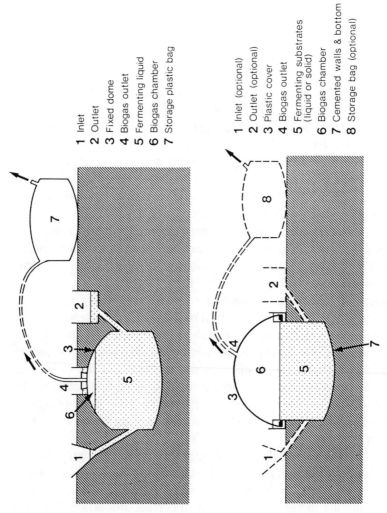

1 Inlet
2 Outlet
3 Fixed dome
4 Biogas outlet
5 Fermenting liquid
6 Biogas chamber
7 Storage plastic bag

1 Inlet (optional)
2 Outlet (optional)
3 Plastic cover
4 Biogas outlet
5 Fermenting substrates (liquid or solid)
6 Biogas chamber
7 Cemented walls & bottom
8 Storage bag (optional)

Figure 3.4: Typical designs of a fixed dome digester with a plastic storage bag and a digester with plastic cover.

Table 3.8

Biogas production rate for principal Chinese feedstocks

Feedstock	Biogas production (l/kg dry weight)	CH$_4$ content (percent)
Carbon-rich		
Grasses	290	70
Tree leaves	150–220	60
Wheat straw	340	60
Corn stover	250	53
Nitrogen-rich		
Pig manure	200–300	60–65
Cow manure	310	60
Horse manure	310	60
Human wastes	240	50

Source: Chengdu Biogas Research Institute.

Sichuanese experience with tens of thousands of digesters led to the following recommendations for optimal loading (water is always 50 percent): 10 percent human excreta, 30 percent manure, 10 percent crop stalks and grasses; or 20 percent human excreta, 30 percent hog manure; or 10 percent each of human and animal excretion, 30 percent marsh grasses. Another popular recommendation for a typical 8 m^3 digester is for 1 ton of grass, 400 kg of cow and pig manure, 200 kg of wheat straw, and 100 kg of human wastes together with 5 tons of water. This mixture would result in a perfect C/N ratio of 28 and in total solid concentration of about 8 percent, again in the middle of the recommended range.

As with the C/N content, feedstocks have widely differing degrees of solidity, from nearly 90 percent in air-dried cereal straws to about 20 percent in human wastes and some drier animal manures to as little as 10 percent in fresh pig manures. Too few solids will result in a sluggish rate of fermentation (which prevents the escape of generated biogas) and clogging. Preferred practice is to maintain solids at around 6 percent in summer and up to double that level in winter. In plastic-covered digesters, up to 40 percent solids can be accommodated, with about 25 percent as optimum.

Anaerobic fermentation can operate within a wide range of temperatures but not below 10°C when mesothermic bacteria stop working. They prefer, however, to decompose the substrate at 30–35°C, and their thermophilic counterparts at 50–55°C. Without external heating the latter range is impractically high even with well-insulated digesters buried in the ground. Without some insulation even the mesophilic range is impossible to maintain over a large portion of populated Chinese territory, and most northern digesters cease operating in winter while the southern ones have much reduced generating rates (fig.3.5).

Continuous methanogenic fermentation requires a neutral or slightly alkaline (pH 6.4–7.6) environment. Levels below pH 6.4 inhibit methanogenic bacteria whereas those above pH 7.6 restrain acidogenic microorganisms critical especially in the early stages of fermentation. Increasing acidity can be easily raised by adding lime water or plant ashes while higher alkalinities can be reduced by addition of night soil, manure, or grass. Proper digester operation also needs regular addition and stirring of the fermenting mixture. Addition of new material should be preceded by removal of the same volume of old mixture from the sludge chamber and followed by thorough and frequent stirring to break up the hardening scum on the top of fermenting liquid. All accumulated sludge should be removed at least twice a year, and the digester should be thoroughly cleaned and seeded with prefermented material to start a new semi-annual cycle.

The advantages of family-scale rural anaerobic fermentation in China are clear and numerous. The process saves irreplaceable fossil fuels as well as slow-growing fuelwood and crop residues; it eliminates many insect pests and diseases and greatly improves the rural hygiene (especially notable is the fact that most *Schistosoma japonicum* eggs are destroyed by fermentation in about a week); it reduces fuel expenditure for peasant families in deforested regions and lightens household labor; and, a consideration as important as the output of clean biogas, it yields an excellent organic fertilizer, still the essential input into China's intensive farming (each family digester can provide up to 100 kg of sludge high in ammonia and phosphorus). Large digesters can produce sufficient amounts of biogas to generate electricity that is used to mechanize some farming operations.

Chinese thus came to consider biogas generation to be not only an effective way of solving energy problems in rural areas that are short of coal, fuelwood, or hydroelectricity but, owing to its other benefits— high quality fertilizer, improved hygiene, and less air pollution—a most desirable component of rural development throughout China. Consequently, China's second national biogas conference held in the

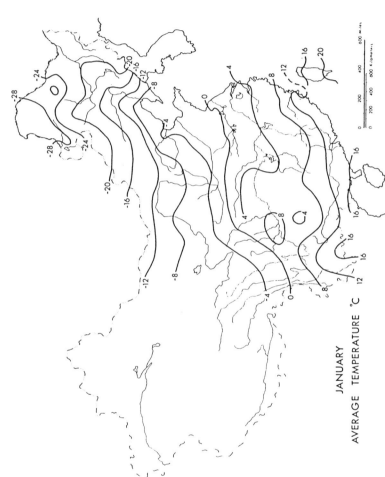

Figure 3.5: Isotherms of average January temperatures show that without heating or heavy insulation biogas generation can continue throughout winters only in the southernmost parts of China.

summer of 1978 heard about plans for 20 million digesters in 1980 and 70 million units by 1985. Yet today there are fewer operating digesters than in 1977, and the program was set back especially in Sichuan, the birthplace and main promoter of the technique: the province had nearly two-thirds of China's units in 1978, but about two-fifths of its peak number of biogas digesters were abandoned by 1982.

While it is still possible to come across some new plans quoting fabulous digester totals by the end of this decade, the skepticism must be deep especially when the statistics of the National Methane Production Leadership Group showed that of the remaining digesters only about 55 percent can be used normally, and among these "not too many can be used to cook rice three times a day, still less everyday for four seasons" (Huang and Zhang 1980). The reasons: the technique, so simple in principle, is rather demanding in practice. Nearly three million digesters failed for several reasons. Leakage of biogas through the covering dome, cracked walls or bottom, improper feedstock adding and mixing practices, shortages of appropriate substrates, formation of heavy scum, and inhibition of bacteria by low temperatures were the leading causes. Unless the digesters are well built (the slightest water and gas leaks ruin the process) and convenient to feed and clean, unless careful attention is paid to proper temperature, C/N ratios, and pH of the fermenting mixture, and unless the digester is frequently fed with the right degradable materials, the units can turn quickly into costly waste pits and are abandoned. Not surprisingly, failures in the second year of operation were common, and for millions of peasants digesters were a burden and costly loss.

In many instances a small family digester was simply of no great benefit compared with the time, effort, and investment put into producing woven baskets, tobacco, eggs, or pork. The long overdue relaxation of "command farming," which led to more food, resulted in the disappearance of many mass campaigns, including the "enthusiastic" building of digesters. More fundamentally, inherent limitations on the efficiency and expansion of the process would keep the contribution of biogas to China's rural energy supply surprisingly low even under the best circumstances.

If half of China's rural families owned a small digester there would be a staggering 80–90 million units for which to find proper feedstocks. Even assuming that enough animal, human, and crop wastes would be a available, the digesters could properly operate for seven to eight months only in southernmost China, just three to five months north of the Chang Jiang; the nationwide weighted average based on Chinese data is seven months. With an average digester volume of 8 m³ and mean generation rate of 0.2 m³ of biogas per m³ of digester this would translate to some 29 billion m³ of biogas a year, equivalent to just 25 million tons of coal equivalent, or some 8 percent of China's current biomass energy use! Even when considering the fact that biogas could be burned more efficiently than straw or wood, the best imaginable contribution could not surpass 15 percent of today's inadequate consumption.

Still, this is a worthwhile approach—but only at a slow and voluntary pace, not in hasty compaigns leaving behind useless expense of labor and materials. And only in locations well suited for sustained generation, that is, throughout the warmer southern provinces where the biogas production can go on, although diminished, even in winter months. In such locations it may also make sense to build larger village-size digesters where the gas can be used for local power generation.

Clearly, the Chinese biogas program does not glitter anymore—but if many Chinese have doubts about the inherent wonders of methanogenic fermentation and about the methods used to promote it in the 1970s, the official facade continues to be one of an exuberant international growth industry: United Nations study and expert missions, cooperation with FAO, large international training courses in Sichuan for agronomists, engineers, and government bureaucrats from Asian and African countries, attendance at international bio-energy meetings. But the only developing countries who might really benefit from the Chinese experience are the pig-breeding cultures with substantial animal numbers that also have a tradition of handling organic wastes and, preferably, do not shun working with human excrements. These requirements shrink the possible candidates to less than a dozen: South Korea, Taiwan, the Philippines, Vietnam, Thailand, Brazil, Colombia, Mexico, and Cuba are the principal choices—but none of these countries has shown an interest even remotely comparable with the scope of China's biogas program. Are the Chinese lessons more relevant as far as the other major attempt at improving the rural energy supply— building small hydrostations—is concerned?

3.1.3 Water power

Widespread construction of small hydrostations has been perhaps the most successful innovation transforming China's rural energy consumption, the most realistic and economically the most sensible choice for the basic electrification of large areas of isolated Chinese countryside. While the Western countries and Japan, where small-scale hydro generation used to enjoy great popularity for decades, moved rapidly to large projects after World War II, China has been developing all sizes of stations, except for the truly giant ones, and as the numbers of small hydros rose to many tens of thousands during the 1970s, many uninformed Westerners came to credit the country with the invention of this appealing concept. The growth during the 1970s was indeed impressive, from about 26,000 in 1970 to almost 90,000 in December 1979 (table 3.9). In terms of installed capacity the growth was even more rapid, from 900 MW in 1970 to 6.33 GW in 1979, which means that the average station size rose from 35 kW in 1970 to 70 kW a decade later.

The greatest possible dependence on local resources, maximum thrift, and speedy construction were the hallmarks of the program. Stations were financed predominantly with local funds, and the state investment went only into the necessary design, equipment manufacturing, or operator training assistance. In general, state contributions have not covered more than one-third of the total investment need. Most of the dams, canals, and dikes for small hydros were built with traditional tools by massed peasant labor. Although some small stations were designed to operate under heads exceeding 100 meters (with water brought through steel or concrete penstocks down a mountainside from a high reservoir), run-of-river projects were common, and most of the plants had generating heads below 10 meters with construction characterized by great simplicity and speed. Compared to large hydro projects, which take at least seven and often ten years to complete, a typical small station can be completed, from design to generation, in two or three years.

Yet another advantage has been a relatively small extent of inundation associated with low dams and the resulting limited need for population relocation. Cement, steel, and timber—three commodities that have always been in short supply in China—were consumed in the minimum amounts. Much of the generating and transmission equipment—small turbines ranging from rather primitive wooden devices to reinforced concrete and metal propellers (fixed-blade Kaplan or Francis turbines seemed to be used most often), generators, transformers, cement poles, wires, and switches—was manufactured on a county or prefectural level. The layout and the equipment of generating halls was simple: belt drives, large flywheels, no turbine brakes, and

Table 3.9

Expansion of China's small hydrostations, 1949–1985

Year	Total number of small hydro stations	Installed capacity Total (MW)	Installed capacity per station (kW)
1949	50	0.5	10
1956	200	3	15
1957	400	6	15
1958	4,700	140	30
1960	9,000	500	56
1965	6,000	300	50
1970	26,000	900	35
1971	35,000	1,200	34
1973	50,000	2,400	48
1975	60,000	3,000	50
1977	80,000	4,000	50
1978	87,000	4,950	57
1979	90,000	6,330	70
1980	88,900	6,930	78
1983	78,500	8,080	103
1985	72,000	9,520	132

Sources: Smil (1981) and Xinhua releases.

minimum instrumentation were common.

Post-1978 changes affected the development of small-scale hydro-stations in several important ways, none being more notable than aban-donment of a large number of the hastily built, inefficient projects. At the end of 1983 there were 76,000 small hydros in China, 14,000 less than at the end of 1979. More than 5,000 new stations were built during those four years, so the total number of stations abandoned during 1979–1983 was close to 20,000, or about one-fifth of the 1979 number. It is not difficult to see the reasons for abandoning so many small projects. Drastic lowering of water storage or a complete desiccation of reservoirs during the severe droughts that afflicted large parts of China in the late 1970s and early 1980s wiped out numerous small projects in several northern, eastern, and south-central provinces. Accelerated silting destroyed the usefulness of many reservoirs, and poor engineer-ing, so common in projects built during the past mass campaigns, has been responsible for the demise of others.

Although the numbers were declining, total installed capacity and mean size kept rising: at the end of 1985, 72,000 stations had 9.5 GW, that is, an average of 132 kW per station. However, the average size of newly completed stations rose to 218 kW in 1981 and 232 kW in 1982, and the 1,150 stations completed during 1983 averaged about 350 kW, with projects of several megawatts becoming relatively common. The importance of larger stations is even better illustrated by the fact that those over 500 kW accounted for 60 percent of all installed capacity in 1983. Consequently, the Chinese definition of a small hydrostation has shifted considerably: in the 1950s it included only projects below 500 kW; in the 1960s the limit went up to 3 MW; and the current definition of small hydrostations embraces all single-generation units not exceeding 6 MW and group (cascade) installations up to 12 MW.

Moreover, at a January 1980 meeting on small hydrostations organized in Chengdu by the Ministry of Water Conservancy and Power, the Bank of China and the Farmers' Bank of China recommended that in all suitable places (i.e., in locations with rich water resources, adequate investment funds, equipment, materials, and skills) the limit of 12 MW should be lifted and the loans should be made available to build larger small stations. China's new-found appreciation of costs and rational economic management are clearly responsible for this move.

The shift toward larger stations is obvious, but modal sizes of small hydro generators remain truly small—below 50 kW—as the higher county, provincial, and national averages reflect inclusion of much larger plants in the published totals. In the rainy South, where most of China's small hydrostations are concentrated, the units tend to be smaller than in the North. In 1983 Guangdong led the provincial totals, as it has for many years, with 14,000 stations and 1,200 MW (85 kW/station), followed by Sichuan with 1,100 MW in more than 7,700 stations (143 kW/station), Hunan with 9,000 stations (900 MW, and 90 kW/station), and Fujian with 8,900 stations with 670 MW (75 kW/station).

Small as these stations still are, many have rated capacities already much beyond the local generation potential: "a big horse pulling a small cart" is an apt Chinese description of this phenomenon (Yu 1983). The low rate of utilization resulting from these arrangements is of increasing concern in China, and attempts are now being made to raise seasonal load as much as practicable. Production of 20 TWh in 1983 implies average load factor of 2,352 hours (or 26.8 percent), and the nationwide average of around 2,000 hours annually during drier years, 2,500 hours during the rainier ones, compares unfavorably to means of 4,000–4,500 hours available for generation in large power plants.

Without better design and more and better transmission, higher load factors will remain elusive. Neither of these improvements will be easy to realize. Contrary to the impressions reported by Westerners after visits to selected show stations, Chinese experts now point out that there is often little difference in the designing effort going into small and large stations, clearly a failure to capitalize on some inherent advantages of small units. Standardization of generating units is obviously an urgent requirement, but with even more stress put on local self-sufficiency in designing, building, and managing the small stations it is far from certain that new, more sophisticated designs will emerge and be widely adopted. Transmission losses in local rural grids have been running as high as 25 percent, and the chronic shortages of poles and wires make the extension of low-voltage links a difficult task. The overwhelming majority of small stations remain unconnected with larger grids.

As for the cost, Chinese are emphatic in stressing the economic viability of small stations although their capital cost is mostly higher or at best roughly the same as in large hydro projects, that is, at least Rmb 1,300 kW (including transmission equipment). Generating costs are, however, somewhat lower than in a large hydrostation and, of course, considerably smaller than in a thermal generating plant. For example, Sichuanese data show costs of Rmb 17.4/1,000 kWh compared to Rmb 69.8/1,000 kWh in small coal-fired stations (Xiao 1983). State subsidies are now limited to Rmb 300/kW, and the new policies encourage not only the traditional investment by counties or villages but also investment by groups of peasants or even single households, yet another manifestation of greater "sideline" specialization in China's countryside.

Clearly, small hydros are in China to stay—and to grow larger and multiply. Of the country's 2,133 counties more than 1,500 now have small hydrostations and nearly 800 rely on them for most of their (still inadequate) supply of electricity. Nationwide almost exactly one-third of electricity consumed in rural areas in 1983 came from small hydros, and long-range plans are to triple the current capacity by the year 2000 when 25 GW in small stations would represent about one-third of power exploitable by such projects.

But the importance of small hydros goes beyond the fact that they have been producing roughly every twentieth kWh in China: in most cases these stations have been the first source of power for the villages and have served as the foundation of the rudimentary electrification of China's countryside. Current plans assign them no smaller role in bringing electricity to 400 million Chinese peasants whose houses are still beyond the reach of light bulbs and power threshers. And besides providing electricity for a wide variety of uses—the most frequent applications are to run irrigation and drainage pumps, food and fodder processing equipment, and to power local small industries, with just a minimum household consumption for weak lighting—many reservoirs of small hydrostations have been helpful in regulating water supplies and preventing floods, always an important consideration in China, and are frequently used to breed fish and other aquatic products. This multiple benefit accruing from small hydro projects is the main reason why they will continue to be built in the decades ahead.

As China's small hydros became such a recurrent example of appropriate technology at least a few sentences on the replicability and engineering contribution of the Chinese experience are in order. Obviously, small hydros should be promoted in all suitable settings in Asia, Africa, and Latin America, but it must be remembered that the basic Chinese advantage, the relatively low capital cost of the projects built with locally available materials by local labor, has much to do with the country's unmatched ancient tradition of hydraulic engineering and with the necessity to manage water resources—and that this experience and urgency is hardly transferrable to different environments where the goal is just power generation and where no peasant has even built a silt dam or dug a canal.

In any case, whatever Chinese can transfer to other poor nations they have been trying to: the International Small Hydropower Generation Technical Centre was jointly set up in China by the United Nations Development Programme and the Chinese government, and bilateral deals to produce and install small hydro machinery are also being pursued. Chinese now have a wide variety of equipment for sale, including eighty-three kinds of turbines and generators ranging from several kW to 10 MW and working with heads of 2.5–400 m. However, U.S., Canadian, and West European companies have rediscovered the appeal of small-scale hydrogeneration, and they now offer a similar range of equipment.

Traditional biomass fuels, biogas, and electricity from small hydrostations are not, of course, the only energizers of the Chinese countryside: the country's extensive coal resources have been tapped by thousands of simple, small open mines and shallow shafts and they, together with coal transfers from larger modern mines and with electricity from regional networks, are powering the now mushrooming rural industrial and service enterprises while the shipments of oil products from state refineries are essential in fueling farm machinery. Only a small part of these inputs reaches households for private consumption.

Before turning to China's urban-industrial energetics I will not only include all of these direct modern energy subsidies in a complete survey of Chinese rural energy consumption but also attempt to quantify all indirect energy costs incurred during production of major farming inputs, above all fertilizers and machinery.

3.1.4 Energy flows in rural China

The easiest task in presenting a complete account of China's rural energetics is first to finish the summary of domestic energy uses. Figures in the last section, based both on the 1979 nationwide survey and on independent calculations using the latest available statistics, added up to about 220 million in crop residues, dried dung, and forest fuels. Addition of biogas, coal wastes, and geothermal heat makes for irrelevantly small increases: errors in estimating amounts of the three-principal biomass fuels are much larger than the aggregate of all other minor flows.

Official statistics on modern commercial energies consumed in the countryside in 1983 show a total of 139 million tce of which only about 45 million tce were used in household combustion and lighting (Deng 1985). On the other hand, at least 3 million tce of wood were burned in brick, tile, and pottery kilns, so that the total household energy use in 1983 came to about 262 million tce—83 percent from biomass, 17 percent from fossil fuels and electricity—and it accounted for nearly 75 percent of all rural primary energy inputs (table 3.10).

Predictably, coal for households is used for heating and cooking in the northern provinces, and virtually all electricity goes for lighting (where one or two 15–30 W bulbs used to be switched on for a few hours a day, 40–100 W lamps are coming with rising affluence) and for rapidly increasing numbers of TVs, tape recorders, and fans (electric rice cookers and other appliances are also spreading, so far only in higher-income regions). Even with these rising modern inputs—in 1979 they totalled merely 36 million tce, four years later they were one-quarter higher—rural energy shortages are losing little in their prevalence and acuteness, largely owing to the continuing low

Table 3.10

Direct energy consumption in China's countryside in 1983

	Amounts consumed	Equivalent energy consumption (10⁶ tce) Total	Households	Production
Biomass energies		220	217	3
Crop residues	230×10^6 t	111	111	—
Dried dung	8×10^6 t	4	4	—
Forest fuels	180×10^6 t	104	101	3
Biogas	1×10^9 cm³	0.6	0.6	—
Commercial energies		139	45	94
Coal	151×10^6 t	108	42	66
Local extraction	102×10^6 t	73	24	49
State mines	49×10^6 t	35	21	74
Oil products	8.4×10^6 t	12	—	12
Electricity	43.5 TWh	19	3	16
Small hydros	20 TWh	8	2	6
State grids	23.5 TWh	11	1	10
Total		359	262	97

Source: Author's estimates based on a variety of Chinese materials.

efficiency of biomass fuel combustion.

With an average overall 10 percent conversion efficiency (at best 10 percent for biomass fuels, up to 15 percent for coal, only about 5 percent for kerosene and electricity illumination), no more than 25 milion tce of useful energy would be available annually, or only about 12 MJ per household daily, still at least 20 percent short of the minimum subsistence need. In section 4.2.5 I will detail the most sensible strategies to close this intractable gap.

Direct energy inputs into rural production have recently grown more rapidly than the household uses, from about 66 million tce in 1979 to roughly 94 million tce in 1983. This more than 40 percent increase in just five years reflected above all the rapid expansion of small and medium-size rural manufactures producing a wide assortment of tools and gadgets both for the domestic market and for exports and relying largely on local coal resources. Naturally, coal also fuels countless village-based manufacturers serving crop production and animal husbandry as well as food processing establishments. Consequently, coal supply by small mines to rural areas rose nearly 2.5 times between 1979 and 1983, and further relatively large increases are certain.

Coal extraction from small coal mines has been through several ups and downs since the early 1950s, with the fluctuations reflecting the prevailing strategic thinking about China's development—including the notoriously wasteful "up" during the reckless Great Leap campaign when the inferior fuel from small mines was used to smelt even more inferior pig iron in a truly deranged Maoist attempt to catch up with the industrialized nations in a lightning dash. Post-1978 large-scale modernization plans could have been expected to deemphasize the importance of small mines, but the *baogan* system gave them an excellent boost.

Of the 50,000 small mines operating in early 1985 about 10,000 were run by individuals in yet another demonstration of flourishing rural entrepreneurship that has been taking the villagers from the fields. No less importantly, economies of scale are making themselves felt: 2,000 mines now have capacities over 30,000 tons of raw coal a year and the largest ones are extracting more than ten times as much, being clearly no longer small enterprises, just rural in the destination of their output.

In terms of equivalent supply, electricity is more important than liquid fuels in rural production: of course, it is perfectly substitutable for the latter in water pumping. In 1983, 56.6 percent of China's 44.64 million ha of irrigated water were watered mechanically (the rest is served by gravity and draft animals), and the country's irrigation and drainage equipment consisted of 6.077 million motors with a total capacity of 78.492 million horsepower (or about 59 GW). Of this total, 52.4 percent were electricity-driven pumps whose operation was severely curtailed by widespread power shortages. Data available for 1982 show that the typical 14 hp (10.5 kW) electrical motor pumped water for only about 560 hours and no more than 660 kW of electricity were expended in irrigating an average hectare. For comparison, the mean for all irrigated cropland in the United States is now at least 2,400 kW.

Energy shortages affect no less the operation of liquid-fueled farm machinery. In 1983, 841,000 large and medium-sized tractors, 2.75 million small and walking tractors, 275,000 trucks, 120 boats, 2.947 million irrigation diesel engines, and tens of thousands of boat tractors, motorized rice transplanters, combines, and farmyard machines had a total capacity of 203.9 million hp (152 GW). If all of this equipment would be used intensively, consumption of refined oil products in rural China would be quite considerable.

Widespread and chronic shortages of electricity and liquid fuels have, however, limited the utilization to a fraction of the installed potential. In 1979, for each kW of capacity in diesel-powered pumps, tractors, and trucks, no more than 2.9 GJ of diesel fuel were available, an amount sufficient for just fifty days of normal operation (Shangguan 1980)—and the official consumption total available for 1983 (see table 3.10) implies no more than 2.3 GJ of liquid fuels per kW of nonelectric farm machinery, enough fuel to operate just for 200 hours and an unmistakable reflection of chronically inadequate refined fuel supply throughout China's economy. The best available estimate is that 40 percent of all Chinese farm machinery has been recently idled by energy shortages.

Interestingly enough, this severe fuel shortage has not much affected the recent performance of Chinese farming, which remains an overwhelmingly manual affair. Except in some model establishments on the northeastern plains, mechanization of fieldwork in China has not generally progressed beyond heavy plowing. In 1983, one-third of all cultivated land was tractor-plowed, but sowing was mechanized on less than 9 percent and harvesting on a mere 3.2 percent. *Baogan* reforms may have greatly increased the demand for small tractors, but more as means of handy transport to the nearest market towns than as field machines. Incentives given to the families have made it profitable to engage in a more intensive cultivation of smaller areas, obviating the need for any significant expansion of mechanized operations. Planting, transplanting, cultivating, weeding, gathering and spreading of organic fertilizers, and harvesting will continue to be done manually or with the help of draft animals on more than 80 percent of China's cropland for at least another decade. Besides plowing and water pumping for irrigation and drainage, mechanization has made significant inroads only in crop processing (grain threshing, oil pressing).

Traditional accounts of energy consumption in farming would end at this point, noting the total of over 90 million tce or, more properly (as most of this figure is coal used in village sideline production), an aggregate of close to 30 million tce consumed in fieldwork, water pumping, and crop processing. But since the early 1970s inquiries of this kind have been extended in two essential directions. First, they were integrated into a much broader evaluation of energy flows through the whole agroecosystem. Second, they were augmented by detailed accounts of indirect energy uses, that is, by calculations of fuel and electricity consumption required to produce the principal modern farming inputs, above all machinery, fertilizers, and pesticides. I will start with this indirect energy cost accounting which is now widely known as process energy analysis.

Before 1978 such an exercise for China had to rest on cumulative assumptions as most of the finer statistics needed for the calculations were not available. Even now the account is far from perfect, but it must be noted that considerable uncertainties continue to exist even in the best Western works of this kind. An interested reader should consult Smil, Nachman, and Long (1983) for the so far most detailed energy analysis of a single crop.

China's agricultural machinery still puts a rather small claim on production energies—and the need would be even smaller if Chinese energy intensities (that is, specific energy consumption per kg of the final product) in smelting metals (most of the mass of farm machinery is, of course, made up of various steels) and assembling the machines were not appreciably higher in comparison with the Western nations. The simplest way to proceed is to apply a representative mean specific weight to a power unit of farm machinery, then, in turn, multiply by an average energy intensity, and finally, adjust the result for typical equipment lifetime.

Total power of Chinese agricultural machinery reached 245 million hp, or 183 GW, in 1983. Averaging across a wide variety of machines is made easier by the fact that only three (admittedly still broad) categories—tractors, motors for irrigation and drainage, and trucks—made up 70 percent of all capacity. After reviewing numerous Chinese tractor, truck, and motor specifications I believe that a mean of 50 kg of steel for each kW of new equipment is fairly representative. Consequently, in 1983, there were at least 9.2 million tons of motorized farm equipment in China, and with no less than 120 MJ of energy needed to produce each kg, the total energy cost would be about 1.1 EJ, the equivalent of roughly 38 million tce. (It will be seen in section 3.2.4 that this mean is most likely on the conservative side as Chinese steel energy intensities were, until recently, truly dismal; of course, most of the machinery now in service was produced before the recent reforms raised the efficiency.

Well-maintained farm equipment can last anywhere between ten and twenty years, and as it is now possible to compare the official totals of tractors and motors in service with their cumulative production, it is easy to see that the Chinese still have about four-fifths of all motorized farm machinery made since 1958 in service, a ratio implying an average lifetime of roughly twenty years. Even a casual observer of Chinese tractors and motors will readily attest to their much patched-up longevity, and the mean of twenty years means that the average annual energy investment in producing machinery is no more than 55 PJ, equal to about 1.9 million tons of standard coal.

To this must be added energy costs of producing large numbers of tractor-towed implements (above all about 1.3 million plows, harrows, and sowing machines used with large and medium machines and 2.6 million implements for small tractors), and of many kinds of smaller nonmechanized field and crop-processing equipment. Assumptions of a total of five million units each weighing 500 kg and requiring 100 MJ/kg result in an aggregate energy cost of 250 PJ. With the twenty-year service period, annualized outlay would be 12.5 PJ (0.43 million tce) for a grand total of only about 67.5 PJ (2.33 million tce) invested each year in farming machinery.

In contrast, fertilizer energy needs are rather considerable, mostly owing to large increases in synthesis of nitrogenous materials whose production more than doubled in the latter half of the 1970s after the completion of a series of large ammonia and urea plants imported from the United States, Japan, France, and the Netherlands and expansion of many smaller domestic factories. The large, new, natural-gas-based plants (M. W. Kellogg design) synthesize ammonia and urea with energy intensities basically equal to the best Western and Japanese levels, but the nationwide average continues to be lowered by the still numerous small, inefficient, largely coal-based facilities where synthesis requirements may be as much as three times higher than those of modern units (Lei 1981).

Detailed performance data published in 1984 make it possible to calculate the two typical means. In 1983 large ammonia plants averaged 41.4 GJ of natural gas and 14.86 kWh of electricity per ton of ammonia for a total energy cost of 41.5 MJ/kg NH_3. As NH_3 is 82 percent nitrogen, the cost per kilogram of the nutrient is almost exactly 50 MJ. This mean must be enlarged by 40 percent, to 70 MJ/kg N, to account for the costs of synthesizing urea, which is the principal product of the new large plants. Unlike NH_3, urea is a solid that can be easily stored, distributed in bags, and applied without special equipment.

In small ammonia plants 1,301 kg of coke and 1,406 kWh of electricity were consumed on the average in 1983 for each ton of ammonia. These rates (taking the official average of 1.43 tons of coal per ton of coke and assuming 25 percent of electricity coming from hydrogeneration and the rest from thermal generation averaging 25 percent conversion efficiency) translate to 70 MJ. Making ammonium bicarbonate, an unstable and rather inferior fertilizer which has been the main product of these small establishments, raises the cost by 30 percent to about 90 MJ/kg N. Total 1983 production of nitrogen fertilizers, equivalent to 11.09 million tons of the nutrient, was split between the two modes of production so that the overall mean was about 80 MJ/kg N and the energy subsidies into domestic synthesis come to approximately 890 PJ. To this must be added the cost of 4.25 million tons of imported, mostly Japanese, urea totalling about 135 PJ.

Compared to this large energy investment in nitrogenous fertilizers (1.025 EJ) costs of phosphorous materials and potassium compounds are low—owing to their inherently lower energy intensities and to their generally inadequate applications in China's farming. While in the early 1980s the worldwide application ratio of the three macronutrients (N:P:K) was approximately 1:0.22:0.31, in China it was a very unbalanced 1:0.11:0.03. In 1983 domestic extraction of phosphates and imports were equivalent to 1.38 million tons of the nutrient, and with average energy cost of 15 MJ/kg only some 20 PJ were invested in the provision of phosphorus. The total for potassium was even lower. With applications of a mere 400,000 tons of the nutrient and costs of just 5 MJ/kg, potassium costs were 2 PJ, a total smaller than the inevitable error in evaluating nitrogen energy needs. Pesticide synthesis totaled 331,000 tons in 1983, and at around 200 MJ/kg the annual energy investment would have been roughly 65 PJ.

All entries may now be listed in a summary of indirect energy subsidies and direct commercial energy flows sustaining China's farming (table 3.11).In 1983 the former added up to about 1.1 EJ, the latter to 860 PJ for a total of 2 EJ or, prorated per unit of cultivated land, about 20 GJ/ha. This calculated aggregate is appreciably higher than the two earlier estimates published by the Chinese (Deng and Zhou 1981; Deng and Wu 1984). The differences are outlined in table 3.12. The greatest discrepancy concerns direct electricity inputs: I have expressed the consumption in terms of energy equivalent needed for generation in thermal power plants (average conversion efficiency of 28 percent) while Deng appears to have used the straight thermal equivalent, disregarding, unrealistically, the losses during thermal generation, which provides three-quarters of China's electricity.

As for the direct fuels, Deng excludes coal altogether whereas I assigned at least a small part of its rural productive consumption to farming tasks. In evaluation of indirect inputs my higher total owes to

Table 3.11

Energy subsidies in China's farming in 1983

Inputs	PJ	GJ/ha
Indirect subsidies	1180	11.8
Machinery	68	0.7
Fertilizers	1047	10.5
Nitrogen	1025	10.3
Phosphorus	20	0.2
Potassium	2	0.0
Pesticides	65	0.6
Direct inputs	860	8.6
Fuels	445	4.5
Oil products	350	3.5
Coal[a]	95	1.0
Electricity[b]	415	4.1
Total	2040	20.4

Source: author's calculations detailed in the text.

[a] Five percent of all commercial coal consumed in rural areas.
[b] Ninety percent of all commercial electricity consumed in rural areas.

Table 3.12

Comparison of three estimates of Chinese farming energy subsidies (all values are in GJ/ha)

	1983	1983 (Deng and Wu 1984)	1978 (Deng and Zhou 1981)
Indirect subsidies	11.8	9.7	9.5
Machinery	0.7	1.7	3.8
Fertilizers	10.5	8.0	5.7
Pesticides	0.6	—	—
Direct inputs	8.6	5.1	5.2
Fuels	4.5	3.3	2.6
Electricity	4.1	1.8	2.6
Total	20.4	14.8	14.7

inclusion of pesticides and higher energy intensities for fertilizer (80 vs. 73.7 MJ/kg for N; 15 vs. 13.4 MJ/kg for P). How Deng arrived at his machinery costs I cannot even guess: his 1983 value is less than half of the 1978 one, and both are much above my fairly liberally calculated value. As he used 84.4 MJ/kg and I converted with 120 MJ/kg, the difference must come from his extremely unrealistic assumptions about the total mass of Chinese farming machinery. Deng's 1983 grand total is clearly too low, and China's real 1983 direct and indirect energy investment in its agriculture totaled almost certainly close to 2 EJ (or 70 million tce, roughly 10.5 percent of the country's primary energy consumption) and hence is prorated to around 20 GJ/ha.

In comparison with eight other nations for which detailed agricultural energy analysis is available, China's total subsidies are at about the same level per hectare of cultivated land as in Egypt (22 GJ) or in France (23 GJ), roughly 40 percent lower than the English inputs (34 GJ), and merely a quarter of Dutch or Israeli farming energy investment (over 80 GJ). However, they are about twice as large as the average U.S. intensity (10 GJ/ha) and an order of magnitude above the Australian and New Zealand inputs (2–3 GJ). China's farming energy subsidies are thus surprisingly high for a country with still only a rudimentary level of field mechanization. This is, of course, largely explainable by the country's extensive and now largely mechanized irrigation (which also accounts for most of the high Israeli intensity) and by its relatively heavy fertilization (which is also the heaviest Dutch farming energy input).

With about 125 kg N/ha of cultivated land Chinese are now fertilizing almost as much as the Japanese (although in terms of average applications per crop they still lag behind as the multicropping ratio is higher in China), and they are well ahead of not only the USSR (about 35 kg N/ha) but also the United States (close to 60 kg N/ha). As a share of total energy use, China's 10 percent going into farming is more than three times the U.S. total and about twice as much as the British share, and it is roughly comparable to French and Dutch expenditures.

This is surely one of the least appreciated realities of modern China: dependence of its farming on nonrenewable fossil fuel energies, providing pumping and motive power and feedstock for synthetic nitrogen, is higher—both in GJ/ha and as a share of total consumption—than in the United States, and it will have to increase substantially to feed the quarter billion people to be added during the coming generation. The Chinese countryside remains critically dependent on biomass fuels, and this means that even in nationwide terms the reliance on renewable energies is still quite large: when added to China's 1983 consumption of 650 million tce of commercial energy, 220 million tce of biomass fuels bring the grand total to 870 million tce, almost exactly 25 percent of national primary energy use. However, the 10 percent of primary commercial energy flowing into agriculture is now no less critical for the survival of more than one billion people, a population too large to be sustained by anything but adequate domestic food production.

Although fossil fuels and electricity now provide irreplaceable energy flows of key importance, animate energies and recycling of organic matter remain essential, and their relative worth is best appreciated through a systematic analysis of principal energy and nutrient fluxes in China's agroecosystem. Figure 3.6 offers a grand picture, from solar radiation to urban food consumption, and the following approximate calculations will show the continuing indispensibility of human and animal labor and of the recycled wastes.

Using three different approaches—typical work rates, all-day energy efficiencies, and calculations of energy available for activity after subtracting maintenance costs from average food intake—I believe that about 450 MJ of useful energy per working adult per year is the most representative mean. With average annual workload of 2,400 hours this translates into personal power rating of about 50 W. Deng and Wu (1984) used 75 W, a mean not unrealistic but almost certainly on the high side. With 310 million people engaged in rural labor, human work in 1983 repesented power of at least 16, or perhaps as much as 20, GW.

In 1983 China had 61.25 million draft animals, mainly cattle, horses, and donkeys, and throughout Jiangnan also water buffaloes. With the exception of water buffaloes and some heavier breeds of northern horses most of China's draft animals are relatively light, and assumption of average power of 400 W per animal (a bit over one-half hp) yields a total rating of about 25 GW; Deng and Wu (1984) are, again, on a liberal side with 650 W per animal. The total 1983 capability of China's human and animal labor thus came to about 45 GW of useful power, equal to about 25 percent of the capacity of all agricultural machinery.

But such a comparison is misleading as the animate capacities are expressed in terms of effective power while the machinery performance, as already pointed out, is greatly limited by electricity and power shortages: the actually available power of Chinese agricultural machinery in 1983 was more likely around 110, rather than the installed 183 GW, and the share of animate power would then be 40 percent. By far the best way to compare the two power sources is to calculate the amount of commercial energy needed to substitute for animate work in fully mechanized farming where there are no draft animals and where human labor figures prominently only owing to its

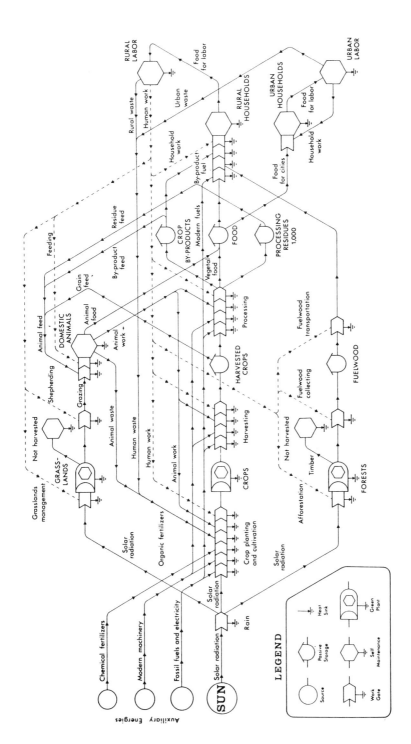

Figure 3.6: Energy flows in China's agro-ecosystem.

irreplaceable control and management function.

Using the average power ratings (50 W for peasants, 400 W for draft animals) and 2,400 hours of work for villagers and 1,100 hours of labor for the beasts, the annual useful animate energy input comes to about 235 PJ. Even when these animate exertions are replaced with machines working with an average 20–25 percent efficiency (a rather liberal allowance for actual field conditions), no less than 950–1,200 PJ of initial fuel and electricity inputs is needed to energize their work, an equivalent of some 30–40 million tce. As the current fuel and electricity consumption by agricultural machinery totals almost 30 million tce, the Chinese farmers would at least have to double their refined fuels and electricity consumption in order to displace animate labor by machinery.

Approximate totals of recycled organic wastes and their macronutrient contents are presented in table 3.13. Led by animal and human excrement and by crop residue, these sources contained in 1983 over 7 million tons of nitrogen, nearly a million tons of phosphorus, and about 4.5 million tons of potassium. In a simple comparison organic recycling would seem to provide at least 35–40 percent of all nitrogen, the same share of phosphorus, and nine-tenths of all potassium applied annually to Chinese crop fields. In reality, large volatilization and leaching losses during storage and fermentation and after application lower the total of actually available nutrients (above all nitrogen) by at least 20 percent and in many circumstances as much as 80 percent. As it is impossible to come up with any representative mean for these ubiquitous losses, one can do no more than estimate that in today's China organic recycling still delivers at least a fifth and perhaps a quarter of all nitrogen, a third of all phosphorus, and four-fifths of all potassium.

Calculating at the prevailing energy cost of synthetic fertilizers (in MJ/kg, 80 for N, 15 for P, and 5 for K), organic recycling saves the Chinese about 260 PJ, or some 9 million tce of mostly natural gas and electricity that would be needed to produce the replacement nutrients. This comparison, of course, ignores those even more important, although not so readily quantifiable, environmental services provided by organic recycling, above all soil moisture retention, improved tilth, and anti-erosion protection. Without these benefits sustained farming is impossible, and it is thus a most unwelcome sign of modernization that the intensity of organic recycling recently has been slipping throughout China.

The two final points I want to make about China's agroecosystemic

Table 3.13

Estimates of annual recycling of organic matter in China in the early 1980s

	Total production (10⁶ t)	Recycled as fertilizer (10⁶ t)	Average nutrient content (percent)			Total annual recycling (10⁶ t)		
			N	P	K	N	P	K
Animal wastes	150[a]	70	5.0	0.8	1.5	3.5	0.6	1.1
Human wastes	370[b]	300	0.6	0.0	0.2	1.8	0.0	0.6
Crop residues	460	210	0.7	0.1	1.2	1.5	0.2	2.5
Oil-seed cakes	6	5	5.0	0.4	1.5	0.2	0.0	0.1
Household garbage	15	10	0.5	0.2	0.8	0.1	0.0	0.1
Mud, silt	—	100	0.2	0.0	0.1	0.2	0.0	0.1
Total						7.3	0.8	4.5

Source: author's calculations based on Smil 1981b.

[a]as dry solids.
[b]as nightsoil.

energetics are to discuss adequacy of food production and compare modern energy subsidies with food outputs. A detailed food balance sheet for 1983 shows a total annual availability of about 4.25 EJ of plant and animals foods, an equivalent of roughly 11.3 MJ (2,710 kcal in the still more common dietary energy measures) per capita a day (table 3.14). Relatively extensive food consumption surveys found average daily per capita intakes at 2,380 kcal, implying a 12 percent loss in distribution, storage, processing, and household waste, a share, as expected, much lower than in Western nations or Japan.

Alternative evaluations of average food energy requirements result in daily needs between 2,200 and 2,400 kcal per capita, indicating a basic adequacy of China's current food production for healthy and vigorous life. This is certainly an impressive achievement: feeding one-fifth of mankind from one-fifteenth of the world's cultivated land and coming within less than 10 percent of average food availability in Japan, a society with per capita income an order of magnitude higher than China! This success must be credited to post-1978 reforms, especially to *baogan daohu*, the household responsibility system that has resulted in a de facto privatization of farming and in unprecedented agricultural output growth.

The impressive average, however, still hides great inter- and intra-

Table 3.14

China's average per capita food availability in 1983

Foodstuffs	Annual per capita availability[a] (kg)	Daily per capita availability[b]					
		Food energy (kcal)		Protein (g)		Lipids (g)	
Rice	108.8	1040		20		3	
Wheat	62.1	595		20		3	
Coarse grains	46.2	440		11		2	
Pulses	2.5	20		2		0	
Potatoes	94.4	180		3		1	
Soybeans	4.3	40		4		3	
Sugar	5.0	50		0		0	
Vegetables	160.5	90		6		1	
Fruits	7.6	10		0		0	
Meat	12.7	90		6		11	
Poultry	1.3	10		1		1	
Fish	4.2	10		2		1	
Eggs	3.0	10		2		1	
Milk	1.7	5		0		1	
Vegetal oils	4.0	90		0		9	
Animal fats	1.5	30		0		3	
Cereals	217.1	2075	(77)	51	(66)	8	(20)
Vegetal foods	495.4	2555	(94)	66	(86)	22	(55)
Animal foods	24.4	155	(6)	11	(14)	18	(45)
Total	519.8	2710		77		40	

Source: Smil (1986).

[a]Calculated by dividing the last column of table 3. by 1,024.95 million: all values rounded to the nearest 0.1 kg.
[b]Standard conversions used throughout; all values rounded to the nearest 5 for kcal and the nearest 1 for protein and lipids.

provincial disparities. Several recent Chinese statements, including the one by Deng Xiaoping, admit that between 90 and 110 million people are not still adequately fed, a proportion confirmed by the latest available provincial grain availability averages. Although there are notable pockets of rural poverty even in the coastal provinces, most of the peasants with inadequate food intakes can be found in the interior crescent arching from Guizhou to Shanxi. Should the rural reforms continue and should the interprovincial food transfers intensify, most of the inadequacies can be gradually eliminated before the end of the century—but such an achievement will also depend on much improved overall environmental management in the deforested, eroded, and, in the North, arid and desertifying agroecosystems.

Finally, a few paragraphs about the overall efficiency of China's agroecosystem. There are several ways to quantify this performance, none of them wholly satisfactory. The broadest measure is to express the efficiency as a share of solar radiation reaching the ground: after all, farming is nothing else but a managed photosynthetic energy conversion. As already noted (in section 2.4), the overall efficiency of China's primary production is a mere 0.15 percent, a disproportionately poor performance owing to the very low productivities of the country's extensive stressed arid and cold ecosystems. With farming the situation is reversed: China's agroecosystem, owing largely to its widespread irrigation, fairly intensive fertilization, and high cropping index, converts considerably more solar radiation into crops than the global average.

With about 4.1×10^{21} J reaching the country's cropfields annually, and with the total 1983 harvest (including crop residues, which are, of course, perfect feeds) at about 13.5 EJ, the conversion efficiency is approximately 0.33 percent. In terms of photosynthetically active radiation (which accounts for about 45 percent of the total spectrum), the share rises to 0.73 percent while the comparable global value is no more than 0.45 percent. A narrower but in many ways more revealing measure contrasts the total managed inputs—animate energies as well as fossil fuels and electricity—with the yield. Using values derived earlier in this chapter (235 PJ for animate and 2 EJ for direct and indirect modern energy subsidies) results in a return of 6 J of crop phytomass for every joule of invested, managed energy.

Of course, such a comparison ignores the fundamentally different qualities of the two energies—food and feed digestible by humans and animals and consumed not simply for its energy content but also for its essential nutrients, on one hand, and fossil fuels and electricity, on the other—and all those conclusions published since the mid-1970s that labeled the agrosystems with low crop energy/subsidy energy ratio as "inefficient" are obviously simplistic and inaccurate. The same charge can be made against the even more restricted ratio where food output is divided only by nonrenewable energy subsidies.

This ratio should reveal the efficiency with which expensive and eventually exhaustible resources are used to increase the yields, but the value is critically dependent on the general orientation of a farming system. Those producing predominantly plant foods (the Chinese agro-system being a perfect example with over 90 percent of all food coming from cereals, tubers, legumes, vegetables, and fruits) will inevitably have higher "returns" than agricultures dominated by animal husbandry (such as all those in all European and North American countries).

Consequently, perhaps the only sensible ratio to use for international comparisons is a simple value of energy subsidies per hectare of cultivated land. This value will, of course, hide great energy input differences among major crops within each country, but it will be a fairly reliable approximation of overall farming intensity. As already noted, the Chinese figure of about 20 GJ/ha is roughly comparable to the Egyptian level and about double the average American intensity. Even if the Chinese conversion inefficiencies, responsible for the relatively high energy cost of nitrogenous fertilizers and machinery, were largely eliminated, the country's much higher fertilizer applications and extensive irrigation would keep it well ahead of the U.S. subsidies.

China's farming will have to become even more of an industrial and urban affair. Photosynthetic conversion in crops will have to be aided more by the fuels extracted in mines and hydrocarbon fields, by electricity generation in thermal and hydrostations, and by fertilizers, pesticides, and machines synthesized and produced in modern plants. The other economy, the urban-industrial one, will thus be even more decisive for the sustenance of rural production.

3.2 Industries and cities

With China's countryside consuming directly only one-fifth of the nation's fossil fuels and electricity, and with the country's huge rural population using less than 10 percent of all modern energies, the disparity between villages and cities remains very large, especially in per capita terms. The following sections will show, however, that the still very inefficient industries, rather than the urban dwellers, are the main consumers of city-bound energies.

On a list of dichotomies characterizing China's post-1949 achievements this industrial-urban disparity is quite notable: impressive quantitative advances in all sectors which made the country the world's third largest producer of primary energy are everywhere in sharp contrast with inferior quality, poor specific performance, inefficient utilization, and widespread shortages. This disparity is perhaps the key to understanding the peculiar weakness of China's seemingly robust and rapidly expanding commercial energy system, and in the following sections, covering individual energy industries, those critical qualitative deficiencies, performance weaknesses, and supply shortages will be given special attention.

3.2.1 Coal as the foundation

In the absence of any substantial hydrocarbon reserves, massive expansion of coal mining was the only sensible option for China of the 1950s when the need for a large amount of coal was driven by requirements of industrialization in general and by Stalinist orientation toward iron, steel, and heavy metal industries in particular. Coal production doubled during the short period of economic recovery between 1949 and 1952, and it doubled again during the First Five-Year Plan (1953–57). During the irrational Great Leap campaigns of 1957–59 raw coal output shot up 2.3 times, but this expansion, coming largely from shallow open pits worked with traditional tools, produced mostly inferior fuel and was clearly unsustainable.

Orderly development resumed after the country emerged from the years of famine and economic disarray in the wake of the Leap's collapse, and by 1970 China was extracting over 300 million tons of raw coal by pushing the development of both large mines under central administration and widespread establishment of small, locally run, pits whose production was to be of critical importance in diminishing the chronic dependence of southern provinces on large-scale coal shipments from the North.

By 1978 the extraction topped 600 million tons (table 3.15), and the first comprehensive proposals for modernization of the coal industry published early in that year envisaged opening of many more small mines in all counties with exploitable coal deposits. The same set of proposals also contained the goal of "basic mechanization" of large mines within a decade and the target of doubling the 1977 output in ten years—and then doubling it again by the end of the century.

Aiming at two successive doublings during such a short period of time and at such huge output levels (from 500 million tons in 1977 to 2 billion by the year 2000) was patently unrealistic, and the goal was dropped before the end of the year. Soon afterward, as the normal economic concerns started finally to prevail over the inefficient and costly Maoist demands of local self-sufficiency and stress on small-

Table 3.15

China's coal production, 1949–1986

Year	Total	Raw coal output Large mines (million t)	Local mines	Coal equivalent (million t)	Percent of total energy production
1949	32.43	30.98	1.45	23.16	96.3
1952	66.49	63.53	2.96	47.47	96.7
1957	130.73	123.23	7.50	93.34	94.9
1965	232.00	198.25	33.75	165.65	68.0
1978	617.86	276.02	341.84	441.15	70.3
1979	635.54	277.77	357.77	453.77	70.2
1980	620.15	275.76	344.39	442.78	69.4
1981	621.63	286.58	335.05	443.84	70.2
1982	665.84	315.00	350.84	475.41	71.2
1983	715.00	363.59	351.41	510.51	71.6
1984	772.00	—	—	551.20	72.0
1985	850.00	—	—	606.90	72.3
1986	870.00	—	—	621.18	72.1

Source: Yuan Guangru (1982), State Statistical Bureau (1986).

scale production at any cost, new priorities were formulated by a new minister, Gao Yangwen, who took control in December 1979.

They had to focus on intense modernization of large ministry-run mines, with special emphasis on expanding coal-dressing capacities and on opening up of new large mines, including surface ones, in regions with the most suitable conditions, above all in the North. For the first time in the PRC's history, Gao's outlines also called for growing exports of coal, coke, and coal-derived chemicals, as well as for development of relatively large-scale coal gasification capabilities. As these expansion and modernization plans would be hard to realize without substantial imports of advanced technology, numerous negotiations started in 1979 aimed not only at particular machinery imports but also at complete mine development packages whose eventual cost would be several billion dollars.

But the most important immediate change in 1979 was to lower sharply the coal extraction growth rate from the excessively high 12.4 percent in 1978. The reasons for this were obvious: too many large mines have ignored for too long the proper balance between tunneling and excavation, and too many accidents were happening in mines neglecting even basic safety precautions. The energy cost of the whole endeavor was dismally high, the quality of output was considered unimportant as long as the planned targets were overfulfilled, and living conditions of miners and their families were overwhelmingly poor. In sum, the rapid growth, the headlong quantitative rush, had no commensurate qualitative infrastructural base assuring sustainable progress in the future.

Gao's new consultative group of one hundred experts prevailed with its advocacy of the necessity to stabilize the output, to readjust the derailed proportion of tunneling and extraction, and to focus on quality as the bases for future orderly expansion. Both 1980 and 1981 outputs were actually a bit lower than the 1979 production (620 and 622 million vs. 635 million tons), but in 1982 the growth resumed at the relatively fast pace of 7.4 percent and China edged out the USSR to become the world's second largest coal producer after the United States. But this position, of which Chinese are now so proud, hides ubiquitous qualitative and technological shortcomings. China is undoubtedly one of the world's three coal super-producers, but otherwise its industry has little in common with its American and Soviet counterparts, as the following parade of comparisons will show in some detail.

To begin with, China's real coal output is considerably smaller than the now regularly released extraction figures indicate: they are all reported in terms of raw coal and must be reduced by about 30 percent to obtain the mass in standard coal equivalent units (fuel with 29 MJ/kg). China's 1983 coal extraction of 715 million tons of raw coal thus equaled only 14.8 EJ, or 510 million tons of standard fuel, while the American output of 712 million tons equaled 22.4 EJ and the Soviet production of 645 million tons was, at 16.4 EJ, still well ahead of the Chinese total despite having a relatively large share of brown coal. (See also table 3.16 comparisons for 1982.)

There is, of course, a good practical reason why Chinese report their output in raw coal: that is how most of the fuel is actually used. At the end of 1983 Chinese had only 110 coal-washing plants which processed 126.88 milion tons so that only 18 percent of that year's output was cleaned and sorted, mostly for coking; with few exceptions even the large, modern power plants burn raw coal! Virtually all of these coal-dressing plants were attached to the largest enterprises among the state-owned mines which produced half of all coal in 1983. Consequently, even in these large collieries only a bit more than one-third of extracted coal was cleaned, and practically the whole output of small local mines was used without any preparation. In contrast, in the other largest coal-

Table 3.16

Comparison of basic statistics for the world's largest coal-mining nations in 1982

	China	USA	USSR	Poland	FRG	UK
Total output (10^6t)	665.8	760.7	647.0	227.0	223.6	124.7
Energy equivalent (10^6tce)	475.4	827.5	565.9	196.9	144.4	143.0
Share of open-cast mining (percent)	2.9	60.1	40.0	16.4	57.0	12.6
Share of mechanical extraction (percent)	40.0	99.0	96.0	96.2	99.7	97.0
Total employees (10^3)	5,500	226	2,310	58	206	270
Underground productivity (t/miner-shift)	0.87	9.98	2.23	3.73	3.39	2.41
Total accidents (deaths/10^6t)	1.5*	0.16	0.96	0.55	0.43	0.36

Source: Rui and Wang (1985); UN (1985).

*Minimum estimate.

mining nations all but a small fraction of extracted coal is washed and sized before combustion.

International comparison of all major qualitative mining indicators shows similarly large gaps (table 3.16). Even in all the ministry-run mines only 21 percent of coal extraction and tunneling were fully mechanized by 1983, compared to nearly total mechanization in all other leading coal-mining nations. The bulk of China's coal is produced with tedious manual labor and, hardly surprisingly, labor productivity is dismal. In 1982 state-run mines employed 4.6 million people and the daily output per miner in large establishments was less than one ton of raw coal (much like in England at the beginning of twentieth century), while even in those European countries where nearly all coal is extracted in old coalfields from relatively thin seams the means are between 2 and 4 tons a day for a miner.

In China's largest and most productive mines in Shanxi province the daily output in 1981 averaged 1.32 tons per miner; in the province's best mine the productivity was just below 3 tons per shift for each underground miner—just a small fraction of the American nationwide mean of nearly 10 tons per shift for each underground miner (in the best mines the productivity surpasses 20 tons a day). The overall national average for the United States is in excess of 15 tons, a result of a large share (60 percent) of extraction coming from surface mines. Open-cast mining has also been producing a steadily growing share of Soviet coal extraction (currently about 40 percent)—yet in China a mere 3 percent of coal output (21.5 million tons) originated in 1983 in fourteen modern surface mines (leaving aside primitive shallow local pits), perhaps the best indicator of the technological backwardness of the country's coal technology.

As for the modern underground extraction methods, the Soviet advisers introduced long-wall mining—a faster, cheaper, safer, and more efficient method than traditional room-and-pillar work—in the 1950s, and the technique now acounts for nine-tenths of output in large state-run mines. Some hydraulic mining is also used, above all in Kailuan collieries. China now produces a wide variety of equipment used in its modern mines, ranging from long-wall assemblies to hoisting devices, but the output is both quantitatively insufficient to mechanize extraction at the desired pace and qualitatively inferior (based on outdated designs and suffering from shortages of high-quality steels) to bring large boosts in the productivity.

These shortcomings have led to increasing imports of advanced machinery for both the underground and the newly promoted surface mining. Great Britain, West Germany, the United States, Japan, and Poland have been the principal suppliers, and these countries will continue to provide most of the imported technology for the planned development of complete large mines. Foreign, above all Japanese, aid is also already used to improve China's inadequate coal transportation capacities. Large regional disparities in coal production—resulting from the highly uneven distribution of the best exploitable reserves (section 2.2.1)—and the fuel's dominant position in the country's economy make coal by far the most important commodity burdening China's railways.

About two-fifths of all tonnage (and 50–70 percent on major North-South trunk railways such as Beijing-Guangdong and Beijing-Shanghai) comprises northern coal moving south an average distance of 400 km in ordinary gondola or hopper cars carrying just 30–60 tons in steam-locomotive-pulled trains of 3,000–4,000 tons. Other large coal-mining nations use special diesel or electricity-powered coal unit trains moving in excess of 10,000 tons in special hopper cars. By far the worst transportation bottleneck has been posed by Shanxi's coal. As stressed before, the province is China's richest depository of excellent bituminous coal, and its annual output had been growing by more than 3 million tons a year between 1949 and 1978 and by an average of 12 million tons during 1979–1984, with most of the increments destined for exports. In 1984, 120 million tons of Shanxi coal (about 75 percent of the total extraction) went to twenty-six different provinces and twenty countries, heavily burdening the province's 3,000 km of railways and 27,000 km of roads. Still, spontaneous combustion of stockpiled coal (by the end of 1983, 27 million tons) has been claiming millions of tons of fuel every year, and the planned grandiose expansion of Shanxi mining would be a futile investment without substantially improved transportation capacities.

And so, finally, a multifaceted effort is now underway to take the coal out of Shanxi economically and reliably. Naturally, the first and foremost method must be unit train shipments: China's first double-track, electrified railway accommodating trains up to 10,000 tons and designed to carry 100 million tons of coal a year will connect Datong fields with the port of Qinhuangdao (Hebei), 639 km to the east. Other railway projects currently underway include a line from Houma (southern Shanxi) to Yueshan (Henan) and from Suo county (northern Shanxi) to Shijiazhuang (Hebei); also, seven old lines are being double-tracked and electrified. At the end of the longest unit train run, Qinhuangdao port had eleven deep-water berths and handled 20 million tons of coal in 1984. Construction of new coal wharves is underway to boost the transfers to southern provinces and exports from a total of 46 million tons in 1985 to 100 million tons in the 1990s (Han 1984).

Huge and accessible deposits combined with qualitative superiority and low extraction costs have brought out again the supremacy of northern coals after decades of on-and-off attempts to make the other parts of the country less dependent on northern shipments. In the early 1950s, before the beginning of China's First Five-Year Plan, the North produced 28 percent of all raw coal and the Central-South 14.5 percent; after two decades of exploration, investment, and promotion of southern mining the ratios were virtually identical at, respectively, 28.9 and 14.4 percent—and by 1983 the North pulled further ahead with 34.7 percent, a share more than twice as large as the Central-South's 15.9 percent.

The North-South disparity in coal extraction proved to be, unfortunately, immune to repeated attempts to reduce it, but another on-and-off strategy has brought a fundamental shift in China's coal industry as the proportion of extraction in medium and small mines has grown from negligible amounts in the early 1950s to about half of all output three decades later. Chinese coal mining is managed at three different levels:

at the top are nearly 600 (562 at the end of 1983) large mines controlled directly by the Ministry of Coal Industry; then come more than 1,600 medium-sized establishments (1,680 in 1983) run by provinces and counties; and finally there are fluctuating numbers—tens of thousands—of small pits which were formerly owned by communes and production brigades but are now increasingly operated by private entrepreneurs or groups.

Most of the output from state-controlled mines is concentrated in eleven mining districts producing more than 10 million tons of raw coal annually and nearly 25 percent of all coal in 1985 (fig. 3.7). Another nineteen mining centers produce between 5 and 10 million tons annually. As already noted, virtually all of this extraction has been from shaft mines with average annual capacity of 630,000 tons for centrally run and 110,000 tons for other state-owned collieries. These enterprises produced 55.5 percent of all Chinese raw coal in 1980, and this share declined to just about 50 percent in 1985 as the latest wave of local coal mining started rolling. Official figures for 1983 put the locally managed extraction at 351.412 million tons, or 49.18 percent of the total, the highest-ever share resulting from the rapid post-1980 expansion.

A minority of these establishments, 2,512 in 1983, were locally managed mines set up with state investment and included in the central output plans. It is not surprising, therefore, that more than half of them (53.4 percent) produced over 150,000 tons a year, and that their average annual extraction surpassed 72,000 tons. In contrast, of the 46,000 small mines only 1,600 were extracting more than 30,000 tons a year, and their average annual production is merely 3,700 tons, or just over 10 tons a day—an equivalent of a single truckload. Most of these small mines are as simple operations as imaginable: open pits or shallow shafts where coal is dug out and removed without any special mining equipment and without even rudimentary safety rules and precautions.

What the Chinese call the "four small items"—winches, pumps, blowers, and mine lamps—were installed in just 4,500 local pits by 1983, and just 4,000 of them put in place the "four eliminations"—that is, they have done away with the single exit from shaft mines, installed some kind of ventilation, and forbidden open-flame illumination and open-flame and sparking blasting fuses. A Chinese coal industry journal may not be wrong for seeing in these changes the beginning of a transformation into normal small-scale production mines, but the task may not be completed for decades and the inefficiencies, waste, and appalling working conditions will remain the mark of small rural

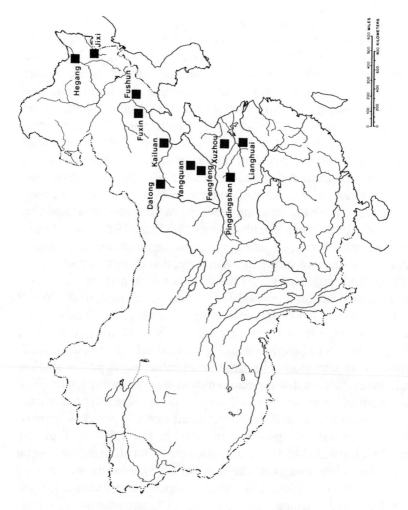

Figure 3.7: Coal-mining centers producing more than ten million tons of raw coal a year.

mining for a long time to come.

This assessment is inevitable in view of the 1983 decision to end the state monopoly on coal mining aimed at relieving the country's chronic energy shortage. On April 22, 1983, the State Council approved the Ministry of Coal Industry's recommendations (here cited from a *Zhongguo meitan bao* editorial of 11 May 1983) to base China's long-term coal expansion once again on "two legs": "While emphasizing development of the country's uniform allocation coal mines, to develop local state-owned coal mines and small coal mines as well."

The new regulations permit private—individual or group—owner-ship of small mines while forbidding "reckless mining and indiscriminate digging" and requiring establishment of "minimal safety conditions." Perhaps most significantly, "coal mines and the masses are to be allowed to use various kinds of transportation equipment for the shipment of coal," and they may haul coal over long distances for sale without interference from any jurisdiction—a practice which inevitably leads to diversion of the rationed diesel fuel and gasoline for profitable trucking to far-away provinces. Predictably, these regulations resulted in a coal rush surpassed only by the Great Leap Forward mania. In March 1985 the director of the State Economic Commission's Energy Bureau stated that more than one million villagers were working in 50,000 small pits (of which more than 13,000 were run by individuals), three times the 1983 total. The number of small mines run by townships also rose, to over 10,000 by May 1985.

The rush is not completely unregulated: the Ministry of Coal Industry set aside large areas with reserves amounting to 35 billion tons just for small-scale production. Peasants must apply to provincial coal resources commissions for permission to start extraction, and local authorities should see to the application of essential technical standards. They are to aid in safety training and should promote the establishment of larger pits to improve efficiency and enhance investment returns. Still, there is little doubt that indiscriminate, wasteful, and dangerous extraction is the norm rather than an exception in thousands of cases. The state readily closes one eye: the new capacities and tens of millions of tons of new output need very little money from its treasury.

Between 1980 and 1982 the large state-owned mines received Rmb 2.57 billion and expanded their output by 23.8 million tons at an average cost of nearly Rmb 108/ton. In 1984 *Zhongguo meitan bao* reported that during the 1970s it cost Rmb 47 to develop one ton of new capacity in state-run local mines while, according to a 1985 Xinhua report, Rmb 287 million of low-interest loans given to Shanxi peasants between 1980 and 1983 boosted the annual output of their small mines by 40 million tons at a cost of a mere Rmb 7.1/ton. After touring Shanxi in the spring of 1985, Gao Yangwen noted that the production cost in small mines was just Rmb 9.86 compared to the province's mean of Rmb 20.

Shanxi's peasant mining has been extolled as a great success story. In 1984 the province's 3,410 rural mines produced 70.65 million tons (out of the total of 178 million tons), nearly as much as the 14 ministry-run large collieries; 79 of Shanxi's 101 counties extract coal, and 51 percent of their peasants' income in 1984 came from coal sales. About 40 million tons of their output was shipped out of the province, mainly to fuel-short Jiangsu and Zhejiang. Other provinces with abundant scattered, shallow coal deposits—Shaanxi, Henan, Gansu, and Guizhou— are encouraged to emulate Shanxi's rush.

Low investment, low production costs, jobs created for peasants whose labor is not required in the privatized farming, rapid easing of local energy shortages, greater interprovincial shipments of scarce fuel, multiplier effects in the economy ranging from new roads, machines, and services to establishment of new local industrial enterprises and manufacturers—all these are appealing and compelling reasons why the promotion of small-scale extraction is now an important part of the national energy policy. In the next chapter (section 4.2.2) I will look at some of the disadvantages of this policy over a longer term. Later (section 5.1) I will also look at the need for reform of dubious energy pricing policies which have generated very high profits for the oil and gas industry but have resulted in meager profits and frequent losses in coal mining.

Characterizing China's coal industry in the mid-1980s is, as with so many segments of the country's energetics, an exercise in contrasts. Coal has always been the prime energizer of China's development, and its consumption will continue to surpass greatly the conversions of hydrocarbons during the remainder of this century. In fact, more is expected of the industry than ever before—and its recent growth may appear to signal a smooth progress under new reformist policies. Yet China's coal industry remains technically backward, inefficient, and unsafe. Coal output is qualitatively much inferior to that of any other large mining nation, its distribution is a chronic problem, its pricing irrational, its future strategies still in flux.

Of course, the prospects would look much better if coal did not have to carry such a large burden, if oil and gas could supply much more than about one-quarter of all primary energy, a share stagnant since the early 1970s. During much of the 1970s such prospects appeared to be imminent; now the outlook is considerably more restrained. Still, hydrocarbon extraction has been of critical importance for the country's industrialization, first obviating costly imports, later earning much foreign exchange, and its future promise is to play a starring role in China's gradual integration into the world economy.

3.2.2 Oil and gas industry

When the PRC was founded in 1949 only three old small oilfields were producing in the Northwest—Laojunmiao in Gansu, Yanshan in Shaanxi, and Dushanzi in Xinjiang—and their total output was merely 100,000 tons a year. Consequently, during the 1950s China was becoming increasingly dependent on oil imports from the USSR—but it was also the Soviet experience with hydrocarbon exploration in continental sediments that led to China's first, and still by far the largest, discovery, the giant Daqing oilfield, an anticlinal structure covering about 1,200 km^2 below the grasslands of southern Heilongjiang. Production at the field started in 1960 using early water injections, another Soviet-introduced technique.

Afterward, China pushed the field's output rapidly to eliminate the Soviet imports (by that time the Sino-Soviet marriage of convenience had turned into a bitter feud) and continued with relatively extensive though shallow (less than 3 km) exploratory drilling, which led eventually to commercial extraction at about twenty minor and five major fields (table 3.17; fig. 3.8). However, Daqing has continued to dominate Chinese crude oil recovery ever since the early 1960s, and its rising output, together with extraction at Shengli oilfield, was behind the rapid increases of nationwide output, the rates surpassing 20 percent annually for many years.

These sustained production gains, contrasting with the supply difficulties in the West after the Yom Kippur War, led to much speculation about China becoming one of the decisive crude oil producers on the global scale by the early 1980s when its growing exports were forecast by some to reach as much as 100 million tons. Collapse of these unrealistic speculations came suddenly: 1978 output growth was down to 11.1 percent, and the 106.15 million tons produced in 1979 were a mere 2 percent higher than in 1978. Chinese crude oil production

Table 3.17

China's principal oilfields

Oilfield	Geological formation	Approximate area (km²)	Province	Counties	Year of discovery
Daqing	Songliao Basin	2,065	Heilongjiang	Anda	1959
Shengli	Jiyang Depression	600	Shandong	Kenli, Lijin	1962
Renqiu	Jizhong Depression	200	Hebei	Renqiu	1975
Liaohe	Lower Liaohe Depression	12,400	Liaoning	Panshan	1967
Zhongyuan	Zhongyuan Depression	5,300	Henan, Shandong	Puyang, Fan, Yanggu	1976

Source: Author's compilation from various Chinese publications.
See also figure 3.8.

stagnated between 101 and 106 million tons until 1983, and the 1986 total topped 130 million tons (table 3.18). No more than about 20 million tons of crude have been exported annually, and news items reporting severe shortages of refined oil products have been as common as those complaining about the shortages of electricity.

What happened has been circumspectly described by the Chinese as "too much concentration on production, too little attention to exploration." Simply, the Chinese behaved just as the no-holds-barred, predatory drillers of the early decades of the American oil industry had: they were sinking as many production wells as possible and pushing their fields with excessive water-flooding while engaging in what amounted—in view of the production levels and increases they wanted to sustain—to only a perfunctory amount of geophysical exploration and wildcat drilling.

Inadequacies of Chinese technology have played an important part in this denouement. Although the majority of basic modern exploration, extraction, transportation, and processing technologies have been either mastered domestically or acquired piecemeal from Japan, Western Europe, and the United States, the overall state of China's petroleum industry is at least two decades behind the Western performance. The gap is especially wide in the areas of computerized geophysical exploration techniques and lightweight rigs capable of drilling up to 6 km. In spite of the growing imports from the West, much of the

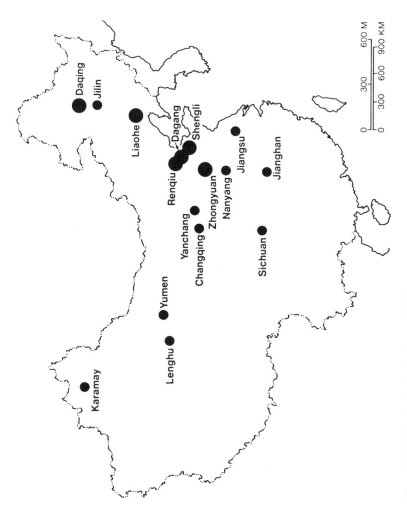

Figure 3.8: China's principal onshore oilfields.

Table 3.18

China's crude oil and natural gas production, 1949–1986

Year	Crude oil output (million t)	Percent of total energy production	Natural gas output (billion m³)	Percent of total energy production
1949	0.12	0.7	—	—
1952	0.44	1.3	—	—
1957	1.46	2.1	0.07	0.1
1965	11.31	8.6	1.10	0.8
1978	104.05	23.7	13.73	2.9
1979	106.15	23.5	14.52	3.0
1980	105.95	23.8	14.27	3.0
1981	101.18	22.9	12.57	2.7
1982	102.12	21.9	11.93	2.4
1983	106.07	21.3	12.21	2.4
1984	114.53	21.3	12.40	2.2
1985	125.00	21.3	12.50	2.0
1986	131.00	21.7	12.70	1.5

Source: SSBC (various years).

industry still has the unmistakable look of the Soviet oil technologies of the 1950s.

And although the Chinese sunk their first offshore wells in 1971 in the shallow Bohai using a Shanghai-made jack-up, their inexperience and inability to undertake large-scale seismic and magnetometric surveys and to work in deeper waters led to perhaps the most fundamental departure from their xenophobic policies and from their repeatedly expressed determination never again to let foreigners exploit China's resources. Chinese offshore waters have become a major scene of exploratory drilling carried out by nearly two dozen companies from eight countries—and the hopes for the new prosperity of China's stagnating oil and gas industry now lie with the large multinational oil companies, yesterday's paragons of capitalist evil (see section 4.2.3).

But even if major discoveries—onshore or offshore—soon bring a new period of production growth, China's petroleum industry will continue to face numerous infrastructural deficiencies owing to its inadequate distribution network and inefficient refining. China's first interprovincial pipeline—1,152 km from Daqing oilfield to Qinhuangdao port in Hebei—was completed only in 1973, and it was 1979 before more than half of the country's crude oil output moved by pipelines.

More than 30,000 railroad tank cars still carry about a third of the production, and north-south transfer proceeds largely by a fleet of small tankers plying the coast.

The Soviets first introduced refining technologies in the 1950s, and these were modernized through Western imports during the 1960s and 1970s; consequently, some of the refineries are quite modern and equipped with good catalytic cracking and hydrofining units. However, the depth and the quality of products from a typical Chinese refinery (a small enterprise processing several hundred thousand to a couple million tons of crude each year) are still inferior in comparison with the output of similar Western installations.

Newly released figures on product yield in crude oil refining show that the share of light and medium products and lubricants stood at 52.22 percent, 6.42 percent below the cut achieved in the early 1950s (Tong 1983). The main reason for this backward trend, sharply contrasting with the efforts of every other major crude oil consumer, is that the artificially low prices made oil a convenient source of industrial and space heat as well as a sought-after fuel for power generation, and this led to rising demand for heavy oil and hence to decline of deep processing.

I will not describe China's oilfields, pipelines, and refineries in detail: since the opening-up of the Chinese petroleum industry to Western and Japanese experts, consultants, and builders, virtually all major fields and enterprises have been visited by foreigners, and the Chinese sources have also published numerous details about the development and conditions of many producing areas and projects. Only the key facts will be given to outline the current distribution and status of China's crude oil and natural gas production.

Concentration of petroleum extraction in a small number of large fields is a fairly usual worldwide occurrence, but in China it is present in a very pronounced manner. In 1985 the largest oilfield produced about 44 percent of all crude, the three largest 75 percent, and the five largest 86 percent of the total flow (table 3.19). Daqing remains by far the largest source (Ding 1983). Every year since 1976 it has pumped out more than 50 million tons a year, and its cumulative output until the end of 1985 was 790 million tons worth over Rmb 70 billion, the largest contribution by a single enterprise to China's economic product.

The field is a single anticlinal structure covering some 1,200 km² and extending 120 km north to south with oil strata in depths between

Table 3.19

Annual crude oil output of China's largest oilfields, 1981–1985

Oilfield	1981	1982	1983	1984	1985
Daqing	51.7	51.9	52.4	53.6	55.1
Shengli	16.1	16.4	18.4	23.0	27.6
Huabei	11.0	11.3	10.6	10.2	10.3
Liaohe	5.0	5.3	6.1	7.7	9.0
Zhongyuan	—	2.3	3.0	4.0	5.1
Dagang	2.5	2.9	2.8	3.2	3.6

Source: Compiled by the author from various Chinese publications.

700 and 1,200 m and with Cretaceous parent rocks amounting to over 12,000 km³ (Yang 1983). Water flooding started in the earliest stages of production, and by 1984 there were 2,000 water injection wells, one every 250 m in rows 600 m apart. Not surprisingly, after two decades of flooding, water content reached 60 percent at the beginning of 1980 and by 1984 was already 71 percent. Excessive flooding led to abandonment of hundreds of wells, and current output of over 50 million tons a year will start declining once the water cut reaches 85 percent. Lowering of soil temperature by up to 8°C has been yet another undesirable complication resulting from excessive flooding, especially when one recalls the high pour point of Daqing oil.

In December 1983 Li Yugeng, the head of Daqing's Oil Management Bureau, stated that the field's output will not fall below 50 million tons a year before 1990, but he also admitted the much higher cost of future production. To pump out the predominantly watery fluid from Daqing's reservoirs he estimated that up to 8,000 new wells were needed between 1981 and 1987, a total equal to twenty years of pre-1981 drilling (Shao 1983). Sharply higher drilling expenditures are paralleled by the cost of electrical pumps and additional gathering lines. Clearly, the field cannot be relied on for any further expansion, and its share in nationwide output will continue to slide.

In contrast, production of the number two field, Shengli, is on the rise. Discovered in 1962 and producing since 1964, Shengli extracts crude oil from wells dispersed over 600 km² on both shores of the Huang He in Shandong near the river's delta. After years of erratic development its output rose to one-fifth of China's total, and in 1985 the Chinese announced a program worth Rmb 25 billion over a five-year period designed to more than double Shengli's annual extraction to nearly 50 million tons. Shengli's crude is mainly transferred south by a 1,000-km-long pipeline connecting Linyi in Shandong with Nanjing in Anhui. Begun in October 1975 and completed in July 1978, the line had to cross railways, highways, and streams almost a thousand times, but it eased greatly the oil distribution in the lower Chang Jiang basin.

Renqiu, or Huabei, oilfield, conveniently located just 150 km south of the capital on the central Hebei plain, has its oil reserves in 30,000 km² of Sinian layers of Paleozoic deposits rather than in Mesozoic and Cenozoic strata of the other eastern fields. Its development has been rapid, with drilling beginning in 1975 and with the whole state investment recovered by the end of 1976. A year later it became China's third largest oilfield with annual extraction surpassing 10 million tons and peaking at 13 million tons in 1979; by 1981 output was down to 11.1 million tons. Two pipelines take the oil south to Nanjing and north to the capital.

Liaohe oilfield includes eight major producing clusters with 1,800 wells and 160 storing and shipping stations in an area of 12,400 km² between Shenyang, Yingkou, and Jinzhou in Liaoning province. In 1980, when its development was completed, the field extracted 5 million tons of crude oil and 1.7 billion m³ of natural gas, and its recent production increases point to a much greater prominence. A short pipeline joins Liaohe with the Daqing-Lüda line for tanker shipments south.

Karamay in Xinjiang is by far the largest producer among the inland fields, and its development has been obviously influenced by the remoteness of the location. Discovered in 1955 and producing since 1958, its output was surpassed by the latest large onshore addition in the eastern third of China, Zhongyuan oilfield, which spreads over 5,300 km² in twelve counties of eastern Henan and western Shandong with hydrocarbons drawn from heavily faulted strata in Puyang, Wenzhong, Wenmingzhai, and Weicheng fields. The extraction started in 1979, and the first announcement about Zhongyuan's output was 2.15 million tons of crude and 0.5 billion m³ of associated gas in 1982.

In March 1983 a State Council directive ordered an accelerated development of the field and named Song Zhenming, the former minister of petroleum, to lead the group charged with the field's rapid buildup. Plans called for verification of 500 million tons of oil and 50 billion m³ of gas by 1985 with oil extraction to reach 5 million tons. Oil is moved by a pipeline from Puyang in Henan to Linyi in Shandong, where it joins the Shengli-Nanjing line; natural gas goes to Kailung in Henan. With the reports of new oilfield discoveries and with extensions of reserves in the producing oilfields the prospects of onshore production look now better than at the beginning of the decade when both output and drilling stagnated.

Drilling activity in the early 1980s stagnated at around 2.5 million m a year for exploratory wells while the total length of developmental wells rose substantially. Some extension and appraisal wells are classified as exploratory wells, however, so there is no direct correspondence with Western statistics. In any case, there are expectations of fairly steady onshore output for the rest of the 1980s as the new discoveries more or less balance the declining extraction from older fields. Offshore drilling is still expected to make the greatest difference, and its most recent development and prospects will be appraised in some detail in section 4.2.3.

No big increases are going to happen anytime soon in the output of natural gas, clearly the weakest part of China's hydrocarbon industry. When compared in terms of energy equivalents, the ratio of crude oil/ natural gas output is just over 1 in the United States and about 1.2 in the USSR. In contrast, in China it is more than 9, indicating both the great backwardness of China's gas industry and its substantial potential. With nearly half of the total output coming from Sichuan's declining fields and used entirely within that province there is an obvious need for diversification of supplies and expansion of extraction. The first large offshore gas discovery in the South China Sea should be just the beginning of such an expansion—although not one without its own considerable problems (see section 4.2.3).

In the mid-1980s China's oil industry clearly ranked among the world's largest. After having moved from the twenty-seventh spot worldwide in 1950 to fifth in 1982, it then dropped a bit to seventh place in 1983, but in 1986 it was again the world's fifth largest, just ahead of Mexico. Since the early 1970s the industry has generated an enormous amount of interest and speculation, best evidenced by the eager participation of numerous Western oil companies in the offshore search. Still, the industry has a long way to go before it could rank with the world's best in terms of the all-important qualitative indicators.

With total output equal to less than one-fifth of the huge Soviet extraction (the world's largest) and one-quarter of American output, China's production relies too heavily on a single giant field whose flow over the next few years can be maintained only with mounting efforts.

The need for source diversification is obvious, but none of the operating onshore fields can supplant Daqing and, at the same time, provide additional output growth. New discoveries are thus imperative, but the best onshore prospects are in remote Xinjiang, where any major finds would occur in the midst of an infrastructural vacuum and would necessitate enormous pipeline investments. This largely explains China's decision to opt for accelerated offshore development where foreign expertise and capital can be used in a more convenient (and more controlled) way to boost the country's oil and gas flows.

Inadequacies of onshore production are further aggravated by wastefulness of the whole extraction-transportation-processing-conversion set-up. Whereas normal hydrocarbon field losses in Western nations are mere fractions of 1 percent, China's average is about 2.3 percent, and the waste is much higher during subsequent transfers. Because the Chinese pipeline network is still so skimpy (only about 100 km for each million tons of extracted crude, compared to about 700 km in the United States), frequent unloading and loading from and to tank cars and trucks as well as poor storage (evaporation, leakage) add up to losses of 6 to 7 percent of extracted crude (Zheng 1982).

Preconversion loss on the order of 10 percent is obviously unacceptably high—and so are the losses in refining, distribution, and storage of liquid fuels. Outdated refinery processes, absence of integrated heat utilization (many improvements have, finally, happened in these two areas since 1979), and excessive construction of small-scale refineries (at the time of mounting crude oil shortages) combine to produce chronically large losses. As for the distribution mess, an extended quote elucidates the situation, which is not going to change radically or anytime soon.

For example, a refinery is subordinate to the leadership of the province, the city's petrochemical departments, and bureaus of several ministries. In addition, such commodity products as gasoline, kerosene, and diesel oil are uniformly produced and sold by the Ministry of Commerce. Some subordinate oil depots are under the jurisdiction of several departments. Three oil depots built at one place and selling the same varieties of petroleum products are operated by three groups of people and each uses its own special railroad lines because one belongs to the commercial bureau, the other to forestry bureau, the third to the agricultural reclamation bureau.

Every time the oil refinery dispatches less than ten oil tank cars, locomotives have to be assigned to send the oil separately to three oil depots. Although the sales of fuels are not large, the three oil depots have a relatively large number of oil tanks. These tanks cannot be filled, and the loss of light oil owing to evaporation over a long period is large. (Zheng 1982)

And yet further losses arise because there are no price differentials for better quality crudes which are refined and used the same way as superior varieties. About the gross inefficiencies in the combustion of refined products much will be said in section 3.2.4.

The overall situation is much like that of the coal industry: inadequate, inefficient, strained infrastructure whose badly needed improvements should be going ahead together with even more costly and demanding—in terms of skills, technology, and capital—expansion and development of new large capacities. As the next section will demonstrate, electricity generation shares all of these troublesome attributes.

3.2.3 Electricity generation

Inadequacy of China's power production is obvious by any standard. Numerous writings since 1979 have repeated the startling fact that at least 20 percent of the country's industrial capacity is idle owing to the permanent shortages of electricity: rationing, rotating allocations, and recurrent inability to hook up even new, costly, imported equipment are common. Although China by 1982 was a $300 billion economy, other nations whose total national product is comparatively large are producing at least three times as much electricity per capita as does the PRC: compared to China's 320 kWh per capita in 1984, Italy generated 3,200 kWh, and Brazil and Mexico produced each about 1,100 kWh.

Comparison of the current output figures with those of the first years of the PRC's existence shows, as in nearly all such cases, an impressive quantitative advance (table 3.20), and there is no shortage of other figures that convey the scale of achievements. Those in hydrogeneration have been especially notable: between 1949 and 1981 some 250,000 construction workers completed 78 large and medium-sized hydrostations, and this task involved moving 200 million m^3 of earth and rock, pouring 30 million m^3 of concrete, and digging over 100 km of tunnels; annual increases in installed capacity and in electricity output averaged, respectively, 16 and 15 percent.

By 1984 China's hydroelectric capacity topped 25 GW, and nearly one quarter of this total was in just 8 large stations with capabilities in excess of 500 MW (table 3.21; fig. 3.9). When the cut-off point is

Table 3.20

China's electricity generation, installed capacity and load factors, 1949–1985

Year	Total	Thermal	Hydro	Hydrogeneration as percent of total primary energy production	Installed capacity (GW) Total	Thermal	Hydro	Capacity utilization (percent) Thermal	Hydro
1949	4.31	3.61	0.70	3.0	1.85	1.60	0.25	25.8	32.0
1952	7.26	6.00	1.26	2.0	1.96	1.62	0.34	42.3	42.3
1957	19.34	14.63	4.71	2.9	4.49	3.42	1.07	48.8	50.2
1965	67.60	57.20	10.40	2.6	—	—	—	—	—
1978	256.6	212.00	44.60	3.1	57.12	39.85	12.27	60.7	41.5
1979	281.9	231.80	50.10	3.3	63.01	43.90	19.11	60.3	29.9
1980	300.6	242.40	58.20	3.8	65.87	45.55	20.32	60.7	32.7
1981	306.7	242.30	64.40	4.2	67.82	46.71	21.11	59.2	37.4
1983	351.4	265.04	86.36	3.7	76.45	52.28	24.17	57.8	40.8
1985	407.3	316.30	91.00	4.4	86.00	60.00	26.00	60.2	40.0

Source: SSB (1986).

Table 3.21

Chinese hydrostations larger than 500 MW

Plant name / River	Province / County	Capacity and units (MW)	Construction period	Area of river basin controlled (km²)	Dam height (m)	Dam length (m)	Dam volume (10⁴m³)	Reservoir capacity (10⁹m³)	Annual output (TWh)
Liujiaxia Huang He	Gansu Yongjing	1160 4 × 225 1 × 260	1958–1974	173,000	147	840	76.0	6.09	5.70
Gezhouba Chang Jiang	Hubei Yichang	965 2 × 170 5 × 125	1970–1981	1,000,000	47		990.0	16.8	5.40
Danjiangkou Han Shui	Hubei Jun	900 6 × 150	1958–1973	95,217	97	2549	292.8	20.89	2.88
Gongzui Dadu He	Sichuan Leshan	700 7 × 100	1966–1979	76,400	85.5	447	74.5	0.36	4.12
Shuifeng Yalu Jiang	Liaoning Kuandian	630 7 × 90	1937–1941	54,235	106	900	340.0	14.70	1.90
Xin'anjiang Xin'an Jiang	Zhejiang Xin'anjiang	652.5 4 × 75 5 × 72.5	1957–1977	10,480	105	462	138.0	22.00	1.86
Wujiangdu Wu Jiang	Guizhou Xifeng	630 3 × 210	1970–1982	27,790	165	—	188	2.3	3.34
Dafengman Songhua Jiang	Jilin Jilin	554 5 × 72.5 1 × 70 2 × 60 1 × 1.5	1937–1958	42,500	100	1030	194.0	1.21	1.89

Source: Pan and Zheng (1982); Lu and Fu (1984).

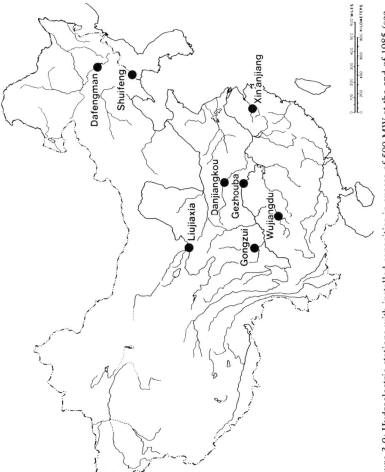

Figure 3.9: Hydroelectric stations with installed capacities in excess of 500 MW at the end of 1985 (see also table 3.21).

Table 3.22

Chinese hydrostations with installed capacity of 500 MW and above under construction in 1985

Plant name River	Province County	Capacity and units (MW)	Construction started	Area of river basin controlled (km²)	Dam height (m)	Dam body (10⁴m³)	Total reservoir capacity (10⁹m³)	Annual output (TWh)
Gezhouba Chang Jiang	Hubei Yichang	2715 19 × 125 2 × 170	1970	1,000,000	47	990	16.8	14.1
Shuikou Min Jiang	Fujian Minqing	1400 7 × 200	1983	—	—	—	2.3	4.95
Longyangxia Huang He	Qinghai Gonghe	1280 4 × 320	1976	131,420	178	154	24.7	5.98
Yantan Hongshui He	Guangxi Bama Yaozu	1100 4 × 275	1985	—	111	—	—	8.0
Manwan Laniang Jiang	Yunnan Yun	1000 5 × 200	1984	—	—	—	—	5.48
Baishan Songhua Jiang	Jilin Huadian	900 3 × 300	1975	19,000	149.5	163.3	6.22	2.0
Tianshengqiao Nanpan Jiang	Yunnan Zhanyi	880 8 × 110	1982	50,194	58	142	0.26	4.83
Ankang Han Shui	Shaanxi Ankang	800 4 × 200	1976	35,700	120	260	3.2	2.8
Tongjiezi Tuo Jiang	Sichuan Fushin	600 4 × 150	1980	76,400	76	253	0.2	3.21
Lubuge Huangni He	Yunnan Luoping	600 4 × 150	·1976	7,300	101	185	0.4	2.75
Dongjiang Le Shui	Hunan Zixing	500 4 × 125	1978	4,719	157	100	9.15	1.32
Wan'an Gan Jiang	Jiangxi Jianggangxan	500	1978	—	56	—	—	—

Source: Pan and Zheng (1982), Tao and Zhang (1982), Mo Guohan (1984). See also figure 3.22.

lowered to 250 MW, the number of large stations rises to 21; there were also about 110 medium plants between 12 and 250 MW (as noted in section 3.1.3, projects below 12 MW are categorized as small ones).

Soon all of these numbers will be rising rapidly as the accelerated construction of large and medium stations will put new capacities into operation. Twelve of the largest projects underway by the end of 1985 are listed in table 3.22 and mapped in figure 3.10. Gezhouba's first stage was already listed in table 3.21 among the completed stations, but here its specifications refer to its full capacity of nearly 3 GW, which will make it the largest operating hydrostation in China. Figure 3.11 charts the station's layout.

The dam cuts the river 3 km below Nanjingguan, the outlet of the steep Xiling gorge, where the stream widens from 200 to 2,200 m and where it is divided into three channels by Gezhouba and Xiba islands. The concrete gravity dam houses two generating stations (the smaller one in the second channel is the first, completed, stage with seven turbogenerators), its central sluice gate can discharge 110,000 m³/s of flood water, and there are three shiplocks (two of them accommodating vessels up to 10,000 tons) and elaborate silt-discharge arrangements.

The top engineering achievements scored so far during the construction of China's large hydrostations include an arched concrete gravity dam of 165 m (a similar 175-m-high structure is now being built) and an earth and rockfill dam of 114 m. The longest diversion tunnel is 8.57 km long (3 11-km-long conduits are under construction), the most voluminous reservoir can store 22 billion m³ of water, the largest operating turbogenerator is rated at 260 MW, and the top annual output of the biggest station is nearly 6 TWh. Impressive as all these figures are in comparison with the state of Chinese hydroengineering just a generation ago, none of these characteristics is outstanding enough to place this facility among the world's top twenty power dam projects.

Fossil-fueled generation, accounting for just over two-thirds of installed capacity and relying primarily on coal, is hardly more advanced. In 1984 there were about seventy thermal stations with capacities above 250 MW, twenty-five of them 500 MW or above; the ones over 600 MW are listed in table 3.23 and mapped in figure 3.12. They display an expected pattern of heavy concentration in the industrialized Northeast, North, and East. Whereas most of these stations consist of 100, 125, and 200 MW turbogenerators and only a handful have some 300 (domestic) and 320 and 350 MW (imported) units, ratings around 400 MW are common throughout Europe, the typical rating of new Ameri-

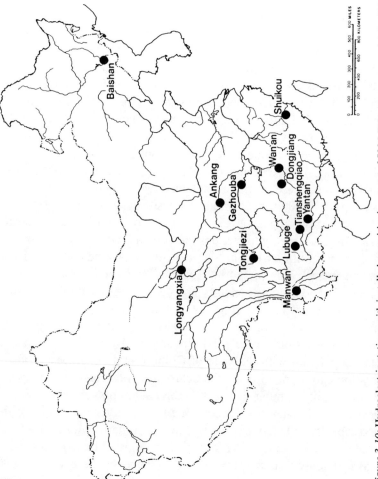

Figure 3.10: Hydroelectric stations with installed capacities in excess of 500 MW under construction in 1985 (see also table 3.22).

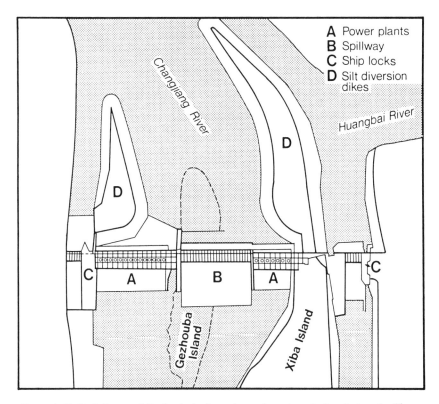

Figure 3.11: Basic layout of Gezhouba hydrostation and water control project on the Chang Jiang.

can thermal units is 500–600 MW (with the largest ones surpassing 1,000 MW), and the Soviets have been assembling their power plants from serialized 400 and 800 MW sets.

Units carrying the burden of Chinese thermal generation are thus too small to deliver the best conversion performance (close to 40 percent), and they cannot be grouped together in very large stations—where the economies of scale are pronounced—owing mainly to the inadequacies of China's transmission technology (as a rule the largest generator in a network should not surpass 5 percent of the system's total capacity), so without interconnections, unit size is severely limited.

Consequently, aggregate ratings of large Chinese stations remain relatively small. Although there are now several hundred thermal stations over 2,000 MW operating in North America, Europe, the USSR, and Asia, the largest Chinese coal-fired power plant in full operation in 1984 rated only 1,100 MW (Qinghe station in Liaoning)—and during

Table 3.23

China's largest thermal generating stations in 1984

Plant	Province (region)	Units (number × MW)	Total capacity (MW)
1. Qinghe	Liaoning (NE)	3 × 200/5 × 100	1100
2. Jianbi	Jiangsu (E)	2 × 300/3 × 100/2 × 50/1 × 25	1025
3. Douhe	Hebei (N)	2 × 250/1 × 200/2 × 125	950
4. Matou	Hebei (N)	3 × 200/2 × 100/2 × 25	850
5. Wangting	Jiangsu (E)	2 × 300/4 × 25/4 × 22/2 × 6	800
6. Huaibei	Anhui (E)	2 × 200/2 × 125/2 × 50	750
7. Baoshan	Shanghai (E)	2 × 350	700
8. Qinshan	Hubei (CS)	1 × 200/2 × 100/4 × 50/2 × 25/1 × 12	662
9. Liaoning	Liaoning (NE)	13 × 50	650
10. Qinling	Shaanxi (NW)	2 × 200/2 × 125	650
11. Dagang	Tianjin (N)	2 × 320	640
12. Shiliquan	Shandong (E)	5 × 125	625
13. Jingmen	Hubei (CS)	2 × 200/2 × 100/1 × 25	625
14. Huainan	Anhui (E)	2 × 125/2 × 120/3 × 25/1 × 12/4 × 6	601

Source: Lu and Fu (1984). Numbers correspond to locations in figure 3.12.

Figure 3.12: China's largest (over 600 MW) thermal generating stations in 1984. The numbers correspond to the entries in table 3.23.

the thirty-five years between 1949 and 1984 China completed fewer than thirty coal-fired mine-mouth stations with capacities in excess of 250 MW. Their total capability is only about a quarter of the nationwide total in thermal power plants—unlike in other large coal-producing nations where mine-mouth plants account for most of the electricity generated from coal. This weakness is finally being remedied through a large-scale program of mine-mouth power plant construction.

Among China's largest coal-fired stations being newly built or expanded as of 1985 (table 3.24, fig. 3.13), only two are near the country's greatest industrial center, Shanghai, where the fuel has to be shipped from remote coalfields. All the other large stations have mine-mouth locations, and several of them will be burning coal from the newly opened surface mines. The first stage of Yuanbaoshan plant already uses lignite from the Yuanbaoshan open pit, Tongliao station also burns lignite from Huolinhe mine, and Shentou will be supplied from Pingshuo mine with excellent bituminous coal. Still, the units under construction are too small (mostly 200 and 300 MW) to match the best Western performances.

As anywhere else, coal burned in Chinese stations, old and new, is often of inferior quality: its mean nationwide energy content is only about 19 MJ/kg, and not infrequently it is subbituminous coal with less than 13 MJ/kg and up to 50 percent ash. Not surprisingly, when these coals are burned in old low- and medium-pressure small-capacity units (as of 1983 about 12 GW, or 23 percent of all thermal capacity, were in this undesirable category), the overall conversion efficiency is quite poor, generally over 550 g of standard coal (or 16.1 MJ) per kWh. Recent installation of scores of larger, high-pressure units brought down the national average of specific coal consumption quite considerably—from 502 g in 1970 to 434 g/kWh in 1983 (both figures refer to performance of large ministry-controlled power stations)—but the latest mean is still about 25 percent higher than the Japanese level, and it implies net conversion efficiency of no more than 28 percent.

Oil-fired stations reached their peak by 1978 with about 12 GW of capacity of which 5,835 MW were in units originally designed for coal burning and converted to oil during the late 1960s and early 1970s. When its crude oil output started to stagnate, China reversed the trend and since 1976 has been converting and reconverting stations to coal firing. The process intensified after 1978 as a part of nationwide effort to conserve energy and to rationalize full conversion effort (see section 3.2.4). Between 1976 and 1981, 3,650 MW of thermal capacity were

Table 3.24

China's largest coal-fired power plants under construction or extension in 1985

Power plant	Province	Installed capacity (MW) Ultimate	First phase	Units (MW)	New or expansion	Mine-mouth or near load-center
1. Pingyu	Anhui	2,400	600	(600)	E	M
2. Datong No. 2	Shanxi	2,400	1,200	200	E	M
3. Shidongkou	Shanghai	2,400	1,200	8 × 300	N	L
4. Yuanbaoshan	Nei Monggol	2,100	(600)	3 × 600,1 × 300	N	M
5. Jianbi	Jiangsu	1,625 (1987)	(1,025)	2 × 300	E	L
6. Douhe	Hebei	1,500 (1986)	(950)	3 × 200	E	M
7. Shentou	Shanxi	1,350	(550)	4 × 200	E	M
8. Xizhou	Jiangsu	1,300 (1987)	(500)	4 × 200	E	M
9. Shiheng	Shandong	1,200	600	4 × 300	N	M
10. Jinzhou	Liaoning	1,200 (1986)	600	6 × 200	N	M
11. Jinxi	Liaoning	1,200	600	6 × 200	N	M
12. Yaomeng	Henan	1,200	(600)	4 × 300	E	M
13. Tongliao	Nei Monggol	800 (1986)	400	4 × 200	N	M

Source: Compiled by the author from various Chinese publications.

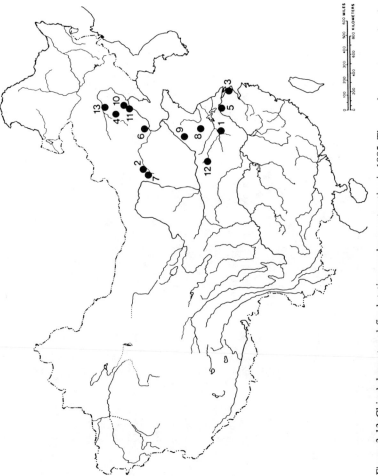

Figure 3.13: China's largest coal-fired stations under construction in 1985. The numbers correspond to the entries in table 3.24.

switched to coal, saving some six million tons of crude oil, and before the end of the 1980s virtually all former oil-fired units should be converted to coal.

No new oil-fueled stations are to be built during the 1980s. Instead, in 1982 the Chinese initiated a relatively large program of nuclear generation to supply the high-load areas far away from major coal-mining centers. As of 1987 one small, domestically designed nuclear power plant and one large, imported plant were under construction, with the first generation from the former expected in 1989, from the latter in 1990–91. Consequently, I will reserve the discussion of Chinese long-term nuclear plans, reasons for their adoption, and their critique for section 4.2.4, which will look at the strategies chosen to quadruple electricity output by the year 2000.

No matter how efficient the generating technology may be, the performance of power systems depends ultimately on transmission and distribution of electricity. Yet nowhere else in the realm of electric industry have the Chinese weaknesses been as retarding as in this very sector. In the mid-1980s 440-kV lines connected national European networks into a huge integrated system transmitting regularly many TWh across boundaries, and Soviets and Canadians have installed direct-current ties of up to 800–900 kV carrying around 1,500 MW over distances of around 1,000 km. Yet China put in its first 534-km-long, 330-kV link only in 1972, and the first 500-kV line, a 595-km-long connection between Yaoming power plant in the coal-mining and power generation center of Pingdingshan in Henan and Wuhan (the capital of Hubei), was completed only in 1981.

Evolution of transmission voltages and their total length are traced in table 3.25. Clearly, 220-kV lines are the principal trunk carriers, and 330 kV will be limited to the northwestern network. As for distribution, the main carriers in urban areas are 10 kV. A nationwide transmission network is still decades away. Currently there are six transprovincial grids: northeastern, northern, eastern, central, southwestern, and northwestern, with the seventh one (southern) to be added soon by connecting Guangdong with Guangxi (table 3.26). Besides these, there are fifteen other grids around China confined to just one province or only a part of it, and only four of these had in 1983 installed capacities above 1,000 MW (Shandong, 3,782; Hunan, 2,830; Yunnan, 1,318; and Fujian, 1,181 MW).

Such a fragmented generation results in obvious inefficiencies and, in the presence of excessively high load factors, in unreliable power

Table 3.25

Development of China's high-voltage transmission, 1949–1983 (all figures are in km)

Voltage (kV)	1949	1955	1965	1975	1983
35–66	4,538	8,788	44,210	121,870	199,004
110	340	917	15,994	48,689	76,205
154	832	1,191	971	894	427
220	765	1,401	3,410	14,201	36,824
330	—	—	—	534	1,085
500	—	—	—	—	1,594
Total above 35	6,475	12,297	64,585	186,188	315,139

Source: Compiled from the Ministry of Water Resources and Electric Power materials.

supply. For example, the northwestern grid, with its large hydro capacity, has had large surpluses of electricity which it could not ship to the chronically power-short northern network just a few hundred km eastward. Some smaller networks have been operating without any reserves, using occasionally as much as 97 percent of their installed capacity, an impossibly high figure in the Western setting.

With recent expansion of generating capacities and the growth of unit and power plant sizes, the long-overdue modernization and upgrading of China's transmission is now underway. During 1985 work was going on in eleven new 500-kV links totaling 4,680 km. In the North the most important are the ties between Shentou and Datong in Shanxi (connecting two large mine-mouth power plants), and between Beijing and Tianjin, an extension of the recently finished 500-kV, 300-km link between Datong and Beijing. Surpluses of Shanxi-generated electricity will thus be available to fill the large supply gaps in the two big northern industrial cities.

Two 500-kV links will also bring more electricity to Shanghai: one from Xuzhou plant in Jiangsu, the other from Pingyu plant in Huainan (Anhui). In the northeast, the port city of Dalian in Liaoning will be connected with Haicheng, the terminal of another 500-kV line from Yuanbaoshan and Jinzhou mine-mouth plants, while Zhuzhou in Hunan, a key railway center on the Beijing-Guangzhou line, will get electricity from Gezhouba station in Hubei. Between 5 and 6 billion kWh of Gezhouba's electricity will be transmitted to the Shanghai area, 1,080 km to the east across Anhui, Jiangsu, and Zhejiang, via China's

Table 3.26

China's largest power grids in 1983

Power grids	Installed capacity (MW)			Annual generation (GWh)		
	Total	Hydro	Thermal	Total	Hydro	Thermal
North China	9840	709	9131	54,829	1171	53,658
Northeast	10,136	2040	8096	53,646	5264	48,382
Northeast (east)	1249	136	1113	6687	457	6230
East China	10,858	1769	9089	58,035	5774	52,261
Fujian	1181	797	384	4756	3390	1366
Shandong	3782	45	3737	21,587	13	21,574
Central China	8554	3129	5425	40,545	15,868	24,677
Hunan	2840	1484	1356	12,282	6732	5550
Guangdong	2101	909	1192	11,412	4373	7039
Guangxi	1273	742	531	4987	3256	1731
Southwest	4860	2406	2454	21,228	10,958	10,270
Yunnan	1318	775	543	5207	2291	2916
Northwest	4744	2212	2532	21,189	10,948	10,241

Source: same as in Table 3.25.

first 500-kV direct-current line to be completed before the end of the 1980s.

In December 1984, a 220-kV link between Shaanxi and Sichuan connected the northwestern and southwestern grids, but it can transmit only 100 MW. A much more powerful tie should be completed by 1988 running from Longyangxia via Xining to Shijiazhuang (Hebei) and the Beijing-Tianjin area. The electricity-deficient northern grid will then be able to receive large hydroenergy surpluses from the Northwest. Studies are now underway to determine if a direct-current link would not be more appropriate to carry electricity from the cluster of new stations on the upper Huang He (see section 4.2.4).

The emergence of 500-kV networks also has clear-cut investment advantages. When using 220 kV as the reference cost, Chinese studies, in accord with Western experience, show that a 330-kV link carrying the same power costs only 77 percent and a 500-kV tie, depending on the number of conductors used, needs only 41–59 percent (Hu and Wang 1982). New high-voltage links will also lower transmission losses, which were exceedingly high during the years of Cultural Revolution mismanagement, as much as 17 percent in large grids, and more than 20 percent in small rural networks. Since the late 1970s the worst inefficiencies have been eliminated, and the average loss in large grids was reduced to an acceptable 8.5 percent. The frequency of most grids has been stabilized and the voltage deviation is kept within 10 percent—but strains remain as electricity supply is still far behind the burgeoning demand.

In 1983 the nationwide shortfall amounted to 40 billion kWh, or a capacity of about 10 GW, leading, as already noted, to a 20 percent reduction in possible industrial output. In some provinces the deficit is even more severe: in Guangdong only 70 percent of current requirements are covered and the province must buy expensive electricity from Hong Kong to ease the shortage.

In Sichuan, where electricity use is still below the nationwide average (in a province possessing the world's largest per capita hydrogeneration potential!), power shortages used to be confined just to the dry season between November and April, but by 1983 a rapidly rising demand made the deficits an ongoing affair: in 1984 power shortfall was about 600 MW during the dry period and 300 MW during the summer.

And yet, incredibly enough, the new capacities under construction are now relatively smaller than in the past. Sichuan's 1981 and 1982 ratios between the growth rate of gross value of industrial and agricultural output and the growth rate of power capacities rose to over 1.6, and in 1983 the ratio reached a post-1949 high of 2.2. Even with accelerated completion of all twelve hydroelectric and thermal power stations now under construction, the province must expect power deficits at least until 1995.

On a national scale the story is uncomfortably similar. The 1980–83 ratio of economic output growth and installed generating capacity growth is nearly 1.9, and little understanding of systems energetics is necessary to appreciate that an electric industry growing at only half the rate of general industrial and farming advance—moreover, already from a level of severe inadequacy—will be a crippling brake on the nation's future economic progress. While the need for the fastest possible installation of new capacities is self-evident, China's output of generating equipment in the early 1980s was smaller, in relative terms, than any time since 1949.

Production of all turbogenerators rose from just 6 MW in 1952 to 198 MW in 1957 and peaked at 6,212 MW in 1979; it then slid to 4,193 MW in 1980, 1,395 MW in 1981, and 1,677 MW in 1982. Since 1983 it has been rising again and it reached 7,120 MW in 1986, but it is still disproportionately small considering China's planned needs. Again, an international comparison starkly brings out the deficiency. Since Japan and the Soviet Union reached 75 GW of installed capacity—China's current level—their annual additions have averaged, respectively, 7.3 and 10 GW, that is, at least two to three times the Chinese 1980–1985 mean. One may argue that the Chinese do not have to replicate either the Japanese or the Soviet experience if they will follow a less energy-intensive route of economic development. In reality, as the next section will show, the PRC has been the least energy-efficient among the world's major economies, in no small part owing to its excessive heavy industrial orientation.

Besides, electrification of the countryside has hardly begun: more than 300 million peasants still do not have even a single light bulb in their houses. Insufficient electricity generation will limit the Chinese modernization drive for the remainder of this century, even should the country's dismal efficiencies improve considerably.

3.2.4 Uses and conversion efficiencies

In view of severe and permanent shortages of fuel and electricity, the waste of these scarce resources during common conversions has been astounding. Traditionally poor management and outdated technologies could not deliver good results during the best times, but the years of political upheaval between 1966 and 1976 led to such incredible deterioration that by 1977–78 indicators of specific energy consumption for most of the common industrial products were worse, and often drastically so, than in 1965. Since 1978, gradual return to better management and continuing energy conservation campaigns have brought many encouraging changes, but the overall performance of China's commercial energetics remains poor.

This is seen quite starkly in international comparisons in table 3.27, where per capita commercial energy consumption and GNP of twelve of the world's most populous nations are used to calculate the overall energy intensity of the economic output. Here it is impossible to go into the reasons for the inherent complexity of the energy intensity ratio: obviously, the measure reflects developmental history and industrial orientation, fuel consumption structure and quality, climate, living standards, habits, and government policies.

Moreover, the well-known uncertainties in preparing GNP accounts for Communist countries and converting them to dollars in the absence

Table 3.27

Per capita energy consumption and GNP and energy intensities in the world's 12 most populous nations in 1982

Country	Per capita commercial energy consumption (kgce)	(GJ)	Per capita GNP US (1982)	Energy intensity of the economy MJ/US$
China	600	17.4	290	60
India	200	5.8	220	26
USSR	6,500	188.5	6,350	30
USA	12,000	348.0	13,180	26
Indonesia	300	8.7	590	15
Brazil	1,100	31.9	2,320	14
Japan	4,500	130.5	8,850	15
Bangladesh	50	1.5	150	10
Nigeria	170	4.9	700	7
Pakistan	220	6.4	340	19
Mexico	1,700	49.3	3,440	14
West Germany	6,000	174.0	10,660	16

Sources: CIA (1983), World Bank (1983), SSB (1985).

of any market-determined exchange rates make the comparisons between centrally planned and Western economies questionable once one goes beyond clear-cut differences. Consequently, even for the countries with highly comparable accounts, differences of a few units cannot be seen as clear bases for sensible ranking, and in China's case the actual performance may be much closer to India's value. But the ratio cannot be dismissed as it does provide important insights.

For virtually all industrialized, as well as industrializing, nations the early 1980s' energy intensity expressed in MJ/$ stands between 10 and 25, with values in the teens showing up most frequently. Chinese performance is unequaled in its inefficiency even if the ratio is adjusted by reducing it by 30–40 percent (i.e., to 36–42 MJ/$). The record would still be the worst one among all listed nations, and those Chinese who are aware of this dismal primacy point out especially the huge difference (as much as fourfold) between their nation and Japan, China's great Asian example.

As energy consumption for energy-intensive products in China's large enterprises is fairly comparable to Indian levels, it is the different industrial orientation (too much stress on heavy sectors) and the high share of inefficient small-scale production that account for most of the

Table 3.28

Comparison of national energy use efficiencies

Consumption sector	China	Japan	USA	UK
		Nationwide first-law conversion efficiencies (percent)		
Industry	35	78	77	67
Thermal electricity generation and transmission	24	30	30	28
Transportation	15	25	25	25
Private use	25	70	70	70
Aggregate mean	30	57	51	40

Source: Yuan Guangru (1982).

Table 3.29

Comparison of efficiencies for major energy convertors (all values are in percent)

	Typical Chinese performance	Typical Western or Japanese level
Large coal-fired power plants	30	35–40
Industrial boilers	56–60	75–80
Industrial ovens	20–30	50–60
Household stoves (furnaces)	15–20	50–60
Railway locomotives (steam vs. diesel)	6–8	25

Source: Yuan Guangru (1982).

disparity, whatever its actual precise level may be. Overall first-law efficiency of China's commercial energy consumption is just 30 percent—compared to Japan's 57 and the United States' 51 percent. Tables 3.28 and 3.29 detail the broad sectoral and major convertor differences, and in the following paragraphs I shall cite numerous examples of widespread inefficiencies, all taken from the now voluminous Chinese literature on the subject.

China—in common with most other industrializing countries and in line with all other, even relatively rich, Communist nations—consumes most of its primary commercial energy in industrial sectors. In 1980, the last year for which detailed sectoral statistics are available, Chinese

Table 3.30

China's sectoral primary energy consumption and energy intensity in 1980.

Sectors	Energy consumption (10^6tce)	(percent)	National income (10^9Rmb)	(percent)	Energy intensity (kgce/Rmb)
Total	568.85	100.0	368.8	100.0	1.54
Industry	349.82	61.5	168.8	45.8	2.07
Heavy	294.68	51.80	98.8	26.8	2.98
Light	55.14	9.69	70.0	18.9	0.79
Households	101.56	17.9	—	—	—
Agriculture	46.95	8.2	144.2	39.1	0.32
Non-energy uses	24.32	4.3	—	—	—
Transportation	23.46	4.1	12.6	3.4	1.86
Construction	8.45	1.5	18.5	5.0	0.46
Commerce	2.13	0.4	24.7	6.7	0.09
Miscellaneous	12.16	2.1	—	—	—

Sources: Zhi (1982), SSB (1984)

industries claimed about 62 percent of all energy; as already noted, this is an extraordinarily high share in comparison with any Western economy. Nearly nine-tenths of this large share went into heavy industrial processes whose output shows, not surprisingly, an extraordinarily high energy intensity (table 3.30), on the average nearly four times higher than for light manufactures.

Chemical plants and metallurgy are the two leading industrial users, and both are fairly inefficient convertors. The chemical industry consumed nearly 15 percent of all energy (about 85 million tce) in 1980, two-fifths of it as coal, one-fifth as oil and gas, the rest mostly as electricity (being its single largest sectoral user). During the chaotic Cultural Revolution years the overall conversion efficiency of the chemical industry deteriorated rather stunningly: between 1965 and 1977 the electricity needed for Rmb 10,000 of chemical products rose by nearly 60 percent, from 5,378 to 8,453 kWh, and a large number of data are now available to show the poor performance of China's large fertilizer industry, which is the main reason for the overall wasteful record.

In 1980 synthetic ammonia plants consumed more than 41 million tce, or nearly half of the sector's total input. As China's synthetic nitrogen output reached 9.99 million tons in that year, this consumption implies an average intensity of 119 MJ/kg N, an incredibly high value in comparison with modern Kellogg or Haldor-Topsøe ammonia plants, which need as little as 30–40 MJ/kg N. Chinese imported a dozen of these large, efficient establishments and put them into operation during the 1970s, but by 1982 no less than 65 percent of all nitrogen was still coming from medium and small coal-based units synthesizing ammonia with dismal efficiencies.

Not surprisingly, as soon as the normal economic concerns, rather than ideologically motivated promotion of local self-sufficiency and small-scale industrialization, started to return to China's long-range planning, the worst of these enterprises were closed (200 between 1978 and 1982), and many of the most glaring inefficiencies were corrected to lower the previous outrageously high energy intensities. According to Lu and Liu (1984), between 1977 and 1982 average coal consumption in small ammonia plants fell by 50 percent and electricity inputs declined by 38 percent—but in 1981 the mean energy intensities were still about 110 MJ/kg for small enterprises, 88 MJ/kg for medium ones, and 50 MJ/kg N for large units (Zhang Zhongji 1982). Further improvements have followed since then—Zhang, Wang, and Xin (1984) reported the mean for small plants at 91 MJ/kg N in 1983—but the whole sector is still nearly twice as energy-intensive as its Western or Japanese counterpart.

The metallurgical industry, with 69 million tce in 1980, consumed 12.2 percent of all primary commercial energy, 60 percent of it as coke and coal, and only 3 percent as oil and natural gas. As in major chemical syntheses, high energy intensities in iron metallurgy have been declining, but they are still much above advanced levels. While elsewhere the use of electricity in steel making has been steadily dropping, in China it actually nearly doubled from 665 kWh per ton in 1965 to 1,102 kWh per ton in 1977. Since then it has been brought back to the vicinity of 625 kWh in 1983, a value much above the current Western levels of 300–450 kWh.

In the late 1970s even large enterprises needed well over two tons of coal to produce one ton of coke, and this rate declined to about 1,430 kg by 1983. Aggregate energy consumption per ton of steel decreased from 2.52 tce in 1978 to 2.04 tce in 1980 and to 1.93 tce in 1983, and in large plants it was as low as 1.2–1.4 tce—all of these rates being considerably higher than typical Western and Japanese requirements of between 0.6 and 0.8 tce per ton of crude steel.

Once again, numerous small iron and steel mills are mainly responsible for the poor nationwide average. While in the early 1980s coke consumption in iron smelting in the industrialized countries ranged mostly between 350 and 470 kg per ton of pig iron, large Chinese furnaces needed an average charge of 535 kg of coke in 1983—but the small ones averaged more than 800 kg. Even if no other examples about energy intensities of large versus small enterprises were cited here, it must be quite clear that the price paid for the Chinese version of "small-is-beautiful" industrialization—in wasted nonrenewable energies, investment, labor, and environmental pollution—has been excessive.

These wasteful performances, summarized in table 3.31, put a great strain on power generation, which, as already noted, is itself far from efficient. Average fuel consumption in large, centrally run thermal stations is now around 430 g of standard coal per kWh, one- to two-fifths above the current American, Soviet, or Japanese levels of 310–350 g/kWh. Yet, again, the difference owes largely to 13 GW of small, outdated medium- and low-pressure generating units which consume at least 500 g of coal equivalent/kWh (economies of scale in thermal generation are quite pronounced up to about 500 MW of unit size, far above the current Chinese mean).

Pervasive inefficiencies of China's industrial energy consumption are perhaps best shown by a rough calculation, published in Beijing in 1980, which asserted that proper operation, maintenance, and management of the existing equipment would have saved annually as much as 40–50 million tons of coal, 3–4 million tons of crude oil, and 20–30 billion kWh of electricity. This totals as much as 60 million tons of coal equivalent, or about one-sixth of China's total industrial energy use. Consequently, Chinese planners put forth relatively high conservation targets, and the improved management together with retirement of some of the most inefficient convertors and installation of modern technologies have been paying off. Many wasteful conversions have been eliminated, but the overall efficiency of energy utilization in industry is still unacceptably low, and vigorous conservation efforts must remain the hallmark of China's long-term energy strategy (see section 4.2.1 for more details).

Household consumption represents the second largest aggregate sectoral flow (table 3.3), but in relative terms it prorates to just a bit more than 1 kgce a day for every Chinese family. More meaningfully, subtracting the roughly 40 million tce of rural consumption would leave some 60 million tce for urban inhabitants, and this amount would prorate (for the 1980 total of 191 million of urban residents) to about

Table 3.31

Comparisons of Chinese specific energy consumption with advanced world levels

Specific energy consumption	Worst performances reported in Chinese literature	Typical late 1970s level	Nationwide consumption		Typical Western and Japanese levels of the early 1980s
			1981	1982	
Coal kg/t of coke	2,500	2,200	—	2,100	1,300–1,500
Coke kg/t of pig iron	800	620	579	577	350–470
Electricity kWh/t of crude steel	1,100	800	651	643	300–450
Total energy GJ/t of ammonia	140	105	—	90	45–55
Electricity kWh/t of ammonia	3,000	2,500	1,445	1,434	40–100
Coal g/kWh of electricity	500	450	440	438	310–350

Sources: SSB (1983) and various Chinese and OECD sources.

315 kgce, or just over 9 GJ per year per capita. To cite just one of many possible contrasts, the same amount of energy will be needed in an American home just to run a standard 2000-W air conditioner during a hot summer—and that family's total household energy use in heating, cooking, lighting, etc. (leaving their car gasoline aside) could easily prorate to 100 GJ per year per capita, an order of magnitude above the Chinese level.

Although the urban household energy shortages are far from the rural desperation, rationing is strict and most Chinese wear warm underwear in order to tolerate the uncomfortably low home temperatures once the summer hot spells are gone. Coal briquettes continue to be practically the only fuel for heating even in the best-off cities as well as for cooking in smaller urban areas, and their combustion in inefficient stoves (10–18 percent efficiencies are typical) is, together with heavy industrial emissions, the main source of China's chronic SO_2 and particulate air pollution, which during winter months can reach levels much higher than the newly promulgated hygienic norms (see section 5.2). A city of one million people needs about half a million tons of raw coal (400,000 tons of standard coal equivalent) annually just for cooking and commercial uses (excluding heating needs), and in several of the largest industrialized cities coal gas and liquified petroleum gases have made substantial inroads in supplying these needs.

In Beijing 800,000 households, that is, about 65 percent of the population in the city proper, used bottled LPG or piped town gas for cooking in 1982. Efforts are underway to extend greatly the municipal coal gas supply: new city gasworks quadrupled the output to 400,000 m^3 a day in 1983, another 240,000 m^3 a day were added during 1984, and a 2 million-m^3-a-day plant is envisaged for the late 1980s.

With 20 kWh a year per capita, urban household use of electricity is very small, mostly for lighting, but until most recently the billing was commonly done on a "lights included" basis rather than by metering, and hence the consumption was frequently at least 20–30 percent, or even 60–100 percent, higher than would be the billed amount. Since 1981 installation of electricity (as well as water) meters has progressed fairly rapidly in most large cities, and so in a few years this infrastructural deficiency will be almost completely eliminated. Recent increases of urban, and perhaps even more so of per capita village, incomes have led to rapidly rising demand for more electric appliances, above all fans and simple washing machines. Nationwide demand for fans is now estimated to be at least two million a year, washing machine sales have surpassed one million a year, and Chinese forecast urban household electricity consumption at 120 kWh per capita, or six times the current level by the year 2000.

Agricultural energy consumption has been covered in section 3.1.4, and hence transportation is the next largest sector to be discussed. Although it is hardly surprising that many new statistics coming recently out of China show disconcerting discrepancies, rarely is the gap as large as the one encountered for transportation energy use. The ranking in table 3.30, prepared by Zhi Luchuan (1982) and accepted by Lan, Lu, and Mao (1984), is, with 23.46 million tce and 4.1 percent of the total primary energy use, only about 55 percent of the value given by Mao and Hu (1984), namely, 43.4 million tce and 7.2 percent of the total. The explanation offered in the first two works is in different classification boundaries, but, unfortunately, I cannot detail where those differences lie exactly.

In any case, the sector's dependence on coal remains very high, nearly three-fifths of all inputs, with virtually all of the rest accounted for by liquid fuels. Steam locomotives, with their inherently low conversion efficiencies (a mere 5 to 9 percent), are an obvious drag on the sector's performance, and its overall poor conversion (about 20 percent) would be even lower if it were not for a relatively large share of waterway transport. In 1983 railway freight transport totaled 664.6 billion tonne-kilometers (including 10 billion tonne-kilometers wasted by moving rocks in unsorted coal!), waterborne shipments amounted to 578.8 billion tonne-kilometers, and the road freight reached only 108.4 billion tonne-kilometers.

As for personal transport, railways dominate with 178 billion passenger-km in 1983, followed by road transportation with 110 billion person-km, but if one assumes that each of China's 100 million bicyclists makes an 8-km trip a day then the total, 292 billion rider-km, surpasses the sum of railway and highway performance, a good illustration of China's poverty. Modernization remedies are straightforward but costly, resting on electrical and diesel locomotives and on increased reliance on diesel-fueled shipping.

Fuel consumption by China's rapidly growing truck, jeep, and passenger car fleets presents a state of an almost incredible wastefulness (Hui 1981). Whereas a typical Western family car will now consume as little as 5 and no more than 8 kg of gasoline per 100 km (i.e., 6–10 liters), Liu (1981) reported that in Liaoning many vehicles consume more than 50 kg of fuel per 100 km, and Yu (1981) quotes the same incredible rates for Beijing. As Yu notes, "few machines in the world consume more gasoline than that." Similarly, while standard fuel consumption by tractors is 1.6 kg/mu, the province's machines consumed more than twice as much. This enormous waste, a result of outdated and poorly maintained machines, has been compounded by stunning mismanagement of vehicles for private use, illegal diversion of the fuel, and incredible mismanagement of shipping operations.

To quote Hui and Li (1981), "it is not unusual for people, motivated by a desire to have a status symbol and to show off, to find excuses to drive tens, hundreds, or even thousands of kilometers for sightseeing pleasure." Needless to say, the cars, the fuel, and the drivers belong to the labor units, not to the tourists: only 60 percent of journeys with publicly owned vehicles are actual transport trips. Oil companies, to meet their sales quotas and to qualify for bonuses, supply fuel to idle, broken-down, or nonexistent vehicles, and this fuel, obviously diverted for private uses, may have totaled as much as 1.4 million tons in the early 1980s. The empty-load rate of operating trucks is at least 50, often 70 percent, and many of these trucks, to avoid the difficulties encountered in shipping by rail, run hundreds or thousands of km to deliver the goods. Annual waste arising from these easily avoidable trips may be in excess of three million tons of fuel (Yu 1981).

Unfortunately, there is more to China's stunning inefficiency of liquid fuel consumption. Unlike some other poor, populous nations (India, above all), China is now a major oil producer, but as the period of rapidly expanding extraction coincided with the years of gross economic mismanagement during the decade of the Cultural Revolution, huge quantities of oil were wasted during that time and the consumption settled into patterns of stunning inefficiency.

Direct burning of unrefined crude oil—a form of truly primitive conversion wasting a limited resource that can be much upgraded by processing for a variety of final markets—has been certainly the most irrational consequence. According to Yang (1982), between 1971 and 1980 China burned a total of 100 million tons of crude oil, an equivalent of one year's extraction by the late 1970s, costing the country Rmb 14 billion more than would have been spent for burning coal instead. In 1980, a year after China's energy conservation program finally got underway, 7 million tons of crude oil were still burned and the total combustion of oil fuels in power plants amounted to 16.4 million tons, in industrial boilers 13 million tons, and the grand aggregate of all liquid fuels, unrefined and refined, burned in China's stationary boilers came to an incredibly high 40 million tons, or 43 percent of domestic consumption. Further oil-to-coal conversion is clearly necessary (see section 4.2.1).

The reasons for China's extraordinarily wasteful energy use fall into at least seven principal categories. Extensive presence of outdated equipment, inadequate maintenance and spotty management, excessive reliance on small-scale industries, and commonly poor quality of the fuel (above all too much raw coal) are the four most obvious reasons an observant visitor could deduce after just looking around. Low energy prices are basically invisible to an outside observer, but they have to answer for much of China's inefficiency (see also section 5.1). With both oil and coal well below the world price there is, naturally, little reason to conserve, and this lack of cost incentive is only strengthened by inflexible central allocations and by the absence of (now finally gradually introduced) management responsibility at lower levels.

Another built-in handicap that is not immediately noticeable is the irrational industrial location: many energy-intensive industries are located along the coast, far away from major energy production centers, necessitating massive coal transfers. On the other hand, many heavy industrial enterprises located deep inland for previously paramount strategic reasons, or growing up on the basis of rashly located small units ("congenital disease," as the Chinese call it), are incompletely equipped, cannot finish their products, and must transfer them for final processing.

Zhang Zhongji (1982) gives what is perhaps the worst example of the latter practice. Each year about 6 million tons of pig iron and steel are shipped to Shanghai, Tianjin, Tangshan, Qingdao, and Lanzhou over an average distance of 800 km to be finished into steel or rolled products. Energy costs of these shipments alone are worth about 1.5 million tce a year, and the resmelting of pig iron and reslabbing of steel needs additional 2 million tce annually.

But by far the most important reason for China's inordinate energy conversion inefficiency is the country's excessive heavy industrial tilt. One can see that China's runaway energy intensity is the inheritance of its Stalinist past, a past which is still uncomfortably present today. Disproportionate stress on heavy industry, and especially the obsession with steel output, not only marked the country's First Five-Year Plan (1953–57), when heavy industry received eight times more investment than light, and the tragic Great Leap Forward, when Mao fantasized about the world being shaken by 60 million tons of Chinese steel by the year 1962, but continued throughout the 1960s and into the 1970s. The light- to heavy-industry investment ratio in 1971–75 was 1:10.2, higher than in 1953–57. And, unfortunately, it marked again the start of the four modernizations campaign in 1978, with the totally unrealistic target of 60 million tons of steel by 1985, and it continues to burden the country.

Moreover, as Feng Baoxing (1979) candidly wrote in *Hongqi*, China's heavy industry is "to a great extent still a kind of self-service industry," contributing more to the perpetuation of its own inefficiency than to the advancement of the rest of the economy. What is obviously needed is a substantial shift to light industry and to diversified farming, and since 1978 there have been encouraging signs of such moves. But an outside observer cannot fail to ask: is it for real this time? Many outsiders share this doubt. To quote Feng Baoxing (1979) once more: "Some comrades raise this question: Is your desire to develop agriculture and light industry genuine or feigned?" An encouraging reversal has been underway since 1978 when heavy sectors accounted for 56.9 percent of all industrial output (a ratio surpassed in the past only in 1971–72 with 57–57.1 percent and during the Great Leap years with a peak of 66.6 percent in 1960). That the shift has been small is not surprising: inertia of complex infrastructures does not allow a rapid turnaround.

A few reversed years are a mere start: a long-term trend is imperative. Should China not only sustain a push toward light industries and diversified, modernized farming but also expand a myriad of the badly inadequate services, its very unfavorable energy intensity would gradually improve. Should this be also coupled with several critical consumption shifts—such as no crude oil to be used for power generation, maximum displacement of fuel oil by coal in the same industry and greater mine-mouth generation based on poorer coals, extended use of gases for urban household and commercial use, and electrification of railways—China's energy intensities could be greatly reduced, laying the ground for a modernization effort surely more sustainable than many designs of the recent past, which still bear a recognizable Stalinist imprint.

MODERNIZATION:
Energy for the Quadrupled Economy

China's return to relatively normal life after the long suffering of the Cultural Revolution and its aftermath started—perhaps not so surprisingly as a reaction to the wasted years—with goals too large to meet. The country was to embark on the road of accelerated economic moderization which was, as repeated in countless proclamations, "to propel it to the front ranks of the world before the end of the century." This Chinese phrasing could be easily dismissed as a mere hyperbolic exhortation—except that some plans laid out during 1978 actually spelled out a variety of gargantuan commitments far beyond the reach of the Chinese economy. Moreover, these plans looked uncomfortably like giant rehashes of the past Great Leap campaigns rather than rational blueprints for sustainable modernization.

No goal was more beholden to the past than the aim to complete several new huge iron and steel complexes by 1985 so that the country's steel output would rise from 25 to 60 million tons in just seven years. The energy requirements generated by such policies would have been enormous, and they were to be met by doubling the 1977 coal output in ten years and then doubling it again by the year 2000. More crude oil was to come from developing ten "Daqings" and thus, implicitly, boosting China's total crude oil flow at least fivefold!

All of these illusory targets had to give way to economic realities. This transformation happened, fortunately, fairly rapidly, with the country entering what was labeled "a period of readjustment," basically a breathing space during which the accent was not on rapid growth rates but rather on consolidating and improving the past achievements through restructuring and qualitative changes before resuming long-term developmental efforts. As the growth rates moderated—national income rose (in constant terms) 7 percent in 1979, 6 percent in 1980, and just 3 percent in 1981—plans were prepared for what is seen as a challenging but manageable task: Deng Xiaoping's goal of quadrupling China's gross annual value of industrial and agricultural production between 1980 and 2000.

This is still a very bold goal—yet one not impossible to reach given the right combination of strategies and changes. Precisely because it fits within the confines of plausibility, Deng's great goal is fascinating to analyze. But no matter what feelings one may have or if unprejudiced appraisal is preferred, one point is indisputable: to make any significant headway will require major transformation *and* expansion of China's energetics.

Consequently, this chapter must be a substantial one. A more traditional treatment would have devoted many more pages to discussions of the past developments and to appraisals of the current situation, and it would have relegated the considerations of plans and possible future trends to a shorter closing chapter. But as China's modernization, undoubtedly the most ambitious, clearly articulated developmental program in history, is so critically dependent on more efficient, more abundant, and more reliable energy flows, I will take up almost as much space assessing options, trends, strategies, and plausibilities of this grand transformation as I have devoted to all the current developments.

4.1 Modernization goals

The general economic objective of China's modernization drive is to quadruple the 1980 national output by the year 2000, a task necessitating an average growth rate of 7.2 percent. This quantitative expansion must be largely driven by wide-ranging upgrading of technological capacities so that by the beginning of the next century production capabilities of the major industrial sectors should match the Western and Japanese levels of the late 1970s and the early 1980s (today they correspond at best to the advanced performance of the 1950s and early 1960s).

If successful, this modernization drive would, after accounting for population growth, boost the average annual per capita income to U.S. $800 (and this figure excludes any contributions of the tertiary, service, sector), making the people, as the current Chinese phrase has it, "comparatively well-off." This achievement, so impressive in its aggregate form, would put the Chinese a generation from now at a level just recently reached by Thailand, the Philippines, or Morocco and already surpassed by nearly fifty lower and upper middle-income developing nations (World Bank 1986).

Much has been written recently by Chinese economists about the realistic nature of this plan and about precedents buttressing the rational hopes for its fulfillment. To cite just one such study, Ren Tao and Pang Yongjie (1983) point out that even if the three years of rehabilitation right after the establishment of the PRC (1949–1952) are excluded (as the rapid growth rates of that period reflected mostly restitution of capacities idled by long civil war rather than new investments), average annual growth of the Chinese economy between 1950 and 1981 was 8.1 percent, nearly a full percentage point ahead of the rate required for the quadrupling by the year 2000.

As it is always more difficult, however, to maintain the past growth rates for several successive doublings, better precedents could be seen by looking at other large economies that quadrupled their product during a similar time span. Ren and Pang (1983) cite examples of the USSR (GNP up 4.25 times in twenty years between 1955 and 1975), Japan (exactly fourfold growth in just fourteen years between 1956 and 1970), and West Germany (fourfold rise in twenty-six years between 1950 and 1976). The last case is an inappropriate one as the period is too long—and, in fact, all the examples are improper as they look at time spans when the three economies were initially much smaller than the Chinese is today.

Once again, one sees the recurrent Chinese ignorance of the base and the sole concentration on growth rate. Chinese GNP reached U.S. $300 billion in 1982—and the same level, expressed in constant (1982) dollars was reached by Japan only in 1963; two decades later, in 1983, that country's GNP was about $1.070 trillion, or 3.58 times larger after the exponential growth rate averaging 6.35 percent. The West German economy first surpassed $(1982)300 billion in 1959 and in the early 1980s stagnated around $(1982)660 billion, that is a 2.2-fold expansion in twenty-four years and a growth rate of 3.28 percent. And the Soviet GDP, using the best available historical series in constant monies (CIA 1982), reached the current Chinese economic output by 1945, which means it took twenty-six years to quadruple its domestic product (an exponential growth rate of 5.33 percent).

Consequently, it is obvious that to go from $(1982)300 billion to 1.2 trillion in two decades, China's performance would have to be better than both the Soviet and the Japanese records. Instead of appraising the probability of such an impressive advance I will reiterate the already mentioned, surprisingly modest per capita implication of this achievement. Without any more digressions, I will focus on the Chinese perceptions of energy fluxes required to achieve the fourfold expansion of the nation's economic product.

4.2 Energy needs and strategies

When current energy supply is so insufficient that no less than one-fifth of industrial capacity is idle and the output of a large number of essential enterprises is determined by their fuel and electricity rations, it is all too obvious that the future production increases of coal, hydrocarbons, and electricity will have to be very large indeed. On the other hand, China's unparalleled energy conversion inefficiencies represent, even after widespread conservation efforts since 1979, a still enormous reservoir of readily available, switchable supply which can run new energy-efficient factories instead of perpetuating outdated fuel-wasting technologies.

And as long-range energy forecasting has been a discordant and overwhelmingly unsuccessful effort even in mature economies, it is not surprising that the current Chinese perceptions of the country's future energy needs have differed quite widely (table 4.1, figure 4.1). I shall look in turn at some typical assumptions published since 1978 before outlining the basic strategies currently dominating the long-range plans laid out by Chinese energy policy makers.

The initial wave of forecasts prepared to establish the energy consumption levels needed to achieve the bold modernization goals showed impossibly huge totals. For example, in one of the most detailed analyses of China's energy situation up to that time Chen, Huang, and Xu (1979) flatly stated that, as the energy/GNP elasticity ratio for developing countries is about 1:1, and as China needs average annual industrial growth of 13.5 percent to bring about the quadrupling of the total economic output, an annual increase of about 80 million tons of coal is called for to sustain this expansion. Indeed, 13.5 percent of 600 million tons of coal equivalent comes to almost exactly 80 million tons, a huge mass of fuel output to add in one year.

These three Chinese economists committed two unpardonable er-

Table 4.1

Comparison of recent Chinese forecasts of primary energy demand by the year 2000.

Authors	Year of the forecast	Analytical method	Primary energy consumption (10⁹tce)
Chen, Huang and Xu	1979	Energy/industrial output elasticity, coefficient 1.0, no conservation	2.400
Gong	1980	Basic needs approach (1.6 tce/capita)	1.936
		Energy/GNP elasticity (6 percent GNP growth, elasticities (1980–1990 1.2, 1990–2000 0.85)	1.860
		Energy/GNP elasticity (8 percent GNP growth)	2.750
Gu and He	1980	Sectoral analysis, target GNP $833/capita, conservation rate 40 percent by 2000	1.390–1.510
Lu and Liu	1981	Input-output analysis, target GNP $1000/capita	1.920
Lu and Zhong	1981	Energy/GNP regression, elasticity coefficient 1–0.8, conservation one percent/year	1.654
Huang and Zhang	1981	Energy/GNP elasticity, coefficient 0.75–.80, conservation 0.5 percent/year	2.400
Chinese Academy of Social Sciences	1985	Regression and basic needs approach (1.5 tce/$1,000 of GNP)	1.560–1.700

Source: Chen, Huang and Xu (1979); Gong (1984); Lan, Lu and Mao (1984); Xinhua, 9 November 1985.

rors: first, they overlooked a simple fact that the elasticity ratio applies to the total economic output rather than just to industrial production. Their second mistake is one to which very large numbers of Chinese planners have been subscribing—and many still do: a general belief in somehow preordained energy/GNP elasticity ratios, particularly in the fact that for developing nations the elasticity cannot be less than one. This would mean, of course, that the quadrupling of the national economic product would have to be driven by quadrupled output of primary energy, and that in the year 2000 China would have to harness 2.4 billion tons of coal equivalent in fossil fuels and hydro and nuclear electricity.

A year later Gong Guangyu (1980) published four alternative forecasts in *Xiandaihua* (Modernization) ranging from 1.86 to 2.75 billion

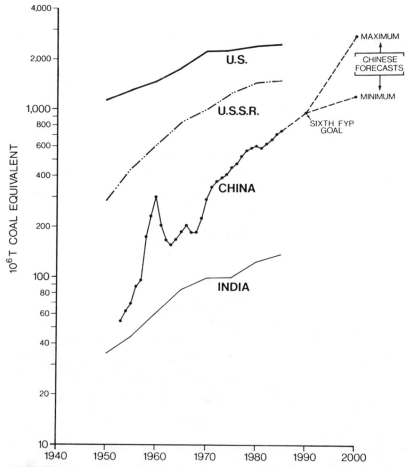

Figure 4.1: Comparison of primary energy consumption in the United States, USSR, China, and India.

tce and concluded that the only way the country can reach average per capita GNP of $1,000 in the year 2000 is to supply the highest forecasted amount. These gross exaggerations did not survive for long: many of the influential Chinese energy planners soon came to realize the impossibility of such a task and have rejected the unwarranted high energy/GNP elasticity ratios.

Developments between 1979 and 1983 showed the Chinese that there is nothing immutably fixed about the relationship of energy consumption and GNP growth. Whereas during 1953–1978 the measure averaged 1.24, it sank to just 0.22 in 1979 and 0.25 1980, became negative in 1981, and then rose in 1982 and 1983, but to no more than, respectively, 0.425 and 0.55. This development, which has been having numerous counterparts in most industrialized as well as industrializing nations around the world, persuaded the Chinese that energy consumption elasticity can be kept below 1 for a rather extended period of time—but not without continuous, vigorous readjustment of the industrial structure, closing down of inefficient small enterprises, technological modernization of major energy intensive processes, and development of many new products and services with relatively low energy content.

How much below 1? Some recent writings have settled on a convenient number of 0.5: quadrupled economy would then need doubled primary energy output, or 1.2 billion tons of coal equivalent by the year 2000. While I absolutely agree with the general tenor of the modified Chinese long-range energy forecasts, above all with their rejection of elasticities at or near unity, I would not be so sanguine as to assume with Ren and Pang (1983) that ''even a conservative estimate suggests that it is entirely possible to reduce the energy consumption of each given unit of industrial products by 50 percent in the twenty years.''

My doubts have nothing to do with the magnitude of the reduction—such a rate of decrease is certainly quite possible considering China's current outrageously high energy content of every GNP yuan. But the change will not come about without sweeping, and hence extremely costly, refurbishing of China's industrial infrastructure. Because only one-third of machinery and equipment in China is at the level of the 1960s and 1970s, whereas two-thirds date back to the 1950s and 1940s, at least half of all fixed assets should be replaced as soon as possible.

Moreover, the process only begins with installing more efficient technologies: assiduous management is the critical continuous need, and there can be no doubt that managing for quality and efficiency has been chronically the least successful part of China's developmental effort, whose notable achievements have come almost solely from concentration on building large, expensive capital projects and turning out large quantities of inferior products.

The choice is, of course, China's to make. Continuation of Stalinist industrialization, further exacerbated by particularly inefficient management, would require at least a matching energy consumption growth with whatever the actual GNP growth rates may be. On the other hand, diversification of the economy and its technological modernization would lead to substantial decline of high energy intensities and to energy elasticities much below the unity.

Putting some reasonable numbers on these improvements—nation-wide conversion mean up by certainly achievable 30 percent, so that the early 1980s' needs could be covered with 450 million rather than 600 million tons of coal equivalent and electricity, and energy/GNP elasticity ratio at sustainable 0.6, that is, an annual energy production growth rate of about 4.3 percent—means that quadrupled GNP by the year 2000 could be supported by just 1.06 billion tons of coal equivalent or about a 1.75-fold expansion of the current usage.

This growth, averaging some 23 million tons of equivalent fuel a year, is still a fairly large quantum of energy to keep on adding—but one clearly within China's capabilities. During 1983–85 it appeared that there was a prevailing consensus in China expecting twofold expansion by the year 2000 (among many others see Zhang 1983, Lu 1984). This goal would obviously require rigorous conservation measures, and it would translate to mean annual additions of 30 million tce, a performance Chinese recognized to be attainable only with extreme exertion (Lu 1984).

The latest Chinese forecasting exercise, a two-year study by the Chinese Academy of Social Sciences released in November 1985, returned to higher values. The forecast assumed that no less than 1.5 tce are necessary to produce a GNP of $1,000 per capita, which would mean an aggregate need of 1.56–1.70 billion tce by the year 2000. Yet the study acknowledged that the actual output cannot be higher than 1.3–1.4 billion tce, leaving a gap of 15–20 percent, a greater relative energy shortage than China experiences today.

Once again, there is nothing preordained about 1.5 tce, and the options remain open to achieve more economic growth with less energy than anticipated by this latest Chinese forecast. Whatever the eventual demand by the year 2000 may be, the Chinese have adopted a set of general strategic approaches toward fulfilling at least the doubling of total energy output. This ambitious goal includes continuation of extensive energy conservation measures; doubling of coal output to 1.2 billion tons (although in 1985 Zhao Ziyang already set the year 1990 for production of 1 billion tons); substantial expansion of crude oil and natural gas production with the as yet unspecified rates depending on the outcome of offshore exploration now in progress; and quadrupling of electricity generation to strengthen what is now China's weakest energy sector. And as these advances would primarily benefit China's industrial and urban energy uses, a comprehensive strategy of energy development must also contain a variety of measures aimed at easing, and eventually eliminating, the country's severe rural fuel shortages and extending electricity to village homes. Each of these five principal thrusts will be now taken up in some detail.

4.2.1 Conserving fuel and electricity

Widespread, and in comparison with industrialized nations often astonishingly large, conversion inefficiencies discussed in section 3.2.4 appear to offer grand potential for savings going still much beyond of what has been achieved since 1978. For many industrial sectors or particular conversion processes these expectations are very much in place, but in a great many other instances future efficiency gains will be at best only marginal. Certainly the best possibilities are in those important industries that are large absolute consumers of energy but whose unit performance is bound to improve quite significantly owing both to improved management and technological modernization of key enterprises and to start-up of new projects built, mostly with foreign help, to perform at or near advanced levels.

Iron and steel industry is the best example in this category. As noted, it is currently the second largest sectoral user of China's industrial energy with about 12 percent of the total, and this high share owes more to its poor conversion efficiency, although it is currently much improved compared to the period before 1977, than to the scale of its output. Between 1978 and 1982 total energy consumed per ton of crude steel in large mills declined by 24 percent, but rich payoffs can still be realized. This can be best illustrated by a detailed comparison of energy intensities of individual steel-making processes in one of China's modern and hence more energy-efficient mills in Wuhan with those of a standard model plant outlined by the International Steel Association in 1976 (Meng and Sheng 1983).

As shown in table 4.2, the overall difference in 1980 was about 425 kg of standard coal per ton of steel as Wuhan's mill was nearly 60 percent more energy-intensive than its model counterpart. Even the least involved intervention—keeping Wuhan's inferior iron/steel and continuous casting ratios and lowering the processing energy uses to the model level—would save about 20 percent of all fuels and electricity with relatively modest investments.

The high level of energy use in Chinese processing is often a matter of obviously poor management rather than outdated equipment (Sun 1983). General enforcement of basic rational management practices—

Table 4.2

Comparison of energy consumption in a large Chinese steel plant and in a model establishment.

Process	Energy consumption (kgce/t steel)	
	Wuhan Steel Plant (1980)	Model (1976) Plant
Coking	104	67
Sintering	138	76
Iron smelting	470	433
Hot rolled plate	141	8
Continuous hot rolling	—	49
Other processes	295	91
Total	1,148	724
Iron/Steel ratio	0.934	0.842

Source: Meng and Sheng (1983).

such as closing down the inefficient capacities—could save up to 20 percent of energy without any major investments. Further savings need changes in production structure and active conservation measures, and these steps, judging by the Japanese experience in the 1970s where the mills started to save from what was already the world's lowest energy intensity, can result in an additional 15 percent savings in three to five years.

A major structural change must involve an improvement in the extremely high pig iron/steel ratio: instead of values between 0.6 and 0.8 common in the Western nations and Japan (precise 1982 values were 0.59 for the United States, 0.78 for Japan, and 0.76 for West Germany), China's pig iron/steel ratio was above 1 until 1980 (1.09 in 1970, 1.06 in 1979), and in 1982 it was still no better than 0.96. Yet every drop of one-tenth in this value would cut about 7 million tons of standard coal (Li and Wei 1983), so that merely through proper recycling China could save, other inefficiencies of the sector notwithstanding, about 15 million tons of standard coal. Furthermore, reducing ash content of coking coal by 1 percent would bring a 2 percent reduction in the coke inputs and 3 percent increase in pig iron output.

The only industry where post-1978 energy savings were even greater than in iron and steel mills was the synthesis of nitrogenous fertilizers largely owing to reduced coal consumption in small ammonia plants and closing down of some of the most outdated enterprises. Still, the opportunities remain very large. According to Lu and Liu (1984), the difference between energy use in average and advanced small synthetic ammonia plants is 69 percent for total coal use and 53 percent for electricity consumption.

Eliminating at least one-quarter of this difference should be generally achievable with better management. Modernization of selected small units and installation of all new ammonia-urea capacities in large, inherently much more efficient plants should result in substantial additional fuel and electricity savings in the years ahead.

On the other hand, there have been several industries where specific energy consumption has actually increased during recent years, most notably coal and oil gas extraction. This happened mainly because the previous neglect of tunneling and exploratory drilling had to be redressed by devoting more resources to these essential preproduction activities. Most notably, electricity consumption in large, ministry-run coal mines rose from 32.08 kWh per ton of raw coal in 1979 to 36.35 kWh in 1983, leaving considerable conservation opportunities throughout the whole industry. They are achievable by replacing, or at least rebuilding and properly maintaining, inefficient ventilators, pumps, and air compressors.

Consumption of coal by the large mines also remains unnecessarily high (and recently rising): at around 400 tons per 10,000 tons of raw coal it has been about 14 million tons a year, or roughly 4 percent of all coal output when expressed in standard fuel terms, the fifth largest final use among industrial sectors (Hao 1984). Replacement of inefficient boilers (the average in large coal mines is now merely 45 percent) by new units, introduction of fluidized combustion, and conversion of surface transport from steam locomotives to diesels are the obvious routes to follow.

Utilization of coal wastes for electricity generation is a concept appealing on several accounts: the "resource" is plentiful, its current storage is objectionable, its conversion has been shown to be technically feasible, and it may even be economically rewarding (Xiao 1984). Accumulated mine waste now amounts to about one billion tons, new waste is generated at a rate of over 100 million tons a year, and more than 15 million tons of it contain over 6 MJ/kg (or over one-fifth of standard coal's heat value), an equivalent of about 5 million tce.

As China's large coal mines used 7.2 million tce in 1984 to generate the needed electricity, it is clear that a large part of this generation could be covered by exploiting the readily available waste. Experimental stations in Yiyang (Hunan), Yongrong (Sichuan), and Pingxiang (Jiangxi) have been using fluidized-bed boilers for several years of stable and profitable generation based on the waste. Investment costs are currently put 50 percent higher than for standard coal-fired stations, but as there is no need to open up new mining capacities and to extract and move the coal, the cost is seen by the Chinese as acceptable, especially as the ash and slag from the burning is suitable for cement production.

In spite of this Chinese enthusiasm I foresee little chance for coming close to the potential utilization capacity. After all, the largest operating boilers have only 6-MW generators, a size too small to benefit from pronounced economies of scale accompanying much larger capacities whose commercial operation in the fluidized-bed mode is not yet an engineering reality. Moreover, large numbers of planned mine-mouth multi-MW stations should be able to deliver the electricity needed by coal mines more economically even when the costs of extraction are considered (there will be, of course, no fuel shipment). Gangue-based generation is thus undoubtedly a sensible local addition with the added environmental benefit—but hardly a major strategic departure.

Overall there is no reason why China's large coal mines should not be able to cut both their raw coal and electricity use by 15–20 percent before the end of the 1980s, savings equivalent to around 2.5 million tons of coal and 2 billion kWh a year. Other sectors with far from exhausted conservation potential are smelting of nonferrous metals, chemical industries, steam generation, transportation, and household combustion. Many energy conservation measures in these important areas are well known, but in Chinese conditions their diffusion will not be easy. For example, using sorted coal in China's locomotives rather than the raw mixture of lumps and dust (whose flying and leaking losses alone amount to several million tons a year) would lower the total consumption by as much as 10 percent.

An obvious measure to increase conversion efficiency in road transport is large-scale introduction of diesel-fueled trucks, buses, and cars, a shift from gasoline which has been underway in most industrialized countries for several decades. But China, as *Renmin ribao* complained in May 1982, has relatively few diesel vehicles and, "owing to the fact that in our country diesel fuel is in shorter supply than gasoline, the motor vehicle industry should take gasoline as the principal fuel" and "diesel vehicles should not be developed in the near future." This is, of course, an undesirable route to take.

Yet another example from the transportation sector has more to do with sensible management than with technical innovation. Jeeps have been commonly used throughout China in place of ordinary cars, and as the specific fuel consumption of Chinese-made jeeps is about one-third higher than that of four-seat sedans, the tens of thousands of units with jeeps outside exploration and mining enterprises should not be allowed to use these terrain vehicles. Yet such a reversal will not travel speedily through the country's bureaucracies. In railroad transport, using screened lump coal instead of raw coal in steam locomotives would save about 15 percent of fuel—but the switch is predicated by the availability of coal-cleaning capacities.

Among chemical syntheses the fiber industry is an important area of large potential savings because its production energy intensities are very high and its output, needed to clothe the huge population, has been rapidly increasing (Sun 1981). The first Chinese syntheses started in 1957, and the output grew from a mere 10,000 tons in 1960 to 100,000 tons in 1970 and 540,700 tons in 1983. Owing to the variety of processes and final products it is not meaningful to quote a typical energy intensity, but most of the values are high or very high (up to 165 MJ/kg).

Thermal energy needed for spinning of synthetic fibers is also high: for acrylic fibers 139 MJ/kg, or 56 percent of total energy consumption; for polyvinyl ones 108 MJ/kg, or 67 percent of all energy. Efficient heat recovery can greatly reduce these needs, but as China's crude oil price is still low in comparison with the world level and the price of synthetic fibers is very high, this artificial, man-made profit hides the widespread inefficiencies throughout the Chinese industry and does not force vigorous conservation efforts.

Substitution of oil combustion in stationary boilers has been one of the top goals of post-1979 conservation campaigns, and this rational conservation strategy should continue. During the five years between 1979 and 1983, 2,679 oil-burning boilers were converted to coal, freeing 11 million tons of crude oil. The cost of these conversions totaled Rmb 1.49 billion while the savings resulting from increasing oil exports and refinery processing surpassed Rmb 4 billion. The official goal set by the State Council is to reduce the stationary oil burning to 20 million tons by 1994, that is, to half of the 1980 level (Li 1984).

Saving 20 million tons of oil between 1980 and 1990 is estimated to cost Rmb 20 billion, but the substitution by coal is to increase direct state revenues by Rmb 7–8 billion every year, and this sum would be considerably larger when the benefits resulting from the processing of 20 million tons of oil and the sale of final products is taken into account. Moveover, in spite of the problems with coal extraction (section 4.2.2), shortages of oil for unsubstitutable final uses are becoming much more acute, and conversions of stationary boilers are the most sensible way to ease these supply pressures. Most notably, the number of cars and trucks on Chinese roads was rising so fast between 1979 and 1985 (when the Chinese imposed strict import controls on all kinds of vehicles) that the average amount of oil distributed per vehicle dropped from 7.1 tons in 1979 to just over 4 tons in 1983.

Complete replacement of thousands of inefficient boilers would lead to dramatic fuel savings, but given the investment constraints these improvements will be realized only very gradually. This concerns above all some 200,000 small, low-efficiency industrial boilers which consume annually about 160 million tons of coal. Many of these units, called "coal tigers" by the Chinese, are of truly venerable antiquity. The best examples I came across were in Sichuan where I was told that a paper mill operates a boiler salvaged from a nineteenth-century ship and that another Chengdu enterprise still stokes a steam generator manufactured in 1864. That such units still must fill the basic production needs is the best illustration of the greatly limited outlook for widespread and rapid replacement by modern boilers.

But just repairing leaky valves and insulating bare steam pipes could add up to 4 million tce a year, and uniformly proper water treatment in industrial boilers could release another 3 million tce. Simplest of all is matching the capacity of boilers with the task, that is, doing away with a common practice of "a big horse drawing a small cart."

Household consumption should be also rationalized. In 1982 urban residents consumed 58.37 million tons of coal, but honeycomb briquettes, burning with 25 percent efficiency, constituted only 24 percent of that large total while the commonly used bulk raw coal delivers heat with no more than 10 percent efficiency. Urban households and enterprises in industrial cities could also use large volumes of gases wastefully discharged each year. Unused coke-oven gas alone totaled 800 million m^3 in 1982, and most of 400 million m^3 of mine gas is also let go. The largest efficiency gains can come only from replacement of coal stoves by gas-burning devices whose conversion rates can equal those achieved in the rich countries.

If it will not be easy to implement myriads of little adjustments concerning utilization of solid and liquid fuels in households, small industrial enterprises, and farming, it should be more bearable to see this diffuse waste as long as China's central planners do their utmost to use the state's investment policies for promotion of labor-intensive light industries rather than for perpetuation of heavy industrial dominance. After all, every shift of 1 percent of the total industrial output from heavy to light industry would, at current levels of production, save annually about 5 million tons of standard coal. Adjusting the proportions of light and heavy industry to the level of the First Five-Year Plan would save as much as 30 million tons of coal equivalent, a revealing fact showing that the Chinese economy became, largely during the 1970s, more Stalinist than during the years it was basically run by the Soviet Stalinist planners.

And it will be necessary to part with a sizable proportion of inefficient small-scale production. In many cases existence of these enterprises will be justifiable even if their energy intensity remains inferior, but eliminating just a third of their current capacity by consolidation into larger units and by expansion of output from modern enterprises could bring aggregate savings of at least 20 million tons of standard coal; one-third reduction of output in small and medium-sized steel mills alone would save 6.4 million tons of standard fuel.

Finally, gradual changes in location of energy-intensive industries would be also very well repaid in energy savings. Large-scale transfers of northern coal to the established industrial centers will have to continue owing to considerable inertial resistance of old production centers to relocation. However, new energy-intensive industries should be increasingly located in the Southwest to take advantage of the region's rich hydroelectricity potential as well as its abundant availability of water and minerals.

To hope that China could, even two decades from now, match Japan's current efficiency of energy utilization would be inexcusable wishful thinking. But there is no doubt that a combination of better management and maintenance, equipment modernization, closing down of the least efficient small-scale enterprises, and a continuing tilt toward more sensible light and heavy industries could realistically result in eventual savings on the order of 200 milion tons of coal equivalent, that is, cutting the current use by one-quarter.

As anywhere else, initial efficiency gains accomplished in China since 1978 have been the easiest ones, and the costs and investment return periods on future savings will be growing. According to Lu and

Liu (1984), savings of 1 tce were realized with just Rmb 160 in 1981 whereas in 1984 their average cost rose to Rmb 300–350. Still, the possibilities remain impressive. Between 1981 and 1985 gains from conservation added up to almost 100 million tons of standard coal, mainly owing to improvements in heavy energy consumption areas of the East and the North where the focus should be on lowering energy intensities of metallurgical, chemical, and building material industries. These measures brought annual declines of 2.6–3.5 percent in energy intensity of total industrial output, with gains in some sectors being as high as 12 percent. Overall, during the first half of the 1980s, gains from conservation provided at least as much energy for economic growth as the harnessing of untapped resources led by coal extraction, to whose future I shall turn next.

4.2.2. Doubling coal output

Unlike the short-lived 1978 announcement of two successive doublings, the current goal of extracting 1.2 billion tons of coal by the year 2000, that is, doubling of the 1980 production, appears here to stay and every commentator, from the minister of coal industry down, has been stressing that it is a realistic target. To reach it will require annual growth of 3.4 percent between 1983 and 2000—and did China's coal extraction not grow by an average of 10 percent a year between 1950 and 1980?

One must agree that it did, but any student of complex systems involving extraction of natural resources knows that the successive doublings are invariably more difficult to achieve: as the infrastructure grows larger it gets both more unwieldy and much more expensive to maintain and expand. Moreover, here is yet another example of the common Chinese preoccupation with growth rates as if they, rather than the base to which they refer, were the essence of the process.

Expanding the output by opening very efficient, completely electrified giant surface mines delivering dressed coal to mine-mouth thermal stations or, via unit trains, for shipments from large coal ports to other parts of the country or abroad is a task requiring incomparably higher levels of capital and operation costs, technical expertise, and assiduous management than giving low-cost loans to peasants with pickaxes and shovels to open up small-outcrop mines and to dig out more fuel which will be used, unprepared and containing often in excess of 50 percent rocks and clay, in local inefficient boilers or whose high waste content will burden the already overloaded long-distance transportation.

Needless to say, if the Chinese are serious about providing energy for economic modernization it is the first kind of extraction they should undertake, not the latter inferior numbers-game. After all, should they just continue to extract their coal as they do today, when they reach 1.2 billion tons, no less than 350 million tons of it would be uncombustible waste! And the final reminder: both of the other two coal superpowers have announced similarly expansive plans for their coal extraction—but both the USSR and the United States have been finding the move toward the billion-ton level much more difficult and much slower than anticipated, notwithstanding their comparatively superior technological investment capability. If it is to be achieved in an efficient, high-quality manner (which would be a real boost to China's modernization), the task is a formidable one, and the outcome must be seen as highly uncertain. Here is how the Chinese propose to do it.

As the possibilities to expand extraction at the existing, already mostly overextended mines (they commonly produce 1.5–2 times the designed capacity) are limited, their output will be expanded just slightly from 344 million tons in 1980 to 400 million tons in 2000, and two-thirds of the 600-million-ton increase would have to come from new collieries. This would necessitate opening up new mines with an average production capacity of 20 million tons every year for the rest of this decade and bringing on line 300 million tons of new capacity during the 1990s. In October 1982 Chen Dun, head of the Capital Construction Department of the Ministry of Coal Industry, outlined the details of fifteen key capital construction projects, listed in tables 4.3 and 4.4 and shown in figure 4.2, to accomplish this goal. No major changes to this plan have been published since.

In a fundamental departure from traditional underground mining, one-third of the new key projects will be large, open-cut mines, four in Nei Monggol and one in Shanxi, with ultimate annual production capacity of over 200 million tons (to be reached no earlier than in the first decade of the next century) (table 4.4). Opening of Huolinhe coalfield on the Horqin grassland in Nei Monggol started in 1981 with the production goal of 3 million tons in 1985. Removal of the overburden at the Yiminhe mine started in 1983 with the goal of 20 million tons a year by 1995. Yuanbaoshan mine should go into production by 1988 with 8 million tons. Junggar mine will be the largest in Nei Monggol with initial output of 25 million tons a year; the only large surface project in Shanxi, the Antaibao (Pingshuo) mine jointly developed by

Table 4.3

Ten coal mining bases chosen as the major centres of modernization

Coal mining base	Province	Principal mining areas	Production capacity (10^6t/year) Current	Planned
1. Eastern Heilongjiang	Heilongjiang	Shuangya, Qitaihe, Jixi, Hegang	30	37
2. Shenyang	Liaoning	Tiefa, Shenbei, Honyang	6	13
3. Hanxing	Hebei	Handan, Fengfeng, Xingtai	14	22
4. Central Shanxi	Shanxi	Gujiao, Huoxian, Xiangning	2	16
5. Southeastern Shanxi	Shanxi	Yangquan, Luan, Jincheng	18	34
6. Weibei	Shaanxi	Tongchuan, Chenghe, Pubai, Hancheng	16	21
7. Yanteng	Shandong	Yanzhou, Jining, Tengxian	6	22
8. Western Henan	Henan	Xinmi, Pingdingshan, Yima, Xinggong	24	38
9. Lianghuai	Anhui	Huainan, Huaibei	17	60
10. Liupanshui	Guizhou, Yunnan	Liuzhi, Panxian, Shuicheng	7	15

Source: Wu (1983) and various Xinhua releases.

Table 4.4

China's five large surface mines under development

Surface mine	Province	Mining area (km²)	Coal reserves (10⁹t)	Heat content (MJ/kg)	Stripping ratio	Annual production capacity (10⁶t/year)	
						initial	ultimate
A Huolinhe	Nei Monggol	540	12.9	11.3	3.5–5.0	3	50
B Yiminhe	Nei Monggol	545	5.0	12.5	1.8–2.5	3	55
C Yuanbaoshan	Nei Monggol	13	5.4	11.3	5.5	3	8
D Junggar	Nei Monggol	1723	3.4	22.8	3.1–6.0	25	60
E Antaibao	Shanxi	376	12.7	29.3	5.0–8.0	15	45

Source: Wu (1983).

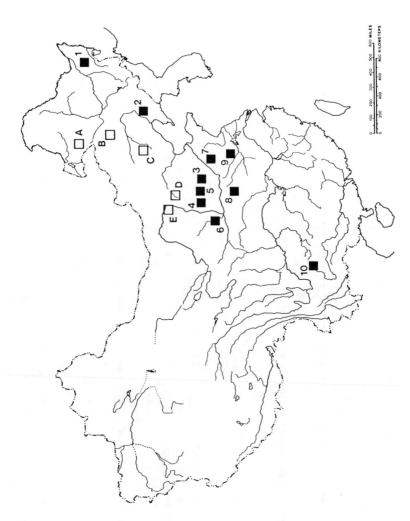

Figure 4.2: Locations of fifteen key projects in China's coal industry (tables 4.3, 4.4).

the Chinese and Occidental Petroleum, should produce 15.3 million tons at the end of the first stage.

At the time of contract signing in June 1985 the Antaibao project was the largest joint venture between the Chinese and a foreign private company, with total investment of $(1984)650 million and Americans (Occidental Petroleum) paying 25 percent of the cost. The open-cast mine will eventually claim an area of 18.6 km² on a barren plateau north of the Great Wall in Pinglu and Shuoxian counties. Verified reserves amount to 450 million tons, and the designed capacity of the project is 15 million tons a year during the fifteen years of joint production. Eventually two other large, open-cut mines should be opened in the area, bringing its total surface-mining capacity to 45 million tons a year.

Of the ten coal-mining centers where new mines should expand the annual output by a total of about 120 million tons a year, Lianghuai in Anhui—which Chinese plan to turn into "the Ruhr" of Asia (Qian and Chen 1984)—Southeastern Shanxi, and the Yanzhou-Tengxian area in Shandong should bring the greatest increments (table 4.3). The announced plans of production increments from old centrally run mines (56 million tons) and from new surface (83 million tons) and underground (120 million tons) projects add up to only 260 million tons, which implies that 340 million tons, or 56 percent of the required increment, would have to come from inefficient, labor-intensive, locally run mines producing inferior fuel.

This simple calculation makes it clear that the doubling plan is critically dependent on small-mine extraction, and the recent Chinese writings profess no concerns about the desirability of its rapid expansion. A *Zhongguo meitan bao* editorial of 15 August 1984 noted with approval that combustion of over 80,000 tons of locally mined coal creates Rmb 100 million of industrial output and brings revenues of Rmb 20 million to the state—while the leftover fuel can fill some gaps in the chronically unfilled unified national distribution scheme (in 1983, 67.4 million tons of local coal were so used). Moreover, local coal mines "have a solid footing in scientific study, coal mechanization, geological surveying, and construction and technical tracking."

After reading, in earlier paragraphs of the same editorial, that the overwhelming majority of these local pits still lack even the most essential mechanization (see section 3.2.1) and ignore basic safety procedures (including such great feats of hazardous economizing as "exploiting the pillars . . . that a large mine would not be able to exploit''), one must wonder about the ''solid footing.'' Nevertheless, local pit extraction is to grow by more than 20 million tons a year ''to reach 450 million tons by 1990, with limitless prospects.''

In 1986 the Chinese press again carried stories of things that should not be happening anymore: mining accidents with numerous casualties as the farmers rush to work in unsafe pits, and open plundering of the resources as mines continue to be set up indiscriminately (*Jingji ribao* reported a case of ''more than ten small coal mines . . . in an area no larger than 5 km²''). That fundamental recurrent question about Chinese intentions returns here once again: is it the quality (economically mined, cleaned, and sorted coal suitable for a wide variety of efficient final uses) or quantity (fuel seemingly cheap but burdened with a large proportion of uncombustibles precluding efficient utilization) that the planners are after?

As far as the shipments from small coal mines are concerned, any beneficial effect diminishes rapidly after a relatively short distance: output of individual local mines is so small that any longer transfers would first require considerable pooling, and even the excessively costly transportation infrastructure would have to be put in place. With such arrangements one cannot imagine what the coal-rich regions would do with scores of millions of tons of coal from small mines not needed locally: in the spring of 1985 these scattered establishments were already stockpiling 47 million tons of coal (which washes away in rain storms and often ignites spontaneously)—and the mass was reported to be rising steadily. The dubious strategy of relying so much on poor-quality coal from small mines in modernizing an economy aiming at substantial efficiency increases and the logistical challenges in integrating this output into the national economy beyond county boundaries are just two of many fundamental problems and complications on the way to doubled coal extraction.

In an unusually expansive interview given by Gao Yangwen to two newsmen from *Liaowang* in 1984, the minister was ''full of confidence'' in doubling the coal output by the end of the century, but he admitted that the whole industry has to ''bear great pressure . . . from many areas, such as fluctuation in output, production accidents, and economic losses. However, the biggest problem remains that of transportation. Out of an annual output of over 600 million tons of coal, over 200 million tons never get delivered to other places because of transportation constraints'' (Huang and Chen 1984).

As already noted (section 3.2.1), shipments out of Shanxi will be decisive, and several railroad projects now underway will about double the total freight capacity to 270 million tons by 1990. About 210 million tons will be reserved for coal—but the plans for 1990 are for total shipments of 400 million tons of coal out Shanxi, and railways alone cannot cope with the expected surge. Consequently, it comes as no surprise that serious considerations have been also given to increased coal shipments by truck. In 1985 there were plans for buying 1,400 heavy-duty trucks within two years. Higher costs aside, the state of the province's roads imposes a severe limitation on these attempts (Cao 1984). Shanxi has only 9,250 km of truck roads, a large part of them steep, twisted, and unfit for heavy coal transport. During 1949–1981 expenditures in Shanxi's construction were Rmb 190 million, a mere 0.75 percent of total capital investment in the province. Major upgrading and construction programs have been proposed, but their costs, after decades of neglect, will be high. Merely to reconstruct 1 km of a tertiary road costs up to Rmb 300,000, so a single upgraded outlet capable of handling 1–2 million tons of coal a year would cost Rmb 20–30 million.

A joint study group of the State Economic Commission and Shanxi institutions suggested using a portion of local funds for coal extraction to build new highways from Jincheng through Zhanglukou to Bo'ai and from Yangcheng through Yadao to Jiyuan, both destinations in Henan where they can link to roads to Shangdong and Jiangsu. Planning for roads to Hebei and Nei Monggol is also underway, but I would question the economic viability of "special highways for coal transport" which are to take Datong coal to Tanggu or Qinhuangdao ports on the Bo Hai. Electrified unit-train runs are not only much less costly to build and operate; they are also much less energy-intensive and much more environmentally acceptable.

Given the huge expected mass of annual shipments from Shanxi, as well as from other inland coal-rich sites, and the fact that these transfers are to be continued well beyond even the most extended planning horizon, there would seem to be a logical place for an innovative transportation that has been recently attracting attention in other large coal-mining nations: slurry (mixture of water and pulverized coal) pipelines. In 1982 the Ministry of Coal Industry initiated feasibility studies for the construction of seven coal slurry pipelines which would, by the end of the century, move coal from Shanxi as well as from other large mining sites (Junggar in Nei Monggol, Liupanshui in Guizhou) to the coast.

Wishful thinking, so frequently encountered among China's long-range planners, is perfectly illustrated by Zhang Deang's (1982) examination of the advantages of slurry pipelines. The first of the five listed benefits is shortening of the transportation route as the grades can be much steeper than for a railroad. True, but this advantage can be easily lost when numerous land disputes force changes in the straightest route: in the United States such challenges were one of the key factors leading to abandonment of the longest planned slurry pipeline from Wyoming to Arkansas, and even in China local and provincial pressures cannot be disregarded in expropriating prime farmland.

The second cited advantage is a "comparatively" low cost. Zhang cites the Black Mesa line investment, which "in terms of a current construction cost of $39 million . . . could be recovered in eight to ten years." This is an unpardonable error as the cited figure represents the line's original cost in the late 1960s—whereas today the same project would require investment higher by more than one order of magnitude (Weil 1983). If key projects worth billions of dollars are being promoted on such a level of "expertise" one must wonder about the sensibility of the whole doubling effort.

Obstacles facing these projects are enormous. Experience with operating long-distance slurry lines is limited to the 440-km Black Mesa line in northern Arizona as other American projects had to be abandoned owing to insurmountable right-of-way problems and environmental lobbying. Costs are in billions of dollars, and considering the unprecedented scale of the Chinese plans preconstruction estimates are certainly too low, an all too frequent occurrence with huge pioneering projects. High water demands, about one ton for each ton of pulverized coal, would only aggravate the already much strained water supply throughout northern China.

The two most seriously considered lines—a 964-km-long pipeline from southeastern Shanxi (Jincheng) to the port of Nantong at the mouth of the Chang Jiang with initial capacity of 15 million tons (eventually to be doubled), and a 700-km-long pipeline from Junggar surface mines in Nei Monggol to Qinhuangdao (carrying 30 million tons a year, most of it delivered to power plants en route)—could not be built without first sorting out considerable bureaucratic conflicts of interest and jurisdictional problems, and then not without extensive American participation ranging from designing, management, and personnel training to delivery of large pumping stations and terminal centrifuges.

Should the Chinese eventually decide to go ahead with these gigantic, expensive, energy-intensive, and untried schemes, the necessarily heavy American involvement would give the participating companies a chance to build and to operate, at least initially, projects that are too controversial and too expensive to be done in the United States—a lucrative and exciting deal, as long as one ignores its broader implications. If the technique cannot find its niche in the United States, is such a poor country as China its best pioneering ground, especially when the gigantic schemes would be set in an already precarious environment?

There is, of course, yet another solution to Shanxi's coal-shipment problem: burn the fuel near the mines and transmit the electricity, an economically desirable solution in accord with the global trend of mine-mouth electricity generation. But, once again, the North's environmental setting must be considered, and that is why later in this chapter (section 4.2.4) I will look in some detail at the gargantuan generation plans for the province and its already strained water balance.

Unfortunately for China's long-range planners, coal transportation is far from being the only major, well-recognized obstacle on a dash to 1.2 billion tons by the year 2000. No less critical will be the effort to shorten construction time of new underground mines (Huang 1983). This period averaged only around forty months for large mines in the 1950s, but it reached seventy-five months by 1976, and by that time even small shaft mines were put into operation only after seventy-four months of construction. By 1980 the mean for all mines topped one hundred months. Better selection of sites for the main and auxiliary shafts, more widespread use of inclined shafts for ascending mining, use of the skip shaft as a return air shaft in appropriate conditions (common in West Germany and Poland), better selection of ventilation site shafts, and utilization of existing mines for new construction are the best approaches to accelerated development.

In new and old mines mechanization of coal extraction, tunneling, loading, and transport must be, obviously, given the highest priority if at least the large enterprises are to improve their productivity and output quality. The key objectives of this effort detailed by Geng Zhaorui (1983) and Fan Weitang (1984) are as follows. Comprehensive mechanization of large mines should rise from 50 percent in 1985 to 70 percent by 1990, and by the year 2000 integrated extraction should be virtually complete. This will require accelerated development of all kinds of coal-cutting machinery, ranging from equipment for full-face extraction of seams up to 4.5 m thick to floor-creeping cutters for very thin seams, and from long-wall hydraulics to short-wall continuous miners in seams with nonrail transport. Concurrent improvements must be achieved in the design and durability of electrical equipment, ceiling supports, work-face transport, and hoisting and ventilating machinery.

Acquisition and absorption of surface mining technology is also a complicated task given its previous near-absence in China (Shi and Fan 1984). The two largest open-cut mines operating in China in the early 1980s had annual capacities of 4–5 million tons and were equipped with single bucket loaders and rails, a simple technology compared to continuous integrated extraction in large (over 10 million tons a year) mines equipped with rotary bucket loaders, conveyor belts and bulldozers or loaders and transport bridges for removing overburden, and large electrical excavators and off-road trucks or electrified rails for shipping coal, arrangements now common in Soviet, European, and American surface mines.

The list of challenges continues. Fundamental safety improvements have been long overdue as the best available estimates indicate that Chinese miners' accidental mortality is an order of magnitude above the American level (in May 1984 Gao Yangwen admitted "the failure of controlling major accidents"). Gas concentrations are high in virtually all of China's large mines (in the early 1980s about 3 million m^3 of gas were expelled from every large colliery), presenting constant dangers of gas bursts and coal slides, and efficient ventilating is a costly affair. Reduction of coal dust explosion and fire risks will require no less investment in dust filtering equipment and fire-fighting systems. Huge investments in coal grading and washing are self-evident in an industry that now cleans and sorts only a small fraction of its output. To allow for more flexible final uses of otherwise cumbersome fuel, Chinese scientists must engage in extensive coal gasification and liquefaction research, and to improve conversion efficiencies and enable the utilization of poorer quality coals great advances are needed in combustion engineering, notably in fluidized bed burning.

The necessity for advanced research and continuous development and introduction of new technologies is obvious to any critical analyst—but not necessarily to every powerful faction of Chinese decision makers. An August 1983 editorial in *Meitan kexue* complained about "some comrades" who think "that since China has a huge population it is only right that we use large work forces," and when the production was pushed to 600 million tons on the basis of backward science and technology there is no reason why the feat cannot be duplicated with yet more human strain and suffering. The dimensions of this major social problem—after all, miners and their families now number over ten million people—were comprehensively illustrated by a review of the situation in Hebei's Fengfeng mines in a provincial newspaper (*Hebei ribao*) in November 1981.

The number of miners directly engaged in coal extraction had been declining owing to sickness, injuries, and disabilities:

> Since the work is hard and conditions are poor, the workers' stamina is easily exhausted and they become very weak. More than 7,000 workers (of the 42,180) have contracted occupational or other diseases . . . After working for an average of 14–15 years, the pitmen . . . have to be transferred . . . about 5 percent of them are unable to do any physical labor yet do not meet the retirement requirements. Miners' children, especially their daughters, have difficulties in getting jobs. The problem of husband and wives living apart is far too common. About 65 percent of pitmen are rural residents . . . most have their families in the countryside . . . Yet, owing to the rapid loss of workface miners . . . the enterprises have to recruit . . . laborers from the countryside.

Hebei is the hinterland of the capital as well as of Tianjin, and the Fengfeng mining bureau is one of the country's eleven largest, with conditions far more advanced than countless interior locations. Still, for many a Chinese bureaucrat, throwing a few extra millions of poor peasants into the "battle of coal"—with all the inevitably depressing consequences—is a highly desirable strategy. What a perfect illustration of the powerful attraction of an old civilization's traditional approach: from the Great Wall masons to Great Leap Forward iron makers to today's coal doublers!

But the rising, better informed managers who had a recent chance to stand at the rim of West Germany's Fortuna open mine, which extracts 50 million tons of lignite a year, or who marveled at American coal combines and augers enabling each worker to produce as much as 20 tons of coal a shift, know differently: "The old road is impassable now. The only way out for the coal industry is to make progress in science and technology." Yet the news and appraisals of recent realities disclose that embarking on the new road has been frustratingly slow and that the prospects of faster advance are blocked by too many obstacles.

There are numerous vivid descriptions of shoddy tunneling (requiring frequent rebuilding of collapsed sections), chaotic management, and rampant stealing at one of the largest newly built mines in Shanxi (Huang Fengchu 1983), with incredible reports about idling and destroyed costly imported equipment (no skilled workers to run it) at the new large Huolinhe surface mine (Zhang and Lin 1983). China's production capacities for new coal-mining machinery are grossly inadequate and its coal-related R & D is extremely poorly staffed and underfunded (Gao Yangwen 1983). Poor mine safety and recent (understandable, I should add) efforts to evade labor assignments to mines further complicate the challenge.

Certainly the gloomiest appraisal emerged from a meeting of a group that should know best: on 6 April 1984 the top men of the Ministry of Coal Industry met with the party's Central Committee bureaucrats in charge of consolidation of industrial work and with representatives of other interested central institutions. A report on this meeting appeared on 14 April 1984 on the first two pages of *Zhongguo meitan bao*, and it should be required reading for all serious students of the Chinese economy. Extensive quotes are a must to appreciate how realistic is the goal of "doubling to assure quadrupling."

Most notably, Gao Yangwen admitted "the lack of stable and firm confidence in achieving the strategic goals of the coal industry." The leading group's "state of shaky confidence . . . was not related to the goal of 1.2 billion tons itself, but to the 800 million tons for unified distribution, as well as to the new construction of 400 million tons. They were especially anxious about the key role of the 200 million tons from open-pit mines." A revealing admission indeed: these top decision makers realize that the "mobilizational coal" extracted by millions of peasants from small mines may push the total to reach the set goal—but they have deep doubts whether at least two-thirds of it can come from large and finally modernized mines.

The leading party group itself "did not have enough of a pioneering spirit and lacked courage in opening up new roads," was very anxious about funding problems (rightly so—financing the world's largest-ever mining expansion in a poor nation in a hurry, with a saturated global coal market, must be an unenviably hard task), and noted how slow, small, and hit-and-miss were the reform steps at lower levels (how could it be otherwise when the leaders themselves repeatedly "surrendered . . . wavered, and retreated").

For all of those foreigners who see the post-1978 changes in China on an irreversible roll, Gao's analysis offers a different perspective: "Sealing off the country, parochial arrogance, and conservative complacency have not been eliminated," nor have the reforms done away with "rigid ideology . . . and there is no management style of working to the finish." Again, what an echo of great mobilizational campaigns whose launching makes greater waves than the follow-up and whose goals just fade away. "Discrimination against intellectuals" (in 1980 a mere 1.9 percent of all mining personnel were engineering experts, but there were many comrades who "have a stronger spirit of backwardness than of renewal and progress"), widespread "serious bureaucratism which manifests itself in irresponsibility and negligence . . . and no distinction between truth and falsehood" complete the image to perfection.

Still, the litany of problems does not end here. Even if the monies were found and the mines were opened up rapidly, mechanized comprehensively, and managed by initiative-taking educated men promoting advanced techniques within a system of flexible responses and incentive rewards, even if the fuel were shipped smoothly wherever needed, the challenge of integrating 1.2 billion tons of coal in a modernizing economy would be still extraordinary, and environmental concerns would become of key importance.

How would China—where today even particulate air pollution is poorly controlled and there are no SO_2 controls and hence ambient SO_2 and particulate matter concentrations are much in excess of new state norms—cope with enormous releases of air pollutants (about 25 million tons of SO_2, more than 100 million tons of fly ash), most of them injected into the atmosphere in dry northern provinces? How could China find the capital to install efficient particulate removal and desulfurization of large combustion sources when the former controls spread throughout the rich world only during the late 1950s–1960s and the latter are still rudimentary even in the world's richest economies, leading to serious concerns about long-term ecosystemic effects of acid deposition?

A closer look at these complications will come later (section 5.2). In concluding this discussion of doubling plans I will avoid any quantitative estimates: I have made it clear that reaching the goal is not important in itself; quality and sustainability are the only two sensible measures. On these scores China's bold coal extraction goals would be an extraordinary challenge even to the other two coal superpowers, which are much richer, technically much more advanced, and infrastructurally much more ready to underwrite such an expansion.

Consequently, I see no way in which China can double its coal output while concurrently transforming the industry into a modernized, efficient, mechanized, and safe endeavor comparable to current achievements of the other two large coal producers. Naturally, demands on the performance of the coal industry would be much lightened by substantial increases in the flow of hydrocarbons, but here, too, I will have to offer a far from ebullient appraisal.

4.2.3 Searching for hydrocarbons

During the last years of the 1970s Chinese were facing several frustrating realities concerning their oil industry. Output at their two largest oilfields (Daqing and Shengli, producing 70 percent of the total extraction) was stagnating. With the exception of conveniently located and relatively rich Zhongyuan oilfield, all other discoveries were yielding only smallish additions of new production capacity, moreover, mostly in difficult-to-develop reservoirs. Geologically most promising unexplored onshore oil-bearing basins appeared to be in Xinjiang, thousands of km away from the industrialized coastal regions. Sedimentary basins offshore were even more promising, but Chinese capacities to explore them and then to develop them were wholly inadequate.

The way out was by breaking with the long-standing proscription of foreigners developing China's natural resources and letting the Western and Japanese oil companies find the offshore hydrocarbons and bring them to market. The first stage of this marriage of convenience was richly rewarding to the Chinese, who lured in the multinationals—eager to have a try at what was perceived by many oilmen as one of the last remaining big plays in relatively easy waters—not by contracts but just by promises.

By July 1979 sixteen groups of foreign oil companies signed agreements to provide geophysical surveys—bearing the entire cost, letting the Chinese sample and learn advanced techniques, and turning over to them all results with the hope of being invited back later for exploratory drilling and production. About 420,000 km^2 of the South China Sea and the southern part of the Yellow Sea were explored by 110,000 km of seismic linear surveys, and after completion of exploration in six of the eight contract areas in April 1980, forty-six companies from twelve countries were invited to submit exploration tenders.

First drilling agreements were signed on a profit-sharing basis with Total China, Elf Aquitaine, and the Japan National Oil Corporation in May 1980, and the first American companies, Altantic Richfield and Santa Fe International, followed a year later, in June 1981, with a memorandum of intent. But these were exceptional early entrants as the true bidding for participation in the exploration of China's continental shelf did not start until March 1982, after the promulgation of new "Regulations of the PRC on the Exploitation of Offshore Petroleum Resources in Cooperation with Foreign Enterprises" on 10 February, and after the establishment of the China National Offshore Oil Corporation (CNOOC), which was put in charge of dealing with foreign participants.

A model exploration contract was revealed in May 1982 and the companies were given until 17 August 1982 to submit their bids. Of the forty-six companies that started the dealing in 1979, thirty-three decided to take a plunge and twenty-five opted for risk sharing in the form of twelve consortia. Finally, during 1983 awarding of exploration blocks got underway, and between 10 May and 2 December contracts were signed with twenty-seven companies from nine countries grouped in nine consortia for eighteen exploration blocks covering a total of 39,199 km² (Jing Wei 1984).

These contracts required the holders to drill 120 exploratory wells within three years at a cost of roughly U.S.\$(1984)1 billion. During 1983 came also the first news of foreign hydrocarbon discoveries. Total China found crude oil (test flow at 450 tons/day) and natural gas (72,000 m³/day) in Weizhou 10-3-3 well and did even better at a nearby site in the Beibu Gulf with Weizhou 10-3-4 flowing 1,158 tons/day of oil and 180,000 m³/day flow through a 1.7-cm choke from a depth below 3,650 m; later it was raised to 1.2 million m³ a day.

Clearly, 1984, the first full year of extensive offshore drilling, looked very promising—although the persistent and deepening glut on the global oil market was making the foreign companies less enthusiastic about the whole Chinese adventure. Chinese, as always fond of military similes, saw the year as "the eve of a massive battle," and the general manager of the Nanhai Western Petroleum Corporation assured a *Beijing Review* reporter that "we have found another battlefield in the South and we are not going to lose. . . . The D-day is not far away."

The analogy was grotesquely inaccurate: large offshore oilfields are not explored and developed by rapid, concentrated, mass assaults—but by a prolonged, incremental process of discovering and verifying new reservoirs and bringing them gradually into production. If anything, this resembles a lengthy, costly, frustrating war rather than a battle. Chinese talked often about the South China Sea as another North Sea. In that case they should have kept in mind that no less than thirteen years elapsed from the first geophysical confirmation of the undersea hydrocarbons to the time when Britain and Norway started to land more than 50 million tons of crude annually.

The realities of 1984 brought a different perspective: after a year of wildcatting in the Zhujiang Basin there were no worthwhile discoveries. Perhaps most disappointing was British Petroleum's failure after spending $55 million on six wells in the Nanhai's most promising offshore structures. As the best prospects yielded no commercial finds, many Western oilmen came to share a feeling that the complex stratigraphy of the Nanhai makes the discovery of a huge oilfield fairly unlikely and that the prospects lie in a multitude of smaller and deeper structures.

In these changed circumstances the China National Offshore Oil Corporation announced the second round of bidding for offshore contract areas on 21 November 1984. The newly opened blocks in the Yinggehai Basin south of Hainan totaled 13,300 km², and a more flexible approach was promised in speeding up the awarding process. In a second stage of the second-round bidding on 30 January 1985, an additional 93,000 km² were opened in the Zhujiang Basin and in parts of the South China Sea.

Among forty foreign oil companies that sought the second-round applications were not only such major old-timers as ARCO, BP, Chevron, ESSO, Occidental, Shell, and Texaco but also Amoco and Union Oil, which participated in geophysical surveys but stayed away from the first-round bidding, and Statoil and Norsk Hydro, two Norwegian companies. Eventually twenty-three oil companies decided to participate, and by the time the first contracts came up for signing in late 1985 the Nanhai prospects brightened considerably owing both to agreements on development of two previous discoveries and to a couple of new, promising finds.

After years of indecision Total China and the Nanhai Western Oil Company finally agreed on trial production from Total's 1981 Weizhou 10-3-3 discovery. The flows of 445 m³ of light crude oil and 51,540 m³ of natural gas a day were recorded in fall 1985, and the production facilities are designed for a maximum flow of 4,100 tons a day, with oil going from an uninhabited platform controlling six wells to a single-point mooring tower connected by a flexible hawser to a 175,000-DWT converted tanker which can be rapidly disconnected before any oncoming typhoon. The trial phase was scheduled to last at least two years during which time the partners hope to recover exploration costs.

Soon after Total's deal came the news of an even bigger arrangement as ARCO, together with Santa Fe International, signed a $500 million contract with CNOOC to develop the Yinggehai gas field discovered in 1983. Production is expected to start in mid-1989 with daily flows up to 8.7 million m^3 by 1992 from a single production and drilling platform. A subsea pipeline will take the gas to Sanya at the southern coast of Hainan, and from there an 80-cm line will distribute it along the Guangdong coast to Guangzhou and Hong Kong to be used in ammonia production, electricity generation, and urban cooking.

Even more encouraging than progress toward commercialization of these earlier discoveries were confirmations of two new substantial finds in October 1985. Phillips has the largest find—its Xijiang 24-3-2 well in the Zhujiang Basin flowed 2,000 tons of oil a day from four petroliferous strata below 1,900 m—while in a neighboring block the Agip-Chevron-Texaco consortium struck oil (at 1,840 tons/day) and gas (265,000 m^3/day) from five strata. The size of the discoveries and their proximity to Hong Kong were of inestimable help for future contract bidding and exploration activity.

Figure 4.3 shows the Nanhai situation at the end of 1985. Most of the 1980 seismic survey contract area has been opened for exploration, but many blocks from the first-round bidding remained available two years after the offering. Confirmed discoveries amounted to oil flows of 6,400 tons a day (about 2.3 million tons a year) and daily gas production of about 9 million m^3 (some 3.3 billion m^3 annually). No big finds were made in 1986. Mildly encouraging would be perhaps the best characterization. Chinese came to realize that the D-day analogy does not fit and have, quite realistically, turned to a meaningful comparison with the North Sea where the British drilled 205 exploratory wells over an area of 240,000 km^2, or one well for every 1,200 km^2.

In contrast, about seventy wells were drilled by the end of 1985 in the Nanhai, one well roughly for every 5,000 km^2. In the Zhujiang Mouth Basin, where five hydrocarbon-bearing structures were discovered by the end of 1985, thirty-four exploratory wells were drilled between 1983 and 1985 over an area of 150,000 km^2, one well for every 4,400 km^2. This clearly indicates that future discoveries are highly prob-

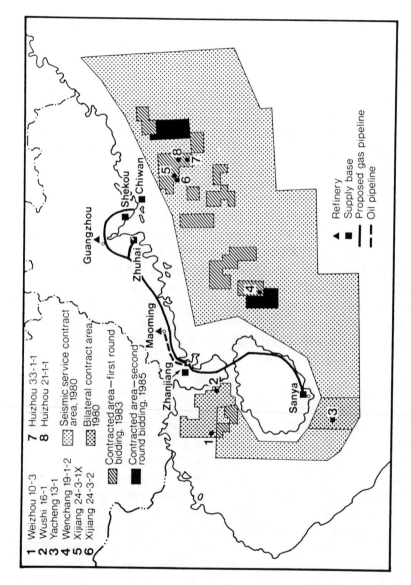

Figure 4.3: Oil and gas exploration in the South China Sea at the end of 1985.

able—although the Chinese interpret the comparison much more optimistically ("China is teeming with offshore oil resources").

But such comparisons can be done for illustrative purposes only. As already noted (section 2.2.2), trusting basin analogies, even after a close stratigraphic evaluation, is a perilous choice. Many promising-looking structures may be in the area but, as BP found off the shore of China after eleven dry wells, none may be petroliferous—or the reserves may be indeed abundant but distributed in scores of disjointed small reservoirs, and development of many marginal oilfields (with total reserves of 10–30 million barrels or about 1.5–4 million tons) is a very different proposition from tapping a few giant structures.

Even the largest Nanhai finds have been smallish compared to the North Sea giants. Weizhou oilfield produced just 160,000 tons in 1986 (0.12 percent of China's total). Total's trial 1985 flow, even if sustained undiminished for thirty years, would yield about 330 million barrels (about 45 million tons) of crude oil while the recoverable reserves in the largest North Sea fields (Statfjord, Brent, Forties) are between 1.8 and 2.6 billion barrels (250–360 million tons). Clearly, if the future Nanhai finds are numerous but confined to smaller, complex reservoirs, development of the basin's hydrocarbons will be a slower-moving process.

There are other important considerations complicating development of the Nanhai's hydrocarbons. First, the South China Sea oil play started unfolding as the global oil market easily reposed on huge production reserves with soft crude oil prices and few signs that economic recovery in the West will push oil demand soon again to its pre-1981 levels. Simply, Chinese are trying to enter the big league when most paying spectators are leaving the bleachers—and when many managers are having second thoughts about enduring frustrations and costs of joint business with the Chinese with less daunting options waiting elsewhere.

After OPEC's loss of its grip on the global oil market and with abundant supply of crude oil depressing the prices below $(1986)15/barrel, who will be waiting for the Chinese crude? Besides, will it be crude? If the North Sea analogy holds there may be plenty of gas, or the finds may be mostly gas. As a Petroleum News commentator remarked in November 1983 "most explorers would prefer that the word not be breathed in polite company."

The reasons are obvious: to repay their expenses foreign companies must export their share of discovered resources—but who wants new huge LNG deliveries and is ready to pay in dollars? Naturally, energy-short Chinese could use all the gas discovered offshore—but there is no infrastructure to deliver the fuel and, even more fundamentally, they are not going to pay hard currency to foreign companies for domestic use as this would defeat the fundamental intent of joint ventures. ARCO's sizable natural gas discovery may be just the beginning of difficult decisions.

Although the development contract is now in place and the Yinggehai gas should flow onshore by 1989, crucial questions remain unanswered: how will the Chinese pay ARCO for the gas (the price, somewhat below the world level, is to be pegged to the price of crude oil)? How will they finance the huge pipeline to bring the gas to onshore markets? What will these markets be: energy-deficient Guangdong, which cannot afford to pay in dollars, or Hong Kong, which can but whose financers look at 1997 and prefer to wait before any long-term commitment? How enticing is the prospect of selling urea made in Guangdong on the well-stocked world fertilizer market?

A host of local difficulties will combine to slow down the development: overlapping, arcane webs of administrative and managerial responsibilities which the Chinese have erected in the area during the past few years; inadequate supply bases—yet continuous Chinese insistence that Hong Kong not play a really major role in supporting the increasing exploration activities in the region; and exasperating complications during the actual joint work where Chinese insist on having too many of their obviously inexperienced and unqualified people.

Coulter's (1984) two papers survey these endless frustrations: little or no influence over which Chinese personnel work where; the impossibility of firing useless workers; poor motivation inherent in a system of lifetime job assignments and rigid wage structures; inability of field managers to take decisions in a system of faceless collective responsibility; and so forth. Many forward-looking Chinese are aware of these restrictive webs. In an August 1984 interview the head of China Nanhai Oil Joint Services Corporation acknowledged, when asked about problems with communication and transport complicating the development of the Nanhai oil, that "there are too many restrictions. There are also people still around with leftist thinking" (Wong 1984). Nobody is able to say how far and how fast these obstacles will recede.

There will be more fluctuations regarding the prospects of the Nanhai oil but it is beyond any doubt that commercial hydrocarbons will flow out of the sea and that it will become an important oil and gas extraction base. But in the mid-1980s it would be preferrable to expect moderate contributions and relatively slow development rather than to engage in yet another round of wishful thinking that first saw China as a new Saudi Arabia a decade ago. If everything goes well, offshore hydrocarbons should be of essential help for China's modernization effort during the next two decades, but they will not be a rapid, magic, all-embracing solution to the country's energy shortages. If things get sticky, for one of many reasons, the vaunted last major offshore play left in Asia may turn out to be a costly flop: by 1995 we will know the outcome.

Compared to the Nanhai, activities in the Bohai appear unexciting. Chinese started the drilling in the bay's shallow waters from small jack-ups in the early 1970s and during the decade discovered three oilfields, Haisi, Chengbei, and Shijiutuo. Japanese have been the only important foreign participants in further exploration and development (French Elf abandoned its concession after drilling just one well), starting with the 1980 contract according to which they bore all the exploration expenses, shared development costs 49/51 percent with China, and were entitled to 42.5 percent of produced oil for fifteen years.

After five years of wildcatting and development the Bohai Gulf started to produce on 1 October 1985 from the Chengbei field, but the costs proved to be much more expensive than envisaged and finds were considerably smaller than expected. Out of twenty-seven wells drilled between 1980 and 1985 at a cost of more than $400 million, seven exploratory wells produced a total of just 4,800 tons/day and the estimates of possible future total extraction fell from the original 55,000 tons/day to a mere 9,700–11,000 tons/day.

Original oil-in-place in the bay is estimated to total about 170 million tons of which some 37 million should be recoverable, and Japan-China Oil Development Corporation plans to get this oil out over a period of about twenty-six years. Clearly, Bohai has not been a failure—but it has not been a great success either: production of less than 1.5 million tons a year for quarter of a century ranks it no higher than below China's sixth largest onshore field and puts it into a very minor category worldwide.

In the coming years there will be more to follow than the still open fate of the Nanhai and orderly, unexciting development of the Bohai: foreign oil companies are moving onshore. This possibility has been rumored for a long time but even after the Chinese opened up the offshore they let in only small groups of foreign experts on specific contracts to help with some onshore problems. Gradually, the foreign technical participation increased, and during 1984 more than twenty foreign seismic, logging, and drilling teams were working in China's onshore fields. Finally, on 10 September 1984 *Renmin ribao* published a report on hearings into the performance of the Ministry of Petroleum Industry stating that "We have to bring in foreign capital, advanced technology, advanced equipment, and advanced management skill and cooperate with foreign companies in exploiting both offshore and onshore oilfields."

In April 1985 the Chinese made the decision official: ten provinces—coastal Jiangsu, Zhejiang, Fujian, and Guangdong and inland Guangxi, Yunnan, Guizhou, Hunan, Jiangxi, and Anhui—covering 1.83 million km² and containing 136 sedimentary basins larger than 200 km² (and 9 over 10,000 km²) were opened for foreign exploration and development. The first contract was signed on 28 May 1985 with four Australian companies to explore an area of about 2,500 km² in the Fushan Depression on the northern shore of Hainan Island just across the strait from Leizhou Peninsula.

By the end of 1986, fifty-two oil companies from thirteen countries made inquiries, and numerous preliminary talks, field visits, and appraisals have taken place, but no new contracts were signed. Onshore contracts are to be based on bilateral negotiations rather than on the bidding competition used offshore in order to speed up the exploration. Still, most of the problems impeding development of offshore resources will also apply in onshore endeavors.

In closing this section I will offer no stunning predictions. Extreme views have not been rare where China's oil is concerned: from widespread belief of poor hydrocarbon endowment to visions of Oriental Saudi Arabia to predictions of rising crude oil imports (the World Bank in its 1982 report predicted that between 1985 and 1990 Chinese oil imports will average at least 14 million tons a year). The realities do not correspond to these prejudiced portions. China appears to be neither so oil-poor nor, especially when its enormous needs are considered, so oil-rich, and later in this decade it is not going to become either a big exporter or a steadily larger importer.

How successful the Nanhai exploration and other offshore and onshore searches will eventually be nobody can tell. The North Sea has made it, slowly but impressively, into the big league—while the Baltimore Canyon, whose stratigraphy looked so much like the eastern coast of the Arabian Peninsula, yielded nothing but a succession of very expensive dry wells. Waiting and watching will have to continue for a long time, but by the mid-1990s it should be possible to say with confidence which way the country's long-term oil fortunes will tilt: a true superpower in the class of the United States (if not of the USSR or Saudi Arabia before its post-1982 production slump), a durable major producer (with extraction at least double the current level supportable for decades), or a minor player, at, or even below, the recent flows.

As critical as the expansion of fossil fuel production will be, Chinese modernization cannot succeed without following the industrial countries in consuming an increasing part of energy in the most convenient and the most flexible form: electricity generation must expand at a faster rate than extraction of coals and hydrocarbons.

4.2.4 Expanding electricity generation

If doubling of coal production in eighteen years presents an extraordinary challenge to China's economy, the official goal of quadrupling electricity generation during the same period appears even more taxing—and, again, Chinese profess great confidence in meeting it. Former Minister of Water Resources and Electric Power Qian Zhengying repeated on numerous occasions that annual generation of 1.2 PWh by installed capacity of 240–260 GW by the year 2000 is entirely possible as China had quadrupled its power output and installed capacity once before, and within a shorter period of time, during the fifteen years between 1966 and 1981.

China's past experience, as repeatedly pointed out, may not be an appropriate guide, but the only two nations that are producing in excess of 1.2 PWh—the United States and the USSR—had quadrupled their output from 300 TWh in eighteen years (the United States between 1946 and 1964, the USSR between 1960 and 1978). Yet this comparison both strengthens and weakens the Chinese case: while it clearly shows that it can be done, it is also a reminder of how much stronger economically and more advanced technologically were the two countries during the years they were producing 300 TWh compared to today's China. Also, as any late-starter, China now has access to more efficient advanced technology whose availability makes the task easier—but acquiring these expensive items may be possible only on a limited scale.

In any case, Chinese strategy rests on two fundamental approaches:

unprecedented concentration on the building of large hydroelectric stations, mainly in the basins of the Chang Jiang and the Hongshui He, and contruction of numerous mine-mouth thermal stations in all major coal-mining areas. Nuclear generation is to play a secondary, but not unimportant, role with several stations built in those parts of the country that lack both hydro potential and major coal resources.

According to Jiang Shengjie (1984), by the year 2000 fossil-fueled generation should increase to 900 TWh (from 242 TWh in 1980) while hydrogeneration should rise to just over 200 TWh (from 58 TWh in 1980), and the remainder of about 100 TWh is to be filled by nuclear generation. Each of these expansions is extremely ambitious, and none has a high chance of being fully realized. The challenge is in both the quantity and the quality of the programs: hundreds of new stations that have to be designed and built must have an average size much larger than those put in place before 1980.

For example, the average size of seventy-eight large and medium hydro stations built before 1981 was only about 160 MW whereas the mean size of thirty future projects for which design and feasibility studies were completed is 1,000 MW (Lu 1984), and a score of these stations will rank with the world's largest hydro installations and would include the single largest generating plant ever built. This, together with the aggregate size and rapidity of the construction effort—about 60 GW in two decades—makes China's hydrogeneration program the greatest engineering undertaking of its kind. In comparison, even such legendary feats as the Tennessee Valley Authority (less than 5 GW in three decades) or the Soviet development of large Siberian rivers (about 20 GW in twenty-five years) appear modest.

Consequently, it may be appropriate to put the hydrogeneration plans at the head of this review. Thermal generation will have to grow even more to provide the bulk of the needed expansion, but it will carry no similarly exciting association of a globally unprecedented task, of capturing the power of many of the best remaining hydro sites on this planet in a country with the world's largest capacity. These grand opportunities require a systematic partitioning in order to describe the principal features of the expansion now underway, and I will follow a Chinese division of the country's hydrogenerating potential into ten major bases unfolding clockwise from the upper Chang Jiang (fig. 4.4). Detailed, collectively written summaries in the August 1982 issue of *Shuili fadian* (Water power generation) and papers by Pan and Zheng (1982), Tao and Zhang (1982), and Zhang Guangdou (1983) are the

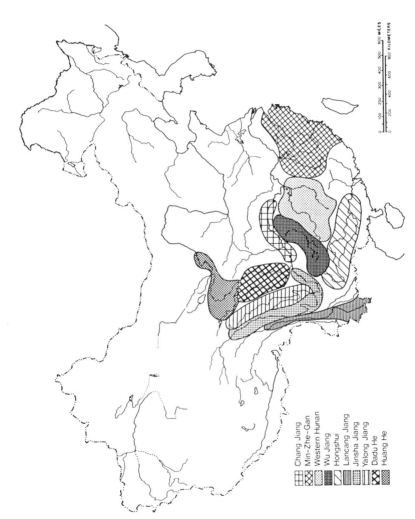

Chang Jiang
Min-Zhe-Gan
Western Hunan
Wu Jiang
Hongshui
Lancang Jiang
Jinsha Jiang
Yalong Jiang
Dadu He
Huang He

Figure 4.4: China's major hydrogeneration bases.

main sources for the following descriptions.

The upper Chang Jiang, a 1,030-km stretch between Yibin in Sichuan and Yichang in Hubei, drains about one million km² and provides opportunities for about 20 GW capable of producing just over 100 TWh a year. So far the only large station in the basin, the first one to dam the Chang Jiang, is Gezhouba (for details see section 3.2.3). Two projects in Sichuan, Zhuyangxi (1.9 GW) and Shipeng (2.13 GW), would dam the river upstream from Chongqing, but it is the prospective fourth dam on the Chang Jiang that is attracting most of the attention.

With 13 GW—and a possibility of further expansion—Sanxia would be the world's largest hydrostation. The project has been under consideration for decades, starting with Guomindang–U.S. Department of Interior appraisals in the 1930s and 1940s, but the enormous cost and unprecedented engineering challenge made it of only theoretical interest. A lesser version of the project was planned with a 130-m-high dam and 10 GW of generating capacity, and a 200-m dam would allow for storage of 73 billion m³, capacity of 25 GW, and annual generation of 100 TWh. Only if Zaire's huge Inga scheme were realized would it surpass the Sanxia capacity.

Set in the famed narrow gorges in western Hubei and eastern Sichuan, the reservoir would also eliminate the long, hazardous, constrained stretch of river shipping, and it would enable 10,000-ton vessels to go all the way to Chongqing. However, the massive capital costs, complications, and risks posed by extensive flooding of farmland and settlements, population relocation, environmental degradation, and countless unforeseen challenges that inevitably accompany execution of such a gargantuan project have acted as powerful brakes on Sanxia's development.

But since Deng Xiaoping's call for swift modernization the project has been persistently moving toward execution as the Chinese hydro engineers have been increasingly preoccupied with researching the options, outlining the alternatives, and getting American consultations. To the powerful faction of the central planners pushing maximum commitment to hydroenergy, Sanxia has become the ultimate goal, a must-do test, a point of honor. In late 1984 feasibility studies were completed for a medium version of Sanxia with a 175-m-high dam at Sandouping, 40 km upstream from Yichang, and total installed capacity of 13 GW (Ji 1984), about 3 percent larger than Itaipu on the Parana between Brazil and Paraguay, currently the world's largest hydrostation.

I will return to Sanxia in the closing chapter of this book when discussing the environmental burdens of energy expansion. But even to an uninitiated observer it must be clear that projects of this magnitude and impact should be approached cautiously rather than treating them as unavoidable stepping stones to modernization—especially when China abounds in excellent sites suitable for building projects that are also very large but much more manageable than Sanxia. As the continuation of the hydropower base review will show, such opportunities can be found in every part of the country except for the North and Northeast.

Min-Zhe-Gan base in the East has only 3.5 percent of China's exploitable hydro potential and already contains the 660-MW Xin'anjiang, 300-MW Fuchian Jiang, and 259-MW Gutian cascade on the Min Jiang. Under construction are Shaxikou (300 MW on the Sha Xi), Jinshuitan (200 MW in the Ou Jiang), and Wan'an (500 MW on the Gang Jiang) as well as the largest site, Shuikou on the Min Jiang, with 1.4 GW. Four river systems in western Hunan and eastern Guizhou have a combined potential about equal to the eastern grouping. The largest generating stations are Zhexi (447.5 MW) and Fangtan (400 MW), and Dongjiang, now under construction, is with 500 MW the second largest of all potential sites. Wuqiangxi on the lower Yuan Jiang with 1–1.75 GW would be the largest, controlling 93 percent of the basin's outflow.

Wu Jiang is major right-bank tributary of the Chang Jiang, and its basin could accommodate about 8.3 GW of installed capacity. Proximity to Chongqing and Guiyang means that extensive development will come early in spite of hydrogeological problems arising from the karst environment in most of the basin. Wujiangdu with 630 MW is the largest completed project, to be dwarfed by the Fengshui (1.2 GW) and Goupitan (2 GW) projects, which are now in design stage.

Hongshui may be fifth on the list of China's large hydrogeneration bases but it is undoubtedly first in terms of recent attention (Weng 1982; Zhou 1985b). In April 1985 a decision was made to accelerate the ambitious construction program in order to put six of the eleven planned stations into operation by the year 2000 (fig. 4.5). The whole program would bring 11.5 GW generating 62.78 MWh a year. The only partially completed projects in 1985 were the first phases of Etan (60 MW out of the eventual 500 MW) and Dahua (300 out of 400 MW) which began generating, respectively, in 1981 and 1983. Construction

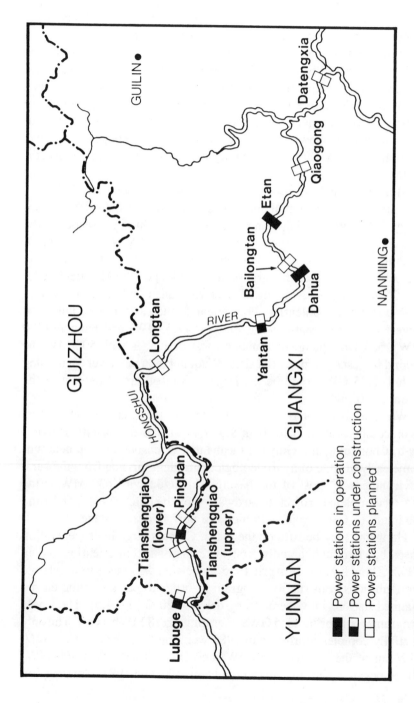

Figure 4.5: Hydrogeneration projects on the Hongshui.

on three other stations started recently: Tianshengqiao's first phase (880 MW) will be completed before Lubuge (600 MW) and the giant Yantan (eventually 1.4 GW).

Lancang Jiang's potential is much larger than Hongshui's and second only to Jinsha Jiang: preliminary appraisals show sites in its basin for 144 hydro stations totaling nearly 25 GW, but their development will be relatively slow owing both to their remoteness and to extremely rugged terrain. The only project underway is Manwan (1.5 GW), which is relatively close to Kunming and whose first generator would start up in 1991. Xiaowan with 4 GW should follow in the 1990s.

Jinsha Jiang's development will be even slower. The potential is unsurpassed with 58.91 GW of developable power above Yibin in Sichuan, but even the smallest of the eight sites under consideration, Banbianjia, has 3 GW, their average is 6.4 GW, and the largest one, Xiluodu, can accommodate 11.4 GW, altogether a clearly unequaled cascade in global comparison. Sichuan would be, obviously, the closest market, but the smaller, though still fairly large, Yalong and Dadu sites are closer to the Red Basin and easier to develop.

Jinsha Jiang's largest tributary, the Yalong Jiang, has 8 percent of China's developable hydro potential (about 25 GW or 152 TWh), but only parts of its southern section, close to the industrial areas of Dukou and Xichang and 300 km (straight-line distance) from Chengdu, will be developed in the foreseeable future. Preliminary plans are for eleven cascades exploiting a total drop of 1.9 km and generating eventually 113 TWh. The largest sites would be Ertan, Jinping I and II (each 3 GW), Yangtanggou and Lianghekou (both 2 GW), Menggushan (1.6 GW), Guandi (1.4 GW), and Dakong (1 GW).

Plans for the Dadu He, the largest tributary of the Ming Jiang, envisage seventeen cascades along 600 km between Shuangjiangkou and Tongjiezi, the largest ones being Jijishaba (2.2 GW), Dagangshan (1.62 GW), Dusong and Houxiyan (both 1.4 GW), and Changshaba (1.24 GW). The first stage of Gongzui (750 MW) is already in operation (the original design was for an ultimate capacity of 2.1 GW) and the 600-MW Tongjiezu is under construction. Proximity to the heavily populated industrial and farming areas of central Sichuan (160–240 km to Chengdu, 285–500 km to Chongqing) will obviously spur the development; moreover, except for a 90-km section, the whole river stretch is already accessible by roads.

The upper course of the Huang He already has four large stations in operation: Liujiaxia (1,225 MW), China's first project exceeding one

GW; Yanguoxia (352 MW) and Bapanxia (180 MW), which are located within a 50-km stretch in the river's bend in Gansu; Qingtongxia (272 MW), which dams the river in Ningxia, and Longyangxia (1,280 MW), which installed its first (of four) 320 MW generator in 1985. The total capacity of these stations, 3.309 GW, would be dwarfed by the group of six additional stations now in the planning and surveying stages.

Laxiwa, with a dam over 200 m, would be by far the largest with more than 3 GW of installed capacity and annual generation of 9.4 TWh. Lijiaxia's corresponding figures would be 1.6 GW and 5.8 TWh, Gongboxia's 1 GW and 4.1 TWh, and Daxia, just northeast of Lanzhou, would add 300 MW. Heishanxia (also called Daliushu) in Ningxia is planned for 1.2–1.4 GW with generation of 4.7–6.6 TWh (Chen 1984). The advantages of developing the upper Huang He cascade are obvious. First, the sites are relatively close to the large population and industrial concentrations of southern Shaanxi, Shanxi, Hebei, Beijing, and Tianjin. This proximity will enable the joining of the northwestern and northern grids, and it will make it possible to use the cascade for coverage of peak loads, to take advantage of the time difference in peak demand periods, and to back up Shanxi's thermal generation base in accidents and emergencies or during high winter needs.

The environmental advantages of the sites are also considerable. Deep gorge locations mean minimum land losses owing to flooding; for example, the 3-GW Laxiwa would flood less than 15 ha of arable land and require relocation of just 100 people. In contrast to the Huang He's middle course where the river cuts through the loess plateau, silting upstream of Ningxia is relatively small: a m^3 of water at Longyangxia averages only 1.1 kg of silt, at Heishanxia about 5.5 kg, compared to at least 50 kg in the southward section between Shaanxi and Shanxi. On the other hand, there are disadvantages of high altitude (above 2.5 km), recurrent severe duststorms from Nei Monggol, and poor transportation access.

All future projects larger than 2,000 MW that are currently in preliminary appraisal or design stage and may be started before the year 2000 are listed in table 4.5 and mapped in figure 4.6. Ten GW in projects under construction as of 1985 will certainly be on line before the year 2000, but even if all 181 projects now in planning and design stages were started and completed (a clearly theoretical if) before the end of the century, the aggregate addition of just over 80 GW would still cover less than half of the planned minimum increment of 180 GW. Consequently, no less than 120 GW would have

Table 4.5

China's largest hydrostations in planning stages

Project	River	Capacity (GW)
1 Sanxia	Chang Jiang	13.0
2 Xiluodu	Jinsha Jiang	11.4
3 Baihetan	Jinsha Jiang	10.1
4 Longtiaoxia	Jinsha Jiang	6.0
5 Xiangjiaba	Jinsha Jiang	5.7
6 Wudongde	Jinsha Jiang	5.6
7 Pichang	Jinsha Jiang	5.5
8 Hongmenkou	Jinsha Jiang	4.0
9 Xiaowan	Lancang Jiang	4.0
10 Longtan	Hongshui	4.0
11 Banbianjia	Jinsha Jiang	3.0
12 Jinping I	Yalong Jiang	3.0
13 Jinping II	Yalong Jiang	3.0
14 Etan	Yalong Jiang	3.0
15 Laxiwa	Huang He	3.0
16 Nuozhadu	Lancang Jiang	2.6
17 Jijiaheba	Dadu He	2.2
18 Shipeng	Chang Jiang	2.1
19 Goupitan	Wu Jiang	2.0
20 Lianghekou	Yalong Jiang	2.0
21 Yangfanggou	Yalong Jiang	2.0

Source: compiled by the author from various Chinese publications.

Note: For location of the stations see figure 4.7.

to come from thermal generation.

Here, in view of China's large coal resources, the choice is obvious: concentrate on increasingly larger mine-mouth stations. As already noted in section 3.2.3, such power plants are now being built at all larger coalfields. But, as also noted, the recent increments of new thermal capacities have been grossly inadequate, and even if the goal of 240 GW in the year 2000 were scaled down to 200 GW, the Chinese still would at least have to double their current rate of additions. Given the country's distribution of rich, economically extractable coal reserves it is not surprising that ever since the beginning of bold modernization plans in the late 1970s Shanxi was chosen to become the country's future unrivaled power base (Jing 1984b, 1984c).

In 1983 the whole province had 2.7 GW of installed capacity gener-

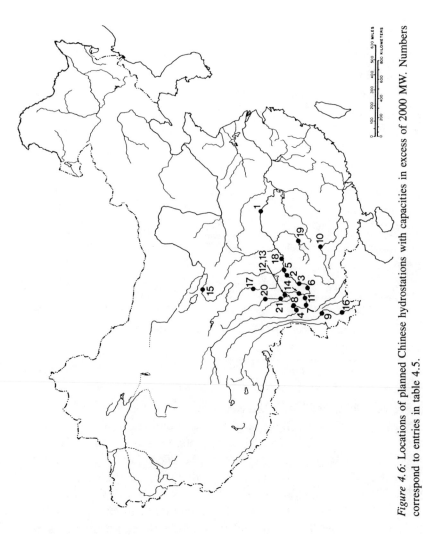

Figure 4.6: Locations of planned Chinese hydrostations with capacities in excess of 2000 MW. Numbers correspond to entries in table 4.5.

ating 15.1 TWh of electricity; these figures represented about 3.5 and 4.3 percent of respective nationwide totals. In contrast, the tentative plan for the expansion of coal-fueled generation envisages production of 85–100 TWh of electricity by the year 2000, or 7–8.5 percent of China's total. This huge jump would come from a series of giant mine-mouth plants dotting all regions of the province. The capacity of stations under construction and in the planning stage shown in figure 4.7 adds up to 24 GW, an equivalent of about 45 percent of China's total 1983 thermal capacity and as much as one-fifth of all thermal capacity growth between 1980 and 2000.

The largest of future Shanxi stations should be a greatly expanded Shentou plant near the Pingshuo surface mine. Its first stage will have 1.35 GW; the second stage, to begin before 1990, will add 2.2 GW; and the third one, after 1990, 2.4 GW for a total of 5.95 GW, a giant station by any standard. And in September 1984 *Shanxi ribao* revealed that the State Planning Commission was proposing another giant station about 100 km west of Shentou in the Baode-Hequ-Pianguan region on the eastern bank of the Huang He. The region has at least 36 billion tons of coal suitable for strip mining, and the Chinese are proposing a large-scale expansion of existing small mines to supply what would be at first a 1.2-GW and eventually a 6-GW station.

By putting between 25 and 30 GW of coal-fueled capacity into an area of about 150,000 km² the Chinese would equal the world's current highest electricity generation densities: at as much as 200 kW/km², Shanxi's rate by the year 2000 would be slightly higher than the early 1980s levels for East Germany and Czechoslovakia and not far from the world's highest thermal power concentrations in Pennsylvania and Ohio (around 280 kW/km²). Needless to say, the environmental implications of this concentration, above all in terms of water balances in a province already suffering through recurrent severe water deficits, would be severe. I will look at them in some detail in section 5.2.

But even if Shanxi were to absorb 30 GW of new thermal capacities before the year 2000—a most improbable assumption once one appreciates that basic infrastructures are still missing in some of the province's areas slated for development of giant projects—this achievement would still leave some 90 GW of thermal units to be located elsewhere around the country, mostly in the North and Northeast. Taking the five provinces in these two regions (Shanxi aside) together with neighboring coal-producing provinces of Henan, Shanghai, and Anhui and assuming that four-fifths of all new coal-fired capacities would be located in

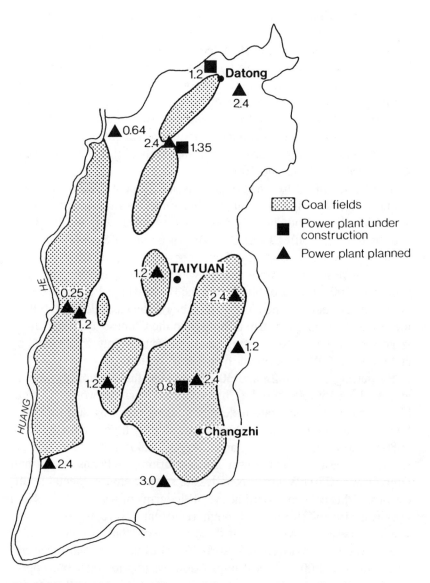

Figure 4.7: Planned locations of large coal-fired power stations in Shanxi.

this area requires additions averaging 9 GW per province before the year 2000, or about a tripling of the current capacities.

Once again, in view of the recent installment record, and with consideration of infrastructural and environmental implications, such an advance appears extremely taxing and its achievement, without substantially raised investments and imports, increasingly unlikely. These slipping prospects of achieving the quadrupling of electricity production through a combination of fossil-fueled and hydrostations must have been on the mind of Beijing decision makers when they opted for nuclear generation—yet its contribution cannot be decisive and other motives must have been no less important.

Even with all plans fulfilled, nuclear generation would deliver at best about 5 percent of electricity by the year 2000, but the proponents of the accelerated program stress that this relatively small contribution would be concentrated in those energy-short coastal regions that produce nearly half of China's national income, and hence it would be of critical importance. Energy-short Taiwan, with its (as of 1986) five operating nuclear stations, is an often-cited example to follow.

The tilt toward nuclear generation started in China in the late 1970s. While doubts about economic viability and worries about operation and waste disposal safety were gradually removing the nuclear industry from the position of a key future provider of electricity in North America and in most of Europe, the Chinese started to publish papers praising "outstanding" merits of fission reactors, dismissing any concerns about accidents by claiming that "safety is guaranteed beforehand in design."

The French nuclear industry, the most vigorous one in the Western world, was seen as the obvious first choice for acquiring fission generation technology. In talks with Framatome, started in late 1978, Chinese were looking at two 900-MW pressurized water reactors (Westinghouse design), but the negotiations were broken off after a few months, and it seemed that the attempt to import a nuclear power plant was just another short-lived ingredient of heady modernization plans of 1978.

But in early 1980 nuclear plans were reborn. The first congress of the Chinese Nuclear Society was held in February and its president, Wang Ganchang, revealed a new plan for China's own nuclear station somewhere in the densely populated coastal area and announced a goal of 10 GW of nuclear power by the year 2000. Officials of the Second Ministry of Machine Building (traditionally responsible for nuclear matters) started to promote fission technology as "the most realistic solution to the nation's energy problems.'' Soon afterward a Nuclear Energy Study Group organized by the State Scientific Commission proposed the building of six nuclear power stations, two each in Guangdong province, in the Jiangsu-Anhui area, and in Liaoning, the three regions with acute shortages of electricity and of local fossil fuels.

Then, during Valerie Giscard d'Estaing's visit to Beijing in October 1980, China agreed in principle to purchase two complete French reactors. Little was heard about any nuclear projects during 1981 when the American Nuclear Society staged a large exhibition in Beijing, and it was only in November 1982 that Xinhua announced the beginning of road and engineering network construction at the site of China's first nuclear power plant.

The station, designed by East China Reactor Design Institute in Shanghai, is located in Qinshan, 11 km southwest of Haiyan (Zhejiang) and, in the same direction, about 120 km from Shanghai, on the northern shore of Hangzhou Bay. This location has the obvious advantage of a coastal setting and proximity to China's largest load center, but—and it can hardly be otherwise in that densely populated part of the country—nearly four million people live within the 50-km radius of the station and over 330,000 people are in settlements within 20 km (Lin, Yu, and Bao 1984).

With 300 MW the Qinshan plant will be a midget in the world comparison as standard generating units are now triple its size. Its heart is a small pressurized-water reactor (PWR), and comparisons in table 4.6 with Japanese Mihama-1 and Swiss Beznau-1 units show how closely the Chinese have followed the foreign patterns. Moreover, several key components, above all the pressure containment vessel and main circulating pumps, are imported. When it becomes operational in 1989 it will expand East China's grid capacity by less than 3 percent at an obviously exorbitant cost. But the decision to promote nuclear generation was not taken on the basis of unequivocal economic advantages: by the early 1980s the whole question of economic viability of nuclear stations had become, in spite of extensive construction and operating experience, highly controversial. While many observers claimed flatly that, at least in the United States where most of the world's reactors are operating, fission generation had failed to pass the market test, others maintained that clear, rational, long-term commitment, standardized design, on-time construction schedules, and, Chernobyl aside, excellent safety record—a combination best manifested by the vigorous French nuclear program—yield indisputable economic results.

Table 4.6

Comparison of Qinshan reactor with similar Japanese and Swiss PWRs

Reactor	Qinshan	Mihama-1	Beznau-1
Location	China	Japan	Switzerland
Thermal power (MWt)	1035	1031	1130
Electric power (MWe)			
Gross	322	340	364
Net	300	320	350
Net efficiency (percent)	31.05	32.0	32.0
Reactor core			
Diameter (m)	2.486	2.450	2.450
Height (m)	2.900	3.050	3.050
Fuel weight (t)	40.32	40.0	45.30
Fuel enrichment (percent)	2.44–3.48	2.27–3.4	2.4–3.0
Pressurized cooling			
Pressure (atm)	155	157	157
Inlet temperature (°C)	288.8	289	284
Outlet temperature (°C)	315.2	317	314
Steam generation			
Steam pressure (atm)	53.5	55	57
Steam temperature (°C)	276.9	270	272

Source: Pan and Zhao (1983).

Promoters of the Chinese nuclear route have said often enough that China's energy development will be patterned after the French example, but one must be highly skeptical about the chances of success for tight schedules in first-ever construction of large reactors in a country of proverbially tentacular bureaucracies where complaints about time and cost overruns for major capital construction projects have been filling the newspaper pages for decades.

In any case, published cost analyses show that in eastern and southern coastal regions PWRs could compete with coal-based generation only when their size rises to 1,000 MW: China's first domestically built plant with 300 MW will be patently uneconomical. According to comparisons prepared by Luo Anren (1983), a 1-GW nuclear station near Shanghai should produce electricity about 22 percent cheaper than the same size coal-fired station (table 4.7)—but Luo, unlike many other nuclear proponents, at least acknowledged that "China has never built a nuclear power plant over 1,000 MW and even design documents for these power plants are not available." Western lessons of extrapolating construction costs of nuclear generation with rising unit size offer plenty of warnings to distrust any such analyses as bases for optimized descision making.

Table 4.7

Comparison of electricity cost in coal-fired and nuclear plants in Shanghai area in the early 1980s (all values are in Rmb/kWh)

Costs	Coal-fired plants		Nuclear plants	
	300 MW	1,000 MW	300 MW	1,000MW
Cost of capital construction	0.734	0.734	1.794	1.223
Cost of fuel	2.924	2.881	3.205	1.661
Total cost excluding electri- city consumed by the plant	3.933	3.846	5.134	2.948
Operating and maintenance costs	0.437	0.427	0.700	0.402
Total cost of electricity	4.370	4.273	5.834	3.350

Source: Luo (1983).

How costly an imported station will be and how rapidly it will get on line will be seen before too long. The Framatome deal has, after years of tangled negotiations, finally entered the construction stage. The site occupies about 200 ha along the shore of Daya Bay in Shenzhen county, a free-trade zone adjacent to Hong Kong and about 100 km southeast of Guangzhou. Peng Xilu, designer of the Chinese nuclear submarine, was put in charge of the project that will be built by a newly set-up Guangdong Nuclear Power Investment Company and the Hong Kong Nuclear Investment Company.

Official announcement of the contract's signing in January 1985 quoted the total cost at $4 billion, and the Chinese plan to repay the necessarily large bank loans by selling about 70 percent of the plant's generation (the two 900-MW PWR will deliver 10 billion kW a year) to Hong Kong starting in 1991 when the first unit is to come on line. Watching Dayawan's progress and eventual performance will obvious-ly be one of the key yardsticks for assessing the future of other Chinese nuclear generating stations.

Puzzling questions must be asked right away. Why build the sta-tion—to relieve Guangdong's severe electricity shortage or to supply Hong Kong? The first reason is *the* rationale for China's planned nuclear projects, yet most of Dayawan's generation will go to Hong Kong. To earn hard currency? Hardly, as those earnings will be needed to repay the foreign-currency loans. Clearly, the most sensible explana-tion is that the Chinese want to use Dayawan for hands-on experience, for acquisition of design, construction, and managerial know-how for their subsequent, domestically built, plants. Walter Patterson (1984) put this all bluntly: "It is difficult to avoid the conclusion that Hong Kong is being used as a cover for an exercise in what can only be called technological piracy."

Both the estimated cost and planned completion of the plant appear dubious. In a 1984 interview Peng Shilu claimed that the actual cost may be 50 percent lower and that the first reactor will generate in just six years, both highly questionable assumptions. Anyway, even if Dayawan generates in 1991, by that time hydrostations on the Hongshui He should be able to cover the current electricity deficit in both Guangdong and Guangxi, making the economic justification of the imported nuclear station even more untenable.

The long-term nuclear energy program formulated in 1983 during a meeting of more than one hundred experts contains eight essential guidelines. First, the PWR will be the choice for the first-generation reactor; second, each planned unit should have installed capacity around 1 GW; and third, the nuclear program should rest both on accelerated introduction of foreign equipment and expertise and on the experience with the domestic prototype 300-MW station.

As for the long-term-capacity plans, about 10 GW should be in operation by the end of the century in energy-short coastal regions. Nuclear fuel for these stations should be supplied indigenously through expanded uranium exploration and application of ultracentrifugal processing. To conserve natural uranium, reprocessing of spent fuel should be seriously considered. Besides fission for generation, nuclear process and district heat application should also be developed in regions short of fossil fuel. Finally, permanent disposal technologies should be adopted at a later time.

Chinese are also planning expansively beyond electricity generation for reactors delivering district heating, providing process heat for industry, and assisting in recovery of the country's abundant heavy oil deposits. A prototype 5-MW low-temperature reactor for district heating is to be built by Beijing's Institute of Nuclear Energy Technology by 1988; it will have three low-pressure cooling loops, and its commercial variant, whose construction was originally planned to start in one of the large northeastern cities before the end of 1980s, should deliver 500 MW of thermal power.

China's first medium-temperature reactor for process steam cogeneration is planned for a petrochemical complex near Shanghai. A 2 × 540-MW plant would deliver a maximum of 125 MW of electricity and 770 tons of steam per hour. Lu (1984) claims that "preliminary benefit-cost analysis seems favorable under the assumption of international market oil price'' and that because ''conservation of petroleum products is highly desired, the high capital investment of small PWR . . . could be tolerated.'' These are, of course, the untested and vulnerable assumptions (oil price has already dropped appreciably!) one always finds whenever promoters of nuclear generation push their favorite schemes. A study of a high-temperature gas reactor (HTGR) for process heat to be used in heavy oil recovery is also underway, but chances of commercialization are even lower than in the case of the cogeneration plant.

But these developments are necessarily far away, and looking back at the fate of similar Western plans of the recent past one can easily conclude that most of them may never be realized as now envisaged. After all, the sequence is not yet clear even for the early 1990s. After completing Qinshan and Dayawan, two stations, each with $2 \times 1,000$ MW PWR, should be built in southern Jiangsu (yet more electricity for Shanghai) and in southern Liaoning, both with key components delivered by a major Western contractor (Framatome, KWU, Westinghouse, etc.), but no firm deals and locations were known by the end of 1986. In fact, there have been increasing signs of second thoughts among Chinese concerning the previously planned rate (10 GW by the year 2000) of nuclear capacity acquisition. The nuclear heat program still has not demonstrated basic economic feasibility, and further discoveries of offshore oil will easily bury any plans for HTGR as a heat source for recovery of heavy onshore crudes.

The latest chapter of China's quest for foreign nuclear technology— large-scale sales of American PWRs—has had many difficulties in getting underway, mainly owing to U.S. concerns about diversions of plutonium and possible proliferation resulting from Chinese exports. A governmental nuclear cooperation agreement, which permits the U.S. nuclear industry to participate in China's nuclear generation program, was finally signed in Washington on 23 July 1985, but any major commercial results of this concord will not be felt before the mid-1990s.

Of all the explicitly quantified modernization goals for the year 2000, quadrupling of electricity generation appears to be most desirable but at the same time most difficult to achieve. With one-third of the twenty-year dash toward modernity gone there is no doubt that the Chinese have been advancing too slowly to achieve that goal—and every year during which they fall behind makes it less probable that the aim can be eventually reached.

Whatever the actual output level in the year 2000, Chinese decision makers, engineers, and managers should watch the quality of the progress: as with all other branches of the country's energetics, somewhat lower output arising from efficient and reliable performance will be preferable to hasty, strained, unsustainable exertion coming closer to a planned target but perpetuating China's chronic industrial afflictions of waste and unreliability.

4.2.5 Providing energy for the countryside

China's modernization plans have a decidedly industrial and urban tilt so that even with coal and oil production doubled and electricity generation quadrupled energy supply in the country's villages would not be greatly improved without extensive efforts to secure a large part of everyday fuel use locally. Modernization would bring a much greater flow of machinery, farm chemicals, and assorted consumer goods—but it would not ease, except in periurban regions, the shortages of cooking and heating fuel, and most of the villages cannot hope to be hooked onto new interprovincial high voltage grids.

Deng Xiaoping's favorite goal of U.S.$1,000 per capita a year by the year 2000 has already been surpassed in Shanghai, China's largest city and its industrial stronghold, which will receive during the next two decades vastly greater supplies of coal, hydro, and nuclear-generated electricity, larger shipments of coal, and, as the Chinese planners fervently hope, a good deal of still to be discovered offshore oil. In contrast, peasants in the mountains of Zhejiang, just a few hundred km away from the city, and tens of millions of rural households around the country where the wealth is today generated at less than one-fifth of Shanghai's level, will still have to rely largely on their own efforts to secure everyday energy needs.

The existing rural energy shortages are so severe and the future needs so enormous that no sensible strategy can abstain from any workable option if it is to succeed eventually. No source and form of energy is sufficiently large, well distributed (or distributable), and suitable to fill and fit the requirements—still so modest but soon to be inevitably higher—of the world's largest rural population, which now finds itself in the midst of rapid modernization. Given the country's extensive coal deposits and hydroenergy resources, both rural coal mining and small-scale electricity generation should keep expanding—

and getting larger in size to take advantage of the economies of scale.

Yet even the greatest practicable expansion of these two obvious sources could not eliminate China's deep rural energy shortages without continuing reliance on biomass fuels, which, in turn, is unthinkable without a major strategic change. Before detailing the genesis, developments, and prospects of such a change—namely, a nationwide policy promoting private fuelwood lots—I will deal with the most appealing, although not necessarily the easiest, way of supply expansion, with a substantial improvement of combustion efficiency.

As in any other poor country where most of the burned biomass is wasted in inefficient combustion, improved kitchen stoves could bring impressive aggregate savings. Universal diffusion of better stoves could cut the current biomass consumption easily by at least 25–30 percent and possibly by up to 35–45 percent; 50 percent savings repeatedly mentioned in Chinese writings are undoubtedly too optimistic as a nationwide average in everyday operations. But even a 30 percent cut would release enough straw to feed at least 25 million head of cattle, and the resulting manure would significantly enlarge the waste-recycling potential by conserving several hundred thousand tons of macronutrients. More efficient stoves would also moderate the rates of deforestation and, later, reduce the area of fuelwood plots needed to provide continuous firewood supply.

Serious Chinese interest in improved stoves dates only to 1979 when a series of tests was done in Shunyi county on the outskirts of the capital to establish the typical combustion efficiencies of various traditional stoves used in northern villages. Predictably, stoves burning crop residues (cornstalks) showed the worst performance with just 8–14 percent efficiency, normal firewood stoves averaged around 15 percent, and their better models with forced ventilation converted 19–21 percent of wood into useful heat. Consequently, assumptions of average nationwide biomass combustion efficiency would not be put higher than 10–12 percent.

Losses of nine-tenths of the fuel's heat content were ascribed to five major design inadequacies: combustion chambers were too large (causing unnecessary heat loss), as were the stoking inlets (allowing excessive cold air intake), no fire grates and, in some cases, no chimneys resulted in poor air circulation, and lack of insulation contributed to further heat loss. Elimination of these faults was the objective of two nationwide design competitions sponsored by the Ministry of Agriculture and judged in 1981 in Zhouhou in Henan (sixty-eight models entered) and in 1982 in Jiangxi.

Fourteen winners of the forty-two entries in the 1982 contest had thermal efficiencies between 32 and 44 percent for firewood stoves and between 26 and 31 percent for stoves burning crop stalks and straw. All of these superior stoves have proper fire grates and chimneys, appropriately sized combustion chambers and fuel inlets, and are designed to operate with 1.5–2.0 volumes of excess air for optimum burn-up; some of the stoves preheat the cold fresh air by leading it along the hot air outlets. Chinese, ever enamored of numerical labels, would like to see all of their improved stoves meeting the "three 10" challenge: boiling 10 jin (5 kg) of water by burning no more than 10 liang (about 400 g) of straw or wood in less than 10 minutes.

The Dancheng county (Henan province) single-pot design (fig. 4.8) meets the criteria by boiling 5 kg of water with 350 g of corn stalks in 9 minutes and consuming only 4 kg of fuelwood for preparation of three meals for a typical five-person family, while a three-pot design from Fengxian county (Jiangsu province), outwardly looking just like countless other traditional large Chinese stoves, can burn any available phytomass with about 40 percent savings (fig. 4.9). Costs of materials have been given as low as Rmb 10 for a small stove, but building a proper larger one would need Rmb 20–40, an amount to be recovered in a year by the saving of nearly a ton of crop residues. An ambitious plan of large-scale diffusion of improved stoves started in 1982 in ninety selected counties around China. By the end of 1983 some 7 million improved stoves were in use (including 3.9 million stoves in the ninety pilot counties), and the goal was put at 25 million by 1985.

Realistic expectations from everyday operation of improved stoves could be no higher than 40 percent savings in comparison with the traditional models: for 25 million units this would be equivalent to about 15 million tons of straw, or less than 7 percent of current consumption, but if all rural households had such stoves annual crop residue savings would reach about 100 million tons, sizable nutrient returns by any standard, and if recycled the effects on soil tilth and moisture retention would be even more beneficial.

However, to diffuse the improved stoves throughout the country and to sustain their performance requires more than just a few competitions and publication of impressive goals in the capital. Fortunately, the organizers seem to have recognized the need for promoting the whole conversion package. Without accessible supplies of quality materials,

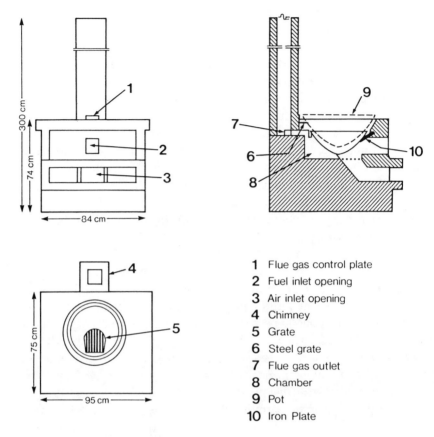

1   Flue gas control plate
2   Fuel inlet opening
3   Air inlet opening
4   Chimney
5   Grate
6   Steel grate
7   Flue gas outlet
8   Chamber
9   Pot
10 Iron Plate

Figure 4.8: Single-pot improved stove from Dancheng county, Henan.

experienced construction, and readily available repair services, the whole program may be short-lived and ineffective. As with so many appealing schemes the real proof of the improved stove superiority will come only after many years of routine use. The awareness is salutary, the initial attempts encouraging, the direction most desirable: for the judgment on the actual savings we will have to wait at least a decade.

But even with outstanding stoves everywhere, elimination of the current fuel shortages and the addition of at least 160–200 million villagers during the next twenty years will require great increases in biomass availability, and only extensive planting of firewood groves and forests can fill this need. Consequently, it is incredible that a regime that was conducting mass campaigns to spread household bio-gas generation kept on forbidding plantings of private fuelwood lots even in dry and extremely heavily eroded regions of the northwestern

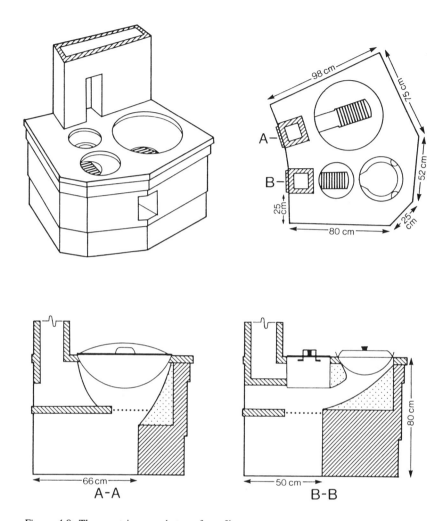

Figure 4.9: Three-pot improved stove from Jiangsu.

interior. The ideological rigidity saw in the ownership of a small wood-lot one of the "last vestiges of burgeois mentality" as it forced peasants to cut out in desperation dry sod or to burn animal dung. Unbelievably enough, reversal of this irrational policy came only in spring 1980, long after other discredited policies were discarded, when the State Council issued a directive about private tree planting. The critical point of the new regulations is that the household ownership of the lot should remain unchanged for decades.

Following this decision one province after another adopted specific regulations. For example, in Heilongjiang each household can get an ownership license for 0.2 ha of land once at least 80 percent of saplings on the lot have survived. As a result, the provincial authorities believed that nearly 700,000 ha of new woodlots would be producing within five years. Similar measures have been adopted in most other provinces, and by the beginning of 1983, 25 percent of China's peasant families were allotted an average of 0.2 ha of hilly or odd land for tree planting.

Given China's extensive area of barren slopeland and some optimistic yield assumptions it is possible to come up with very impressive appraisals of the woodlots' potential. According to repeated official claims there are nearly 85 million ha of hills and slopes suitable for afforestation which could yield, with just 5 dry tons/ha, some 425 million tons of wood a year (about 7.6 EJ), enough to satisfy basic energy requirements for 200 million Chinese households expected by the year 2000 as long as the wood is burned in improved stoves with at least 18 percent efficiency, certainly a practical possibility. This scenario, however, will not become a reality.

The ultimate Chinese goal is to set aside a firewood grove for three-quarters of 170 million rural households so that by the end of the century the area with newly planted trees would cover 27–33 million ha. The higher value would equal the total afforested in three decades of repeated communal mass-planting campaigns from which only about one-third of the trees have survived! In contrast, the private plantings could survive and be productive in just a few years owing to, in the words of a vice-chairman of the State Agricultural Commission, the "assiduous care" the families devote to their trees (Zhang Pinghua 1981).

Realistic assumptions must be made in estimating the eventual sustainable yields from these extensive plantings, and the grand total will be critically dependent above all on the regional distribution of private fuelwood plantations and on the choice of tree species. Available statistics show, not surprisingly, that the densely populated East and North have, respectively, only about 11 and 13 percent of all barren land suitable for fuelwood planting, while the Northeast has nearly 18, the Central South 19, and the Southwest almost 27 percent of the total (Huang 1982).

Naturally, the best growing conditions for various fast-maturing shrubs and trees are in the South—but there in many areas the warmer climate and greater availability of crop residues and slopeland grasses make the need for additional fuel less pressing than in the devegetated, cold North. Moreover, there is simply no suitable land available throughout extensive stretches of intensively cultivated coastal lowlands while numerous counties in the relatively sparsely populated interior cannot possibly use all the odd land available for tree planting.

Consequently, the simplest assumption that the provincial distribution of 25–30 million ha of fuelwood forests will more or less resemble the rural population pattern would be in considerable error. Similarly, the choice of planted species can make a substantial difference, especially in the South where the annual dry yields can range from just around 5 tons for some pines to more than 20 tons/ha for some acacias (*Acacia auriculiformis*) and rapidly growing leucaenas (*Leucaena leucocephala*) and casuarinas (*Casuarina equisetifolia*); in the North yields in excess of 7.5 tons/ha would be the exception no matter what kind of fuelwood species is grown (table 4.8).

I shall assume that by the end of the century only half, rather than three-quarters, of all rural families will have a private fuelwood lot. With the lots averaging 0.2 ha, these roughly 100 million families would tend 20 million ha of fast-growing trees and shrubs, and even when assuming, fairly conservatively, that the average annual phytomass yield will be just 5 dry tons per hectare these woodlots, once established (usually after four to six years), could produce each year 100 million tons of wood equivalent to about 1.8 EJ. As discussed earlier (section 3.1.1), the minimum daily rural requirement is now nearly 19 MJ of effective energy per family; consequently, at least 680 PJ of useful energy would be needed by those 100 million families owning firewood lots. With widespread adoption of improved stoves burning the wood with 25 percent efficiency, the useful output would amount to some 450 PJ or almost exactly two-thirds of the essential requirement.

If China's other forests were managed properly they could yield easily at least 400 kg of dry woody phytomass (tree tops, branches, bark, stumps) per hectare for household combustion (indeed, in many instances these firewood harvests can surpass 500 kg/ha) and add nearly 800 PJ of sustainable harvests. With, again, 25 percent combustion efficiency, some 200 PJ of effective energy would bring the total to about 650 PJ, or within less than 5 percent of the need. The best conclusion is that by the year 2000 a combination of extensive fuelwood plantings, proper forest management, and improved combustion efficiency could, with fairly conservative assumptions, provide all the essential household fuel needs for half of China's rural population— and do so in a sustainable way, without overcutting, illegal felling, and spreading deforestation and erosion. Clearly, the potential is impres-

Table 4.8

Fast growing trees and shrubs suitable for fuelwood planting in China

Region Species	Annual dry yield (t/ha)
Northeast	
Poplars (*Populus* sp.)	2–13
Willows (*Salix* sp.)	2–8
Birches (*Betula* sp.)	2–6
Northwest	
Narrow-leaved oleaster (*Elaeagnus* sp.)	6–9
Tamarisk (*Tamarix ramosissima*)	5–15
Saksaul (*Haloxylon ammondendron*)	5–7.5
North	
Acacias (*Acacia* sp.)	5–7.5
False indigo	5–7.5
Tamarisk (*Tamarix ramosissima*)	5–15
Poplars (*Populus* sp.)	2–8
Willows (*Salix* sp.)	2–8
South	
Acacias (*Acacia* sp.)	15–24
Eucalypts (*Eucalyptus* sp.)	15–22
Casuarina (*Casuarina equisetifolia*)	15–22
Leucaena (*Leucaena leucocephala*)	15–22
Mimosa (*Mimosa* sp.)	11–18
Tan oak (*Lithocarpus thalassica*)	20–24
Pines (*Pinus* sp.)	5–9

Sources: National Exhibition of Rural Energy (1982); Smil (1983).

sively large, but when realistically appraised it is not large enough to offer a complete solution.

The other half of China's peasantry (or, with more forgiving assumptions, only a third or a quarter) will have to turn to better exploitation of other local resources, but millions of villagers living on the large river and coastal plains, where the high population density and intensive farming leave little space for private household woodlots, can still benefit from an extensive agroforestry effort. Although Chinese have planted large numbers of trees along canals and roads and between fields (the official total is more than 12 billion since 1958), much more could still be done. For example, in eastern China's Jiangsu-Shandong-Henan plain farmland networked with trees is still only about two-fifths of the possible total (Hao 1981). There is also a large potential for multipurpose use of fruit and oil trees planted in backyards and on odd land: cultivation of Chinese dates, tea-oil and tung-oil trees, olives, apples, pears, persimmons, walnuts, chestnuts, and lichees has been neglected during the decades of the "grain-first" policy, but all of these are valuable tree crops whose pruning provides welcome fuelwood and whose cultivation is now again expanding in private ownership.

Eventual success of woodlot plantings will depend above all on the permanence of private ownership. Foresters worldwide have learned that if trees are to grow to maturity they must be cared for by people who own them, and the Chinese have finally recognized this necessity by allowing familial inheritance of the lots by giving titles for up to fifty years. A great deal of research on optimal selection of the best tree and shrub species, on introduction of new plants, and on proper woodlot management in different regions will also be essential, as will the establishment of numerous nurseries and provision of county-based and itinerant consulting services. The desirability of the success is obvious, not only to relieve the chronic severe rural energy shortage but, no less importantly, to aid in restoring environments capable of supporting intensive farm production.

An essential part of the restoration is, of course, gradual reduction and eventual cessation of direct crop residue burning. The only proper way in which some residues may be burned—most of them should be directly recycled in the fields—is indirectly, by generating biogas and hence conserving the macronutrients. But before appraising the future of China's biogas production I have to focus on the two more important sources that, together with woodfuel from private lots, will be decisive in determining the adequacy of rural energy supply: coal extraction in small mines and small-scale hydroelectricity generation.

Rural modernization requires more than just an indiscriminate increase of total energy consumption: in a country where about two-fifths of all peasants still have no electricity in their homes, multiple rise of rural electricity generation is imperative to banish the dark evenings and to enable widespread diffusion of numerous electrical appliances, ranging from fans to rice cookers. With a mere 11 percent of hydrogeneration potential exploitable by small stations currently producing electricity, opportunities for future construction of power plants with capacities ranging (to eliminate less economical very small units) from several hundred kW to about 10 MW remain exceedingly rich—and they should be pursued extensively and accompanied by improved transmission and distribution grids and by their gradual integration into larger, multicounty networks, a development that would greatly increase the load factors and reliability of supply and allow a faster achievement of electrification goals.

Another critical consideration is the avoidance of redundant construction of small hydrostations in the watersheds of medium and large projects. Flooding of small plants, accompanied by disputes about proper compensation, has been recently on the increase. Tu (1982) estimated that if the compensation payments and the financial aid given by the state to small stations are added together, the costs of flooding of thousands of small stations may eventually reach billions of Rmb.

Newly announced criteria for rural electrification stipulate that a county can be considered electrified when more than 90 percent of homes use electricity for low power tasks such as lighting, radios, and TVs, more than 50 percent of homes have electric fans, and more than 20 percent use seasonal excess electricity for cooking and heating water for at least half a year, and when power needs for food and feed processing (grain husking and milling, fodder grinding, oil pressing), irrigation, and small industrial manufacture are "basically satisfied" (Xiao Dianhua 1983). With current Chinese consumption and output levels these requirements would imply the need for about 100 kW per capita a year or some 100 W/capita installed in small hydrostations.

As the current annual rural electricity consumption (43.5 TWh in 1983) prorates to less than 60 kW per capita, complete rural electrification would need, with rural population up by 25 percent two decades from now, roughly 4.5 times larger generation—but not necessarily that much more installed capacity. Larger hydrostations and network integration could raise the load factor by at least 10–20 percent, and, of course, not all rural inhabitants need to be, or can be, supplied by hydroelectricity. Consequently, a 3.5–4-fold expansion of small hydrostations might do to achieve the goal of basic rural electrification, a challenging but not impossible task.

After reviewing the current "coal rush" in the Chinese countryside (section 4.2.2) it must be obvious that coal should go a long way toward easing the rural energy supplies, but I do not know of any estimate or formula that would enable one to apportion the future output among the productive and household uses, especially as a far from insignificant share of rural consumption comes also from state-run mines. Currently about two-fifths of all rural coal consumption goes to households and, in turn, a bit over one-fifth of all coal extraction reaches the countryside. If these shares would remain unchanged by the year 2000, with the 1.2-billion-ton target fulfilled, then about 70 million tons of standard coal would be available for household use—and just a 20 percent increase would raise it to 85 million tce.

Similar uncertainties concern the generation of biogas, although in this case even a large relative range makes a rather small absolute difference. Even a tenfold expansion of the 1983 level of methanogenic fermentation would add annually no more than 6 million tce to the aggregate rural household supply. Numerous scenarios of future rural energy availability can be constructed—and the Chinese have recently published their share of often excessively expansive forecasts—but I will offer just one estimate as an anchor for contemplating other more or less appealing alternatives. The scenario is a case of successful, extensive local fuel production (woodlots), conservation (improved stoves), and expansion of modern supply (local coal and hydroelectricity), a combination of realistically achievable results.

Complete elimination of crop residue burning by the end of the century is highly unlikely: if it were halved (to 25 percent of the harvest) it would provide, assuming total cereal output around 600 million tons, about 70 million tce. Successful diffusion of private woodlots to half of all rural households would bring in at least 60 million tce, and sustainable forest phytomass harvests will add another 30 million tce. Methanogenic fermentation could hardly contribute more than 5 million tce, and hydroelectricity from small stations and provincial networks could, at best, add up to an equivalent of 15 million tons of standard coal. As noted, a gradual increase (20 percent in seventeen years) of the current consumption shares would make available about 85 million tce from coal mines.

The grand total would then be some 265 million tce—fortuitously a sum nearly identical with the 1983 aggregate but one obtained without any deforestation and with doubled crop residue recycling! Moreover, when assuming that average combustion efficiencies would rise from the current weighted mean of 13 percent (10 percent crop residues, 15 percent wood, 17 percent coal) to 18 percent (overall 40 percent improvement), the effective energy in the year 2000 would be nearly 50 million tce compared to just 34 million tce in 1983.

In per capita terms even when assuming merely 1 percent annual population growth, the total would be just about 20 percent higher: roughly 1.5 vs. 1.25 GJ of effective energy. This would be, of course, just enough to satisfy the minimum cooking and heating requirements as defined today—while still relying heavily on crop residues. Complete elimination of crop residue combustion would demand an additional supply of some 70 million tons of standard coal for household combustion.

This fairly optimistic scenario offers no great promises. In terms of household energy use even a combination of successful vigorous innovations and supply expansions would not lift an average Chinese peasant much beyond the minimum subsistence level. In real terms 1.5 GJ of effective energy available per capita in the year 2000 would still equal no more than 800 g of standard coal or 1.5 kg of straw per day per capita, energy a typical North American suburbanite may spend in driving just 5 km to a nearby shopping center. But there would be a critical qualitative difference as the new total would be obtained without destructive devegetation of China's countryside and with considerably better agroecosystemic management.

If one wants to remain realistic it would be possible to be only a bit more optimistic, but a gloomier scenario may not be anymore unlikely than the just outlined successful case: a slower increase of crop residue availability owing to problems with further intensification of farming and to greater diffusion of short-stalked grain varieties; continuing stagnation of the biogas program; disappointing performance of private woodlots caused by improper choice of species and slackened management of policy reversals; insufficient diffusion and declining performance of new stoves; and, after an initial rush, a slower expansion of coal supply for domestic use.

These developments, coupled with faster population growth (for example, 1.4 rather than 1.0 percent would add another 65 million villagers between 1983 and 2000), would make the next two decades yet another generation of chronic fuel shortages and of even greater degradation of the already deteriorated environment—and leave Chinese villagers worse off than today, a difficult state to imagine. Much needed improvements are certainly achievable, but doubts remain. Only concerted efforts can succeed, and there is no room for complacent forecasts: of all the needed advances this one may be the most difficult to make—yet in simple human terms it has no more pressing counterpart.

5 THE OUTLOOK:
Appraising the Limitations

The future prosperity of the United States, Canada, Japan, and the richest countries of Western Europe may be contemplated without calling for any substantial energy consumption increases. The recent experience is encouraging: as the prices of traditionally cheap energy rose after 1973 these nations responded with a combination of conservation measures, technical advances, and structural shifts. They lowered energy intensities of their economic products to such an extent that a decade after the first OPEC jolt they were consuming the same amount of energy as in 1973—yet their combined gross economic product was 20 percent higher! Possibilities for further improvements are easily discernible. They may not come rapidly with falling energy prices, but it is not difficult to show that the rich Western industrialized nations could maintain their high standard of living and support modest economic growth for the remainder of this century without using any more energy than in 1985.

China's outlook is fundamentally different. Its per capita energy consumption is an order of magnitude below the rich Western levels (and only about a third of the global average), most of its modern infrastructures are yet to be put in place (China's railway network, for example, when measured in km/km², has the density of U.S. railroads in the early 1870s), and bold modernization plans are expected to usher in "basic" prosperity for more than 1.2 billion people just a generation from now. No matter how successful the Chinese are in reducing their wasteful conversion and lowering future energy intensities the imperative is clear: energy consumption will rise appreciably.

Although there can be no doubt about the necessity of the growth there is little certainty even about its approximate target. A close link between energy consumption and economic modernization cannot be doubted, but its nature cannot be forced into any simplistic formulations. Economists have relied too heavily, and most often unprofitably, on energy/economy elasticity coefficients (see section 4.2)—yet these are not preordained and immutable. They arise from particular energy use structure and efficiency, industrial orientation, climate, the nature of settlements, and life styles. Consequently, one can find countries with nearly identical GNP per capita and similar climates yet with significantly different energy use (e.g., Canada and Sweden, Czechoslovakia and Austria), or nations that consume about the same total amounts of energy yet differ greatly in economic output (China and Japan in the late 1970s are, of course, the best example).

In general it may be true that for industrializing nations energy/GNP elasticities are higher than for mature industrialized societies, but precise levels are not determined by any abstract formula or by a given stage of development but, as already stressed (section 4.2), by strategies adopted for the future economic growth. Not surprisingly, long-range energy forecasts published in China since 1978 reflect all the misunderstandings, simplifications, and biases commonly encountered in such exercises, and, as reviewed, the totals needed by the year 2000 range from just 1.2 to 2.7 billion tce.

All the forecasts above 1.6 billion tce by the year 2000 are useful merely as examples of incorrigible ignorance of economic and technical realities or as fine specimens of wishful thinking. This is the most fundamental limitation shared by all complex systems: their growth rates must moderate as their size increases. I will not engage in lengthy speculations about what will be China's most likely energy consumption level by the year 2000. What is important is to show the limitations of even excessively optimistic achievements. In 1985 China's annual primary energy consumption prorated to just 19 GJ per capita. Only if the total energy use were to reach 1.6 billion tce by the year 2000 and if the population did not surpass 1.2 billion would per capita consumption double to 38 GJ. Global plots of energy consumption versus life expectancy, infant mortality, and literacy (the three measures used to define the widely used Physical Quality of Life Index) show that increases above 35–40 GJ bring only relatively small improvements—and that annual consumption around 40 GJ may be seen as the level satisfying basic human needs. If one accepts this conclusion, by the year 2000

China may just fit into that category if everything works out extraordinarily well.

Yet as noted earlier, Chinese planners are now aiming realistically at annual consumption of 1.2 billion tce by the year 2000, and this aggregate, with 1.25 billion people, would result in only 28 GJ per capita, just short of 50 percent above the 1985 level. And a closer look at quality of life indicators reveals an indefensible weakness of literacy as one of the three determining measures. Substitution of a much more meaningful indicator, share of young adults enrolled in institutions of higher learning, uncovers China's specific weakness which will inexorably limit the country's quest for real modernization.

While most of the better-off industrializing countries send 15–20 percent of young adults to universities and colleges (Egypt and Mexico 15, South Korea 18) and India's figure is now close to 10 percent, the Chinese share in the early 1980s stood at a mere 1 percent. Even if China reaches the average basic needs level of 35–40 GJ per capita by the year 2000 will it be able to give a postsecondary education to 15–20 percent of its young people, as at least twenty industrializing countries are already doing today?

China's bold goals are impressive only when one considers the rapid planned growth of already huge aggregates. In per capita energy consumption and personal income the most likely outcomes have the country a generation from now reaching a level recently attained by nearly two score industrializing nations—although health indicators may be at a relatively higher and the educational ones at a considerably lower level. This comparison is helpful to appreciate better the enormity of China's modernization task and its fundamental limitations. Even when very successful the generation-long effort will put the country merely at the doorstep of true prosperity.

And mere continuation of post-1978 changes would not result in a successful outcome. If reforms and innovations introduced since 1978 are not just the beginnings of a process that must be both broadened and deepened, the expectation for the year 2000 will have to be lowered substantially.

5.1 Reforms and innovations

The task is extraordinary: a fundamental restructuring of a rigid economic system in order to quadruple the national product of the world's most populous nation in a single generation. Rural reforms, resulting in impressively rapid increases of productivity and food availability (Smil 1985), have been easier to introduce and to deepen than the restructuring of urban industrial activities, which should diffuse relatively independent enterprise management and local responsibility for profits and losses, change the country's irrational pricing, and loosen the market forces.

In energy industries the need for these reforms is especially acute. Poor product quality and high consumption of raw materials—in Zhao's (1985) words "the fatal weaknesses of our economy"—as well as backwardness in technology and even a greater lag in management are nearly ubiquitous characteristics of China's energy procurement. Their correction will require not only better management approaches but also huge investment in technical innovation, a necessity impossible without large-scale imports and technology transfer, a requirement difficult to finance in a country that, again in Zhao's words, "will suffer shortages of foreign exchange for a long time."

Consequently, in this section I will touch all of the principal reform and innovation concerns that will determine the success of China's modernization drive in energy industries: improvements of product quality and lowering of specific consumption, elimination of outdated processes and introduction of flexible management, reforms of irrational price structure, necessity of foreign inputs, and inadequacy of domestic financing. Separating all these points makes sense for purposes of systematic discussion, but in reality most of them are closely linked.

For example, a better quality of bituminous coal (cleaned, washed, uniformly crushed) would lower its specific consumption (per ton-km) in locomotives—but even so many old machines scrapped during modernization of transportation infrastructures will be replaced by more efficient diesel or electric locomotives, whose attractiveness may further increase after low coal prices are finally raised but whose large-scale diffusion may require major purchases abroad (as has been recently the case).

As repeatedly noted, Chinese preoccupation with quantitative achievements has resulted in a nearly universal neglect of quality, a disparity demonstrated by such diverse phenomena as voluminous shipments of raw coal, uncritical commitment to massive construction of small hydro stations, or production of inferior (but highly energy-intensive) nitrogenous fertilizers. Considering the continuing key importance of coal for China's economy, rapid and massive introduction of coal cleaning and preparation facilities would be the most important step toward raising the quality of China's primary energy output.

Yet the planned rate of introduction of new coal washing and sorting capacities means that at least half the coal from large mines still will not be cleaned and prepared by the end of the century, and the continuing prominence of small local pits, where installation of coal preparation equipment is hardly a viable economic option, means that by the year 2000 most of the Chinese coal will still be used in raw form. The economic and environmental burdens of this chronic quality lag will be staggering. Assuming the output of 1.2 billion tons a year, no less than 300–350 million tons of incombustible waste will be shipped from the mining regions, and combustion of this raw coal will add millions of tons of fly ash to the atmosphere as it is most unlikely that installation of air pollution controls would be rapid enough to reverse this trend.

Improvements in product quality are also imperative as far as the inputs into energy production and conversion are concerned. In Chinese publications one can find complaints about poor quality of just about any common equipment, from drills to turbogenerators, from trucks to refinery columns. Many gross failings are now being eliminated, but seemingly small inadequacies built permanently in the systems which will not be easily eradicated add up to considerable losses.

For example, improper hydraulic design, testing, and manufacturing have combined to produce maximum turbine efficiencies 1–7 percent lower than the Western standard. As a result, in the early 1980s China's large hydrogenerating stations produced each year almost 2 TWh of electricity less than they could have done with proper turbines, a loss equivalent to an annual production of a typical 500-MW hydrostation. Moreover, the low efficiency of hydraulic turbines worsens the flow conditions which increase cavitation damage and necessitate extensive repairs. Chinese turbines suffer about ten times more cavitation damage than Western units, and they have to be taken out of operation for a couple months of repairs after just 5,000–8,000 hours, or roughly one-half to two years (Shen and Guo 1982). Losses of designed output are obviously large, on the order of 6 to 10 percent nationwide, up to 40 percent for the worst afflicted stations.

And there are reports indicating that even the latest Chinese generating machinery has serious quality problems. On 18 April 1985 *China Daily* reported that cracks were found in the rotary blades of Dahua's first three generators, in one case after only 510 hours of operation. What quality price will be paid for the rush to fulfill the ambitious quantitative goals of quadrupling? Clearly, quality improvements will have to remain a constant preoccupation of Chinese energetics if its performance by the beginning of the next century is to resemble that of a fairly advanced industrial power rather than the current pattern of large but inferior outputs.

High-quality machinery inputs and excellent fuel and electricity outputs would make little difference if China's excessive energy intensities were not reduced substantially. Various examples of high specific energy consumption have been cited in the previous chapters, and they indicate well the huge potential for further efficiency gains. Lowering of energy intensities must start with energy industries themselves: coal consumption in coal mining, oil and natural gas waste in hydrocarbon extraction, and consumption of electricity by generating plants are all unnecessarily too high.

Naturally, better management can go a long way toward solving the kindred problems of poor product quality and high energy intensity. After more than three decades of rigid central planning and incentive-less command work, opportunities for flexible, incentive-driven, market-responsive management are ubiquitous. Some simple, rational decisions impermissible under the previous set-ups can result in literally immediate impressive efficiency gains while other changes are still clearly too far-reaching to be adopted by an economy still so much rooted in the centrally planned orthodoxy.

Any serious student of Communist planning and management appreciates the formidable obstacles facing the Chinese industrial reforms. Their diffusion and effective execution will be incomparably more difficult than the rural transformation resting on rather straightforward private initiative of hard-working or eagerly enterprising villagers. Chinese leaders readily acknowledge the difference, seeing the urban-industrial reforms as "a tremendous, complicated task of social systems engineering" (Zhao 1985).

Given the dismal state of Chinese management, improvements can be recommended wherever one turns. Cogeneration—the use of exhaust steam and hot water—in urban-based power plants can raise significantly the overall conversion efficiencies while reducing air pollution. Installation of household electricity meters can save much energy in permanently strained systems (it is certainly one of the most incredible management lapses that until very recently millions of urban households had no meters and were billed simply on the "light-included" basis—in a country of chronic electricity shortages). Reorganization of industrial processes can release relatively large amounts of previously wasted fuel (as in doing away with most of the pig-iron shipments caused by regional absence of integrated steel-making facilities).

But rather than continuing with numerous other specific examples of improved management, I want to focus on the general problem of proper size in Chinese energetics. Scale of operations has a critical role in production efficiency, and it is unfortunate that the Chinese have had a proclivity toward far from optimal extreme solutions; there has been too much promotion of obviously inefficient small-scale operations and too much preoccupation with giant projects; this irrational dichotomy is still much alive in the modernization designs.

Taking the examples from the most insufficient branch of China's energetics, there is little doubt that the often extreme smallness is incompatible with optimizing management as far as the tens of thousands of rural hydrostations are concerned. These stations commonly lack any regulating reservoirs, generating surpluses of electricity during wet seasons and often standing idle during long dry spells. Integration of scores or hundreds of small stations into larger country-size grids is the essential step toward rational utilization—but it obviously requires relatively high levels of coordination supported by automation and investment into higher voltage transmission and switching equipment. However, remote locations in mountainous areas would make many link-ups possible only with long lines experiencing large losses.

In thermal generation the largest domestically produced 200-MW and 300-MW units are too small to serve as the most efficient baseload generators in the networks expanding beyond 10 GW, and the lack of interconnections among the country's grids is another example of unrealized economies of large scale. On the other hand, the recent preoccupation with the construction of Sanxia and with the early start of other giant hydro projects makes little sense in a country so richly endowed with scores of smaller, although still very large, hydro sites: why spend extraordinary monies for projects that cannot be completed in less than a decade when smaller dams would generate the same amount of electricity sooner and with much less environmental impact?

There are other general management concerns that need clarification and establishment of a sensible course. Why not, in a system that "leaks" more than any other national energy conversion, plug the holes before pouring in more electricity from economically and environmentally dubious nuclear generation? Why channel more energy into synthesis of nitrogen when chronic deficiencies of phosphorus and potassium make it impossible for crops to use much of the nitrogen efficiently? These questions cannot be avoided—and wrong answers will only deepen China's unenviable record of industrial energy mismanagement.

But even the best management has its limits: both the product quality and energy intensity improvements often can be effected only through elimination of outdated equipment and processes. That the boilers of nineteenth-century vintage and pickax-and-shovel mining must go is obvious, but the Chinese infrastructural modernization is made much more difficult owing to the fact that the country needs to replace the mainstays of its energy production and conversion. Large numbers of drilling rigs, coal mining machinery, locomotives, boilers, and turbogenerators made in China during the past two decades are derived from the Soviet, Czech, East German, Polish, or Hungarian designs transferred to China in the 1950s and most often corresponding to the Western levels of the 1930s and 1940s.

Such a pedigree is obviously unsuitable to become the base of effective modernization, and the recent diverse acquisitions of foreign technology, ranging from American drill bits and West German coal combines to Swiss turbogenerators and Italian petrochemical processes, are telling testimonies about the nearly universal need for foreign inputs. Indeed, a detailed systematic survey of Chinese energy technologies, similar to the one I undertook a few years ago (Smil 1980), shows that there is no important area of modern energetics where the Chinese would not need considerable transfers of foreign products, processes, and know-how if they are to realize most of their ambitious developmental plans.

In coal mining the indispensable imports include large overburden-removal machinery (bucket excavators or draglines), heavy off-road trucks, and mine locomotives for new surface mines, fully automated long-wall workfaces and ventilation and hoisting equipment for underground collieries, and coal preparation facilities for both kinds of extraction. In the oil and gas industry the import needs extend to every operation: in exploration they range from advanced geophysical techniques to large mainframe computers; in drilling, from light-weight rigs to mud-handling equipment; in production, from offshore platforms and mooring systems to reservoir management know-how; in transportation, from design of long-distance pipelines to gas compressors; and in conversion, from computerized refinery controls to pollution-control techniques. Thermal electricity generation needs better boilers and turbogenerators, hydrogeneration needs more efficient turbines and reservoir management, and transmission cannot progress without advanced high-voltage lines and direct-current links.

Chinese have been importing in all of these categories, setting up joint production ventures, receiving advanced training, asking for consultations. Compared to the last years of Mao's reign the volume of these activities in the early 1980s is staggering; compared to the needs of an economy aiming at efficient quadrupling it is greatly inadequate, and shortages of foreign exchange are an obvious limitation to the needed expansion.

In spite of recent rapid expansion (exports up from less than US $14 billion in 1979 to US $30.9 billion in 1986, imports during the same period rising from US $17.2 billion to US $42.9 billion), China remains a marginal trading nation: its total annual foreign trade turnover is of the same order of magnitude as that of Brazil, East Germany, or, a most illustrative comparison, Taiwan. Given the country's enormous and diverse import requirements—recently the largest purchases among industrial products have not been complete sets of equipment but rolled steel, nitrogenous fertilizers, copper and its alloys, and chemicals—it is obvious that modernization of energy industries can claim only a small part of overall imports.

Not surprisingly, the Chinese have tried to fill as many gaps as possible by low-interest borrowing abroad—the best recent examples being the deals to build the Daya nuclear station in Guangdong and a series of World Bank loans for construction of large hydrostations—or by joint energy development ventures. In the latter category they have successfully attracted every major Western oil company to contribute to an unprecedented free gift of geophysical exploration in the South China Sea, and now they hope for multibillion dollar investment in developing the first discoveries. Japanese have already committed about three billion dollars for development of Bohai, Daqing, and Dagang oilfields.

The totals of these loans and joint ventures are impressive proof of the fundamental turnaround in Chinese developmental policies, which until 1978 saw this kind of foreign participation as a signal embodiment of imperialist outreach—but compared to the aggregate investment needs the sums are still very small. How much bigger they could grow will depend on the Chinese tolerance of foreign debt (so far they appear to be unwilling to carry out half as much as South Korea does) and on the changing perception of the desirable level of foreign involvement in developing the country's critical industries.

This is perhaps the most appropriate place to assess briefly the potential of energy exports to earn foreign exchange. China has evolved into a growing energy exporter (in 1983 crude oil and coal imports brought the country 21 percent of all foreign trade earnings), but its share of the global fuel market is minuscule (less than two percent), and its huge domestic demand means that the future shipments will be relatively limited. This is especially true for crude oil, and doubly so if the world oil market remains soft for an extended period as the Chinese crudes have no superior attributes (being fairly heavy and highly waxy) to attract preferential demand.

Coal shipments reached the record high of 7.567 million tons in 1985, mainly to Japan, but the discussed problem with shipping of Shanxi coal, sharp competition from Australia in the East Asian market, and, as with oil, the general weakness of the global coal market are hardly a combination affording expansive export forecasts. Exchange of foreign investment for fuel exports will be thus of only a very modest help in modernizing both coal and oil and gas industries.

Most of the financing will have to be internal, and although the shares are up, there is little doubt that energy industries are not receiving, and will not soon receive, funds sufficient to meet the ambitious long-term goals. Coal, oil, gas, and electricity absorbed nearly 29 percent of all capital construction investment in industrial sectors in the First Five-Year Plan (1953–57), and although this share has gradually grown to 38.5 percent during the Sixth Five-Year Plan (1981–85), the total remains inadequate. I will demonstrate this shortfall once again with an example from China's most lagging energy sector.

Average investment cost in hydrogeneration was Rmb 1,560/kW in the early 1980s, while the new thermal capacities cost Rmb 700-800/ kW but construction of the requisite mining and transportation infrastructure doubled the expenditure so that a kilowatt of new thermal capacity had a virtually identical cost at around Rmb 1,500 (Lu 1985). Naturally, eventual installation of fuel gas desulfurization systems would increase this cost by at least 20–25 percent.

Staying with the average of Rmb 1,500/kW, construction of the new desired capacity of 180 GW between 1980 and 2000 would require aggregate investment of at least Rmb 270 billion, or an average commitment of over Rmb 13 billion a year for two decades. Yet between 1981 and 1985 the total investment in electricity generation was set at

Rmb 20.73 billion or just around Rmb 4 billion a year. Even if one-third of investments in coal mining were added to these figures (to account for the cost of new production capacities destined for thermal generation), the totals of Rmb 5–6 billion would be still less than half the required level. Clearly, the goal of 240 GW by the year 2000 could be reached only with improbably high investment acceleration in the years ahead.

An economist surveying the state of Chinese energy industries would see an effective cure for most of its ills in a thorough reform of the irrational price structure. Better management, including the abandonment of outdated processes, lower energy intensities, and higher product qualities, would follow automatically in a market-dominated set-up with energy prices reflecting production costs, qualities, and desirabilities of various forms of fuels and electricity rather than central dictates. Many Chinese economists have extolled the great virtues of stable, centrally set energy pricing which insulated the country from fluctuations brought by the post-1973 rise and post-1984 fall of world energy prices—but more recent evaluations had to admit that the system is far from optimal and that it needs fundamental readjustment (Lan, Yu, and Mao 1984; Xu Yongxi 1981).

Coal prices were readjusted three times in the past (1965, 1979, and 1985), but the present price averaging Rmb 23 per ton is indefensibly low. To begin with, the country's lowest-cost producer, Xishan mine in Shanxi, needed Rmb 13.27 in 1982 to produce a t of bituminous coal while the average for the province's large ministry-run mines was Rmb 16.31. As China's definition of cost excludes capital interest and resource rent as well as all prospecting and exploration expenses, it is clear that the real cost even in the country's best, most productive large mines is barely below the fixed sale price.

Even with the truncated definition of costs, low coal prices mean that about half of all coal mines, including many large modern collieries, have been operating with a loss. Very low transportation tariffs have been further distorting the coal prices in regions requiring large volumes of long-distance shipments (above all in the East). Yet another revealing illustration of coal's cheapness is the comparison of coal and electricity prices in China and Japan. Japan's household electricity price for an equivalent amount of thermal energy is only 1.9 times that of coal while in China the difference is more than 40-fold (Lu and Fu 1984).

In contrast, the crude oil price of Rmb 100 per ton is much above the average production cost, and the Ministry of Oil Industry has been turning out huge profits each year. But, as with the coal price, the crude oil price is much below the equilibrium price: demand for both fuels induced by their respective prices is much higher than what can be produced, and there is little incentive for development of new resources and energy conservation. In terms of energy equivalents, one GJ of coal costs about Rmb 1.1 while one GJ of crude oil is priced at about Rmb 2.4. Using official exchange rates these costs would translate to just around $(1985)0.50 for one GJ of coal and $1.20 for one GJ of crude oil—while the average world prices for the two commodities were, respectively, nearly $2 and $5 per GJ, levels roughly four times higher than the fixed domestic prices.

This large differential creates an illusion of profitability in exports of energy-intensive items and contributes greatly to perpetuation of the heavy industrial orientation of the Chinese economy. On the other hand, if the enterprises could sell any surpluses of energy allocated to them by the center directly on the foreign market, incentives for conservation would be very strong indeed. Electricity pricing is hardly more sensible. The price is fixed at Rmb 0.07/kWh, which gives a good investment return in generating plants—yet again the value is much below the equilibrium. There is no distinction between base load and peak load charges and between hydro and thermal generation, and chronic shortages require constant, complex rationing.

The need for the price reforms is now widely acknowledged in China, but the concerns about economic and social dislocations ranging from higher inflation to elimination of numerous enterprises and higher unemployment and lessened competitiveness on foreign markets will mean tardy progress. Lan, Yu, and Mao (1984) summarized the dilemma well: "Although China's pricing authorities have recognized the need for energy price adjustment and initiated extensive investigations of the actual costs of thousands of major commodities, they are hesitant in taking action."

The first steps have been taken by creating parallel price systems. After they exhausted their fuel quota purchased at fixed prices, enterprises now have the option of buying on a "free" market where prices are several times higher. For example, allocated light diesel oil costs Rmb 300 per ton but its contract price is Rmb 800. Still, many enterprises producing goods for export or heavily sought-after on the domestic market have been using this option repeatedly. Similarly, in the summer of 1985 the State Council abolished the center's monopoly on large-scale electricity generation. Local governments and departments are now allowed to construct and operate their own plants, also as joint ventures with foreign companies, and to fix their rates according to local supply and demand conditions.

Chinese see these arrangements as temporary measures to be eliminated by the gradual rise of fixed energy prices once again promised by Zhao Ziyang in his outline of 1986–1990 plans. The sooner the changes start, the better: no argument for the preservation of the current arrangements should obscure the high price China pays for the arbitrary pricing in economic efficiency and coexistence of crippling energy shortages and appalling energy waste.

Progress in most of the areas discussed in this section will not be rapid. Fostering economic reforms and technical innovations is not a *métier* of one-party regimes in general and of the monumental Chinese bureaucracy in particular. The recent successes in agricultural production should not be taken as a harbinger of the pace and extent of future industrial reforms. Their actual progress and impact cannot be safely predicted even by their authors and promoters.

Reading Deng Xiaoping's speeches and interviews I am repeatedly struck by the improvisational nature of the changes transforming China: "We still have to work out specific rules and regulations by trial and error" (Deng 1985). Even the supreme leader himself has little specific appreciation of where things will be just five years ahead. The process that has been underway since 1978 has acquired momentum, and features that were unpredictable during its genesis, but changing rules and regulations can at any time lessen or reverse its undoubted achievements.

Deng does not even want to admit such a possibility: "As far as China is concerned, there is no other road China can take. Other roads will lead only to poverty and backwardness." Unfortunately, the history of modern China offers no analogies of clean breaks and sustained advances. Speaking of inadmissibility of other roads is very much in the manner of denying the existence of ghosts: if they do not flit about, why speak of them? They do—and China can take other roads, some of them much more sensible than the current reforms (entailing, unthinkably for Deng, the end to one-party dictatorship), others painfully regressive (with the party's suffocating control rampant again).

But no matter what the rules, choices, and courses are, the country's energetics will remain a critical determinant of modernization outcomes. And even if all quality, efficiency, management, technology, and investment concerns were tackled with skill and foresight, there would remain a large class of phenomena that would complicate, alter, and limit China's developmental plan. Before closing this book, therefore, I have to discuss the environmental consequences and implications of China's energy modernization.

5.2 Environmental complications

The swell of environmental awareness that engulfed Western nations in the late 1960s and early 1970s brought fundamental changes to the ways of planning, building, and operating energy industries. Environmental implications of energy projects have assumed a role as important as—and not infrequently clearly much more decisive than—the traditional engineering and financial concerns.

The extent of land dereliction and possibilities of recultivation after surface coal mining, oil spills from tanker shipments, air pollution arising from coal combustion in power plants (especially the releases of sulfur and nitrogen oxides, precursors of acidifying sulfates and nitrates), ecosystemic changes brought by construction of large dams, safety concerns about operation of nuclear plants and long-term disposal of radioactive wastes—all these and scores of other factors became prominent in determining the very existence, location, size, and operating modes of energy projects throughout the Western world.

Chinese have become alert to these concerns only since 1978, but since then there has been enough attention not only in scientific journals but also in mass-circulation periodicals to indicate sufficient awareness of the impacts and complications waiting ahead if environmental considerations are ignored or belittled. That some bureaucratic factions promoting their particular schemes continue to ignore these newly issued warnings is hardly surprising. Given China's dichotomy of energy consumption, the two principal categories of environmental problems arising from the provision and use of fuels manifest themselves in very different ways.

In the countryside excessive burning of biomass (described in detail in section 3.1.1) results in many-faceted environmental degradation embracing deforestation, accelerated erosion, increased silting of streams, aggravation of seasonal floods, local climatic changes, deterioration of soil structure and organic matter content, loss of plant nutrients, lowered crop yields, and extinction of species. In mining, industrial, and urban areas, China's extraordinarily high reliance on coal combustion is all too perceptible owing to air pollution levels which now have few counterparts even in a global comparison.

As noted in section 3.1.1, there are no reliable figures to apportion the causes of China's extensive deforestation, but the rising rural fuelwood demand must have been responsible for a major part of the often irreparable losses. I have reviewed numerous environmental consequences of Chinese deforestation elsewhere (Smil 1984), so I will mention here just one downstream link through which demand for fuelwood affects the capacity of another energy-harnessing activity. Erosion of exposed deforested slopes has been generally the worst consequence of deforestation leading inevitably to faster silting of reservoirs. Consequently, at the beginning of the 1980s an equivalent of about one-third of the newly impounded reservoir volume was eliminated each year through sedimentation (Kinzelbach 1983).

Environmental costs of burning crop residues are quantifiable with a satisfactory degree of accuracy. Current combustion of some 230 million tons deprives Chinese fields of about 1.6 million t of nitrogen, 230,000 tons of phosphorus, and 2.8 million tons of potassium—and it has also nontrivial energy use implications: when calculated at prevailing energy costs (80 MJ/kg N, 15 MJ/kg P, and 5 MJ/kg K), fertilizers supplying the same amount of nutrients need about 150 PJ of feedstock and process energy, an equivalent of about 5 million tce—but synthetic chemicals would not bring the benefits of higher water retention, effective anti-erosion protection, and organic matter replenishment conferred by the recycled straws and stalks.

As outlined in section 4.2.5, excessive use of biomass fuels, and hence its environmental impacts, can be corrected by widespread adoption of improved stoves and planting of private fuelwood lots. These measures require extensive organizational, consulting, and service support and cannot succeed without ongoing commitment of tens of millions of everyday users and producers—yet they do not need any sophisticated inputs and their costs are mostly in cheap rural labor. This is in great contrast to measures needed to alleviate the high environmental penalty paid for China's dependence on coal: some of them do not call for advanced engineering but all require considerable to very expensive investments in appropriate control technologies.

These should begin with massive expansion of China's wholly inadequate coal-processing facilities. Proper sorting, washing, and cleaning of coal can reduce significantly both its ash and inorganic sulfur content and increase the fuel's combustion efficiency. Improvements of dismal combustion efficiencies through replacement of outdated boilers, better management, and diffusion of larger, inherently more efficient units, accompanied by installation of modern electrostatic precipitators to eliminate most fly ash emissions, must be the centerpiece of air pollution control. To believe that Chinese planners could start thinking seriously about installation of flue gas desulfurization equipment would be nothing but wishful thinking: these devices are far from universal even in the richest coal-burning nations.

That China has an acute need for broad-ranging air pollution control can be readily seen by international comparisons of both emissions and ground-level concentrations. With combustion of roughly 800 million tons of coal, annual emissions of particulates amount to about 50 million tons (of which fly ash is about 15 million tons), and those of sulfur dioxide to 15–17 million tons. In contrast, in the United States, with higher coal combustion (especially when compared on the energy equivalent basis—see section 3.2.1), annual particulate emissions do not exceed 15 million tons because uncontrolled small sources have mostly substituted less-polluting hydrocarbons for coal, and all large combustion units have efficient electrostatic precipitators. In China only a few of the latest imported units are equipped with these efficient (99 percent +) controls: most power plants have only mechanical dust separators removing only about 80 percent of fly ash.

Not surprisingly, particulate concentrations in Chinese industrial and urban areas are commonly at levels encountered in Europe and North America two generations ago, before the advent of widespread air pollution controls. While the Chinese allowable limit for particulate fall-out is 3 t/km•month, residental areas of large cities receive between 10 and 100 tons and in many industrial areas the rates are commonly in hundreds of tons and even much over 1,000 tons a month. In terms of airborne particulate matter the hygienic norm of 0.15 g/m^3 is commonly surpassed up to tenfold in residential and up to twentyfold in industrial areas. High residential concentrations are above all a seasonal phenomenon arising from combustion of raw coal, coal dust, or poor quality briquettes in small, inefficient household stoves.

This combustion also explains why during winter months residential areas have higher SO_2 concentrations than many industrial regions: uncontrolled emissions near the ground produce higher atmospheric levels of the gas, especially during nighttime inversions, than those from much taller industrial and power plant chimneys, which can be considerably diluted before reaching the ground. Daily averages of SO_2

in residential areas of China's thirty largest cities are mostly between 100 and 400 $\mu g/m^3$ with some annual means surpassing $500\mu g/m^3$ while winter means in northern cities are as high as 2,000 $\mu g/m^3$—compared to North American urban levels between 20 and 100 $\mu g/m^3$.

Incomplete combustion of coal also generates relatively large quantities of benzo(a)-pyrene, a polycyclic aromatic hydrocarbon with strong carcinogenic effects: its concentrations during the heating period in northern cities are as high as 5–10 $\mu g/100$ m^3 with peaks in industrial cities surpassing 20 $\mu g/100$ m^3 (Lan, Lu, and Mao 1984). Obviously, such high concentrations of particulates, SO_2, and aromatic hydrocarbons have contributed to increased respiratory, cardiac, and cancer morbidity and mortality in China's large cities. For example, cancer mortality is four to six times higher in urban areas than in the countryside.

Another worrisome environmental consequence of poor efficiency and combustion concerns the quality of indoor air during winter months in the North. Lu and Fu (1984) published results of extensive measurements in Beijing and Shenyang which show that cooking and heating with small, pot-bellied coal stoves raises the indoor concentrations of carbon monoxide to 15-28 mg/m^3 so that carboxyhemoglobin levels surpassed 4 percent in 20 percent of the 7,000 investigated people and 2 percent in 81 percent of cases (observable effects on human mental and motor performance start at between 2 and 3 percent).

The latest Western air pollution concern is also making itself felt in parts of China. Acid deposition—resulting largely from conversion of sulfur and nitrogen oxides (emitted by combustion of coal in stationary sources and liquid fuels in cars) to acidifying sulfates and nitrates which may be transported far away from the source areas and raise the acidity of susceptible lakes (with attendant change of species composition) and endanger the growth of coniferous forests—is being increasingly encountered in China.

In the North long dry spells and the presence of large quantities of airborne terrigenic alkaline matter (from the devegetated surfaces) which can readily neutralize the acid substances have counteracted the copious generation of acidifying compounds. In the rainy East both Shanghai and Nanjing have had occasional periods of acid precipitation, but the problem is worst in the Southwest where heavy seasonal rains and coals with high sulfur content combine to produce high acidities, with pH values as low as 4.0 in Chongqing.

Chinese modernization plans would inevitably intensify some air pollution problems. With substitution of coal by gaseous fuels (natural gas, LPG, coal gas) in household urban combustion and with increasing shares of coal being burned in large stationary sources equipped with efficient electrostatic precipitators, emissions of fly ash and airborne particulates should be on the decline, as should be the urban levels of sulfur dioxide. Total emissions of SO_2, however, will increase almost proportionately with rising coal combustion, and by the year 2000 they may be double the 1980 volume. As they will be increasingly emitted from large stationary sources with tall stacks, the potential for regional acidification will grow and it will be intensified owing to the planned concentration of coal-fired generating capacities in several northern provinces. The effects would be most pronounced in Shanxi, Hebei, Henan, Shandong, and Anhui during summer months when millions of tons of SO_2 emitted from large power plants into the wet and sunny atmosphere would undergo rapid photo-oxidation to sulfates which would spread acid precipitation over most of Shanxi and much of the North China Plain and Shandong peninsula.

The other major atmospheric deterioration will be the diffusion and aggravation of photochemical smog. Until the early 1980s this condition was limited to summer months in Lanzhou where high concentration of hydrocarbons and intensive insolation produced photo-oxidant levels comparable to those encountered during North American smogs. However, growing numbers of cars, trucks, and buses in urban areas, their poor maintenance, and traffic congestion resulting from the sudden rise of traffic are already bringing higher seasonal smog levels to many large cities. With more cars and more oil flowing in from future offshore discoveries many Southern cities may have a chronic summer smog problem before the year 2000.

Intended quadrupling of thermal electricity generation would also put a huge additional demand on the already strained water supplies. Thermal generation is invariably the largest industrial user of water. Depending on the average conversion efficiency and the degree of recycling in cooling towers and ponds, modern coal-fired stations need 100-200 liters of water for each kWh, or roughly 0.6-1.2 billion m^3 for each GW of installed capacity. In the early 1980s Chinese thermal power plants used nearly 30 billion m^3, putting them close to the lower end of the indicated range.

Should thermal capacities at least triple by the year 2000, water demand, even with additional conservation, would rise to no less than

75 billion m³ a year. When distributed fairly evenly around the country this would be an easily manageable increase, but contemplated regional concentration would start encountering obvious water availability limits. As with SO_2 emissions, Shanxi would be the most troubled province. The province's total available water resources are 17.18 billion m³: 11.68 billion m³ of surface and 5.5 billion m³ of underground water; the total agricultural, industrial, and household consumption is 6.4 billion m³ (Hu 1983).

This may seem to offer further considerable utilization potential—but of the total runoff only about 7 billion m³ are practically harnessible, and in dry years there are just 6 billion m³ available for the whole province. Severe water shortages are thus Shanxi's norm: only one-quarter of cropfields have irrigation water throughout the growing season; Taiyuan, the province's largest city, has a chronic 20 percent shortage for its waterworks; and some four million people in Shanxi's mountains have difficulty getting even enough of drinking water. Over-exploitation of underground waters has extended over more than 3,000 km² with spreading surface subsidence (Xia 1983).

If all the envisaged coal-fired stations were built, 20–24 GW of thermal capacity would, even with consumption at just 0.6 billion m³/GW, require no less than 12 billion m³, nearly twice the currently available total withdrawal. Where would the sharply increased requirements for expanded coal mining, chemical and other industries, new housing, and farm irrigation come from? And, as will be recalled, many Chinese planners still want to use slurry pipelines to ship Shanxi's coal eastward! Reread, please, the last two paragraphs—and reflect on the sanity of those grandiose plans.

And there are other environmental complications arising from expanded coal extraction and thermal electricity generation. Over 1 billion tons of mining waste are already piled up around China's collieries, occupying over 7,000 ha of land and contributing to atmospheric pollution owing to spontaneous combustion and dust generation. The current generation rate of these wastes is about 70 million tons a year, and with expanded production and coal preparation it will more than double by the late 1990s.

Installation of efficient electrostatic precipitators in power plants and on large industrial boilers will reduce airborne particulates but will greatly increase the amount of captured fly-ash that must be stored, usually by ponding near the plants, claiming large areas of flat land over the lifetime of the projects. Assuming that each 1,000-MW power plant needs at least 200 ha for thirty-year ponding of fly-ash, no less than 24,000 ha of flat, potentially cultivable land would be needed between 1980 and 2000 if all the planned coal-fired power plants were to capture their fly-ash.

Shipment of increasing volumes of northern coals eastward and southward will necessitate construction of new railroads or double-tracking of old ones, and these projects will claim relatively large areas of flat land (with clearances between 5 and 10 m). Much larger areas of grasslands and uplands will be destroyed as China's surface coal mining expands from its current low share of a mere 3 percent to some 15 percent by the year 2000. The volumes of acid mine drainage will increase, damaging underground waters and nearby watercourses.

The two principal alternatives to coal-fired generation—hydrostations and nuclear power plants—carry their own considerable environmental problems. Compared to extraction, transportation, and conversion of coal, hydroelectricity generation appears to be environmentally much more benign, but environmental considerations must be of great concern in planning for hydrogeneration capacities. Most Chinese rivers have large seasonal runoff fluctuations with as much as 70 percent of the annual flow occurring during the three to five wet months, and to even out at least partially this irregularity requires construction of large reservoirs at the upstream sites. Recurring droughts, recently exacerbated by widespread deforestation, can reduce electricity supply in provinces heavily dependent on hydrogeneration and create seasonal power shortages (recently in Yunnan and Sichuan).

But the effects cut the other way as well. Although a newly created reservoir may seem to be a definite environmental asset with its flood-control capacity, moderating microclimatic influence, and opportunities for irrigation, agriculture, and recreation, there are considerable costs to pay, ranging from common losses of good farmland to rarer but all the more worrisome reservoir-induced earthquakes.

Flooding of fertile alluvial fields in a country where there are only 500 m² of arable land per capita in the most densely settled provinces and where every large project may require resettling of tens of thousands of people is necessarily of great concern in China. According to Weng (1982), since 1957 generation of every 100 GWh in large and medium-sized hydrostations has required flooding of 50 ha and displacement of 560 people. Applied to the annual generation of nearly 60 TWh in 1980, these specific rates would translate to total losses of

30,000 ha and resettlement of 336,000 people.

Very large projects now under construction or in planning stages would make relatively higher demands, and this has been one of the reasons why the preference in building high dams with large reservoirs is given to upstream sites in mountainous locations and why the still plentiful hydrogeneration opportunities in lower stream stretches will be developed mostly as run-of-the-river stations with minimized land requirements. Still, the farmland losses and resettlement costs for the two decades would add up to significant totals.

I have not come across any published aggregate figures, but a fairly reliable estimate can be made by prorating the past claims. As outlined in section 4.2.4, by the year 2000 new hydrogenerating capacities could add up at best to 80 GW and produce about 240 TWh more electricity than in 1980. If the historic averages were to apply, no less than 120,000 ha of farmland would be flooded between 1980 and 2000 and 1.3 million people would have to be resettled. In reality, it is rather unlikely that all of the planned projects will be built—so soon or ever—and many large reservoirs in deep valleys in mountainous areas will certainly flood relatively less land than small reservoirs built before 1980.

For example, four major dams of the Hongshui cascade will claim only 20 ha of land and dislocate about 370 persons for every 100 TWh (Weng 1982), the values, respectively, 60 and 33 percent lower than the pre-1980 mean. On the other hand, the Sanxia, even when limited to 13 GW capacity, would flood 44,000 ha of farmland, most of it in Sichuan, already China's most populous province with arable land per capita much below the nationwide average. Moreover, it would necessitate resettling of nearly two million people as the reservoir's waters would flood not only riverside villages but also ten cities and parts of eight others (including Chongqing). Relocation of settlements, factories, transport, and communication links may cost as much as $3.5 billion.

Whatever the precise eventual figures are, the orders of magnitude are unmistakable: before the end of the century China's ambitious hydrogeneration program will claim 10^5 ha of farmland (100,000–150,000 ha is the most likely range) and force the resettlement of 10^6 people (1–1.5 million appears to be the minimum) at a cost of billions of dollars ($4–5 billion would be a likely range). The farmland loss may seem small as it is a mere 0.1 percent of the current nationwide total, but most of that land is in the high-yielding category and with an easy access to transportation.

Troublesome as the losses of farmland and the needs of massive resettlement are, they are not the most important environmental worries associated with the construction of large hydrostations: in China silting is indisputably the leading problem. The middle course of the Huang He basin, cutting through the world's most extensive deposits of easily erodible loess, is, of course, the best-known global example of erosion and silting, and the first Chinese attempt to dam the river just at a point where it is leaving the loess deposits turned out to be a hazardous experiment that ended in a huge economic loss.

Sino-Soviet designs for the Sanmenxia dam in a Henan gorge about 120 km downstream from the river's rectangular eastward bend did not envisage any major silting problems for a 1.1-GW project: protective measures upstream (ranging from small silt check dams to slope grassing) were to lower the silting rate to such an extent that the generation could last for fifty to seventy years. But when the reservoir started to fill in the early 1960s more than 90 percent of the inflowing silt was retained, raising the water levels upstream into the valley of the Wei He and encroaching on Xi'an. To avoid extremely costly environmental damages the dam had to be pierced by a large sluicing opening, additional outlets were cut into the shoulder rocks, and the Sanmenxia was turned into a low head run-of-the-river plant with capacity of just 200 MW and without any major capability for seasonal flood storage.

Although it is true that the Huang He's mid- and low-course silt load is exceptionally huge, the recent decades of environmental degradation have increased silt loading of many previously unburdened rivers throughout the southern half of China. Widespread deforestation, cropping of slopelands, and overgrazing increased the erosion rates while extensive filling of alluvial lakes raised the amount of silt moving downstream through river channels.

Consequently, Danjiangkou, so far China's most voluminous reservoir in the Han Shui in Hubei, lost one-seventh of its capacity in just a decade, silt content of seven major rivers in the Chang Jiang basin rose by about 25 percent during the past three decades, and the Yangzi itself now carries nearly 650 million tons of silt a year as it leaves Sichuan and before it enters the gorges, almost 25 percent above the value of 525 million tons used in the original design of Gezhouba in the 1960s (Xu 1981). Hongshui is also increasingly silty (Weng 1982).

The total design capacity of China's eleven largest reservoirs completed by the early 1980s was 37 billion m³ but silting, proceeding at an average rate of 850 million m³ a year, had already taken up 10 billion m³ by 1982, and such large projects as Yanguoxia (originally 352 MW), Qingtongxia (design capacity 272 MW), and the second cascade on the Yili He have completely lost their regulatory function and can generate electricity only from runoff water (Shen and Guyo 1982).

Silting is also a major reason of damming up of downstream tail-water which reduces designed generating heads (other causes are care-less pileups of construction debris below the dam and retention of construction weirs). The problem is worst at Liujiaxia where the gener-ating head was reduced by 4 to 6 m. In the early 1980s loss of genera-tion owing to the damming of tailwater added up to between 290 and 420 million kWh a year in China's eleven largest stations, the equiv-alent of 1.5–2.2 percent of their designed capacity.

Other environmental and engineering complications besides the shortened life of reservoirs and the loss of generating capacity range from retention of nutrients and accelerated shoreline erosion to abra-sion of turbine blades. Egypt's High Dam cutting the Nile at Aswan has become a textbook example of costly consequences of nutrient retention and coastline erosion. Previously thriving fishing in the Mediterranean waters nearly disappeared, and accelerated erosion of the Nile Delta moves Egypt's coastline relentlessly southward as salt water intrudes farther inland.

The analogy with the Chang Jiang's possible fate after the Sanxia is made even more worrisome by three facts. First, recycling of organic nutrients, including river mud, is already in decline in China's inten-sively cultivated alluvial plains. More importantly, China's richest fishing grounds off the coasts of Jiangsu and Zhejiang obviously de-pend on the influx of riverine nutrients, and their reduction may speed up the decline of coastal East China Sea fishing, which already suffers from excessive netting. Finally, and perhaps most importantly, during dry spells salt water has already backed up far enough to affect Shang-hai's drinking supply.

Sanxia would also bring geoengineering worries present in many smaller projects but rarely carrying the likelihood of major risks. According to the United States' Three Gorges Working Group (com-posed of representatives of two governmental agencies and more than half a dozen private companies), the area to be flooded can experience landslides large enough to pose a significant safety threat (it was a large rockslide that swept water over the Vaiont dam in 1963 and killed 2,600 people downstream). More importantly, large dams can induce earth-quakes in seismically unstable regions and, to begin with, they should be designed to withstand tremors likely to occur only once in ten thousand years—yet according to the American report Sanxia's current design could cope with only a one-in-one-hundred-years earthquake.

Little needs to be written about environmental implications of nuclear power generation after a decade that has seen the Chernobyl tragedy, Three Mile Island and other lesser accidents in the United States and the near-demise of nuclear generation in several Western countries, a turnaround caused by doubts about economic viability of fission generation, but above all by widespread concern about operating safety and by lasting uncertainties about modes of final, environmentally benign disposal of high-level radioactive wastes.

While the Chinese nuclear faction may spread complacent notions about the infallibility of fission reactors, planned siting of nuclear power plants in the fuel-deficient but industrialized and very densely populated eastern, southern, and northeastern locations will not be looked on with indifference by those who appreciate the relatively high degree of reliablity achieved in nuclear generation—but who are also aware of the very real possibilities of accidental malfunctions and human operating errors.

As noted at the outset of this section, few of the solutions available for alleviation or elimination of numerous environmental problems associated with modern energetics are cheap. But Chinese will have to start taking these costly steps by setting aside steadily increasing portions of their investments in new energy production capacities for environmental protection and pollution control: it is an indispensable part of sustainable strategies of energy development, and its neglect will claim a much costlier rectification in the not too distant future.

5.3 Sustainable strategies

The years since 1973 have seen the birth and demise of more energy forecasts, projects, and policies than the preceding three decades of rapidly expanding energy supplies fueling the post–World War II prosperity. Where are the forecasts of crude oil at $100 per barrel by 1985, the plans for military takeover of Saudi oilfields, Nixon's Project Independence, and Carter's synthetic fuel extravaganza? After OPEC's first round of price increases the Chinese ascribed the Western discomfort and fears to the inherent failings of doomed capitalism—but a mere five years later they were busily wooing the multinational oil companies, former paragons of capitalist vices, to help them capitalize on the booming oil market.

This was just one of many spectacular Chinese policy twists of the recent past. Where are the late 1970s' goals of ten Daqings and quadrupled coal extraction by the year 2000? What huge gaps separate today's realities from plans for massive crude-oil exports to Japan or from forecasts of tens of millions of small biogas digesters? In China as well as in the West, the challenge is to formulate long-term strategies that could be translated into sustainable practices. This requires sound fundamental analyses on which to base clear but flexible objectives.

Encouragingly, the new spirit of "seeking truth from the facts," although far from permeating everyday Chinese practices, has brought many thorough, penetrating, and pointed analyses of the country's failings and aspirations, and an unprecedented outpouring of criticism and polemic writings have uncovered many untenable fallacies and suggested more sensible alternatives. Naturally, this refreshing wave of candid and critical analyses and proposals could not sweep away all the deeply embedded bureaucratic biases, factional preferences, and doctrinaire formulas.

But I have to conclude that by and large the top Chinese policy makers now have access to plenty of critical evaluations that put long-term energy planning on foundations not substantially different from those in many rich industrialized countries and that make it possible to come up with sound, sustainable policies. That many decisions still prove to be unrealistic and their fate is short-lived (exaggerated plans for nuclear generation are perhaps the best latest example) is hardly a specifically Chinese failing. A brief review of the principal recent trends and policies, with some critical observation, may therefore be a fitting conclusion to this book.

The Chinese decision to continue with coal as the main energizer of their economic development is inevitable given the country's huge deposits of five bituminous coals as well as of lignites extractable in giant surface mines. Many complications, however, ranging from the necessity of large-scale, long-distance transfers of northern coal to the risks of acid deposition caused by combustion in new large thermal stations, will make both the planned doubling of coal output (especially if the quality is to increase considerably) and largely coal-based quadrupling of power generation taxing challenges. Much greater attention to environmental consequences of coal-fired generation will be necessary: costly but essential, it will prevent large-scale environmental degradation.

The outlook for the oil and gas industry is basically fairly favorable, although the chances of truly spectacular offshore discoveries are rapidly disappearing. Offshore drilling is coming up with first, relatively small, commercial discoveries—but it will be the end of this decade before the actual capacities of China's offshore basins are known with certainty, enabling long-range planning. Until then the current policies of conversion from oil to coal and maximum oil conservation should rightly continue.

New thermal generation capacities alone could not cover the huge anticipated demand and hence the stress on accelerated construction of large hydroelectric stations is a rational component of the modernization drive. What is questionable is the strong preference for giant, multigigawatt projects in a country that could, more speedily and most likely also more economically, develop first plenty of smaller large sites with capacities in hundreds of MW. The current enthusiasm for construction of nuclear power stations in densely settled coastal regions appears to me to be another questionable move which the high expenditures may soon reduce to much more modest proportions than originally planned.

Even a complete success of modernization in the coal, oil and gas, and power generation industries would not fundamentally alter the everyday rural energy supply: it would bring more fertilizer and machinery but it would not make cooking and heating any easier. Consequently, to ensure that four-fifths of China's population will fully benefit from economic modernization, workable ways must be tried to expand rural energy supply without further environmental degradation.

No single form of energy will be sufficient for the task. More coal from better-run small coal mines, more electricity from larger hydrostations, and more biogas from properly built and operated family digesters will be helpful, but for the near future the two centerpieces of China's rural development strategy must be the greatest possible extension of private fuelwood lots, including agroforestry plantings, and an extensive effort to introduce higher efficiency stoves.

If very successful, this combined approach might eliminate most of the current overexploitation of biomass fuels, above all the burning of crop residues, by the end of the century while raising modestly the average per capita energy availabilities. Even then the Chinese rural energy use would remain a very frugal affair and chances for radical improvement are low for yet another generation. On reflection, there appears to be no sensible alternative to this combined woodfuel-coal-hydroelectricity-biogas-improved stoves approach.

Failure of this combination would, especially when combined with higher than anticipated rural population growth rates, deepen the prevailing energy shortages to a truly unimaginable degree. After all, in today's China there are already regions where firewood is more expensive than grain! Clearly, as far as an average Chinese is concerned, the country's success in turning the bold modernization plants into reality will be determined more by the achievements in alleviating the rural energy crisis and the accompanying environmental degradation than by the advances in acquiring assorted high technologies.

First things first: the country can move ahead without nuclear power plants or oversize steel mills which it is now busily constructing, but all technological achievements and rising output statistics for industrial products will be much flawed victories when half a billion people are not able to cook their morning gruel for weeks.

All the right ingredients of sensible long-range energy policy appear to be recognized and promoted by the current pragmatic leadership: extensive energy conservation, mechanization of coal mining, joint ventures with experienced foreign companies to develop offshore hydrocarbons, expansion of electricity generation by building minemouth stations and hydroelectric plants, belated but genuine attention to rural energy shortages, gradual reforms of the irrational energy price structure, and the necessity to increase household energy use. But other things will determine the outcome: ability to set a sustainable pace of development (in a society whose economy has shown more, and greater, fluctuations during the past thirty-five years than any other of its size worldwide); achievements in genuine absorption of advanced foreign technologies (in a country where many skills are nonexistent, where motivation of common workers has been exceedingly low, where technical personnel amount to just a few percent of labor force, and where a whole generation of young people missed systematic higher education); successes in everyday management of countless interlocking tasks (in a nation where mobilizational, mass-scale construction has always mattered more than the quality and sustainability of the projects); and the degree of workable long-term compromise between the ruling rigid orthodoxy and pragmatic flexibility required to meet evolving societal and economic needs (in a country famous for its repeated stunning reversals of dictatorial policies).

Perhaps the strangest thing about post-1949 China is how abundant have been both its successes *and* its failures. Looking ahead one sees the obvious potential, notes the recent recognition of realities, and approves of many plans—but one also feels the weight of limitations not easy to shed in a dash toward quadrupled economy within a generation. *You yi li bi you yi bi,* where there are advantages there must be disadvantages, goes an ancient saying. Chinese possess plenty of both—and I am sure the outcome of the great modernization drive will duly reflect the mixture.

REFERENCES

Bai, Yiliang, ed. 1985. *Geological Map of China.* Hong Kong: Petroleum News Southeast Asia.

Beijing Planetarium. 1977. "Solar Radiation and Its Uses." *Dili zhishi* (Geographical Knowledge) 12, pp. 25–27.

Cao Wenlong. 1984. "How to Speed Shanxi Road Building to Expand Coal Transport." *Guangming ribao* (Guangming Daily) 31 January 1984, p. 2.

Carin, R. 1969. *Power Industry in Communist China.* Hong Kong: Union Research Institute.

Central Intelligence Agency. 1976. *China: The Coal Industry.* Washington, D.C.: CIA.

———. 1977. *China: Oil Production Prospects.* Washington, D.C.: CIA.

———. 1979. *Chinese Coal Industry: Prospects over the Next Decade.* Washington, D.C.: CIA.

———. 1980. *Electric Power for China's Modernization: The Hydroelectric Option.* Washington, D.C.: CIA.

———. 1982. *USSR: Measures of Economic Growth and Development, 1950–80.* Washington, D.C.: CIA.

———. 1984. *Handbook of Economic Statistics, 1984.* Washington, D.C.: CIA.

Chen Ruchen and Xiao Zhiping. 1979. *Digesters for Developing Countries.* Guangzhou: Guangzhou Institute of Energy Conversion.

Chen Shangkui. 1984. "Accelerated Construction of Hydropower Base on the Upper Huang He." *Kexue shiyan* (Scientific Experiment) 3, pp. 4–5.

Chen Xi, Huang Zhijie, and Xu Junzhang. 1979. "Effective Use of Energy Sources Is Very Important in Developing the National Economy." *Jingji yanjiu* (Economic Research) 5, pp. 20–24.

Cheng, Chu-yuan. 1976. *China's Petroleum Industry.* New York: Praeger.

———. 1984. *The Demand and Supply of Primary Energy in Mainland China.* Taipei: Chung-hua Institute for Economic Research.

Clarke, W. W. 1978. "China's Electric Power Industry." In *Chinese Economy Post-Mao,* Joint Economic Committee of the U.S. Congress, Washington, D.C.: GPO, pp. 403–35.

Clauser, T. 1981. "Small Hydro Stations Power China's Growth." *Petroleum News* 11, pp. 20–21.

Coulter, J. 1984. "China Contracts—Shortening the Odds." *Petroleum News* 3, pp. 6–7; 4, pp. 14–15.

Deng Keyun. 1985. "Developing Rural Energy Resources." *Beijing Review* 28 (21), pp. 23–25.

Deng Keyun and Zhou Qingche. 1981. "A Discussion of the Methods of Solving China's Rural Energy Crisis." In *Beyond the Energy Crisis*, vol. 1, ed. R. A. Fazzolare and C. B. Smith. New York: Pergamon Press, pp. 85–91.

Deng Keyun and Wu Changlin. 1984. "Rural Energy Utilization in China." Paper prepared for Energy Research Group, International Development Research Center, Ottawa.

Deng Xiaoping. 1985a. "Current Policies Will Continue." *Beijing Review* 28 (4), p. 15.

————. 1985b. "Speech at the CPC National Conference." *Beijing Review* 28 (39), pp. 15–18.

Ding Yaolin. 1983. "Daqing Oilfield Today." *Beijing Review* 26(13), pp. 23–25.

Djurović, M. 1979. "Mini Hydro Plants Boost China's Power Supply." *Energy International* 16 (11), pp. 44–46.

El-Hinnawi, E. 1977. *China Study Tour on Energy and Environment. Small Hydropower Schemes.* A Technical Report. Nairobi: UNEP.

Fan Weitang. 1984. "On Research and Development in Coal Industry." *Meitan kexue jishu* (Coal Science and Technology) 10, pp. 3–8.

Fang Rukang. 1984. "The Current Situation and National Utilization of Energy Resources in China." *Dili yanjiu* (Geographical Research) 3 (4), pp. 25–38.

Feng Baoxing. 1979. "Bear in Mind Historical Lessons in the Lopsided Development of Heavy Industry." *Hongqi* (Red Flag) 12, pp. 14–17.

Fingar, T. 1980. *Energy and Development: China's Strategy for the 1980s.* Occasional paper of the Northeast Asia-United States Forum on International Policy, Stanford University, Stanford, Calif.

————. 1983. *Energy in China: Paradoxes, Policies and Prospects,* Washington, D.C.: The China Council of the Asia Society.

Food and Agriculture Organization. In Food and Agriculture Organization. 1977. *China: Recycling of Organic Wastes in Agriculture.* Rome: FAO.

Food and Agriculture Organization and United Nations Development Programme. 1978. *China: Recycling of Organic Wastes in Agriculture.* Rome: FAO.

Gao Yangwen. 1983. "Rely on Scientific and Technological Progress to Initiate a New Phase of the Coal Industry and to Realize the Doubling of Coal Output." *Zhongguo meitan bao* (China's Coal News), 20 July 1983, pp. 1–2.

Geng Zhaorui. 1983. "Prospects for Developing Mechanization of China's Coal Industry in the 1980s." *Shijie meitan jishu* (World Coal Technology) 7, pp. 5–9.

Gong Bao, Lu Weide, and Tian Xiaoping. 1984. "Recent Advances in Solar Energy Utilization in China." Paper prepared for Energy Research Group, International Development Research Center, Ottawa.

Gong Guangyu. 1980. "China's Energy Needs in the Year 2000." *Xiandaihua* (Modernization) 9, pp. 1, 9.

Han Baocheng. 1984. "Qinhuangdao—China's Key Energy Port." *Beijing Review* 27 (52), pp. 23–29.

Hangzhou Regional Centre for Small Hydro Power. 1985. *Small Hydro Power in China: Survey.* Intermediate Technology Publications, London.

Hao Fengyin. 1984. "Energy Conservation Measures in the Coal Industry." *Neng yuan* (Journal of Energy) 1, pp. 7–8.

Hao Yushan. 1981. "Survey of Afforestation of the Jiangsu-Shanghai-Shandong-Henan Plain." *Zhongguo linye* (China's Forestry) 9, pp. 6–8.

Hu Benzhe. 1983. "Study on Methods of Coal Transportation in Shanxi Energy Base." *Neng yuan* (Journal of Energy) 4, pp. 1–3, 17.

Hu Daoji and Wang Zun. 1982. "Development of Extra-High Voltage AC and DC Transmission." *Dianli jishu* (Electric Power) 9, pp. 73–78.

Huang Fengchu. 1983. "Solving Key Project's Problems of Bad Management and Inferior Quality." *Renmin ribao* (People's Daily), 3 July 1983, p. 1.

Huang Fengchu and Chen Hongyi. 1984. "Advance Toward the Target of an Annual Output of 1.2 Billion Tons of Coal—An Interview with Gao Yangwen, Minister of Coal Industry." *Liaowang* (Outlook) 20, pp. 11–12.

Huang Heyu. 1982. "The Present Situation and Prospects of Developing Our Nation's Firewood Energy." *Neng yuan* (Journal of Energy) 2, pp. 40–43.

Huang Mingfu. 1983. "The Technological Approach to Shortening the Time for Underground Mine Construction." *Shijie meitan jishu* (World Coal Technology) 9, pp. 2–6.

Huang Zhijie and Chang Zhengmin. 1980. "Development of Methane Is an Important Task in Solving the Rural Energy Problem." *Hongqi* (Red Flag) 1980 (21), pp. 39–41.

Hui Yangmin. 1981. "Immediate Action Needs to Be Taken to Correct the Waste of Gasoline in Motor Vehicles." *Renmin ribao* (People's Daily) 13 February 1981, p. 1.

Ikonnikov, A. B. 1975. *Mineral Resources of China*. Boulder, Colo.: Geological Society of America.

Ji Shi. 1984. "The Hydropower Base on the Upper Course of Chang Jiang." *Shuili fadian* (Water Power Generation) 12, p. 63.

Jiang Shengjie. 1984. "Developing China's Nuclear Power Industry." *Beijing Review* 27 (25), pp. 17–20.

Jing Hua. 1981. "Small Hydropower Stations." *Beijing Review* 24 (32), pp. 22–29.

Jing Wei. 1984a. "The Eve of a Massive Battle." *Beijing Review* 27 (15), pp. 19–22.

————. 1984b. "China's Biggest Energy-producing Centre." *Beijing Review* 27 (49), pp. 16–18.

————. 1984c. "Large-scale Development Mapped Out." *Beijing Review* 27 (51), pp. 23–26.

Kinzelbach, W. K. H. 1983. "China: Energy and Environment." *Environmental Management* 7, pp.303–310.

Lan Tianfang, Lu Yingzhong, and Mao Yushi. 1984. "China's Energy Economy." Paper prepared for Energy Research Group, International Development Research Center, Ottawa.

Li Desheng. 1982. "Tectonic Types of Oil and Gas Basins in China." *Shiyou xuebao* (Acta Petrolei Sinica) 3, pp. 1–11.

Li Guangan and Wei Ligun. 1983. "Energy—The Key to Economic Development Strategy." *Jingji yanjiu* (Economic Studies) 11, pp. 10–16.

Li Peng. 1983. "To Invigorate the Economy We Must First Develop Electricity." *Hongqi* (Red Flag) 18, 17–22, 29.

Li Renjun. 1984. "Creating a New Situation in Using Coal Unstead of Oil." *Neng yuan* (Journal of Energy) 6, pp. 1–3.

Li Wenyan and Chan Hang. 1983. "A Preliminary Study of the Energy-Economic Regionalization of China." *Dili xuebao* (Acta Geographica Sinica) 4, pp. 327–40.

Li Yufeng. 1979. "Only by Concentrating Forces on Extracting Coal in the North Can We Obtain Fast Results." *Renmin ribao* (People's Daily) 1979, p. 3.

Li Zhenrong. 1984. "Preliminary Conclusions about the Design and Operation of the Jiangxia Experimental Tidal Station." *Shuili fadian* (Water Power Generation) 4, pp. 12–18.

Lin Weixian, Yu Ouyang, and Bao Feng. 1984. "Site Selection for Qinshan Nuclear Power Plant." *He kexue yu gongcheng* (Chinese Journal of Nuclear Science and Engineering) 11, pp. 16–20.

Ling, H. C. 1975. *The Petroleum Industry of the People's Republic of China.* Stanford: Stanford University Press.

Liu Zhongxian. 1981. "Petroleum Products Must Be Controlled as well as Foodstuffs." *Liaoning ribao* (Liaoning Daily), 5 January 1981, p. 2.

Lu Changmiao and Fu Lixen. 1984. "Exploring Directions for Developing Civilian Energy Resources in China." *Zhongguo huanjing kexue* (Environmental Sciences in China) 5, pp. 34–37.

Lu Qi. 1984. "Energy Conservation and Its Prospects." *Beijing Review* 27 (46), p. 20–23.

Lu Qi and Liu Xueyi. 1984. "Industrial Energy Consumption and Conservation in China." Paper prepared for Energy Research Group, International Development Research Center, Ottawa.

Lu Qinpei. 1984. "Prospects for Hydropower Development to the Year 2000." *Shuili fadian* (Water Power Generation) 10, pp. 15–20.

Lu Yingzhong. 1984. "The Development of Nuclear Energy in China." Paper prepared for Energy Research Group, International Development Research Center, Ottawa.

Luo Anren. 1983. "An Economic Comparison Between Nuclear and Coal Power Plants in Southeast China." *Hedongli gongcheng* (Nuclear Power Engineering) 6, pp. 43–50.

Ma Shijun and Chang Shuzong. 1980. "It Is of Immediate Urgency to Protect Our Environment and Natural Resources." *Jingji guanli* (Economic Management) 10, pp. 28–29, 39.

Ma Yunliang. 1982. "Standard of Construction of Our Nation's Water Conservancy and Hydraulic Power Projects and Major Achievements." *Shuili fadian* (Water Power Generation) 8, pp. 24–32, 41.

Mao Yushi and Hu Guangdong. 1984. "China's Transport and Its Energy Use." Paper prepared for Energy Research Group, International Development Research Center, Ottawa.

McGarry, M. G., and J. Stainforth, eds. 1978. *Compost, Fertilizer, and Biogas Production from Human and Farm Wastes in the People's Republic of China.* Ottawa: IDRC.

Melent'ev, L. A., and H. A. Makarov. 1983. *Energeticheskii kompleks SSSR.* Moscow: Ekonomika.

Meng Renlun and Sheng Changzhi. 1983. "The Direction of Energy Conservation for the Iron and Steel Industry." *Neng yuan* (Journal of Energy) 5, pp. 1–2, 18.

Meyerhoff, A. A., and J. O. Willums. 1976. "Petroleum Geology and Industry of the People's Republic of China." *CCOP Technical Bulletin* 10, pp. 103–112.

Ministry of Coal Industry. 1982. "China's Coal Industry." In *Zhongguo jingji nianjian* (China's Economic Yearbook). Bejing: State Statistical Bureau, pp. v105–v108.

Ministry of Petroleum Industry. 1982. "China's Petroleum Industry." In *Zhongguo jingji nianjian* (China's Economic Yearbook). Beijing: State Statistical Bureau, pp. v98–v100.

Mo Guohan. 1984. "Economic Considerations of Shuikou Reservoir Flooding." *Shuili fadian* (Water Power Generation) 6, pp. 14–16, 63.

Nickum, J. E. 1977. *Hydraulic Engineering and Water Resources in the People's Republic of China.* US-China Relations Program, Stanford University, Calif.

Office of Technology Assessment. 1985. *Energy Technology Transfer to China.* Washington, D.C.: OTA.

Pan Jiazheng and Zheng Shunwei. 1982. "Construction of Large Dams at Our Nation's Hydroelectric Power Stations." *Shuili fadian* (Water Power Generation) 8, pp. 14–23.

Pan Xiren and Zhao Jiarui. 1983. "The Main Design Features of 300 MW PWR Power Station." *Hedongli gongcheng* (Nuclear Power Engineering) 4, pp. 1–6.

Patterson, W. 1984. "Questioning the Answers." *Petroleum News* 1984 (8), p. 6.

Qian Zhengying. 1982. "Concentrate More Efforts on Quickening Hydropower Construction." *Shuili fadian* (Water Power Generation) 1982 (8), p. 3–4.

Qing Changgeng. 1982. "The Development of Water Turbine Generators and Their Accessory Equipment in Our Nation." *Shuili fadian* (Water Power Generation) 8, pp. 48–53.

Ren Tao and Pang Yongjie. 1983. "Can the Coal for 2000 Be Reached?" *Beijing Review* 26 (9), pp. 12–15.

Ren Xiang, Yang Qilong, and Tang Ninghua. 1984. "Geothermal Energy in China." Paper prepared for Energy Research Group, International Development Research Center, Ottawa.

Rui Susheng and Wang Qingyi. 1985. "Impact of New Technological Revolution on China's Coal Industry." *Meitan jishu* (World Coal Technology) 2, pp. 3–6.

Shangguan Changjun. 1980. "Ways Must Be Found to Solve Energy Problems in Rural Areas." *Nongye jingji wenti* (Agricultural Economic Issues) 4, pp. 1056-1058.

Shao Lei. 1983. "Stable Production of Oil at Daqing Relies on Scientific and Technological Progress." *Renmin ribao* (People's Daily), 17 December 1983, p. 1.

Shen Xinxiang and Guo Zhongxing. 1982. "Take Active Measures to Increase the Output of Existing Hydroelectric Power Stations." *Shuili fadian* (Water Power Generation) 9, pp. 3–6.

Shi Wen. 1982. "Use of New and Renewable Energy Resources in China." *Beijing Review*. 25 (16), pp. 18–20.

Shi Yuqian and Fan Qiwan. 1984. "An Inquiry into the Direction of Technological Development in China's Surface Coal Mines." *Meitan kexue jishu* (Coal Science and Technology) 5, pp. 34–41.

Smil, V. 1976. *China's Energy*. New York: Praeger.

————. 1977. "Intermediate Energy Technology in China." *The Bulletin of the Atomic Scientists* 33 (2), pp. 25–31.

————. 1978. "China's Energetics: A System Analysis." In *Chinese Economy Post-Mao*. Washington, D.C.: Joint Economic Committee of the U.S. Congress, U.S. ATO, pp. 323–69.

————. 1979. "Energy Flows in Rural China." *Human Ecology* 7, pp. 119–133.

————. 1980. "Energy." In *Science in Contemporary China*, ed. L. A. Orleans. Stanford: Stanford University Press, pp. 407–34.

————. 1981a. "Energy Development in China: The Need for a Coherent Policy." *Energy Policy* 9, pp. 113–26.

————. 1981b. "China's Agro-ecosystem." *Agro-Ecosystems* 7, pp. 27–46.

————. 1982a. "Energy in Rural China." In *Improving World Energy Production and Productivity*, ed. L. A. Clinard, M. R. English, and R. A. Bohm. Cambridge, Mass.: Ballinger, pp. 309–28.

————. 1982b. "Chinese Biogas Program Sputters." *Soft Energy Notes* 5 (3), pp. 88–90.

————. 1983. *Biomass Energies Resources, Links, Constraints*. New York: Plenum Press.

————. 1984. *The Bad Earth: Environmental Degradation in China*. Armonk, N.Y.: M. E. Sharpe.

————. 1985. "China's Food." *Scientific American* 253 (6), pp. 116–24.

Smil, V., and K. Woodard. 1977. "Perspectives on Energy in the People's Republic of China." *Annual Review of Energy* 2, pp. 307–42.

————. 1986. "Food Production and Quality of Diet in China." *Population and Development Review* 12 (1), pp. 25-45.

Smil, V., P. Nachman, and T. V. Long. 1983. *Energy Analysis in Agriculture*. Boulder, Colo.: Westview Press.

State Bureau of Geology. 1979. *Hydrogeologic Atlas of the People's Republic of China*. Beijing: State Bureau of Geology.

State Statistical Bureau. 1985. *Zhongguo tongji zhaiyao 1985* (Chinese Statistical Abstract 1985). Beijing: SSB.

Sun Hongzheng. 1983. "Economic Operation Is a Key Link in Energy Conservation." *Neng yuan* (Journal of Energy) 5, pp. 38–39.

Sun Shoukang. 1981. "On the Question of Energy Conservation in Synthetic Fiber Production." *Fangzhi xuebao* (Journal of Textile Research) 6, pp. 67–69.

Tao Jingliang and Zhang Jihua. 1982. "Hydroelectric Power Stations in Construction." *Shuili fadian* (Water Power Generation) 3, pp. 45–46, 53.

Taylor, R. P. 1982. *Rural Energy Development in China*. Washington, D.C.: Resources for the Future.

Tong Yihao. 1983. "An Investigation Into the Effective Use of 100 Million Tons of Crude Oil." *Neng yuan* (Journal of Energy) 3, pp. 1–4.

Tu Hua. 1982. "We Must Prevent Redundant Construction of Small Hydroelectric Power Stations." *Neng yuan* (Journal of Energy) 4, pp 4–5, 39.

United Nations. 1983. *Yearbook of World Energy Statistics*. New York: United Nations.

Van Buren, A., ed. 1979. *A Chinese Biogas Manual*. London: Intermediate Technology Publications.

Wang Bingzhong, Anang Fuguo, and Li Lixian. 1980. "Solar Energy Resources in China." *Acta Energiae Solaris Sinica* 1 (1), pp. 1–9.

Wang Jiansan, Zhang Renjie, and Yang Shengzhuan. 1982. "Views on Some Specific Problems in Designing Thermal Power Plants." *Dianli jishu* (Electric Power) 10, pp. 1–6.

Wang, K. P. 1975. *The People's Republic of China: A New Industrial Power with a Strong Mineral Base*. Washington, D.C.: GPO.

Wang Menkui. 1980. "Pay Attention to Solving Rural Energy Problems." *Guangming ribao* (Guangming Daily), 19 July 1980, p. 4.

Wang Shengpei. 1982. "Development of Hydroelectric Power Science and Technology in Our Nation." *Shuili fadian* (Water Power Generation) 8, pp. 33–40.

Wang Zingyi and Gu Jian. 1983. "How Will China Solve Energy Problem?" *Beijing Review* 26 (35), pp. 13–18.

Weil, M. 1983. "Coal Slurry in China." *The China Business Review* 10 (4), pp. 21–24.

Weng Changpu. 1982. "Experience in the Planning of Comprehensive Use of the Hongshui." *Neng yuan* (Journal of Energy) 1, pp. 8–11.

Weng Wenbo. 1982. "The Prospects of China's Natural Gas Industry." *Shiyou kantan yu kaifa* (Petroleum Exploration and Development) 1982 (6), pp. 1–8.

Weng Yongxi, Wang Zhishan, Huang Juanguan and Zhu Jianing. 1981. "Views on Strategic Problems in China's Agricultural Development." *Jingji yanjiu* (Economic Studies) 1981 (11), pp. 13–22.

Williams, B. A. 1975. "The Chinese Petroleum Industry: Growth and Prospects." In *China: A Reassessment of the Economy*. Washington, D.C.: GPO, pp. 225–63.

Wong Kwok Wah. 1984. "Dividing up Responsibility." *Petroleum News* 8, pp. 63–64.

Woodard, K. 1980. *The International Energy Relations of China*. Stanford: Stanford University Press.

World Bank. 1986. *World Development Report 1986*. New York: Oxford University Press.

World Energy Conference. 1983. *Survey of Energy Resources*. London: WED.

Wu Jing. 1983. "Prospects of China's Coal Industry." *Beijing Review 26* (37), pp. 14–16.

Wu Wen. 1984. "Biomass Utilization in China." Paper prepared for Energy Research Group, International Development Research Center, Ottawa.

Wu Wen and Chen Enjian. 1982. *Our Views on the Resolution of China's Rural Energy Requirements*. Guangzhou:Guangzhou Institute of Energy Conversion.

Wu, Yuanli, with H. C. Ling. 1963. *Economic Development and the Use of Energy Resources in Communist China*. New York: F. A. Praeger.

Wu Zhixiang. 1983. "The Five Large Open-Pit Coal Mines in the Modernization of China's Coal Industry." *Shijie meitan jishu* (World Coal Technology) 2, pp. 6–8.

Wu Zhonghua. 1980. "Solving the Energy Crisis from the Viewpoint of Energy Science and Technology." *Hongqi* (Red Flag) 17.

Xia Guocai. 1983. "Accelerating the Development of an Energy and Heavy-Chemical Base in Shanxi Is a Major Strategic Decision in China's Modernization Progress." *Zhongguo jingji ribao* (Chinese Economic Daily) 3, pp. 27–29.

Xiao Dianhua. 1983. "The Development of Small-scale Hydropower and Its Characteristics in China." *Shuili shuidian jishu* (Water Resources and Hydropower) 6, pp. 7–11.

Xiao Han. 1978. "Developing Coal Industry at High Speed." *Peking Review* 21 (8), pp. 5–7.

Xiao Shi. 1984. "Bright Prospects for Using Gangue to Generate Electricity." *Guangming ribao* (Guangming Daily), 23 April 1984, p. 2.

Xu Dixin. 1981. "The Position and Role of Forests in the National Economy." *Hongqi* (Red Flag) 23, pp. 40–45.

Xu Junzhang. 1982. "The Current Situation and Prospects for Saving Energy in China." Paper prepared for Workshop on Energy Power in the United States and China, Beijing, September 1982.

Xu Qiwang. 1984. "Development and Research on Oceanic Energy Resources in China." *Neng yuan* (Journal of Energy) 1, pp. 9–11.

Xu Yongxi. 1984. "Symposium Discusses Electricity Pricing Issues." *Dianli jishu* (Electric Power) 11, pp. 5–10.

Yang Bo. 1982. "Strive to Reduce the Burning of Oil and Strive Diligently to Conserve Use of Oil." *Neng yuan* (Journal of Energy) 2, pp. 1–4.

Yang Jinhe and Chen Wenmin. 1982. "Basic Characteristics and Main Uses of China's Coal." *Meitan kexue jishu* (Coal Science and Technology) 3, pp. 2–9.

Yang Wuyang and Dong Liming. 1980. "Wind Regime in Urban Planning and Industrial Distribution." *Scientia Sinica* 23, pp. 766–73.

Year 2000 Report Group. 1984. *China in the Year 2000*. Science and Technology Publishing, Beijing.

Yu Guangqian. 1981. "Stricter Controls Are Needed to Curb Gasoline Waste by Motor Vehicles." *Renmin ribao* (People's Daily), 13 February 1981, p. 2.

Yu Kaiquan. 1983. "Some Opinions on Accelerating Development of Small-scale Hydropower in China." *Shuili shuidian jishu* (Water Resources and Hydropower) 6, pp. 59–61.

Yuan Guangru. 1982. "A Survey of China's Energy Industry." In *Zhongguo jingji nianjian* (China's Economic Yearbook). Beijing: State Statistical Bureau, pp. v96–v98.

Zhang Changsong. 1982. "Twenty-year Outlook for China." *Shijie meitan jishu* (World Coal Technology) 11, pp. 2–5, 19.

Zhang Deang. 1982. "Development of Pipeline Transportation—A Look at the Problem of Transporting Shanxi's Coal Energy." *Jishu jingji yu guanli yangjiu* (Research in Economics and Management Technology) 1, pp. 27–29.

Zhang Guangdou. 1983. "Some Views on Accelerating Hydropower Development." *Shuili fadian* (Water Power Generation) 5, pp. 3–4.

Zhang Pinghua. 1981. "Conscientiously Implement Private Woodlots and Energetically Raise Fuelwood and Charcoal Forests." *Zhongguo linye* (China's Forestry) 3, pp. 4–5.

Zhang Qinghai. 1981. "Practical Solutions to Rural Energy Problem in Acid Areas of Northwest China." *Nongye jingji wenti* (Agricultural Economic Issues) 10, pp. 57–58.

Zhang Xuanguo. 1983. "Weaknesses in Technology Hamper Progress at Huolinhe Coal Mine." *Renmin ribao* (People's Daily), 29 July 1983, p. 2.

Zhang Zhijian, Wang Jiacheng, and Xin Dingguo. 1984. "China Has Bright Energy Future but the Tasks Ahead Are Arduous." *Neng yuan* (Journal of Energy) 5, pp. 1–16.

Zhang Zhongji. 1982. "Vigorously Tap the Potential of Energy Conservation." *Tongji* (Statistics) 1, pp. 10–12.

Zhao Zengguang. 1982. "Reviewing the Development of Small Scale Hydroelectric Power in Our Nation Over the Past Thirty Years." *Shuili fadian* (Water Power Generation) 8, pp. 54–56.

Zhao Ziyang. 1985. *Explanation of the Proposal for the Seventh Five-Year Plan.* Beijing: Xinhua.

Zheng Bingqiang. 1982. "Improve Comprehensive Utilization, Use 100 Million Tons of Oil Economically." *Neng yuan* (Energy Sources) 3, pp. 13–15.

Zhi Luchuan. 1982. "Ways to Improve Energy Efficiency as Judged by China's Energy Balance Sheet for 1980." Cited in Lan, Lu, and Mao (1984).

Zhou Wenbin. 1980. "Putting Utilization of Solar Energy on Tiber's Agenda." *Guangming ribao* (Guangming Daily), 13 July 1980, p. 3.

Zhou Zheng. 1985a. "Gezhouba Hydroelectric Project Revisited." *Beijing Review* 28 (27), pp. 16–19.

————. 1985b. "The Hongshui River: A Mighty Powerhouse." *Beijing Review* 28 (26), pp. 14–18.

Zhu Xiaozhong, Ding Guangquan, and Eugene Chang. 1984. "How Small Hydro Power Is Helping China's Rural Electrification Pogramme." Paper prepared for Energy Research Group, International Development Research Center, Ottawa.

Zhu Yajie and Wang Qingyi. 1984. "Energy Policy Study in China." Paper prepared for Energy Research Group, International Development Research Center, Ottawa.

APPENDICES

Appendix A   Information sources   239

Appendix B1   China's provinces   242

Appendix B2   China's largest cities   243

Appendix B3   China's economic regions   244

Appendix C   Key economic indicators for the PRC, 1949–1986   245

Appendix D   Energy units   246

APPENDIX A

Information Sources

Three collections of Chinese news agency releases, nationwide and provincial broadcasts, and writings on a wide variety of topics, ranging from general political items appearing in the dailies to highly technical papers published in scientific journals, are regularly published in English translation, and they form an indispensable information basis for any serious student of contemporary China. These collections are: *British Broadcasting Corporation Summary of World Broadcasts*, Part 3, The Far East, Daily Report and Weekly Economic Supplement; *Foreign Broadcast Information Service*, Daily Report; and *Joint Publications Research Service*, China Report, Economic Affairs (available only on microfiche). All three collections have been recently carrying a large amount of translations on energy matters.

In China, where virtually all major decisions are taken by the central bureaucracies to conform with the Communist Party's precepts, important plans and policies are not revealed in technical publications but rather in the party's daily *Renmin ribao* (People's Daily) or in its monthly *Hongqi* (Red Flag) and in often lengthy releases of the official news agency *Xinhua* (New China News Agency). Hence a regular perusal of these three sources is imperative to keep current with the latest Chinese happenings and intentions.

Essential statistical sources are the *Zhongguo tongji zhaiyao* (China Statistical Abstract), published annually by the State Statistical Bureau, and *Zhongguo jingji nianjian* (China Economic Yearbook), which contains a large number of review articles on all aspects of China's development. Since 1979 the State Statistical Bureau has been releasing, usually in spring, increasingly detailed reports on the results of the previous year's economic performance; these reports contain all essential macroeconomic statistics and are easily accessible in *Beijing Review*.

New specialized statistical yearbooks are indispensable for any detailed studies of major economic sectors. The most important sources for energy studies are *Zhongguo nongye nianjian* (China Agricultural Yearbook) and two volumes conveniently available in English editions, *China Coal Industry Yearbook* (compiled by the Ministry of Coal Industry and published and distributed by Hong Kong's Economic Information Agency) and *Electric Power Industry in China* (published also in Hong Kong by Canal Promotion Centre).

Publication of virtually all economic technical and scientific journals was suspended between the years 1958 and 1976 but restored rapidly before the end of the 1970s, and many new journals, mostly monthlies, have been added. Just the key ones are listed here by topics. General economic problems: *Jingji guanli* (Economic Management), *Jingji yanjiu* (Economic Research). General energy studies: *Neng yuan*, (Journal of Energy) *Xin neng yuan* (New Energy

Sources), *Jie neng* (Energy Conservation). Coal industry: *Zhongguo meitan bao* (China's Coal News), *Meitan kexue jishu* (Coal Science and Technology), *Shijie meitan jishu* (World Coal Technology). Oil and gas industry: *Shiyou xuebao* (Acta Petrolei Sinica), *Shiyou kantan yu kaifa* (Petroleum Exploration and Development). Electricity generation: *Dianli jishu* (Electric Power), *Dongli gongcheng* (Power Engineering), *Shuili fadian* (Water Power Generation), *Shuili shudian jishu* (Water Resources and Hydropower).

Those who seek information on China's energy that has already been systematically evaluated and analyzed can now choose from an increasing variety of writings—but they must keep in mind that while the qualitative appraisals contained in pre-1979 writings may be quite correct their detailed quantitative foundations have become in many cases obsolete after the publication of regular official statistics was renewed in 1979.

Two books provide systematic looks at all important aspects of Chinese energy resources, production, and utilization since the founding of the PRC: Wu with Ling (1963) covered in detail the decade of rapid initial industrialization of the 1950s while Smil (1976) surveyed all major developments until early 1976. Woodard's (1980) book is also a general review carried up to the late 1970s but one heavily tilted toward international implications of China's energy production. Cheng (1984) focuses on the demand and supply of primary commercial energy and Beijing's Year 2000 Report Group (1984) puts China's future energy needs into a wider perspective. Book chapters, workshop records, and review papers giving broader appraisals of Chinese energy situation are Smil and Woodard (1977), Fingar (1980, 1983), Smil (1978, 1980, 1981a, 1981b), Yuan Guangru (1982), Wang and Gu (1983), Li and Chen (1983), Li and Wei (1983), Fang (1984), Lan and Lu (1984), Zhang, Wang, and Xin (1984), Zhu and Wang (1984), and OTA (1985).

Books, monographs, documents, book chapters, and key review papers focusing on individual sectors of Chinese energetics will be listed chronologically by sectors. On coal they are Ikonnikov (1975), Wang (1975), CIA (1976, 1979), Xiao Han (1978), Li Yufeng (1979), Ministry of Coal Industry (1982), Zhang Changsong (1982), Wu Jing (1983), Gao Yangwen (1983), and Rui and Wang (1985). On hydrocarbons the main entries should include Ling (1975), Williams (1975), Cheng (1976), Meyerhoff and Willums (1976), CIA (1977), Ministry of Petroleum Industry (1982), Zheng Bingqiang (1982), Weng Wenbo (1982), and excellent annual reviews in *Petroleum News*.

On electricity Carin (1969), Clarke (1978), CIA (1980), Wang, Zhang, and Yang (1982), Li Peng (1983), and Jiang (1984). A special issue of *Shuili fadian* published in August 1982 contains several detailed reviews of China's achievements in hydrogeneration since the founding of the PRC: Qian Zhenggying (1982), Ma Yunliang (1982), and Wang Shengpei (1982) provide a general overview, Pan Jiazheng and Zheng Shunwei (1982) look at construction of large dams, Qing Changgeng (1982) describes the development of hydraulic turbogenerators, and Zhao Zengguang (1982) reviews the progress in small-scale hydro construction. Lu Yingzhong (1984) offers a detailed review of nuclear plans.

Energy conservation and improvement of conversion efficiencies are detailed in Chen, Huang, and Xu (1979), Wu Zhonghua (1980), Xu Junzhang (1982), Zhang Zhongji (1982), Lu and Liu (1984), and Lu (1984). Systematic appraisals of rural energy based on a multitude of Chinese sources are contained in Smil (1978, 1979, 1982, 1984) and Taylor (1982). Important Chinese reviews are those of Shangguan (1980), Wang Menkui (1980), Deng and Zhou (1981), Weng et al. (1981), Zhang Pinghua (1981), Shi Wen (1982), Wu and Chen (1982), Huang (1982), Wu (1984), Deng and Wu (1984), and Deng (1985).

Rich literature in English, including a complete translation of a popular Sichuanese manual, is now available to describe design, operation, and advantages of biogas digesters. The principal entries are Smil (1977, 1982, 1983), FAO (1977), FAO and UNDP (1978), McGarry and Stainforth (1978), Chen and Xiao (1979), and Van Buren (1979). Over the years much has been also written on small hydrogeneration with the main sources in English being Nickum (1977), El-Hinnawi (1977), Djurovic (1979), Clauser (1981), Jing Hua (1981), Zhu, Ding, and Chang (1984) and Hangzhou Regional Centre for Small Hydro Power (1985).

Appendix B1

China's provinces

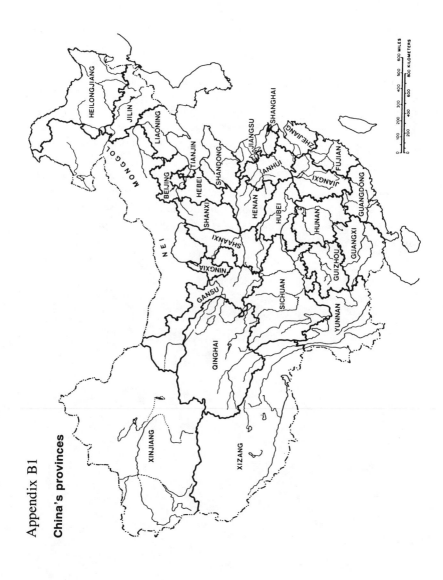

Appendix B2

China's largest cities

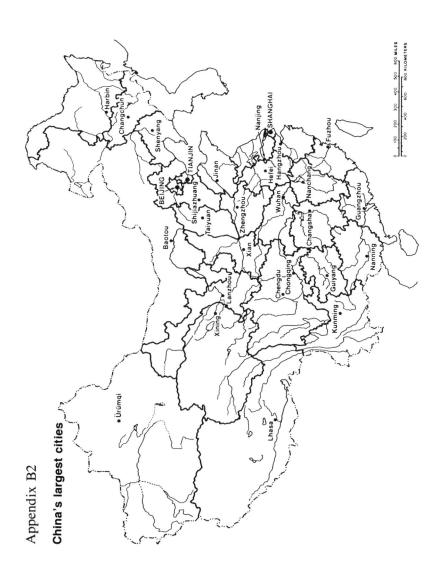

244

Appendix B3

China's economic regions

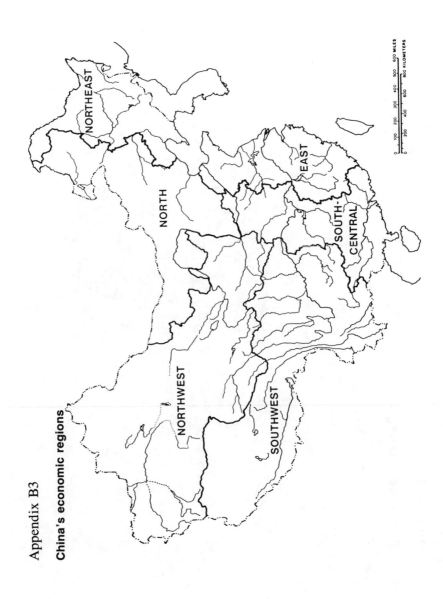

Appendix C

Key economic indicators for the PRC, 1949–1986

Year	Population	National economic product Total (10⁹Rmb)	Per capita (Rmb)	Grain output Total (10⁶t)	Per capita (kg)	Primary energy production Total (10⁶tce)	Per capita (kgce)
1949	541.67	—	—	108.10	200	23.74	44
1952	574.82	101.5	177	158.20	275	48.71	85
1957	645.53	160.6	249	188.30	292	98.61	153
1965	725.36	269.5	372	221.70	305	188.24	260
1970	829.92	380.0	458	239.96	289	309.90	373
1975	924.20	537.9	582	284.52	308	487.54	528
1978	962.59	684.6	711	304.77	317	627.70	652
1979	975.42	764.2	783	332.10	340	645.62	662
1980	987.05	849.6	861	320.56	325	637.21	646
1981	1,000.72	904.8	904	325.02	325	632.32	632
1982	1,015.40	789.1	974	353.43	348	667.22	657
1983	1,024.95	1,105.2	1,078	387.28	378	713.00	696
1984	1,036.04	1,283.5	1,239	407.12	393	766.00	739
1985	1,046.39	1,624.2	1,552	378.98	362	839.00	802
1986	1,060.08	1,877.4	1,771	391.09	369	862.00	813

Source: State Statistical Bureau (various years).

APPENDIX D

Energy units

In the International System of Units the basic energy unit is the joule (J) and basic power measure is the watt (W). One watt equals 1J/sec and hence one joule is one watt/sec. Principal common conversions for both units, as well as multiplication prefixes, are shown below.

In practice, energy performance at the national level is most commonly given in terms of fuel equivalents, coal, or oil. Standard coal contains 7,000 kcal or 29 MJ/kg, standard crude oil has 10,000 kcal or 42 MJ/kg, and natural gas is converted at 9,300 kcal or 39 MJ/m³. Chinese energy statistics are, for obvious reasons, in coal equivalents. A multiplier of 0.714 is used to convert one ton of Chinese raw coal to standard fuel while crude-oil output must be multiplied by 1.429 and natural-gas output (in m³) by 1.33 to arrive at the common denominator in coal equivalents.

Energy conversions

From / To Multiply by	J	Kcal	kWh	Btu
Joule (J)	1	2.389×10^{-4}	2.389×10^{-7}	9.486×10^{-4}
Kilocalorie (kcal)	4186	1	1.1628×10^{-3}	3.9685
Kilowatt·hour (kWh)	3.6×10^{6}	860	1	3412.8
British thermal unit (Btu)	1055	0.252	2.928×10^{-4}	1

Power conversions

From / To Multiply by	W	hp	kcal/min	Btu/min
Watt (W)	1	1.36×10^{-3}	1.433×10^{-2}	5.688×10^{-2}
Horsepower (hp)	7.45.7	1	10.68	42.44
Kilocalories/minute (kcal/min)	69.783	9.351×10^{-2}	1	3.9865
British thermal units/minute (Btu/min)	17.58	2.356×10^{-2}	0.252	1

Energy equivalents of principal fuels

Fuels	Energy equivalents MJ	Mcal
Bituminous coals (kg)	20–33	4.7–7.9
Brown coals, lignites (kg)	8–20	1.9–4.7
Standard coal (kgce)	29	7
Crude oils (kg)	42–44	10–10.5
Gasoline (litre)	34–35	8.1–8.4
Natural gas (m³)	37–39	8.8–9.3
Fuelwoods, air-dry (kg)	14–17	3.3–4.1
Crop residues, air-dry (kg)	12–16	2.9–3.8
Dried dung (kg)	11–14	2.6–3.3

Prefixes

Factor by which unit is multiplied	Prefix	Symbol
10	deka	d
10^2	hecto	h
10^3	kilo	k
10^6	mega	M
10^9	giga	G
10^{12}	tera	T
10^{15}	peta	P
10^{18}	exa	E

INDEX

Agriculture
    energy consumption, 70-80, 83-84, 129
    fertilizers, 74-77, 80-81, 124-125, 143, 215
    food production, 81-83
    machinery, 71-74
Air pollution, 161, 216-218

Biogas, 54-63, 198-199
Biomass, 19-24, 70
    biogas, 54-63, 198-199
    crop residues, 48-51, 197, 213
    fuelwood, 51-53, 193-197

Coal
    electricity generation, 114-116
    consumption, 70-71
    mining, 32, 85-95, 148-162
    large mines, 88-89, 91-93, 149-153, 157-160
    preparation, 87
    resources, 30-35
    small mines, 70-71, 91-94, 153-154, 198
    transportation, 89-90, 129, 154-157
Cooking, 13, 46, 49, 62, 128, 190-193
Crop residues, 48-51, 197, 215
Crude oil
    combustion, 130-131, 145-146
    electricity generation, 114, 117
    extraction, 95-102, 162-171
    offshore, 37, 98, 162-170
    oilfields, 95-97, 99-102, 163-169

refining, 99, 103-104
    resources, 35-40

Daqing, 39-40, 95-96, 99-100
Domestic animals, 50-52, 59, 78-81

Economy
    agriculture, 45-46
    energy intensity, 121-128
    GNP, 3, 136-140, 202
    growth, 135-137
    income, 3, 45-47
    planning, 4-5, 131-132, 139, 146-147, 158-160, 224-225, 227
    prices, 211-213
    reforms, 5, 134-136, 203-213
    trade, 208-210
Ecosystems, 20, 83
Electricity
    consumption, 120, 124-129, 143-144, 198
    costs, 210-211
    fossil-fueled, 109, 111-117
    geothermal, 15-17
    large hydro, 104-111, 172-180, 220-223
    mine-mouth, 114-115
    nuclear, 183-188
    small hydro, 63-69, 197-198, 207
    solar, 13-14
    wind, 14
    thermal, 109, 111-117, 172, 181-183, 207, 218-220
    transmission, 117-119

Energy
 conservation, 126, 141-148, 206-207
 consumption, 4, 8-9, 43-44, 46-54,
  70-80, 83-84, 121-132, 136-
  146, 202-203
 costs, 73-77, 80, 122, 124-128, 141-
  145, 186, 210
 forecasts, 136-141
 international comparisons, 4, 8, 10,
  17, 19-21, 24, 28, 31, 43-
  44, 75, 77, 87-88, 102, 104, 109,
  111, 121-123, 171
 prices, 211-213
 units, 246-247
Environmental degradation, 214-224

Food, 81-83
Forests, 20-23, 53-54
Fossil fuels: *see* coal; crude oil; natural
  gas; peat
Fuelwood, 23, 51-53, 193-197

Geothermal energy, 15-19
Gezhouba, 106-109, 111, 118

Hot springs, 15
Hydrocarbons: *see* crude oil; natural gas
Hydroenergy
 generation, 104-111, 172-180, 220-
  223
 resources, 24-29
 small-scale generation, 63-69, 197-
  198, 207
Hydrostations
 large, 106-111, 174-180
 small, 63-69, 197-198, 207

Industry
 energy consumption, 123-127
 planning, 4-5, 131-132, 139, 146-
  147, 158-160, 224-225, 227
 iron and steel, 125-127, 133, 141-142

Natural gas, 39-40, 102, 165, 167-168
Nei Monggol, 14, 21, 33, 149, 151-152
Nuclear energy, 183-188, 224

Peat, 40

Photovoltaics, 13-14
Pipelines, 98, 103, 155-157
Population, 45, 78-80
Power plants: *see* hydrostations; electric-
  ity generation

Renewable energies, 9-30
 biogas, 54-63, 198-199
 biomass, 19-24
 crop residues, 48-51, 197, 215
 fuelwood, 23, 51-53, 193-197
 geothermal, 15-19
 hydroenergy, 24-29
 solar conversions, 13-14
 tides, 29-30
 wind, 14
Rivers, 24-27, 173-178
Rural energy
 biogas, 54-63, 198-199
 consumption, 44-49, 54, 69-80, 189-
  200, 226-227
 crop residues, 48-51, 197, 215
 flows, 69-80
 fuelwood, 51-53, 193-197

San Xia (Three gorges), 27, 174-175,
  223-224
Shanxi, 33, 88-90, 94, 149-153, 155,
  179, 181-183, 219
Shengli, 39-40, 95-96, 100-101
Sichuan, 10, 21, 30, 55, 62, 102, 120
Silting, 222-223
Solar radiation, 10-14
South China Sea, 37, 162-168
Stoves, 190-193

Tidal energy, 29-30
Transmission, 117-119
Turbogenerators, 106, 108-112, 120-
  121, 205-206

Uranium, 40

Water, 218-219
Water power: *see* hydroenergy
Wind energy, 14

Xizang (Tibet), 10, 13, 15, 17, 49